she's
all
that

kristin billerbeck

Other Books by Kristin Billerbeck

she's all that

kristin billerbeck

INTEGRITY®

PUBLISHERS

Nashville

Library of Congress Cataloging-in-Publication Data

Billerbeck, Kristin.
  She's all that / by Kristin Billerbeck.
      p. cm.
  Summary: "The first novel in the Spa Girls Collection, She's All That, focuses on Lilly Jacobs, a San Francisco fashion designer determined that her "bad hair" is the root source of her problems"—Provided by publisher.

  ISBN 1-59145-328-3 (trade paper)

  1. Women fashion designers—Fiction. 2. San Francisco (Calif.)—Fiction. 3. Hairdressing--Fiction. 4. Hair—Fiction. I. Title.
  PS3602.I44S537 2005
  813'.54—dc22
                                            2005008312

Dedication

To Beth Harke, my best friend since I was four. The spa and Kristin don't really mesh because I am way too hyper. Although Beth loves me, she is not planning anymore spa trips with me. I think "over my dead body" might have been her actual words. Between my inability to relax and the middle-aged bald guy macking at the pool with his girlfriend, that was really enough of the Spa experience for us. However, she continues to tell me how great the spa trips are with her other friends. I wonder what's up with that?

Love you, girlfriend!

Acknowledgments

No man is an island (whatever that means) and no writer can do it without a team of experts. Thank you to my brainstorming team and writing playgroup: Colleen Coble, Diann Hunt, and Denise Hunter. My agent, Jeana Ledbetter, who puts up with me—and trust me, that ain't easy. My editors Natalie Gillespie and Angela DePriest—these girls rock. And finally, to my faithful readers who keep me enthused and younger than my advancing age, especially Alisa Smith and Miss Michigan 2004, Kelli Talicska.

chapter 1

Bad hair ruined my life. Oh, I know what you're thinking: it's physically impossible for bad hair to ruin your life. But if I didn't have frizzy, bushy, mushroom-shaped hair, I wouldn't need thermal reconditioning every four months. And if I didn't need thermal reconditioning, I wouldn't have been at the salon for five hours when my boss gave my promotion to another designer.

My boss, Sara Lang: "I'm sorry, Lilly, but you just don't have the distinction in your designs."

I beg to differ. My designs cover every pertinent part. How many others can claim that simple fact?

"Okay, thank you." *Wimp. Wimp. Wimp.*

Here's the kicker, though, the determining factor in my day of total humiliation and ruination: if I hadn't gone to my boyfriend's house after the news to cry on his shoulder, I would have never known about Katrina. Katrina, who is apparently his new girlfriend. The one he claims he's been trying to tell me about, so that I would know that I am officially, oh-by-the-way, the *ex*-girlfriend. Minor oversight on his part, I'm certain.

I'd like to say I'm crushed about Robert being my ex. I mean, it's sort of pathetic that he was part of my life for a few months, and my only answer to this unexpected Katrina surprise was a wave of the hand and a thoroughly disgusted, "What*ever*" (with a shrug for emphasis). Robert was more dinner companion than boyfriend, and that's about it. He was straight and a Christian. Let's face it, living in San Francisco and working in the fashion industry, that was really all he needed to be.

In terms of a long-term romantic future, I had higher hopes for myself—despite being continually stymied by my lack of speaking ability in the presence of men I find attractive. Generally, I date men I'm not all that attracted to. It's just easier, because at some point you have to talk to them, and with a mouth that doesn't function properly in front of guys I find, well, *hot*, this is an issue. Whereas, if I'm not looking at potential husband material, the words flow like Niagara. Granted, this dilemma doesn't bring me the passion of a Cary Grant movie, but it does suffice if I want to get out of the house once in a while.

So currently, I am Lilly Jacobs, single girl nearing thirty and fledgling fashion designer. Not *Lilly Jacobs for Sara Lang Couture*, or even the future *Mrs. Robert Hazelton*—but I am still, and most importantly, a card-carrying member of the Spa Girls.

I unlock the litany of latches on my loft studio apartment, flop onto my futon, and call Morgan, my best college friend and fellow Spa Girl, on her cell. "I need a spa date! Fast."

"Lilly, just a minute," Morgan whispers. I hear some shuffling, and then Morgan is back on the line. "I'm at a political luncheon for a would-be senator. Woefully boring, and really, will the Republicans ever win in San Francisco? Talk about a waste of time."

"What are you there for, then?" I ask, annoyed that the Republicans are interfering with my crisis.

"I'm wearing this fabulous teardrop necklace with an

incredible pink diamond. Daddy just got it in from Australia. I've already had a few comments," Morgan says. "I bet it's sold by dinnertime."

I sigh aloud. *Could our lives be any more divergent?*

Morgan Malliard is a tall, willowy, blond jewelry heiress officially known about town as the "Ice Queen" for her ever-changing diamond collection provided by her father's fashion-able Union Square store. And what better item to soothe an aching Republican in Liberal Central than a fabulous diamond, the cost of which would bring many people's problems to an end? And most small countries' problems, as well.

"Which do you want to hear first?" I ask. "The bad news? Or the really bad news?" Personally, I think the fact that I'm still sleeping on a futon and am about to turn thirty speaks pretty loudly for my fate. *But wait, there's more!*

"Give me any bad news that involves Robert. I never liked him. Too blah—like a white wall amidst Ralph Lauren paint colors. He gives nerds a bad name. There *is* bad news about Robert, isn't there?" she asks hopefully.

I sigh again. "Yes, that's the pseudo-bad news. He has a girlfriend."

"A girlfriend who is not you, I'm assuming."

"Correct."

Morgan lets out a restrained, "Yes!"

"Could I get some sympathy here? I have been seeing him for three months." But even I have trouble feeling too sorry for myself. This is the equivalent of saying I've been seeing my second cousin for months. It doesn't really invoke sympathy. Just sort of a sad disgust.

"Seeing him only when you had nothing better to do," Morgan retorts. "Give me a break. It's not like we're talking about the great love of your life. What's the *really* bad news?"

"Shane Wesley got my promotion today."

"No! Oh, Lilly!"

"Yep. Another bald, gay man who represents the fashion industry better than me. It's my hair, I just know it."

"Would you stop? You have great hair. Felicity made a mint on hair just like yours. Remember, she even got in trouble for cutting it off."

"Um, back to me here," I say, looking for my dose of sympathy and wallowing in my narcissism for the moment. After all, I earned it fair and square.

"Sorry. I'm sorry about the promotion." Morgan sounds like she's going to cry for me. "I know how much you wanted it and deserved it. I wish you'd let me help you, Lilly. I've told you that a million times. I'll wear anything you ask. Your designs would be mentioned in the society pages. For the four people who read that page, it would be great!"

"Thanks for the offer, Morgan, but no. I want to do this by myself. I want to be so good that I can write my own ticket. Like Tom Ford. Only not male. And not gay. More like Vera Wang, I guess. Maybe I could do for the bolero jacket what she did for the wedding gown."

"The bolero jacket?"

"Okay, what about the woven hat?"

"Like J.Lo and Mariah Carey? Not exactly strutting down the couture runway, Lilly. You do need a spa weekend. You're delirious."

"Yeah. I'm desperate, Morgan. I need truffles, exfoliation, and gallons of Diet Pepsi to drown my sorrows. And pickles. Could we get some pickles too?"

"You better warn Poppy if you're bringing the hard stuff. She'll want you to sip detox tea, you know that. There will be ginseng and chamomile for all, but there will definitely *not* be Diet Pepsi. Somehow I'm thinking cured, dead cucumbers are not on the menu either."

"Can you call Poppy for me?" I whine like the worm I am. "It's been a really bad day."

"Lilly, I've got news for you. She knows you drink Diet Pepsi—and the pickle thing? Well, you're on your own there, because that's just weird." Morgan pauses for a moment. "I wonder how many people in this ballroom have ever even eaten a really good pickle."

"Have you?" I ask.

"No, not really. It's not the most feminine of snacks, Lilly. I mean, if you were here at this Republican soiree with me, would you feel comfortable chomping on a pickle?"

"It's *the* most feminine of snacks. Think of all the pregnant women who will settle for nothing else. I'll bring you one this weekend."

"That's all right, Lil. If you were pregnant, maybe I'd understand, but as a consolation for losing Robert? Please. He's not even worth good chocolate. A Hershey bar and I'd be over him."

"If I'm going nowhere in my career," I remind her, "I might as well be bloated, but happy, from a salty foodfest. I just hate to upset Poppy. You call her. She wants me to be healthy and 'in touch with my temple as God created it.' She'll think I've fallen off the wagon if she hears about the soda."

"I'm hanging up now. The senator wannabe is wrapping up. Call Poppy, and I'll make the reservations for the spa. But no more whining over Robert. I'm not wasting any more energy there."

I hang up and shift on my lumpy futon. Who invented this trash piece of furniture anyway? It's so college years. So I-can't-afford-life. Yet I have an MBA from Stanford—granted, it's a degree currently gathering dust since I chucked finance for fashion three years ago. I bet you I'm the only MBA from Stanford sleeping on a futon! Can you spell L-O-S-E-R?

I imagine that if I'd had two parents, or even if I grew up

in a mansion like Morgan with only *one* doting parent, I wouldn't still be sleeping on a futon. Life is full of inequity, I suppose.

I dial up our other friend from college and Spa Girl extraordinaire, Poppy Clayton.

"Dr. Poppy's office."

Poppy, a chiropractor, won't let people call her Doctor Clayton. She always was an open book. At Stanford, they called her "Granola Girl." She was the Birkenstock-clad, tie-dye-wearing freak show who seemed entirely too flaky for her biology major. Poppy was the girl who missed the turnoff for Berkeley and ended up on Stanford's campus by mistake. After college, the medical community and its lack of heart soon broke Poppy's, and she ended up in alternative medicine. I can't imagine her really doing anything else. She thinks pharmaceuticals are of the devil.

"Hi, Emma," I say to her front desk gal. "Is Poppy there? It's Lilly."

"Yeah, hang on." Emma is munching some kind of food in my ear. That woman, while lithe as a bean pole, never stops eating. She'd make a great model, but alas, she doesn't believe in the false Hollywood image. Neither do I, but I'm not averse to simple vanity. If I ate nothing but sawdust so I could somehow end up looking like Emma, I'd at least use it to my advantage. Emma is thin, yet she actually has a figure. I admit it; I covet the image. I'm thin, but in a lanky, childlike way, definitely not an Uma Thurman/Jennifer Aniston way. More like a "Have you entered puberty yet?" sort of way.

Poppy comes on the line with her deep, breathy voice. "Lilly? Is everything all right?"

"Spa weekend," I croak dramatically, in the kind of voice you use when you call in fake-sick. Not that I've ever done that, mind you.

"Oh, no. What's happened?" Poppy immediately goes into doctor mode, ready to cure my ails with some sort of foul-tasting herb.

"Shane got my job, and Robert has another girlfriend—a *Katrina*," I add for emphasis. I'm hoping giving her a name will allow Poppy to ignore my soon-to-be-confessed need for pickles and diet soda.

"Robert had extremely bad energy. You didn't want to marry him, so I'm glad to hear this. He would have sucked the life right out of you. He was an energy vacuum, utterly ruthless, like one of those new Dyson versions with the continuous suction. He would have removed everything."

"Whatever," I say, not willing to listen to her "light is energy" mantra. "It's my hair. It's all because of my hair. I was getting it straightened when the promotion happened." *Why did God bless me with this "crown of glory" anyway?*

Poppy's voice is low and calm. "I imagine they took advantage of your being gone, not that you lost the job because you were gone. And, Lilly, your hair is a gift. Remember, God made you special," she says, sounding remarkably like Bob the Tomato. "Your designs are fabulous, Lilly. I think God's just giving you a place of rest before He launches you, so you're ready to take off. He wants you to stay humble."

See? This is why my Spa Girls are my best friends. With Poppy and Morgan, I am already Vera Wang. It's just a matter of proving it to the rest of the world. They were like that in college, too, when they thought I'd be the next Greenspan or Forbes, trumping those men in the finance world. You know, with friends like this, I've slowly begun to forget all the ugly names I was called in my childhood, the taunting for my out-of-control hair piled atop my lanky frame. Names like "Q-tip" and "Don King" and, my least favorite, "Einstein." I'm mostly over it now, but I have to admit, one look in the mirror on a bad hair day, and I still hear the echoes of those kids calling me those names. And I feel like an awkward fourth grader again.

"I've got four patients right now; can we talk later?" Poppy asks peacefully. Poppy doesn't know stress. She's probably got four people freaking out, waiting to get back to work while she calmly moves about her office at the approximate speed of those last five minutes of winding down in yoga class. She is *shavasana* personified.

"You go, Poppy," I say, out of mercy for her patients. "Will we see you tomorrow afternoon?"

"Count me in for the spa. It's time we all detoxed together." She hangs up on me, and I'm deliriously happy for the moment. I didn't even have to start the Diet Pepsi excuses, and I'm going to smuggle in chocolate truffles on my Spa Girl getaway while I drink green tea with a smile on my face.

So here I am. Three years have passed me by since I left a "real job" to start at the bottom of the fashion world, and so far my name—well, my designs—are not up in lights. I am alone in a dingy apartment with only the roar of the nearby freeway and the musty stench of the moist San Francisco air to keep me company. I grab my ever-present can of Lysol and spray with vengeance. The antiseptic smell soon stings my nose, and I can breathe again. I wonder if you can get addicted to Lysol.

I look at the fabrics splayed all over my cement-block, fashion district loft/warehouse. Remember how in old schools, the windows were up where you couldn't actually see out of them? You got it. That's my loft. Cement. Ugly. Windowless. Well, not windowless if you're willing to climb a twenty-foot ladder for just the freeway view.

The colorful fabrics—scraps from work—almost make

the place livable. They remind me I am at least working in my dream industry. The dream job will come. My big break is just around the bend. It has to be. See, there's an ugly little secret in the couture industry: the geeks of the world rule the runways. And I, most certainly, am a geek. I did not live firmly planted in the world of dweeb in high school for nothing. My fame awaits me. I am getting closer. All the snickering laughter from the homecoming princesses, and now—although they don't know it yet—I am telling *them* what to wear. Chock it up to all those days spent drawing, creating the magical outfit that would make the doofs of the world, like me, suddenly acceptable.

Sophisticated. Elegant. Flawless. Best of the Season.

These are the words used to describe the gowns in my employer's current collection. Actually, the gowns *I* created under her name, Sara Lang. *Lilly Jacobs.* Doesn't it just sound like a Saks Fifth Avenue Collection? Then the loft door jingles, and my passionate daydream is cut short.

Kim Robinson, my roommate and fellow grunt at Sara Lang Couture, comes in and tosses her keys on one of our lone pieces of furniture: an old sewing table retrieved one time from near the dumpster. "Are you all right?" she asks.

"I'm fine," I say, thinking, *How fine can I be? I'm the most overeducated, underemployed person on Sara Lang's payroll.* "Did anyone say anything about me not getting the job?" I ask.

"Just murmurs. No more than normal when someone gets promoted. We meowed and then cleared out."

"I have to leave Sara Lang, don't I? I mean, it's now or never."

"It's obvious what Sara thinks, Lilly. You'll find something else. Maybe under someone else's wing, you'll find more options. Or you can always go back to fi—"

"Don't even utter the word!"

I start pacing the whole twelve-hundred square feet of our loft—my high-heeled feet clacking on the cement floor with an eerie echo. "Nana's gonna pass out when she finds out I didn't get the promotion. I've been telling her this is it for us." My Nana sold her house to pay for my education. She put up with my little design stint, thinking I'd be over it by now and back to finance—and good shoes. Alas, I'm a stubborn thing, and I really thought this dream was what I was meant to do. Nana, who raised me since I was a baby, seems to take a more practical view of God at work. "What does Sara Lang know anyhow? I can do this."

"*Please*, Lilly. Spare me the *Evita* speech. You're best friends with Morgan Malliard. Let her wear your stuff, for crying out loud! Then, you'll *know* if you have the talent or not, 'cause you'll read about it on the society pages the very next day." Kim's got her head in the fridge, looking for a nonexistent snack. "That ridiculous pride of yours is going to keep Nana in a rental the rest of her life! If I had a friendship like yours, I'd use it! I sure wouldn't let Sara Lang get any more of the credit. The last time that woman touched a sewing machine, it had foot pedals! She couldn't use a computerized model if you locked her away with it for a year."

I sigh. "You're probably right." Of course she's right. No one likes a whiner, and I'm sort of dwelling in that place right now. I'm the antithesis of yoga-calm Poppy. I'm Jazzercise on steroids.

I just can't use Morgan, though. Not after watching her own father toss her out into society to be devoured like she was a piece of meat thrown to lions. Morgan has been used enough. Her father actually asks her to preen when dirty old men salivate over her—thinking perhaps the additional testosterone will pry open their moth-ridden wallets. *Ick! No,*

I just can't do that to Morgan. If anything, I need to help her escape her gilded cage. Not add padding to the nest.

Morgan is so beautiful, so put-together that when she befriended me in college, it made me forget I was an object of scorn, laughed at for my hair. Hanging around Morgan Malliard made me feel like the princess she is. She made me feel important. Naturally, I knew Jesus loves me for who I am, but in college, having Morgan and Poppy as friends was like having Jesus in the flesh, right in the dorm. They made me feel loved and accepted more than anyone ever had. They still do.

"She'd put a sack on for you, Lilly," Kim says of Morgan, and I know it's true, which is the exact reason I won't ask. Kim always seems like she doesn't pay attention to anything going on around her, but she sees a lot more than she lets on. She's the first to claim ignorance in any given situation and go on about her GED or lack of good breeding, but she's got more sense than half the men in the Financial District, generally speaking. That's not to say she doesn't have her issues.

My Spa Girls seem to inhabit a different universe from Kim and me. Morgan Malliard lives in a mansion on Nob Hill, wearing her father's jewelry for a living at different social events. Poppy Clayton heals people by cracking their bones and doling out sage biblical wisdom, along with botanical herbs. I live a different existence, with debt the size of California itself, a futon, and an expensive education—that's doing *what* for me again?

My Nana, who raised me, is living in a six-hundred-square-foot attached studio, for which I feel fully responsible. She sold her house when my undergraduate scholarship ran out—never even told me she was selling, though it had been my childhood residence and the only place I knew as home. She didn't put a sign out or anything. Just one day she had her crumbling foundation, Formica-countered house, and the next day she had a cashier's check for $375,000 after taxes and mortgages. Welcome to the Bay Area. Doesn't that sound like a mint? Yeah, it did to us too. Once upon a time, before I slept on a futon.

I grab my bag, a freebie that has Sara Lang written across it. *Ugh, like I needed that.* I spray it with Lysol just to show Sara what I actually think of her. "I'm going to the spa this weekend," I say to Kim. *Translation: Don't get drunk. I won't be here to drive you home.* "Morgan's paying for it yet again. You'd think with all the spa dates I need, God would have seen fit to provide me a better income."

Kim is moving around the room with an iPod bud in one ear. "Quite frankly, if I had a friend like Morgan, I'd harass her to no end until she wore my designs. What would I have to lose?"

This from the woman who thinks being the designated driver is the job description for roommate. And I don't even have a car!

"Is this what you planned for your life? Living in an airplane that never leaves the runway? That's what it sounds like." Kim yanks her hair up into a ponytail, pulls out the earbud, and changes the now-heated subject. "What are you doing *until* this weekend? Are you showing up at work tomorrow? What are you going to wear?"

"Of course I'm showing up. I can't pay for all this luxury," I sweep my hands around the dumpy room, "without a job."

"I'm going out with the gang tonight," Kim explains. "We're going to diss Shane at Happy Hour. Want to come? Free food."

"No thanks." I look down at my Bible and a twinge of guilt suddenly explodes within. "Maybe Shane deserved that promotion."

She lifts an eyebrow. "Being a Christian doesn't mean you should lie just to be nice. Am I right? Besides, he'll be worried about our opinions tomorrow, so I figure that gives us this one day to vent, but good. And what better way than over cosmopolitans and free food?"

I toss the Sara Lang bag on the bed and grab some microwave popcorn while Kim gets dressed in her "bedroom," better known as behind the Chinese silk screen partition—a Poppy hand-me-down. I chug my first Diet Pepsi of the binge. My eye wanders to a picture next to the fridge: Poppy, Morgan, and me in Stanford sweatshirts with mud packs on our faces.

What a weird threesome: Morgan, the aloof, nearly friendless princess everyone loved to hate; Poppy, the flaky, hemp-wearing Stevie Nicks of the late 1990s; and me, at Stanford on a government grant, meeting their "affordable-education" quota. Three misfits brought together out of sheer necessity (no one else wanted anything to do with us). It's amazing what social ineptitude can do for female bonding.

We three dateless wonders somehow all ended up at a Stanford social, but there must have been something better going on somewhere else because we were the crowd. We had a dorm lounge, a TV/VCR combo and *Edward Scissorhands* all to ourselves. We bonded over Johnny Depp sighs, Now & Laters, and our love for Jesus.

Most importantly, that night we learned that all of us were raised without a mother. Mine ran off when my dad was killed and left me with my Nana. Poppy's was in and out of her life in between communes, and Morgan's died young from an unexpected stroke. It was enough to bond us for life. And it did.

Since that time, I've realized that it wasn't all that accidental that the three of us are dateless. Morgan runs everything past her overbearing and ridiculous father, who never approves of anyone without a solid portfolio and an advanced age. Poppy, meanwhile, often runs dates off with her alternative-medicine diatribe, telling them how their headaches are caused by poor liver function and the like. She makes men feel completely emasculated, as though she's saying, "You are absolutely void of testosterone. I cannot find a male hormone within you."

Me? As I've said, I am incapable of speaking properly when attracted to a man, so I tend to stick with men I'm not attracted to. With all our quirks, this makes for a rather passionless existence for all three of us. So rather than plan our weddings, we go to the spa and whine about the complete and utter lack of available men in San Francisco. When crises arise, we head to Spa Del Mar in central California. It's a pretty cheesy spa, as far as luxury goes, but now that we (meaning Poppy and Morgan) can afford better, we're too attached to our precious, dumpy Del Mar. Morgan always pays for my portion of the spa. She insists, and I've stopped fighting her. It's like paying for 7-11 coffee for me: insignificant to her bank account. If we were going to the Golden Door or something, I could understand, but Spa Del Mar? Not an issue.

Kim emerges from behind the screen wearing a micro-mini skirt, a faux fur jacket, and a matching furry purse. She takes notice of my silent disapproval. "Just never mind. It's what I'm wearing. At least I have a place to go."

"Suit yourself," I say. *Or not*, I add silently, unwrapping the popcorn and putting the bag in the microwave.

Someone knocks at the door. "That must be my ride." Kim opens the door, and her expression visibly falls. It's Nate, our upstairs neighbor. He looks at Kim's skirt, or should I say lack of skirt, and I see his face contort in confusion.

"Hi, Nate," I say from the kitchenette.

"Hey, gals." Nate lets himself in, as Kim has deemed his presence unimportant in her life and has walked away with the door open. "I just wanted to come by and let you know someone tried to break into my place today. The police came, but if you hear anything suspicious, just call them, okay?"

Nate has completely remodeled his loft, and it looks like something out of an architectural magazine. He's also an engineer, so the entire contents of his office look like a Best Buy store. Ah, the soothing style of slick, black particle board. Trendy, and oh-so-practical.

We, by contrast, have a TV set. An old nineteen-inch TV set. With rabbit ears—pointed ineffectively at the raised window.

"I don't think the burglars will be by here, Nate," I counter. "I mean, I bet they could get a whopping fifty cents for that sewing table on eBay. With shipping, it's completely worthless. Sadly, I think we're safe."

"I just don't like you two down here alone. You want to borrow Charley for a couple days?" Nate asks.

Charley, his mutt who smells worse than my musty loft? The dog with a draining ear issue? "No, thanks. I'm going away this weekend, so just keep an eye on Kim. Kim, do you want Charley?"

Kim wanders back into the loft. "I can handle myself. I'll wait for my ride downstairs." Kim rolls her eyes. Nate is about as mainstream as they come, and therefore of no interest to Kim. She tends to lean toward bad boys who ride "hogs" and who are more covered by tattoos than not.

Kim breezes by Nate, and he watches her go down the hallway. "She'll have plenty of offers for rides in that getup." He shakes his head.

"You're probably right, but you can't tell Kim anything. At least she's not driving, so I can keep my ten o'clock bedtime. Come on in for some popcorn. It's almost done," I say, listening to the quick succession of pops in the microwave.

Nate saunters in, wearing his UC Davis sweatshirt and a

pair of holey jeans. He's just heavenly to look at, sort of a cross between Hugh Grant and Bill Gates. I wish he was my type, but he's too into electronics and technological advancements for me. A conversation with him always includes acronyms that make me think he's speaking another language. MIS, IT, JPEG—it all gives me a vicious headache.

Maybe working with creative types is warping me, but life with Nate has got to be exasperating. And with Charley as part of the deal? It's simply not negotiable. There's not enough Lysol in the world. Nate has a view of the Bay Bridge and a complete lack of desire to "venture out" into the beautiful city he takes for granted. He'd rather see the world through the Internet, international phone calls, and ethnic takeout. His speed dial reads like a mall food court:

Pradeep (chicken tandoori)

Rupert (shepherd's pie)

Hao (sweet and sour pork)

Junien (brie—not mall court fare, but what else do the French eat?)

"So where you going this weekend?" Nate goes to my fridge and pulls out a Diet Pepsi for himself.

"It's a Spa Girls weekend." Even as I say it, I feel my body relax.

"Ah, girls and goop. Doesn't get much better than that, huh?" He takes a swig of soda.

It sure doesn't. I flop onto my futon and grin at him. "If you're destined to be a loser in this lifetime, a chemical peel can at least make you look good while you're at it."

chapter 2

nly half a day of work. That's what I tell myself to gear up for the coming storm. I can feel the squall in the air as I think about my ride to work on Muni, San Francisco's glorious (not!) public transportation. I wish I could sneak Lysol aboard. Or I should at least remember to wipe Vicks VapoRub under my nose to ward off the lovely combination of body odor, sweat, and stale cigarettes that stick with you long after you and Muni go your separate ways. The gift that keeps on giving. I sit down at the sewing table for a gourmet breakfast of generic Grape-Nuts. *Someday,* I think, *I'll be able to afford the real thing.*

It's only a mere few hours until the smell of peppermint foot salts will put an end to this misery I call daily reality. It's depressing that I should be wasting my freshly-straightened hair on this day, but as I said, if I hadn't been out of the office thermal-reconditioning—I might be the hot, new, young designer at Sara Lang.

Kim gets up, looking like the kiss of death. Her ashen skin and bed head plastered with last night's gel give me a run for my money. She is smacking her tongue against the roof of her dry mouth, and I have to say, it's grossing me out.

"Do you have to do that?" I ask. "I'm eating."

"My mouth is like the Sahara. Too much alcohol last night. I always regret that."

I raise my eyebrows at her. "You're not twenty-one anymore, Kim. I think your body's rebelling. I know mine is. Sit down, and enjoy some fiber with me."

She rubs her forehead. "It's downhill from here, isn't it, Lil? First, we're eating fiber. Next thing you know, we're drinking prune juice and doing crafts in the rec room." She lets her head fall in her hands. "Once, we were the talk of the town. The young designers coming in to take Sara Lang into the next millennium. Remember, they even did a story in the *Chronicle*. Now we're has-beens and we haven't even been anywhere."

"We're not has-beens. They say fifty is the new thirty, so I figure we've got a good twenty years left to make it."

"Shoot me if I try that long." Kim cradles her head in her hands. "At this rate I won't even be able to afford good plastic surgery when this job has sucked out my very essence. I'll be visiting one of those guys who advertises on billboards: "FACE LIFTS: $4,000." She pulls her jet-black hair up, yanking her face unnaturally tight. "I'm going to get myself a respectable job that pays. I'm tired of walking by the window at Saks and drooling. Heck, the windows at Macy's! Pretty soon, I'm going to be drooling over the windows at Target. And they don't even have windows," she moans.

"You're just saying all this because it's the morning after the Shane debacle. We've had other designers rise beside us. It's our turn, Kim! Sara's making big changes, and this could be our opportunity. Maybe Shane got the job because Sara has something better for us."

"No, Lilly, the Lang train has passed us by, and we're pathetically sitting on the platform waiting for the next. Only, it's not coming. It's been and gone. Sara herself is becoming passé, which is the only reason she promoted one of us in the first place. She needs someone young to remind her that people actually have a social life beyond ruining their daughter's lives."

"You'll feel better after you brush your teeth," I say, hoping the reminder of minty-fresh breath will spark some action.

Kim grabs me by the shoulders and jolts me back into the moment. "What part of this are you not getting? We've wasted three years! Not to mention that you are wasting your college education and missing out on a decent job handling other people's money! Avoiding dog-breath is not going to fix this. Good oral hygiene is not our problem, Lilly." She looks at my collection of Lysol cans. "There is not a spray available that can wipe away the infection we know as Sara Lang. It's over. She's taken over, like a resistant strain of bacteria. She's impervious to antibiotics."

"We're on the brink of something big, Kim. I feel it." But do I really? Or am I just avoiding the obvious: that maybe it's time for a real job. "I had a plan. Granted, this diversion wasn't in it, but we can take our designs to our own business. We've got everything we need. My sketching, your computer experience. All we need is a tad more work on color and we're gone! This is the springboard to greatness, don't you see?"

"This is why you should drink, Lilly. At least the delusions I live under are fun. Listen to you, Pollyanna! And the thing is, *you* don't even believe it. There's no way you could."

She's right. I hate that. Even with a hangover and eight piercings, Kim makes sense. I'm twenty-nine with a master's degree, and I can't afford windows. I can barely pay to maintain my mop. Without a steady dose of pomade and hours in the stylist's chair, I'm Lilly from high school again, the girl with big hair and bad clothes.

The alternative, a real job, is too painful to think about.

Proving my Nana right after all these years would be like taking my last gasping breath before allowing my face to disappear into the quicksand. I just can't do it. I have to try one last time. It *has* to be my turn. I can't bear to think of the contingency plan. Working in finance was like being monetarily rewarded for a lack of creativity.

I stand up and take my bowl to the sink. "We're going to make it, Kim."

"We're not, Lilly. We didn't, in fact." Kim tries to smooth a brush through her dyed tresses, but it appears something has encrusted from the night before, and she throws the brush across the room.

"So I'll give you, maybe we're not going to make it at Sara Lang. Maybe our time's up there, but we're not giving up for the likes of Shane Wesley. He's not the designer he thinks he is," I say, feeling guilty for finally admitting the truth out loud.

"Think practically. Your grandmother is not getting any younger. Would you have her retire here in this dump with us? As if *you* don't deaden the party as it is, we need a seventy-five-year-old woman cramping our style?" Kim rolls her eyes.

"I'm leaving for work," I say, parking the dirty dish in the sink as she so often does for me. "Are you coming?"

"No. I quit. Why should I suffer the humiliation of Shane in my job? In your job? He'll be walking around dressed like Steven Tyler, bossing anything that moves, whisking his scarf around like the drama queen he is. You *know* he'll have a scarf today. I don't have it in me to watch. There's not enough hangover left. I'd have to start from scratch to stomach it, and I'm broke."

"What if it is our turn, Kim? And we get off the highway one exit too soon?" I don't want her to give up. Part of the reason is that if Kim gives up, I might give up, and I'll be back crunching numbers for the rest of my days. I'll be waiting for the accountant of my dreams to darken my wood-paneled doorway.

"Lilly," Kim says as if I'm slow. "There are illegal aliens in L.A. sweatshops doing our jobs. Your degrees are being wasted, my talent is evaporating, and you think ignoring these things will make them go away. We either go with some dignity intact or we suck up to Shane, pretend nothing happened, and see how long Sara will let us hang around. What's it gonna be? Self-respect or perpetual failure?"

I look around at our hovel. "You mean there are consequences worse than this?" I pick up my Sara Lang bag, toss it over my shoulder, and head for the door. "I'll see you at work. I'll make excuses for you being late."

"I'm not coming, Lilly. Have some dignity, will you?"

"Dignity can wait. I need a paycheck."

"Everyone who has gotten a promotion is gone, Lilly. It's like Sara's chaining us, and this is our last chance to break free! You're handing her your wrists and begging her to lock you up!"

I think about this. I felt locked up when I was in finance. Deciding whether people like James Huntington III would make more money with a sagging property as a tax write-off or with a 1031 exchange for a high-end rental that would bring in more income...*that* was locked up. It's not that James Huntington III doesn't have the right to make as much money as he pleases. This is a free country, and capitalism is an important part of that. I just had no passion for that life, other than pleasing my Nana. She seems to think that if I get rich, all of my problems would be solved.

But I'm a poor excuse for a rich person. I don't have the right hair, for one thing. Money just doesn't motivate me, which is a problem when you're in finance. I didn't really care if James Huntington III made more money. He'd buy a new

Mercedes convertible to use on the weekends, and I'd feel empty inside. Even if I could buy a new Mercedes, what's the point?

Being a real, live fairy godmother, transforming an ugly duckling into a beautiful swan with the right design, the right fabric—*that* was my dream. That would give me total job satisfaction. So I prayed for God to make my path and purpose clear. I prayed while bent over my sewing machine, and I realized that I felt the most alive when I was creating something out of material, when there was something beautiful at the end. So I jumped the finance ship and hopped aboard the world of fashion—at Sara Lang. I would have worked for Sara for free if I could still eat. Three years later, I'm still barely making ends meet, but I love what I do. I take problems and construct solutions out of fabric. Sure, it's a small thing in the scheme of life, but it's important to me.

"I'll see you, Kim. I'm off to the office," I say, tucking my Bible under my arm. I'm going to need all the ammunition I can get today.

After a harrowing ride on Muni, I open the office door to see everyone swarming Shane's desk, fawning over him. *Gag.* The fiber cereal is roiling, and I'm wishing I ate Cap'n Crunch instead of wasting anything healthy on this day. Shane is completely in his element, laughing uproariously and sharing the design that cinched the job for him. I amble to my desk, limp with disbelief. *Oh yeah, Shane will do for design what Mad Max did for buttless chaps. You know, God, there are days I just don't get what You're doing in my life.*

"Lil-lyyy!" I hear Shane yell with overemphasized vowels. "Aren't you going to congratulate me?"

"I did. Yesterday. Remember?" *I fear that's all I can stomach without retching.*

"Oh, so you did. I must have been so impressed by your

freshly-pressed hair that I forgot. You really give us a shock when you get that done. It makes us all fear the run on John Frieda products will temporarily lower the Dow Jones!" He laughs aloud. Now I'll admit I keep my share of John Frieda products in my office, but do I look through the baker's dozen of pill bottles in his desk? No, I don't.

I have never once made fun of his fake lisp, or his penchant for evening eye makeup during the day. Not even of his inability to eat lunch without wearing some of it. And yet every chance this man gets, he picks on my Achilles heel: my hair. *If them's not fighting words, I don't know what is. I mean, at least I have hair.*

I land a playful slap on his arm. "You're so funny, Shane." On that note, I saunter—at least I aim for a saunter—over to my desk and unpack the variety of fabrics from the canvas bag. I've picked some great material for the next spring collection, and I'm betting the whole bundle on spring. If it doesn't happen then, I'll give up. *Color,* I think to myself. *I have to understand color better!*

Shane follows me into the office. "You're not going with that, are you?" He bunches up his nose, as if something smells even more overwhelming than his cologne. "Lavender is so last year."

"It's from last year," I counter. "I use scraps to create my design. It's easier on Sara's budget that way. If we're ever going to go public, we need to be conscious of costs." But as I say it, I wonder if my need for cheap—excuse me, *cost effectiveness*—is getting in the way of my learning the full spectrum of color. *Besides, I sorta like lavender.*

"Little old ladies worry about budget. You're designing couture, Lilly; act like it. Or next thing you know, you'll be designing painted T-shirts with matching leggings for the Pier 39 set," he says, referring to San Francisco's tourists. "Now that you're a part of my team, it's important we're on the same page."

"We'll never be on the same page, Shane." As I stare at him, I think, *At least I hope we'll never be on the same page.* Shane's love in life is the society set, and this is his route into the realm of people he hopes to hang around and model his life after.

Me? I just want to dress them and run for cover.

"I suggest you bookmark my page, Lilly, because I am taking this company to the next level, and only those of the highest caliber are coming with me." He snaps his fingers back and forth in the air.

Is it possible that rolling your eyes too much can lead to permanent brain damage? I say nothing as Shane gets to the door, his navy-outlined eyes threatening me.

"Don't give me that look, Lilly. Your association with greatness means nothing to me. Unlike Sara, I'm not afraid to fire you because you're friends with Morgan Malliard."

I gasp. My fingers fly up to cover my mouth, but it's too late. "Morgan Malliard wouldn't wear anything you designed if her life depended on it!" I hiss. Mostly because I'd kill her if she did, but also because she has taste. Shane's style emulates the Bratz doll, for those with fathers who have more cents than sense. Those willing to pay for the hoochie couture look. I understand Sara's rationale behind Shane's promotion. She's going after the Paris Hilton type, becoming the Chanel for the spoiled generation. A business model that makes my Stanford MBA curl on the wall. *Can you say "fad," "trend," and "soon-to-be irrelevant"?* Instead of her former understated elegance, Sara and Shane have recently marketed stick-figure jeans and skull-and-crossbone T-shirts.

There's a reason for Sara's abrupt left-turn in fashion, her attempt to appeal to a different kind of clientele. Sara's husband left her for a hoochie couture type. Now, if you'd ever seen

Sara talk to her husband (or should I say yell mercilessly?), you'd understand that his acquiring the underage girlfriend was merely a symptom of the marital problem. Not that Jeff Lang is innocent, mind you, but it takes two to tango. Once he left, Sara had only one thought: revenge. When she was ordered to pay alimony, I think her dream became for Jeff "the lying, cheating scum" Lang to see every young woman's bum covered with his ex-wife's signature. Hence the jeans.

At some point, of course, she will want to return to opera gowns and wedding dresses. At least, one can only hope.

Shane leaves my office and goes running to his desk where his fans await him. *He's all bark.*

Now Sara Lang walks quietly into my office and shuts the door behind her. To say that Sara would eat her young is, of course, an exaggeration. But she would steal her daughter's boyfriend. I watched the attempt. When young Lina, a mousy antithesis of her mother, came in with a new beau, Sara did everything she could to wrench the boy's attention away from her daughter. To his credit, he rebuffed my boss's advances, and he's been my hero ever since. But seeing that side of Sara opened a whole new world for me.

I realized some people are just narcissistic to the core. The world does not turn unless it's in relation to them. Oh, I know that everyone's a sinner. That's plain scripture. I understand it well, in fact, but some people are hideously egotistic and never take another's well-being into account, even their own flesh and blood. That's my boss in a nutshell, and it ain't pretty. I've seen the most gentle people feel sorry for her and try to soften her heart, only to run screaming at something she does. She's known for toddler-like tantrums, screaming expletives at employees, and now for keeping her ex-husband on a very short financial leash.

Looks-wise, Sara Lang is above average, though past her

prime and a big fan of the chemical peel and Botox. It's not her looks though, that garner attention. She oozes sensuality and speaks to men without talking. It used to work like a charm. Now it's just sort of pathetic, especially with her face not moving the way it once did when it wasn't full of muscle zapper. She's no Demi Moore, and the schmoozing talk with a hint of more to come is just plain frightening to men. I know it's certainly terrifying to watch.

Sara leans against my office wall, pausing dramatically to give me the effect that she really is upset the promotion did not go to me. "I'm sure you're wondering why Shane got the promotion," Sara says, pacing the four square feet in my office, trailing her hand along my sewing machine. I see her eyes stop on the couture gown sketch on my desk, but I quickly turn it over.

"I figure you must have your reasons," I state coolly. "Yesterday, you said something about my designs not being unique. You've been more than clear that you're fond of his talent over mine."

"As you know, I'm thinking of taking this company public soon."

"I've heard rumors." Though in my heart, I know with the new hoochie direction, this company's like an anchor on a kite string. It's not going anywhere because it completely strays from her customer base: San Francisco's sophisticate crowd.

"I need a chief financial officer who knows the business," Sara says, smacking her glossy, freshly Restylane-pumped lips. "A CFO who has the education to please investors. Something akin to an MBA from Stanford." She looks pointedly at me and crosses her arms, letting her black-manicured hands slide down her arms like two long-legged spiders.

"I'm a designer, Sara, not a CFO." I grab a stack of papers

and smack them against my desk like the local TV news anchor.

"You can design when there's time, but a CFO has so much more say in the direction of a company." She slides a paper in front of me like a bad car salesman. "This is what our CFO will make."

My heart begins to palpitate as I look at the number. My mind reels: *my Nana's home...designer handbags...windows...a pair of Giuseppe Zanotti stilettos.* I had all those things once, but they came with a life I hated.

I slide the paper back toward her. "Why not hire an experienced CFO?" I ask, leery. *Sara is as cheap as a Vegas showgirl.* Remember when Courtney Love turned couture? Didn't exactly take, and Sara's sudden turnaround in wanting to keep me is, most likely, no different. I should have listened to Kim and stayed home today.

"Lilly, you've done a great deal for this company. Don't think I haven't noticed how you've managed the collections financially. I think this is your true gift. If designing comes, great, but this is where I need you. This is where the company needs you."

My true gift? Is it? Part of me wants to salute and tell her, "Lilly Jacobs, reporting for duty." But I revert to my overly cautious self. "Can I have the weekend to think about it?" *The Spa Girls will know what I should do.* I hate to think I can be bought, but staring at this number, I'm thinking maybe it's easier than I thought to purchase Lilly Jacobs. The idea of staying in design at a decent salary, even if it's not exactly the job I want...well...it's tempting, I'll admit. I picture myself walking up with a Marc Jacobs bag, and it's nearly over.

"Take the weekend," Sara says agreeably. "If you're worried about the public offering, you won't have to go through that. The venture capitalists will put someone in place who specializes in going public when the time is right. If I didn't think you were capable of the job, Lilly, I wouldn't offer it." Sara licks her lips, which is like watching a dog eat peanut butter. "Is Kim in yet?"

I stammer a minute. "No, but she's coming. Muni was having big issues today." *Not a lie; Muni always has issues. Not the least of which is the smell.*

Just as I say it, Kim comes sauntering into the office, carrying a Starbucks cup (a splurge for her). I feel my shoulders relax. Slowly, Kim looks into my doorway and smiles at me. I feel a spark of hope ignite.

chapter 3

Spa Del Mar's brochure reads like this: *Nestled in the wooded hills of the Central California Coastal Range, Spa Del Mar offers an extraordinary healing retreat away from the busyness of life and the bustle of the city. Your peaceful accommodations include freedom from ringing phones, unpleasant smog, and traffic jams. Enjoy the tranquil setting of our redwood hot tubs with soothing mineral water, and experience our therapeutic massages and state-of-the-art skin care. Retreat to our labyrinth meditation garden to allow nature's serenity to soothe your soul.*

Translation: *Spa Del Mar is in the middle of nowhere. We haven't got any phones or televisions because we can't afford an operator or the cable bill. When you think you're bored out of your skull, take a dunk in our redwood hot tub with sulfur water that smells like rotten eggs, and select from two spa treatments: facial or massage. Take your pick. We make decision-making easy here at Spa Del Mar because we only offer two choices. It's all we're legally entitled to perform. When you're done with that, you can fight for the single bench under the sycamore tree outside.*

Altogether, Spa Del Mar is so not state-of-the-art. But we love it.

After a four-hour ride, we drive up to the spa's front door in Morgan's BMW, which is the size of a small airplane and has just as many buttons. You might think that a bellman would come running out, wearing a red suit with smart, gold buttons. But no, at Spa Del Mar you park the car and schlep your own bags up the hill to the speckled Formica front counter. Spa Del Mar runs your credit card (or in this instance, Morgan's credit card) through that machine that still uses carbon, and we're on our way—with a complimentary warm bottle of mineral water and a key. (Apparently, cold water can upset your digestive tract.)

Spa Del Mar's well-appointed balcony room (which we get every time) includes two lawn chairs and a plastic table outside, plus two queen beds decorated in a palette of seafoam and jungle green inside. Whichever one of us really *needs* the spa weekend gets a bed to herself. This time, that would be me. See? There are distinct advantages to being a failure and having hair that ruins your life. Naturally, since I'm not able to pay, I don't call too many spa weekends of my own, but I knew it was bad when my straightened hair didn't even cheer me up. This weekend was a necessity.

It may sound like Spa Del Mar is a complete dump, but it's not. It's beautiful, with canopied sycamores and oaks and lush greenery surrounding—even a jacaranda tree that is bright purple when it blooms. The room is clean and neat, just nothing fancy. Plus, it has windows! Still, it is a bit shocking that Morgan is willing to come here. I think she equates it to "roughing it." The evenings are spent enjoying fine spa cuisine by a chef from California's wine country. Throw in plenty of giggling and those forbidden organic truffles, and how could I not love it?

"All right, Lilly. We're here." Morgan turns around on the stairwell and stares at me. "Are you ready to talk? We've given you the entire drive, and you haven't said a word."

"You need to talk about it before you have the first spa

treatment. The release of emotion starts the detox process," Poppy adds.

"Can we get in the room first?" I say. I don't want to let on that my contraband jug of pickles and two liters of Diet Pepsi in the bag slung over my shoulder are killing me. Then again, I don't want to discuss my personal life on the stairwell, either.

Poppy opens the door and kicks off her earthy Clarks clogs. She breathes in deeply and lifts her hands to the ceiling. "I love this air. We really should do this more often. Mmm. It smells like they sprayed eucalyptus oil." She opens the sliding glass door to our balcony, sniffs the sulfur from the hot tub below, and covers her nose. "Ugh, maybe not *that* air."

"Come on, crisis meeting." Morgan yanks the desk chair onto the balcony. All three of us take our places for the official "Spa Girls Board of Directors Meeting" where we discuss the reasons for the trip. Of course, we all know the reasons, and we're only rehashing old information, but venting is a necessary part of a Spa Girls Weekend.

We sit and look at each other. *We're here.* I'm significantly calmer knowing I'm here, and that I can always come here if I need to. And that my Spa Girls will always be on my side. Once, in college, there was this guy I was interested in, and I followed him to class. He caught me trailing him, turned around sharply, and said, "Stop following me, Afro girl! You need a muzzle on that thing!" I was heartbroken and humiliated.

The next day, Morgan dressed up in heels and a skirt and accidentally-on-purpose dropped her art history paper in front of him. When he saw the endless legs attached to the heels on the absolute vision before him, he became speechless and bent down immediately to pick it up. Morgan cut him off in mid-bend. "Don't touch my paper," she said. "I don't know where you've been. And I don't want to." Then, with a flick of her luxurious hair, she picked up her paper and sashayed off.

It was a small thing. The guy never knew she had anything to do with me or his rude comment the day before. I'm sure he didn't even get it, but her gesture made me feel six feet tall, with naturally sleek hair, and ready for the cover of *Vogue*. Poppy and I stood by laughing, entranced by our friend's unselfish-yet-childish act.

"It feels good to be here, doesn't it?" I ask. "It's been too long."

"Let's hit it!" Morgan says, clapping her manicured hands together. "First, we need to give thanks that Lilly dumped Robert. I've been praying for that for ages."

"Is that biblically acceptable? Praying for me to dump someone?" I ask.

"Take it up with God, Lilly," Poppy says.

Morgan holds up a palm. "First of all, do not say he dumped you. I will not allow you to be dumped by a drone who thought Denny's was an appropriate date night choice in San Francisco. The finest culinary fare in the world, and he thinks letting you choose the chicken-fried steak is going all out. He *so* did not dump you. I will not give him the satisfaction of dumping you."

"Okay," I shrug. "But he sort of did."

Poppy starts to crack up.

"Besides, I like chicken-fried steak," I admit.

"Next subject," Morgan says.

"Well," I say. "We have an array of choices. We can start with my pathetic career, move on to my nonexistent love life, or if we're really feeling lottery-lucky, we can go with my hair. The *root* of all my issues." I look at Poppy, and her mouth is open. "And if you say one thing about my negative energy, you're gonna feel my negative energy in the form of a palm!"

Poppy puts her hands up in surrender and giggles. "Listen, I'd rather have a nonexistent love life *without* a boyfriend than *with* one!" She clears her throat. "Robert…really, Lilly, if we're going to discuss pathetic…besides, neither one of us would have attended a wedding to that dimwit. He made Alan Greenspan look like the life of the party."

"He was bald," I explain, because for me that's a good thing. Massive hair plus no hair equals children with normal hair, right? Because I would never inflict any child with my mop—and the life that goes with it.

"Lilly, I've tried to explain genetics to you," Poppy says. "It doesn't matter if your husband is bald; you could still have a child with curly hair."

I cover my ears. "I'm not listening."

"I think we need to pray about our attitudes first." Morgan bows her head and recites a prayer for me and my attitude.

She'd have an attitude, too, if she was living on a twin-sized futon with a hand-me-down silkscreen partition defining her bedroom. She'd have an attitude if she wanted to keep doing a job so badly that she was willing to work for the Wicked Witch of the West to do it, to abandon all pride and decent pay. These silent surrenders cause attitude to build up like a water balloon hooked up to a spigot.

"Do you have anything to add?" Poppy asks at the end of prayer.

"Do I ever!" I say, but quickly shut up as I see them both with their hands clasped in prayer. It wasn't the kind of thing I could add during prayer time. Apparently, the attitude request hasn't kicked in with God yet.

Poppy clears her throat. "Good, we should get started with our facials and come back with some solutions for you, Lilly. The natural oils will allow our brains to focus on solutions."

"Solutions? My life has solutions? Other than the kind with the acrid smell that calm my hair, you mean? A solution where I don't look like Howard Stern?"

"Quit your whining. You're burdening me." Poppy breathes in deeply through her nose. Now I know she sounds like a complete Californian, but Poppy really just likes to bug us with her energy talk. She knows we're only so open to the idea of light as energy, God's first building particle, being the healing life source of it all. So she loves to bring it up. Constantly. Just to challenge our grounded and conservative ways. She's also always bringing us some new elixir that has the consistency of yogurt and is the sickly green color of Shrek.

"I'm entitled to a bit of whining. Tell me something in my life that's actually on target." They both stay silent. "See? You got nothing. Oh yeah, I deserve to whine. Bring out the pickles."

"Pickles? Lilly, you didn't bring the pickles!" Morgan says.

I clutch my Sara Lang bag close to my heart.

"You'll get a yeast imbalance," Poppy says, reaching out for the bag, which I yank closer. "The human body is made up of a careful balance of good yeast and bad—"

"Stop it," I say calmly, not relinquishing my grip. "Vinegar is a preservative. How do you know that my body won't have a half-life of forty billion years from my pickle fetish? Maybe I'll outlast you both. Preserved like well-oiled wood."

"Gross," Morgan says.

Poppy grabs the handles and darn if that Pilates isn't making her tough. She wrestles it free. "You're not eating this poison." She gasps as she looks inside the bag. "And diet soda? You've got to be kidding me. Toxic, Lilly! It's important for your future children. So important, in fact—" She rushes through the bathroom door with my coveted bag and locks it with a loud click.

I bang on it. "Open this door. Right now, Poppy! I mean it!" I pound again, and I can hear her in there fiddling. Then my ears pick up a sudden swoosh of liquid. "I want my pickles! You better not have done anything to—"

In another moment, she calmly opens the door and exhales with yoga intensity.

"What did you do?" I ask. "Ugh!" We're overcome with the sour vinegar smell emanating from the bathroom. "You did not ruin my pickles!"

"I'm going to prove to you what you're doing to the lining of your stomach. Just a little science experiment worthy of my Stanford biology undergrad work."

I gasp as I see the sink filled with my pickles. Covered in a hazy brown sauce of diet soda. I have to admit, it is a revolting sight. "What did you do?"

"By the end of the weekend, those pickles will be a ghastly color, and the carbonation and fake sugar will have eaten holes right through them. That's what you're doing to your stomach." Poppy flicks back her hair. "No wonder you stress about simple matters. Your body is completely overloaded from garbage, and the good bacteria can't overtake the bad in those quantities."

"That is disgusting," Morgan comments in her cool manner, as she looks at the sickly display of my snack life. "We are not going to smell that all weekend just for the sake of science, Poppy. Let them out of their misery. She can't eat them now anyway."

"What would I do with them?" Poppy asks.

"Get a garbage bag or something. I am not brushing my teeth over pickles drenched in diet soda."

I slam the door on the bathroom to avoid the smell and point at the Spa Girls, who are now seriously on my bad side. "You two are *so* not friends. We came here for me. And I wanted pickles! What kind of friends would deny their friend the wallowing she so richly deserves?" I slink to the floor. "Where did my friends go?"

"Where did your *friends* go?" Morgan blinks wildly. "You

wanted Steve Collins in college, and we protected you from that as well," Morgan reminds me. "And Robert, Lilly? Completely not worth damaging your stomach lining for. Clearly, you're not the best judge of what's best for you lately. You need us, face it. You would have been in Florida eating the early bird specials by the time you were thirty. We're rejoicing in the loss of Robert, because he was a loser with a capital *L*, only out of his mother's house because this area actually rewards geeks with good pay. And if you're going to harm yourself, use chocolate like normal women."

I'm still not over the pickles. "You two can afford nice things. I can afford pickles. I can't believe you would be so cruel. It seems to me we all had a fetish for Now & Laters in college. Just because you got money and changed your habits, now I'm supposed to follow suit? How about a little commiseration? Alms for the poor and all that!"

Poppy slides down beside me. "It's good to unleash this anger. Tell us about Sara Lang now," she says with a Zen-like quality.

I'll admit, I'm fired up just hearing that woman's name. "She's evil. When I think about her black nails and her scary, icy-blue eyes over the well-concealed eye bags—and to give my job to that man!" *If you can call someone who wears more eyeliner than me a man.* "She actually thinks twenty-five-year-old men want her, when they laugh at her!"

"What else? Let it out."

"She thinks I can be bought. She offered me big money to be her CFO. As if I'd do a job I hate *and* work for her!"

"What did you say?" Morgan asks.

"She offered me a finance job," I repeat. Their looks of pity quickly dissipate.

"Are you going to take it?" Poppy says as she puts her hair into a clip. Poppy has the most beautiful hair you've ever seen. It's an incredible hue of natural red, and it falls down her back in gentle curls. She's got a speckling of freckles across her nose and deep blue eyes. In other words, she's everything I'm not. And she wastes it in bad cotton clothing. *So criminal.*

"No! I didn't accept it." I cross my arms, waiting to hear another reason besides my own happiness to turn down a solid salary. I'm definitely tempted. Then I notice my friends aren't jumping on the supportive band wagon. "Do you think I should do it?"

"You don't want to do finance," Morgan shrugs. "You could have gone back to finance years ago. What have these years of training been about? All those years of learning how to make computer patterns! How to drape a fabric with CAD? No, you definitely can't take it. You have to try."

Wouldn't it be nice to actually think everyone has options? Of course, I do have options. They just require living in poverty a little longer. In my mind, I was on my way to a pair of fashionable walking shoes…maybe Borns, or the like.

"I don't *want* to do it!" I exclaim. "But I want to make a decent living wage, and I'm tempted. I want to pay my Nana back so she can have a decent place again." But in reality, I'm not too tempted. Fabric makes me feel alive. Finance…well, finance makes me feel nothing, quite frankly.

"Your Nana has a great place. There aren't many grandmothers who live in a marina studio apartment overlooking the San Francisco Bay. I don't think she's in nearly the hurry for that money that you think she's in."

It's not just Nana. It's my own selfish desires too. "I saw on *Oprah* that when you turn your passion into work, you make it. Did Oprah lie to me, girls? I mean, I don't want a BMW or anything, but a Marc Jacobs bag is tempting. Being able to sit in a luxurious salon, while I get my hair straightened—is tempting. Being able to afford a respectable vice, like

Starbucks, is tempting!" I pull the paper out of my pocket and show Poppy. "Look at this salary. It actually qualifies as a salary."

"You gave up that salary because you wanted to design. Right?" Poppy blinks her big, blue eyes and avoids the number. "I can get you a job in finance. Working for a normal boss if that's what you want. I have a ton of patients in high-tech finance. Don't take a job doing something you hate, for someone you ha—aren't fond of."

"Poppy's right, Lil," Morgan says. "You hate finance. You could have done that years ago. Not to mention that Shane Wesley will remind you every day that he was Sara's choice. You'll live with your failure every day. You want to design. You want to do what you love. What have all these years on Highway 101 been about if you're going to quit now?"

Of course, I know all this. I just want to be told I'm right. There are no better words in the English language than, "You're right, Lilly." So I sink onto the bed, and listen while my Spa Girls tell me all the things I already know.

I give them a little more ammunition. "Three years ago, I was young and I had more determination and confidence. I'm twenty-nine now, and I have no windows. A girl my age should definitely be able to afford windows." I look at Morgan, who is studying the carpet.

"If there was something I wanted, Lilly," Morgan's cheek twitches, "I'd do it. At least you still have a *little* determination left. You brought the pickles, didn't you? You haven't lost all your will or you wouldn't have been willing to fight Granola Girl."

"Hey!" Poppy shouts.

"I've got my facial appointment now." I stand up, taking one last sniff of the gone-but-not-forgotten pickles. "I'll be back, and you're driving me to the store to get some pickles, Morgan."

"Am not."

"Are so."

She takes her car keys out of her expensive handbag, and dangles them over the balcony, right over the sulfur-ridden hot tub on the floor below. As I lunge for them, she drops them into the water.

"The remote is electronic. You'll ruin it!" I say, shocked that she would be so callous with her own property.

"So be it. Daddy will FedEx me new ones."

I don't say what I want to. Wouldn't be considered Christian. I just hike down the stairs for my facial. Life will look better when I'm well-moisturized and fresh as a cucumber.

As I lay smothered in a mango elastin-regenerating fruit mask, I feel myself exhale the pressures of the week. Life looks clearer from under a layer of fruit. I *do* hate finance. I love design. I love the way it makes me feel to see my dresses hanging on a Saks Fifth Avenue mannequin. To see the female form evolve into something breathtaking when draped in a beautiful, elegant silk. God created such beauty. It's my calling to clothe it.

ashion is my calling," I say as I get back to the room, convicted as only a cleansing facial can convict a person of depth and truth. Sure, I act like they convinced me, but what are friends for, if not for solid affirmation? They scratch my back; I scratch theirs.

"A good handbag is my calling," Morgan says, looking up from her romantic suspense novel.

"A perfectly-curved spine is my calling," Poppy adds, dropping her *Health* magazine.

"No, wait. My calling is finding the perfect man and learning how to make a pot roast without the cook on duty," Morgan winks. "Romance can't blossom with a cook for chaperone or on an empty stomach." We all laugh at the thought of Morgan in an apron.

"Do you even know how to turn on the oven?" I ask.

"Okay," Poppy interrupts, "then my true calling is finding the perfect man and not laying him out on a table to crack his back within the first ten minutes of meeting him. Romance can't blossom with a man lying prostrate before you." We all gaze at her. "It's true. A guy doesn't want a girl who can snap him like a stalk of celery."

"Well, now there's a shocker," Morgan giggles. "Twisting a

man like a pretzel is not good for romance. Go figure."

"Oh, we're talking our *real* callings," I say. "*Pardonez moi,*
I misunderstood. Forget fashion, then. Mine is meeting a man
I find attractive, and not uttering something unintelligible.
Not being Cyrano de Bergerac—except replace the bad nose
with bad hair—that's my calling. Oh, and wearing couture
while I do it."

"Well, good," Morgan sighs. "Now that we have that out
of the way, and Lilly has decided to leave finance behind her,
back there with her knowledge of geography, we're all set."

"Excuse me. I know every back road on the San Francisco
Peninsula." I cross my arms.

"Where's Missouri?" Poppy asks.

I pause before saying confidently, "It's in the middle."

"The middle of what?"

"Duh, the country," I answer. "I'm a native Californian.
Why do I need to know where Missouri is? It's one of those
middle states."

"We're all native Californians, Lilly. Who is more organic
Californian than Poppy? I bet she knows where Missouri is."

"I do," Poppy sits up straight. "It's on the Mississippi River."

"See? In the middle," I say with more confidence than I feel.

"The middle of the country more toward the left or the
right?" Morgan asks.

Ack, a little lost here. It's a fifty-fifty shot, and I'm a gambling
girl. "The left."

"Wrong!" Poppy and Morgan say in unison, falling into
giggles. It's a big joke that I can find any alley in the City, but
I cannot tell you how to get to Nevada, our neighboring state.
Since I don't own a car, it doesn't get me into much trouble.

"I meant if you were facing south." I raise my eyebrows
and cross my arms.

Morgan throws a pillow at me, "You are so full of it, Lilly."

"I've got my facial appointment now." Poppy stands up and grabs her spa robe that comes with the room. There's only one esthetician at Spa Del Mar, so we have to take turns. "How was that reenergizing mask, Lilly? Should I get that one?"

"Energizing. Not sure about the *re* part, but doesn't my face look like that battery bunny? Pink and moist? I just keep going and going…"

Poppy rolls her eyes. "You need your curls back. Only you would complain that you don't have money for a decent vice and then pay to have your hair straightened like a wet dog. How can you have such good taste in couture and such bad taste in your coiffure?" She slaps her knee. "Hey, I made a rhyme!"

"I thought you had a facial."

"I'm going." Poppy exits, and Morgan breaks into giggles again.

"She's right. You do sort of look like a wet dog." Morgan wrinkles her nose. "I've always wondered how you can notice the difference in stitching on a dress, but can't see that your hair looks glued to your head in that style. You have great hair, but you *pay* for bad hair."

People who have manageable hair always say things like this. It doesn't occur to them that when your hair enters a room before you, it's not a good thing. Most likely, they can use a barrette without their hair exploding out of it. They don't need an industrial strength comb to brush their hair.

"It will fill out a little. It's freshly straightened." I shrug. "Take your shampoo commercial hair away from me."

But Morgan's not letting up. "You know how on *The Swan* they put those same hair extensions on the girls, and it makes them sort of look like cross-dressers?"

"No, I don't get that channel," I lie.

"But you know what I'm talking about. They make the

girls all look the same with bad, fake hair dye and long hair. Like all women should have long hair. It's so neanderthal."

"More neanderthal than just major surgery to enter a beauty pageant, you mean?"

"I like that part," Morgan says in all honesty. "I like knowing there are women in society willing to undergo torture to look good. It's interesting to see how much pain is involved. I don't know if I'd do it."

"You're sadistic."

"Like you don't watch. I know you get that channel. They give all those girls the round water-balloon chest—you know, the 1980s chest. Implants have come a long way, baby. Someone needs to tell them you don't need to look like you're going to tip over."

"Excuse me, darling, but I couldn't help but notice that your implants are entirely out of fashion," I say with a fake, hoity-toity English accent. "Don't you know natural is in?"

"I'm serious."

"You would totally do plastic surgery, Morgan. You'll do it, and you'll be the first to lie about it. By the time we're fifty, you'll have that surprised look all the time that says, '*Lilly, did I invite you to dinner?*' when you answer the door. There isn't a vainer person on earth, and when that first wrinkle appears, you'll be clambering to the front of the line at the top plastic surgeon's office. Shocked that life should leave any sort of mark on you."

She throws another pillow at me. "I'm vain? Vainer than spending five hours in a salon chair to look like a wet dog, you mean?"

"Like those highlights of yours are real. How long do those take?" I ask. "In human hours, not dog hours!"

Morgan's mouth tightens. "None of your business."

"See, you're totally vain. What other woman would keep

it a secret from her best friends that she gets highlights? Like we couldn't tell anyway? You think because you hide out in those exclusive salons you can put something past Poppy and me? Ha! Chunky blond highlights do not occur in nature on someone older than three years of age. Not even for you, Morgan."

"I'm not trying to put something past you, Lilly. I was just taught you don't discuss private things." Morgan rises and glides across the room like she's on a runway.

We laugh at our discussion. The fact is, we're both vain. Only Poppy is free of society's preoccupation with looks. If there was one hairdresser left in San Francisco with one good treatment left in him, Morgan and I would probably battle to the death for chunky blond highlights or straightening.

"I have your care package. Although I'm not sure I want to give it to you. You deserve to wallow in bad soap and cheap shampoo."

I jump up. "Please give it to me! I'll be good, I promise."

Morgan puts together a luxury-item basket for me whenever we see each other. Shampoos from luxury resorts she's stayed in, toss-off cashmere sweaters she's tired of, and fancy chocolates she may have been given. Her figure is actually affected by such things, but when you have the figure of your standard thirteen-year-old like I do, not so much.

Morgan brings out a hat box covered in shopping bag design, and I can hardly wait to tear into it. "Ooh, what did you bring me?" This is better than gifts from Santa. This is stuff I can actually use!

"Calm down, it's nothing special."

She always says that. And it always rocks! "I'm calm," I say, though I'm practically panting like the dog they say my hair resembles.

She opens the box and hands me my first freebie, a small

sampler of Jane Iredale mineral foundation. "Ah!" I scream. "I *so* love this stuff! Where'd you get it?" I hold it up to the mirror, and it matches my tone perfectly.

"They gave it to me when I was looking for a darker color for summer. It was too dark. Okay, next. A Mac lipstick that was too brown for me." She hands it over.

"*Wooo-hooo!* I love this stuff too!" It sticks like glue, and you never have to reapply.

Morgan proceeds to take out endless items from her magic bag of tricks.

Small bottles of Bed Head shampoo: "My hairstylist gave it to me for my birthday. It flattens my hair." *Not a problem for me.* Perlier honey Italian bath soap: "I don't have time for baths." *I'll make time.* Lancome perfume: "It smells too citrusy for me." *Bring on the lime!* And the *piece de resistance*: a Marc Jacobs pebbled pink leather handbag!

I grab the bag and begin dancing with it. "No way! You're getting rid of this?"

"I'm done with it."

"Must I hurt you?" I clutch the bag close. "I was just lamenting how my job didn't let me afford a Marc Jacobs bag, and God provided!" I hold the purse in front of me and inspect it, not finding a single flaw. "Did you even use this?"

"I did. It wasn't structured enough for me. I like a more structured bag."

"Look at this stitching!" I kiss the bag.

"I'm sure when you get to heaven, God will be quite satisfied to know your Marc Jacobs prayer was answered, Lilly." Morgan rolls her eyes.

"You have not been given, because you have not asked," I say, paraphrasing Scripture. "God knows I'm materialistic and a wee bit shallow. He's working on me, but in the meantime, He totally got me a Marc Jacobs bag! My God rocks! Oh, I've got a present for you too." I rummage through my bag, now lightened since the Diet Pepsi and pickles have been destroyed. I pull out a pair of long-legged deep blue jeans. "I made these for you. I noticed your jeans were too short last time I saw you. When you have those legs, you should definitely take advantage and show them off."

"Lilly!" She holds up the jeans, and I can just tell they're going to be a perfect fit. I smile confidently. *She's going to stop traffic in those.* "They're perfect. I can't believe you can make a pair of jeans. They're just as soft as a baby's bottom. What are they made of?"

"They're stone-washed, and hand-hewn. The material was left over from these awful things Shane is making, so I took the scraps and dyed them a decent color."

"They're gorgeous. Thank you." She pulls the jeans to her chest. "Listen, Lilly." Morgan's tone turns serious, and when I look at her, she's lost all traces of her smile. "I have something to ask you."

I feel my way down to the bed. "What?"

"I heard at the gym that my dad owes someone. Just whispers, it's probably nothing more than gossip, but I need you to ask Sara about it before you decide to leave."

"You think she'd know anything?"

"That Union Square merchants' group is really tight. She might. He'd never tell me if it was true, and I don't want to find anything out from the *Chronicle*, if you know what I'm saying."

"Sure," I say.

"I just didn't want you to get on bad terms with Sara before you got a chance to ask."

"Bad terms? What makes you think I'll be on bad terms with her?"

"Has anyone ever quit that she didn't try to ruin?"

I open my mouth to recite a list of Sara Lang protégés who've made it, but the realization strikes me: there are none.

Morgan nods. "There are some women you just fear for good reason. I think she's one of them."

"I can handle Sara Lang." I feel my back straighten even as I say it. *I imagine that's what Superman thought before he came into contact with kryptonite too.*

chapter 5

S ome girls just develop later," my Nana used to say.
Here's the rest of that advice: "Some girls don't develop at all. Some girls stay stick-straight and will only require a training bra for the rest of their natural-born lives."

That's me.

But let's make it complete. Top this little-boy figure with a mop of wild, frizzy curls, and add the nickname "Q-tip" to the recipe. Send her to school in homemade miniskirts from the clearance polyester fabric bolts, and be sure and plop big, ol' brown clodhopper shoes on her, so her toothpick legs can get the full brunt of junior high ridicule.

Before it sounds like my youth was no more than a tale of utter woe, there is a silver lining to my billowy, gray cloud. In the fashion industry, they covet the woman's boyish figure. Granted, you have to be about five inches taller than I am, but still, I felt like I glimpsed my future when I saw an emaciated model with a dress hanging off her like an elegant sheath. (This was before the era of emaciated bodies *plus* enormous fake implants, à la Jessica Rabbit, so I was given hope without the desire for plastic surgery. I'm not big on pain.)

I wanted to look like the gaunt models in *Vogue* and wear

tweeds and silks and be proud of my gangly frame. But first, I had to cover it up with something more than a miniskirt.

When I created my first pair of jeans, I knew I'd found my calling. Denim was my friend—it took my scrawny legs and swallowed them from visual range. When the jeans got too short, I added cool plaid cuffs. Eventually, I cut the jeans at the knees and made capris fashionable at school. There was simply no end to my freedom with fabric. Fashion was my saving grace until Nana introduced me to Jesus.

Speaking of my Nana, my heart beats rapidly. Spa weekend came to its glorious conclusion, and now it's time to explain to her that I've been offered a real job where I actually use my degree again (the easy part). And that I'm turning it down (the hard part). I've brought the Marc Jacobs handbag just to prove I have everything I need right now.

I pause on Nana's landing before actually knocking on her door. *She'll understand*, I tell myself. *She just wants me to be happy*. But then I think back to those large, leather brown shoes with the miniskirt and wonder if that's true.

Nana lives in a lower apartment of a single journalist's home. She's in one of the swankiest parts of the City, the Marina. The area was ravaged in certain parts by the Loma Prieta earthquake in 1989. I figure that's how the journalist must have afforded it. He probably bought it condemned in 1990. Max Schwartz is a television critic for the *San Mateo Times*. In other words, as long as people can still *read* about television, Nana has a home.

I knock on her door. Nothing.

Knock again. Nothing.

Banging now. I think Nana is going deaf. "Nana!" I shout.

"Are you looking for Mildred?" A voice from overhead calls after me. It's the TV dork. He's typical for what you imagine a journalist might look like. Fairly small in stature with a goatee trying to make him appear so anti-establishment; dark, closely-cropped hair; oversized glasses. But his strong, straight jaw is somewhat unexpected. He appears intellectual, but of course, he writes about today's television shows. Since critiquing *America's Top Model* doesn't exactly attract the Pulitzer Prize Committee, he's got a steady nine-to-five and not much opportunity for advancement. We have that much in common. A life without passion, but a job like the other drones in the Bay Area. The biggest difference? He's got a majestic view of the San Francisco Bay and a job after Monday. "Do you know where my grandmother is?" I shout up at him.

"She's up here. I'm getting ready for the new television season."

Sigh. And my Nana is up there—why?

"She's making a roast chicken," Max adds.

Of course she is. "Can I come up?"

"Yeah." He buzzes a gate, and I gain entry to his elitist iron staircase. At the top of the stairwell, he rubs his hand through his hair, then thrusts it toward me. Noticing his *faux pas*, he wipes his hand on his jeans and tries again.

I take his hand. "Good to see you, Max."

"You too, Lilly. Your grandmother was just talking about you. Saying you're still trying the fashion thing."

"Yep, still working at it. Rome wasn't built in a day and all that."

"How long do you think you'll give it?"

I open my mouth, but nothing good will come out, so I snap it shut. I walk into Max's house, which is one-fifth living area, four-fifths television screen. My Nana is bent over the stove, a big commercial Wolf one, which is entirely strange, but considering the television, I question nothing. Nana has two oven mitts on her hands and props the chicken on the stovetop.

"Nana, what's going on? I pounded on your door."

"What do you mean, what's going on? I wasn't home. It's August. Nearly time for the new fall preview schedule. Do you live in a hole?"

"I just don't watch much TV." I shrug to Max. "The rabbit ears, you know. It's not really a *season* at my house." I look at Max, and he winks at me. *Oh brother.*

"Look at that television." Nana waves a wooden spoon out of the salad bowl towards the enormous flat screen that could double for a drive-in should they ever come back into vogue. "The paper bought him that. Isn't that incredible? Our Max, he knows how to watch television."

What a gift.

"Lilly, have you met Valeria?" Max asks as a tall, lithe figure emerges from the living room easy chair. She's got that exotic look, perhaps a mixture of Indian and something else. She could model if she didn't have such an expansive chest. *Sigh.*

"Nice to meet you." I smile at Valeria, rhymes with malaria, trying not to gaze down at my own chest. Or lack thereof. I suddenly feel very deflated and for more reasons than just Sara Lang.

"Your Nana has makes me right at home here in San Francisco. She makes me to learn to cook." Valeria's broken English only makes her that much more exotic.

She's in her early twenties, I would say. Max is in his mid-thirties—and a geek. Have I mentioned that? This is the inequity in the world that makes you want to give up on the male species altogether.

"Really?" I say to gorgeous Valeria. "Nana's helping you cook?" *Just what the world needs, a goddess who can cook.* "Where are you from?"

"I am Russian. My father was Indian," she says with the accent you expect from an übermodel.

"Wonderful. Glad to have you here." I grab my grand-mother's arm. "I need to speak with you about something."

"After dinner. Sit down, it's ready."

"I'm not hungry, Nana. It's sort of important."

"That's why you're so skinny; you never eat. Don't be rude. It's been ages since Max has seen you, and I don't want Valeria to think I didn't raise you right. Max always asks what you're up to, don't you, Max?"

"I'm skinny because of genetics," I explain to Valeria, as if she has any interest or desire to know about my DNA structure.

She smiles condescendingly. Like we don't have a complete lack of eligible bachelors here in the City, we have to import beautiful women from other countries to completely throw our chances out the fifty-fourth story window? *Melting pot, my foot!* The immigration laws should definitely say something about being homely or married. It's one or the other, people! Good-looking? Available? No entry. I mean, doesn't the Statue of Liberty even say that? "Give me your tired, your poor, your homely…" Something like that.

"It's good to eat and enjoy; that's what Solomon says in Ecclesiastes. He was the wisest man in all the Bible," Nana continues as she puts more dishes on the table.

Valeria whips out a new place setting, and I sit down. *I know when I'm beat, and my education has nothing on Solomon. I don't need the sermon to that effect.* If I want to have a conver-sation with my Nana, I will be eating.

"I'm here every Sunday night, Lilly. If you ever came to see me, you'd know that. Max, do you want wine?" Nana is poised with a bottle opener.

"No, thanks. Valeria might." Max sits down and grabs Valeria's hand.

"Is Valeria old enough to drink?" I ask, and everyone stares at me. Apparently, this was not the choicest of commentary.

Here I thought I was doing well avoiding her statuesque figure.

Valeria shakes her head to wine, and our whole dysfunctional party sits down for dinner. Max and his very warped harem. *Where's Dr. Phil when you need him?*

"Where have you been, Lilly? It's been a long time since I've seen you around," Max comments, while scooping up some salad.

"I spent the weekend at a spa with my girlfriends. But I've been working a lot. I was hoping for a promotion, but I didn't get it, so now I have to make other plans." Here's where I stuff an oversized piece of French bread in the mouth.

"That's because she's not using the degrees she earned." My grandmother sits down. "Hold hands; we're going to pray." We do. She does. She's back to nagging. "That incredible brain God blessed her with, and she's going to be a hunchback as much as she bends over that sewing machine and sketch book and now, the computer too." She directs her attention toward me. "Is that what you want?" Nana shakes her head. "A Stanford education she doesn't even use. Valeria, if your grandmother worked herself to the bone for your education, you would use it, no?"

When I say that my Nana gave up everything for me to be educated, including her home for my master's degree, I neglect to mention that I will hear of nothing else for the rest of my natural born days. When my Nana is gone, her words will haunt me like the *Telltale Heart* under the planks. *Thump-thump. Thump-thump. Fi-Nance. Fi-Nance.*

"So, Nana, don't you think Valeria and Max might want to be alone?" I ask, hoping we can excuse ourselves.

"It's dinner time," she says, as if without her, Max and Valeria might starve. "It's Sunday night. We watch the new pilots on DVD from the affiliates. I can't give Max my opinion without seeing the shows."

"Nana, Max gets paid for *his* opinion—not yours."

"Little good it would do him without me. He hasn't lived life. What does he know about quality television? He was a mere baby when Vietnam happened. He needs me."

Quality television, a definite oxymoron. Oh please, mother earth. Swallow me up into the deep crevice that is the San Andreas Fault. Dare I point out that *Desperate Housewives* and the significance of the Vietnam War have very little in common?

And then it dawns on me that this is my moment! Everyone is very lost in their own lives. They don't have time for the insignificance of mine. If I tell Nana my plans in front of Max and Valeria, I have the buffer I need. The highway median of a human sort.

Just as I see Nana fork the first piece of chicken into her mouth, I speak. "So Nana, Sara offered me a finance job." Wait for it. "But I'm not taking it. I'm going to be starting my own business within six months." Now keep in mind, I've just said this with the same tone I'd say, "Nana, I'm taking the garbage out."

Nana starts to cough, choke actually, and Max rises up to tap her back. He's hovering over her, waiting for her to recover, slapping her as she coughs. Nana gulps some water, and now all three of them look at me as if I'm the human form of evil.

"My own design business," I clarify.

"We know what you mean, Lilly," Max says. "Just where will you get the money to start a business?"

Shoot. I never counted on Mr. Television piping up. This must have been one of the past plots on *CSI: Miami* or something. Or did *The Apprentice* offer some sort of business advice last week?

"I'm planning for capital now. That's using my degrees." Little white lie here, but if I tell Nana I have no business model, she might feign another heart arrhythmia and next thing you know, I'll be waiting for my exorcism. Clearly, I can cross Max off my potential investor list, considering his collateral is probably the sum total of that television set. Now everyone has stopped eating, waiting for me to say something more.

Valeria is shaking her head as if to say, *Ah, you ignorant Americans.*

My Nana's mouth is still open, and she shoves her plate away. "I'm not hungry anymore."

"Nana, I thought you wanted me out of Sara Lang?" *That's right. Go with Plan A. Nana's ideas are always best.*

"I want you out of design. You're getting too old to be playing these games, Lilly. It's time you found a real job with your education. You were always telling me about those boys who got this degree and that but never got a job! How is this any different?"

I bite my lip. "I never really wanted to do finance, Nana." I've tried to tell her this before, naturally, but Nana has a special way of avoiding words she doesn't want to hear. I don't want to hurt her; this is the woman who raised me when no one else would! But again, I can't devote my life to getting James Huntington III a new Mercedes either.

"I'm sorry, Max." My Nana puts on her low *I-didn't-raise-her-like-this* tone. "Lilly seems to bring a tornado with her *when* she graces us with her presence. She's not good for the digestive system." Nana turns back to me. "Sometimes, Lillian Jacobs, life isn't about what we want. Sometimes it's about what's best for us. It's fine to have dreams when you're young, but you also need to think about a pension at some point. You're not getting any younger."

Why? Why didn't I stand up to Nana when I was eighteen before my undergraduate? Why not when I was twenty-three and getting ready for my masters? Why now, when it's all said and done? I know why, of course. She's my Nana, the only constant

I've ever had in my life, and I'd do almost anything to make her happy.

"I'm sorry." I stand up. "Forgive me, Max. I didn't mean to ruin your dinner." I turn back to Nana. "I'm irresponsible; I'll give you that, but finance makes me feel worthless, Nana. I can't be someone I'm not just for money. Fashion is my calling," I say weakly. It sounded so much better in front of Poppy and Morgan.

"Poppycock." Nana slams her hand down. "I wanted to be Esther Williams too. The terrible thing was, I couldn't swim. But oh, I could have kissed that Van Johnson all right. I could have made his toes curl."

Oh, ick. I put my hand up. "Oversharing, Nana."

"Lillian Jacobs, the world is your oyster. Quit throwing your pearls before swine."

"Nana, that makes absolutely no sense."

"Just go." Nana closes her eyes, and I can see she's had her fill of me.

I hate to see her disappointed. I want to tell her right now, *Forget everything, I'll take the job. It's not too late.* But I can't get the words out.

I walk out of Max's house slowly, hoping my grandmother will stop me, but she never does. She just grumbles to Max and Valeria about how ungrateful I am. When I reach the porch, I look back at the door. My eyes start to sting. Suddenly, my calling feels incredibly selfish. One thing is certain: my Nana's money was not free—it has a distinct, reverse-mortgage feel.

"Maybe having a real job again wouldn't be so bad. I'm older now. More mature," I mumble.

Max follows me out. "I wanted to get the gate for you."

"So as not to let it hit me on the way out?" I ask.

"I'm sorry, Lilly. I wasn't thinking." Max actually looks

repentant, and my heart softens toward him just a little. He lives with my Nana. I have to admire him for that feat—more difficult than any Bond stunt.

I shake my head. "It's not your problem." He lets me out of the gate, and looks at me through the bars. "I suppose you think I should go back into finance too?"

Max laughs. "You really have no idea who I am, do you?"

"Should I?"

"I think you should do what you want in terms of jobs. You're a grown woman." He pulls off his glasses, and his eyes crease with a smile. "You're always welcome here."

I smile back. *There's a special place in heaven for a man who puts up with Nana.* I look up to the blue sky, quickly being covered by the evening fog, and mutter, "I never meant to call him a geek, Lord. Forgive me."

have just nullified my weekend with a guilt-induced trip to Nana's—do the math.

Spa Girls Weekend:	*10*
Effects of Spa Girls Weekend after	
visiting my grandma:	*-10*
	0
Complexion after facials and bloating	
ratios after no pickle binges:	*10*
Forehead crinkle desperately needing	
Botox after Nana visit:	*-10*
	0

The fact is, I cannot ever do what I want with her approval. She'll live as long as Moses, so waiting it out isn't an option—and how wrong is that anyway? Nana wants me to be a banker, which strikes me as extremely odd. One gander at my apartment would tell her that I have no clue what to do with money, considering that I have none. People who "get" money have a gift, one which I'm clearly missing, in favor of the gift for how to cover my lanky frame—and calm the stormy sea that is my wavy coiffure. And frankly, that's the gift I needed.

After a harrowing mid-evening bus ride, I unlatch the locks on my door. The locks make it appear to the ignorant that we have something valuable behind the door—which we don't. But they came with the place. Even though we only lock three of them, they are trying my patience after my evening. I mean, Max-the-TV-King is dating a foreign Angelina Jolie, and they'll probably give my grandmother "great grandchildren." And even though we're not related, it will be one more aspect of my open failure to Nana. I'm through the second lock when Nate opens the door.

I look around him. "Nope, no nice computers or television sets. I am definitely on the right floor."

Nate shrugs. "Kim called me to be her designated driver tonight. She's on her bed, laughing wildly at something now. And she smells like the gutter." Nate hands me my Lysol bottle, which I've traded in for the essential oils mist that Poppy gave me to "get off the hard stuff." Nate continues. "I thought I'd wait until you got home, if it wasn't too late, just to make sure she didn't try to escape or anything. I've never seen her this bad."

I can hear my roommate talking to herself and giggling uproariously.

"You should have seen the bar she was in. I would think you could catch something just by walking in." Nate's top lip curls. "I'm glad you didn't pick her up. What a dump."

"Sorry, Nate. I was at my grandmother's."

"No problem. I wasn't doing anything, just watching *Desperate Housewives* in TiVo, which says a lot about my own life, wouldn't you say?"

"Sort of, but at least you don't get paid for watching it."

"Huh?"

"Never mind."

"How was your girls-and-goop weekend?" Nate asks, and isn't it cool he remembered?

"Nullified by my Nana. As most moments of joy are in my life." I plop my stuff down in the entry and head to the kitchen. I'm dying for Diet Pepsi. "Do you want something to drink? Or a pickle, maybe?"

"I made some espresso for Kim. Do you want some? You look like you could use a cup. Or a pot."

"But we don't have a coffee maker," I say, pointing out the obvious.

"I brought my espresso maker down when Kim got settled. All it did was prolong her sleeping it off, but I didn't know what else to do for her. Kim sure knows how to make a guy feel useless."

He brought his espresso maker down! For some reason this makes me want to cry. Why can't I be attracted to nice guys like this? "Nate," I say, with a well of tears in my eyes.

"Don't say that I'm a nice guy, Lilly. No guy wants to be told they're nice! It's like being told that you're a golden retriever, when women want a bulldog. So just hold that thought because I'm embarking on a new life. I'm going to be the complete jerk from here on out. Kim's rescue was my last attempt at knight in shining armor. I'm going for Bond from here on out."

I start to laugh. "You gotta lose Charley then, Nate. No jerk puts up with a dog whose ear drains and smells like something Roto-Rooter comes to fix."

He thinks about this for a minute. "Yeah, that's my trouble, huh? I'm a sucker for the dog. Charley's not leaving. He's more welcome than any woman. I'll have to be jerk enough to over-come him. I'm not really a leather jacket sort." He rubs his chin. "I was thinking jeans with a tight T-shirt."

"So, Marlon Brando in *On the Waterfront*?"

"Sort of. Maybe Brad Pitt to bring it into the modern era."

"He wore a dress in *Troy*. Too metrosexual. What about George Clooney?" I think about this. "Nah, too noncommittal. You'd never pull it off."

"That's it: George Clooney, or Simon Cowell from *American Idol*. That's what I'm going for: noncommittal. I want women to fear me, think I'm completely unattainable, a guy who will always have a twenty-something babe on my arm no matter how old I get." He swings his hand through the air. "Line up to get your heart broken. You know, Trump without the comb-over."

I shake my head. "It's not possible. The dog gives you away. If you can commit to a dog, a woman is the next logical step. A guy with a dog is practically begging for a woman in his life. The only thing worse giving you away is the loft you own. Owning your own place, having a dog—you practically scream 'Desperately ready to commit!'"

"I don't believe it. Bond probably had a dog."

"Bond definitely did *not* have a dog. He was attached to his sports cars and martinis, remember? Besides, I've always imagined Bond with terrible breath for some reason. You're not Bond. You're minty-fresh."

"Your nose," Nate taps me on the tip of it, "is in the wrong business. You should be in perfume. Although you've probably done lifelong damage from all the Lysol you inhale. You're probably killing off brain cells at a rapid rate, which might explain your dog issue."

"Speaking of smells." I grab my handy can of essential oils spray and give the loft a thorough spraying, but it's not strong enough, and I'm quickly reaching for the Lysol. "Can you show me how to use this machine? The espresso smells even better than Lysol. Could it be that a little coffee pod could spare me buying Lysol in bulk?" I walk over to the gleaming, stainless steel espresso machine. It glistens with opportunity, and I reach out to stroke it.

He walks over. "No pods. Okay, you take some ground coffee. Only freshly-ground, *capisce*?"

"*Capisce*," I echo. "You're so metrosexual," I purr, which just cracks him up.

"You tamp it down." As I watch Nate, his eyes meet mine. I don't think I've ever looked him in the eye. They're hazel, and there's a spark in them that belies his boring exterior. My mouth is hanging open as I study him as if for the first time, and suddenly, we both snap our attention back to the machine. He finishes the rest of the espresso lesson without saying a word. "Everything here seems to be fine now. I'm going upstairs." He looks toward Kim, whose voice has gotten considerably less bubbly. "You have got to get her help, Lilly."

I nod. "I know."

Nate hands me the espresso with a perfect blanket of cream in an espresso cup. A jerk would never own a specialized espresso cup. That's as metrosexual as they come. The strong espresso scent beckons my nose. I can hear Poppy's liver warnings as I taste my first sip. "It's heavenly."

Nate nods nervously and heads for the door.

"Do you have to rush off? Come sit down for a while." I pat the kitchen chair.

Nate shakes his head. "I've got to get back to Charley."

I think I scared him. I'm not usually so needy, but man, tonight I'm like Anna Nicole Smith-needy. "Your espresso machine!" I shout after him.

"I'll get it tomorrow." The last part is muffled behind the closed door.

I just noticed the color of his eyes, for goodness sakes. I wasn't going to maul him. Maybe I'm giving off desperate vibes, like the wives he's been watching on television. I'll admit I'm depressed after seeing Nana. It seems as though she respects everyone else's career, but nothing is good enough for me. She can actually fawn over a guy who sits on his duff and watches TV for a living, but thinks fashion design is akin to street-walking for me. I know she wants what's best for me, but why do I have to fit in such a small round hole when I am clearly a square peg?

I look down at the new dog pillow I'm making for Charley because of his ear drains. I hate for the poor thing to have a smelly bed, and washing it doesn't work, so I make Charley a fresh doggie bed every month.

Kim comes staggering out from behind the screen, her shirt hanging off one shoulder. "I need another drink. Tail of the dog and all that."

"You need to go back to bed," I say, tempted to aim the Lysol can at her. Now I may not be CFO material, but I know enough not to have alcohol in the apartment. "We've got nothing but Diet Pepsi. Go brush your teeth. You'll feel better."

"Lilly's answer to everything: oral hygiene." She starts to giggle, brings her fingers gingerly up to her mouth, and burps.

"Attractive."

"I met this amazing guy tonight. Hot…cute…straight."

"And this is your way of impressing him? Calling poor Nate to come rescue you? You're going to make that man move, Kim. We'll never be able to watch reality TV again if Nate moves, and all we have is these rabbit ears."

"You're so self-fightush and jealous. My hottie already text-messhaged me. Said he'd call tomorrow."

"You gave our number to some guy in a bar!" I can't help it. I roll my eyes and sigh.

"'s not like that."

"Kim! What's it like then?" I hate to sound like the girl's mother, but could she get a clue? Doesn't she watch *Law and Order: SVU*?

"I told you, he was shtraight. You'd slike him. No tattoos. He had his hair combed, and looked good. For once, I was astracted to a straight man. One doesn't let opporstunidty like that passh by." She burps again and giggles.

When Jennifer, our former roommate, lived with us, Kim would go out drinking maybe once every two months, and she never came home sloshed. I don't expect her to live the life of some goody-two-shoes Christian, but if she's going to give our number out, I just ask that she'd be sober. This lifestyle doesn't agree with her, but she's not ready to go church-hopping either. I look at the dishes piled in the sink. An entire weekend's worth. Including the cup I placed there on Friday.

"Nate wants me," Kim says as she meanders back to bed. "It took all his shelf-control not to take advatash tonight. I'm s-hot."

She's shot all right. "Maybe it was just animal magnetism drawing him to you—because you smell like Charley!" I call out to her. "And I'm not self-righteous, Kim. I just don't find being drunk a positive attribute for you. You're going to have a headache the size of the Golden Gate tomorrow. You can't afford Starbucks every day, you know." I'm assuming straight-boy paid for her drinks tonight. It's the next day that presents her with the financial problem when she pays to fend off the results.

Kim's chattiness dissipates, and she slinks back down on her bed, kicking the silk screen partition over with a bang. Her bedroom now completely lacks privacy. "Nate made me espresso. He so wantsh me," she says as she cuddles up with her pillow. Tonight, I could use a dose of Kim's reality. It would be nice to believe someone wanted me. Judging from Nate's hasty exit, it appears my luck with men hasn't changed. And, see? It was right after I found him attractive. It's a curse!

"I need a spa weekend to recover from my spa weekend." I'm talking to the espresso machine when our phone rings. "Hello."

"Hey, baby, it's Jason." *Slimy and yet oh-so-smarmy.*

I'm assuming Jason is hot, cute, straight-boy, and I can't help myself. "I told you not to call me here. What if my husband answered? I mean, he's on patrol tonight, but he could have been home already."

Click.

One problem solved. Only 861 more to go. I start to clean up the dishes Kim has left over the weekend, and I realize: something has got to change. There is not one thing in my life that I'm proud of at the moment. Besides my friendship with the Spa Girls that is, but Poppy lives forty miles away in Cupertino, and Morgan runs with a crowd who would rather entertain Paris Hilton's chihuahua than me.

am fired. It has such a *David Copperfield* feel, doesn't it? Sara didn't want to hear my excuses. She didn't want to hear my goals, my dreams, or what I planned to do with myself. She just wanted me out of the office without any of her equipment, even a ball point pen. I went without so much as a cardboard box to remember my years there. I didn't even have the forethought to grab the classifieds. Kim was fired too. For insubordination when telling Sara what an idiot she was to fire me, but Kim thought that was cause for celebration, and laughingly left the office with a friend's Starbucks card.

I'm unsure of my next move. Right now, I'm sitting on a wood beam at the edge of the Embarcadero Pier, under the Bay Bridge. Luxury cars and eighteen-wheelers, all with places to go are overhead, and I'm down here. With the roar of traffic, the scent of salty sea air, the bark of sea lions, and the call of the gulls, I am aimless. But I feel slightly giddy. *I did it*, I think. I stood up to my Nana and Sara Lang. I feel like I could do anything!

Fashion is a tough business. I always knew that, and maybe I set my hopes too high by working for Sara Lang and listening to the reviewers about my work. You know what they say: you're never as bad or as good as they say you are.

A big Beemer drives onto the Pier, right under the large "No Parking" sign, and Morgan emerges in a pale pink suit and stilettos to die for. "I got your call, Lilly. Came as soon as I could. Woo-hoo! You're fired; let's go play!" She rushes towards me, and we giggle. I have no job, but like Morgan's hero, Scarlett O'Hara, I'll think about that another day.

"This so sucks," I say, still slightly in disbelief that Sara had the nerve to fire me. "My designs have made her in the last year. I feel like such a complete loser. I just couldn't get onto Muni and prove it to myself further." I didn't want to quit. I wanted to stay and glean what I could from Sara's brilliant use of color, but it wasn't enough for Sara. I didn't show complete and utter submission to the queen.

"Sara's the loser. You're going to make it, Lilly. But you go ahead and wallow in it; it will make the success all the sweeter when it comes."

But I'm probably not going to wallow, and I might not even succeed. I'm going to go home, scan the want-ads for a finance job, and sew in my spare time. Just like I used to do.

Seeing Morgan's deep blue eyes filled with sorrow, I realize I've really messed up. "I forgot to ask Sara about your dad."

"It's no big deal about my dad, Lilly. I'm sure I don't want to know anyway."

"So, what now?" I ask, looking for a little direction in my life, thankful Nana and Sara aren't here to give it.

"So we'll go out to a fabulous dinner, and you won't have to get up in the morning and schlep on Muni to Union Square. Look at the bright side."

I look out over the San Francisco Bay and see the myriad of sailboats and ferries bustling back and forth. "Even those boats have purpose, and they're not even human. A Christian girl's purpose should really include more than trying to avoid bad smells and keeping her hair in line, shouldn't it? I mean, those skills don't exactly bring up the whole salt-and-light feeling, do they?" I look at Morgan, and she rolls her eyes at me.

"Are you done now?"

"I guess."

"Who has worked in the children's Sunday school since she was thirteen?"

"Poppy."

"Oh, right. Okay, who has worked at the soup kitchen, even though the smell of the meals made her sick?"

"You know, that doesn't really make me sound all that charitable. I know you're trying to help, but getting sickened by the smell of the food at the soup kitchen? You can't make me sound better than that?"

"At the moment, no I can't. You're ticking me off, Lilly."

"Sorry."

"I've got a good one. Okay, who is thrilled to get the latest giveaways from Estée Lauder when I buy make-up?"

I look at her, confused.

"You're content with a little, Lilly."

"Oh, yeah. I am, huh?"

"You are! Oh wait, wait. I have a better one." Morgan flips back her blond hair with her manicured nails. "Who takes care of her Nana and helps her with rent, even though she's mean as a pit bull?"

"I do!"

"That's right, Lilly, you do! And anyone who has a heart for that woman? Well, I'm just sure God has something special planned for you."

We both start to giggle when a policeman pulls up behind Morgan's BMW. "This your car?" he asks while stepping out of his patrol car.

"It is, officer," Morgan purrs. "I'm here to pick up my

friend. Oh my, there's a No Parking sign there! Oh, I'm so sorry, sir. We'll get out of here right away." Morgan yanks me toward the car, and the officer waves back at her.

"It's all right, miss. No harm done."

We get into the car, and she backs it up onto the Embarcadero. Cars start honking, and Morgan just keeps on pulling out. "Morgan, you're going to get us killed!" I say, looking back at the busy street and the angry members of car society.

"Oh come on, like it's going to hurt them to stop for a second while we back out." She continues to pull out, and I just slink down in my seat. She pulls forward, finally, and looks over at me. "Let's go shopping."

"Morgan, you usually don't celebrate losing a job by going shopping."

"Actually, I have found there isn't a lot in life that can't be solved by a very good shopping trip."

I roll my eyes.

"Can't we at least go to lunch?"

"Fine, but not one of those expensive places where I'll feel ashamed to be dressed in denim, okay?"

"Those jeans are awesome, Lilly. You have to make me another pair. Oh my goodness, they're like my secret weapon. I love them!"

"I'm sure I'll have the time on my hands now. I'll see if there's any denim left in the apartment." We drive to a little hole-in-the-wall café that Morgan likes, and for the first time in a long time, I realize I am free. Granted, my rent is not, and a job search is imminent, but this is what faith is about, right? God will provide. He cares for the birds of the air; how much more a daughter of the King with really bad hair?

chapter 8

I, Lilly Jacobs, have two desires in a husband. One, he must be Christian. Two, he's got to be bald by age twenty-eight, because that is the only genetic combination I'm willing to consider, should I procreate. I will not put another generation through a lifetime with this hair. It's in that freshly-straightened phase where it hangs around my face like a wet Afghan dog. So *attractive*.

I should be over it. I'll grant you that. I'm almost thirty and I'm reliving junior high every day, but in the finance world it's so important to conform. That's where I got in the habit of straightening it. And like any addiction, now I've got to have it.

Kim walks up behind me in the only mirror we own. "It's a wonder you have any hair left at all, the way you obsess over it."

"I can fling it today!" I answer excitedly. I hold up my palms. "What else do I have to be excited about today?"

"My sister's a hairdresser, and she says it's better to have too much than not enough."

"You have a sister?" I turn around and face Kim, and it dawns on me how little I really know about her. I inherited her as a roommate, and since our social circles don't exactly collide, other than the occasional after-work get-together, we tend to keep a shallow relationship outside the office. I thought I knew everything about her by osmosis.

"A half-sister," Kim corrects.

"Where are you going?" I ask, seeing she's dressed in what you might call "hoochie festive" this time.

"I've got a date. Remember that guy I met in the bar? He called the wrong number, but he text-messaged me. I told him I lost my job," Kim shrugs. "So we're going walking out on Angel Island and then to dinner. Should be fun."

"How are you going to hike in those boots?"

Kim looks down. "Oh yeah, maybe you're right."

"Jeans would be good," I say, hoping to send a message like any teenager's mother would.

"I'll never wear denim again after that nightmare with Sara. Why can't she just go out and buy a Mercedes convertible, like most disgruntled socialites? She has to put half her employees out of business?"

I'm still fixated on the miniskirt. "Aren't you a little worried about Angel Island being too remote? You've only just met this guy, and it's a tad isolated out there. What if you miss the last ferry coming back?"

"There's a reason I don't live with my mother." Kim strips herself of her boots and miniskirt and searches for something more appropriate. It's always amazing to watch her dress, because she's colorblind, yet can match things perfectly because she's learned to deal with it. Amazing testimony to the triumphant human spirit. If only she didn't think "flesh" matches everything so well.

"So, does he have a job?" I ask, waiting for her to bite my head off.

"He does, Mom. He's in sales."

"Sales of what?"

"It's complicated, he says. I'll find out more on our walk."

Lord, have mercy.

Back to daydreams of my future husband before I was so rudely interrupted by visions of Kim in her hiking mini. Nate has a friend, Michael Sloan, who's trying to get back into the dating field after his divorce. Not bald, not Christian—not an option for life. But he's available tonight and wanting to try out his gentlemanly manners and a trendy new restaurant. How wrong can it possibly go? Since I'm jobless, and an expensive (but free to me) meal is not completely unpalatable, I'm throwing caution to the wind and going anyway. It will expand my horizons, which isn't too hard since I have no windows through which to have horizons. I go behind the screened partition to dress and pass Kim, now in capris and a halter top.

"Don't worry. I'm putting a leather jacket over it."

Yeah, that'll help. "I didn't say a thing!" I exclaim before opening my closet, an unfinished armoire from Ikea.

Kim's watching the news when I come out.

"This guy's actually picking you up? That's a good sign." I'm a little impressed. Kim never manages to meet men who think anything more than honking the horn is necessary.

"Is that what you're wearing?" she asks me.

"You don't like it?" I'm fingering the light summer wool jacket I made for myself. It has big, boisterous buttons all the way down, is cut short at the waist, and I have a darling peasant shirt hanging out. *Very cute!*

Kim shrugs. "It just doesn't really say anything. It looks like something you'd wear out with your dad."

By this I'm guessing she means it doesn't say, *Here are my "attributes" for your perusal.* "Well, Kim, how do you say, 'I'm here for the free meal'? Maybe a necklace that says, 'Feed Me'?"

"You are a designer. I just thought you might want to make a statement on your date out in the real world. It's not like you have all that many, and if he's taking you somewhere nice, someone might see the outfit."

"Oh, right," I say, sorry I snapped at her. "I like this jacket, and it's not really a date. It's more of a test-drive, really, and I could get a date if I wanted one. Need I remind you of Robert?" *Was it not me who had the most recent boyfriend?*

"Right. Big-spender Robert, who worried that if he went out, his wallet might explode on impact with air? That date?"

I purse my lips together. "You don't have to get nasty about it." I could tell her of hot, cute, straight-boy calling here in the middle of the night, but then I'd have to admit my getting rid of him. Well, I thought I'd gotten rid of him.

Kim rolls her eyes and flicks on the VCR. "Have you seen this *Dr. 90210*? Nate taped it for me."

I look at the television to see them cutting into human flesh. "Eww, what is that?"

"It's this plastic surgery show."

"Can they do anything for hair?" I sit down next to her.

"Only if you're losing it. Hair transplants. Saw it on *Extreme Makeover*."

"See, that is so unfair. If you're losing it, you can wear a wig, but if you have too much, there is no way to cut it that looks good without balding yourself. Layering makes it stick out farther, having it long makes you look like Shaggy on *Scooby Doo*. You either thermal recondition and straighten it to straw, or you live with it—and I'd like to have *some* curl."

Kim focuses back on the TV. "This girl's getting butt implants." Kim points the remote at the TV.

"No way! They do not make butt implants."

"Seriously. She wants to be like J.Lo."

I think I'm going to be sick. "I told Sara the other day, when she was designing jeans with pockets, that no one wants a bigger backside. I hope she doesn't see this." I flinch at the sight of this poor girl on television. "That is disgusting. Can you imagine how that must hurt?" I'm squirming in my chair. Feeling my hair, I'm thankful I can sit for five hours in a salon and temporarily solve my problem without surgical additions or removals.

"She's Hispanic. Says it's important in her culture."

"I'll buy that she wants more bum, but cultural? This world is way too politically correct if we're blaming weird plastic surgery on culture. Maybe we need a new culture." As I'm watching, it dawns on me. "Kim, we could make jeans that solve her problem. This is a fashion dilemma, *not* a surgical dilemma. Just sew a little rubbery material in the right places and—"

"You really need a job, Lilly. This girl wants to be naked in a magazine," Kim informs me. "Jeans aren't going to take care of her problem."

I hold my hands up. "Right. I'm really doubting she can blame that on the Hispanic culture." I'm disgusted with the show and get up before I get sucked into seeing the end results. When I want to look at a girl's "after" in that region, I've got more problems than I need.

The doorbell rings, and Kim and I stare at each other. "It must be for you, Lilly. My date isn't due for another half hour."

"Please let him look like that guy on *Alias*," I say out loud.

Kim opens the door, and behold: *Michael Moore in a suit.* She can barely contain her giggles. "Lilly, your date's here!"

"Hi," I say with way too much enthusiasm as I click off the obscene television show.

"Lilly," he holds out flowers. "I brought you some lilies."

Okay, nice gesture even though they represent DEATH in the Asian culture. I'll let this one go. It *is* my name.

"Michael, it's nice to meet you." As soon as the name

Michael is out of my mouth, Kim breaks into loud laughter again. The thing is, Robert sort of looked like a bald Michael Moore, so you might think this is my type.

"Are you ready?" Michael asks me without the hint of a smile.

"Oh yes, let me put these in water." I grab a Big Gulp cup out of the cabinet and fill it with water, thinking this is probably not the best way to go about impressing a guy, putting his death flowers in a plastic tumbler. But my options are limited. This was nice of Nate, I keep trying to remember. I'm going to help Michael with his manners, and then say goodnight. No difficulties there. I am the Miss Manners of the dating world.

As we walk out the door, I know Kim will be on the phone immediately to Nate to tell him her impression of my date. I'm supposed to get back to Nate and give him a score on Michael and whether he's ready to be back in the dating world again. Somehow, I like the power this affords me. It makes me forget there could be reciprocal scoring here.

We get to Michael's car: a Buick LeSabre that any grandfather would be proud to own. It smells of leather, maneuvers the road like a barge, and boasts big dashboard numbers for those nearly blind consumers. It probably has its own zip code as well.

"We're going to Entrée," Michael says, in a voice that sounds lower than a limbo stick. *He's got to be making that voice up.*

"How'd you manage to get a table there?" I ask, trying not to sound overly impressed. Do you have any idea how long it's been since I've eaten a salad? One that wasn't a few wilted pieces of iceberg drowning in the house dressing? I can feel my mouth salivating at the thought of a real meal, and at the same time hoping I don't get used to it.

I thought I could handle this. I thought I could go on a date with no expectations and no feelings and eat a decent dinner with a new friend, but I can't. I've tasted rejection my entire life, and sure, maybe that sounds overly dramatic, but being in this car, having watched Michael look at my outfit and my cheap shoes with scuff marks, clearly wondering if I was good enough for Entrée. *I just can't take it.*

Michael stretches his arm out confidently along the bench seat. Luckily, the car is so huge, I manage to wiggle out of grasp range. "So, you know how Entrée is nearly impossible to get into? Well, I've been reserving a restaurant every month. It forces me to get a date and keep it, regardless of how I'm feeling about women."

"That's nice," I say, hoping he won't elaborate. He begins to elaborate.

"Some days I just don't feel like ever seeing another female. I want to take that rib of Adam's and stomp on it before woman gets created." Michael laughs. "Nate told me you were a Bible thumper, so I thought you'd like that analogy."

Next subject, please! "I was sorry to hear you're divorced. That must be rough."

"I'm sorry to hear you're unemployed."

He doesn't sound all that sorry. "Yeah, thanks. Hopefully, this is a foray into something bigger."

"San Francisco is land of the entrepreneur. If you can afford the employee taxes, you can make it work. What's on your mind? Stocks? Real estate? What are you hoping to invest in?"

"I'm actually raising capital right now," I say, curious to know if not buying Big Gulps actually warrants the term "raising capital." Considering I only gave them up yesterday, probably not. "For fashion design," I continue.

"Waste of time. The last thing women need is another

frock. I've got a lot of friends in venture capital when you come up with a marketable idea."

Frock? What is this, 1810?

We drive to the financial district and the newest restaurant to receive acclaim in the City. No easy task in San Francisco. Whatever Michael's downfall is, it's not frugality. He pays for valet parking, and the Buick boat is whisked off, leaving us amidst the horns and city noises of San Francisco.

Michael puts his hand in the small of my back and leads me inside the restaurant. It's like being in a 1960s Bond movie at a supper club. The décor is modern, with straight lines everywhere and unexpected orange boxed lights in the ceiling. Small pendant lights hang haphazardly around the room, like a wave of brightened triangular balloons. There are men in tuxedos. Granted, they're the waiters, but still. I'm half-expecting Austin Powers to join us under the orange glow of the period lighting, and I'm hearing that theme music in my head.

The thing that really gets me is the smell. It's like heaven, a mixture of garlic and cilantro and I can see the fresh crab lined on ice, but can't smell those thankfully. My mouth is watering, and I don't even want a pickle! See? I'm only attached to cured cucumbers when I can't afford the good life. This is the life I was born to live!

"I'm Bond. James Bond," I whisper to Michael.

"What?"

I shake my head, embarrassed by my attempt at humor. "Nothing. I thought the place looked like a Bond set."

Slight smile, then it's back to scanning the room to see who might recognize him.

The mâitre d' seats us in chairs that are black and Asian in influence. Bamboo boxes cordon off tables, and the rustic orange must provide some really great *feng shui* vibes. The waiter places the linen napkin on my lap, and I feel a little violated. *Who needs help with a napkin?* See, there are advantages to Denny's—your personal space is not invaded for manners' sake.

"So Nate tells me you have a Stanford education," Michael says, while checking the cleanliness of his butter knife.

"I'm a fashion designer," I say, squaring my shoulders as if to say, *Check out this jacket!* "My gowns can be seen in San Francisco's Saks under the name Sara Lang Couture," I boast proudly. But you know what they say about pride and the fall.

"Fascinating," he says. "Tell me what you majored in at Stanford. I went to Berkeley," he says condescendingly. *Ah, the old Cal/Stanford rivalry—how droll.* Have I been transported back to high school and the popular table?

Fine, he wants impressive. I'll give him impressive. "I majored in finance as an undergrad, went on to get my masters in business administration, but I went to design school at night. Design has always been my passion. When I was a small girl—"

"What are you doing with the degrees? It seems sort of pointless to get them and not use them."

"I've been designing for Sara Lang. Have you heard of her? She's quite famous with operagoers. San Francisco's premier designer, actually. I use my business skills every day."

"When you were working, you mean?"

"I guess I do mean that, yes."

"Nate told me you could discuss what I do: tax law."

"Is there a quiz?" It's a joke, but obviously not all that funny to Michael. Michael is a bit self-absorbed. This meal is suddenly not feeling free. Pretty costly, actually. Sort of like my education.

"I'm curious because my wife was not too bright. I think it hurt me with clients, and I want to ensure that I don't get caught in that same predicament. You understand."

"We're just having dinner, right? After all, I shouldn't send away too many clients with one dinner." *And trust me, you're feeling like a one-date guy. That is, if the gal makes it through the first one at all.*

"The thing is, women present themselves one way, and turn into *another*. Do you remember the movie *Gremlins*?"

"No."

"Well, you couldn't expose these cute little creatures to light or feed them at night. There was just a whole bunch of rules, or they turned monstrous. I feel like that's how life with my ex-wife was. If I didn't do something right, I paid for an eternity when she turned into the ugly, scary gremlin."

"So how did she turn on you?" *This, I gotta hear. You know it's not his fault!*

"All my wife wanted to do was spend my money. It was like going to work and leaving a running faucet. I didn't know what disaster I'd come home to—more shoes, garden hoses littering the backyard, new flowers—"

"Was she into couture?" I ask understandingly. I've seen many a wife drain their husband's wallets at Sara Lang.

"She went to Target three times a week. Every time it cost me fifty dollars. That's $150 a week."

How much did it cost to divorce her? "She spent $150 a week? In San Francisco? Good luck finding one more frugal than that."

For the first time, Michael breaks a smile.

"What did she do, your wife?"

"Nothing. I just told you; she spent my money."

Gosh, I'm feeling for the gal. *A few trips to Target?* "Maybe she was bored. What did she do before she married you?"

"I met her in a shop. She was selling high-end candles."

There's your first clue, dude. She was in retail. "I've seen women in Sara Lang's shop spend more than $10,000 a day in clothes, so $150 doesn't sound like that much to me, actually." *And I'm poor.*

"It's the respect issue. A woman needs to respect that her husband is out working hard to earn money."

"Women nest. Maybe she was nesting, getting ready for the children to come and all."

"No, no children. Did Nate say something about kids?"

"He didn't tell you I want a bunch?" I look up dreamily. "Oh yeah, I was an only child, so I want about six, and just constant noise in the house. I want to be the neighborhood home where all the kids congregate, and other people's kids call me Mom J or whatever my last name is."

Houston, we've lost contact. Hallelujah! I believe the marriage discussion is officially over. We are officially unengaged.

I look up and, to my shock, see Morgan walk in with a man who must be twice her age. "Um, excuse me, will you?" I stand up.

"You know her?" Michael asks me.

"A little. She's an acquaintance." An acquaintance who's one of my best friends, but we'll let that go as I'm not willing to share anything more with Michael.

Michael pulls a card out from his chest pocket. "Give her my card, will you? Tell her I'm available, and my divorce is final." Michael begins to nod and rub his chin. "Morgan Malliard would definitely help my business prospects."

Must...hurt...him. "You know, I don't think I will do that." I hand him back the card. "She's out for a meal, and she's not looking for companionship from what I understand. I've never known Morgan to be without a date."

See, there really is no such thing as a free lunch. Or dinner.

I walk over to Morgan, and she has the oddest expression. Dumbfounded, perhaps. "Morgan?" I say.

She squires me away from the old man. "I'll be right there," she says to her date, before looking at me as if I'm guilty of the ultimate betrayal. "What are you doing here?"

"Once in a while, they let me out for good behavior." I giggle. "I'm on a date." I wave a hand in the direction of Mr. Sloan.

Morgan looks over and asks, "Is that Robert's brother?"

"Just never mind. What are you doing here?"

"Just pretend you didn't see me, okay?"

"But Morgan, I—"

Morgan rushes off behind her "date," and he pushes the chair in while she sits down. I'm standing alone in the middle of the restaurant now, and I can see faces staring. I march over to her table, but I can see by the look in her eye she's serious, so I back away slowly.

I lift my lapels and look at one of the women staring hard. "Couture," I say, fingering the jacket.

I walk back to the tax attorney sheepishly.

"She's busy," I explain.

"Okay, let's order." Translation: "Let's get this over with." *I couldn't agree more.*

"I'm not really that hungry—just a soup and salad for me."

"You really should put some meat on your bones if you want a man."

"Thank you. I'll take that into consideration."

"Seriously, a guy will think you've got anorexia and can't carry a baby. I assume most of the religious sorts are interested in that. Want you barefoot and pregnant and all that."

I'm going to kill Nate, and then I'm going to find him a nice girl who works for the IRS.

I drop my head in my hands, trying to regroup and praying silently that this date could just end. I knew better, I knew better, I knew better...

"Lilly?" Robert, my formerly beloved "white wall" is standing in front of me with Katrina on his arm. *This is why I have no friends. They're all in fancy restaurants I can't afford! And why didn't Robert ever take me to a place like this?*

"Robert," I say, and I force myself to add, "Katrina."

"Who's your friend?" Robert asks, and I look over. Michael has shoved an entire breadstick in his mouth, and what didn't fit he's now wearing on the front of his suit.

"Michael Sloan, this is Robert and his girlfriend, Katrina."

"Pleasure," Robert says as he thrusts out his hand.

Michael wipes his hand across his chest and reaches for Robert. I look over at Morgan, and she's got her hand in the old man's clutches. *What the heck?*

"Lilly, it was good to see you," Katrina says while yanking Robert away.

"Yeah, you too," I say absently, still mystified by Morgan and her nameless geriatric.

The soup arrives, and I have to admit I've lost my appetite, but I'm going to consume every bite lest I get the anorexic sermon again. Although I evidently know a rather large proportion of the restaurant patrons here with me, I have never felt more alone. I shove another spoonful of soup in my mouth. *Nate, you are so gonna pay for this.*

chapter 9

When I get home, I slam the door hard. "Nate!" I scream, knowing he's there. I watch his popcorn fly since I've scared him, but now he's laughing. So is Kim as they sit in front of some fuzzy television show. "So you both think this is funny."

"You dating Michael Moore's twin? Um, yeah, we think that's funny. It's like there's this endless parade of them waiting to date you." Kim pops a piece of popcorn in her mouth. "For one thing, going out of here you looked like Shrek and his Q-tip." She laughs. "I'm sorry, you just got your hair straightened. Shrek and his toothpick!"

"Are you trying to help, Kim? I thought you had a date."

"Didn't work out," she says cryptically.

"Nate, do you want to explain this?" I ask, tapping my toe. "Because Nate knows Michael's size has nothing to do with his downfall. I like teddy bear men. Grizzlies, not so much."

"I know you'd be content to sit in this box every night, Lilly. I thought I'd do you a favor and move you forward. You waste so much time being too *above* dating. I figured you'd get that first nervous tension out of your system after Robert, and you'd be fine." Nate shrugs. "Plus, if you could survive a date with Michael Sloan, you'd be ready!" Nate turns back to Kim.

"The women at work just hate him. He was hired as a consultant, and the women scurry away like rats when he comes to the office. He's as abrasive as a scouring pad." Nate and Kim are both cracking up.

"You *knew* that? Nate, how could you? I thought this was for Michael," I say in all innocence. "You told me you thought he was looking to see what he did wrong with women?"

"Michael? Oh no, Michael doesn't do anything wrong. It's always the women. More than half of the American population has the problem, but not Michael. Michael's perfect." Nate and Kim break into laughter again. "But you're such a sweetheart, Lilly. I knew if he couldn't make it with you for an evening, he might listen to reason. The women at my office thank you."

"I cannot believe you let me go out into the night with that man!" I'm stunned. Nate does not have a mean streak in his body. At least I thought he didn't, but he's sitting on the Goodwill sofa cackling, like all the kids in seventh grade did.

"He's perfectly harmless. I'd never put you in danger, and I figured you'd eat well. Maybe bring us dessert as a thank you," Nate says. "You didn't bring us dessert, did you?"

"Michael would have thought I was going home to eat it and throw it up. He's convinced I'm anorexic or bulimic. I heard about the benefits of nutrition all night! Ugh, I had indigestion before the meal started! That was my last mercy date, you understand?" I bend over to point my finger in Nate's chest. "I'm not desperate!" I cry urgently. I stand up straight, dropping my finger to the side. "Besides, I've got to concentrate on my business, not men. I've got to find capital, and that's my goal right now. Romance can wait."

Don't I sound so strong? Romance can wait. As if I have a choice.

"Didn't you ask Michael for money? We figured you'd at least make the most of your time there," Kim says. "You're so pathetic, Lilly. You just sort of expect the money to drop out of the sky because you need it."

"Michael didn't really understand ball gowns as an investment opportunity. He had a little issue with women spending his money."

"Don't they all," Kim says.

Kim looks good. She's happy and glowing, and her coloring is back to normal. Nate definitely brings out the best in her. "Why do you two watch television down here when Nate has all the best equipment upstairs?"

"Nate's place stinks," Kim says. "No offense, Nate. Lilly, you gotta finish Charley's new bed."

"Charley can't help it," Nate shrugs. "It's his ears." He pauses. "The vet says he's not sure he'd survive an operation to fix them. I keep Lysol at the door. Do you want me to buy Vicks VapoRub for when you come over, Lilly?"

Yeah, he's not a nice guy at all. I smile at him and see his espresso machine is still here. "Can I make one?" I ask, pointing at the gleaming machine.

"Be my guest," Nate says. "I bought you fresh coffee today. Kim says I can't have my machine back. I can only come down here and visit it." He laughs. "You'll be sorry if I wander down in my boxers for my morning java."

"Oh, trust me, *you'll* be the sorry one," Kim says. "By the way, Robert called right after you left. I told him you were on a date. He commented that you moved on quickly."

"You're kidding! I *saw* him on my date. Did you tell him where I was?"

"I didn't know where you were, Lilly."

It pains me to admit this. "He took her to Entrée," I say sullenly. "I was only worth Lyon's or Denny's."

Nate gets up and puts his arm around me. "You're worth Entrée in our book, Lilly."

"What did he want?" I ask, knowing that hearing from an ex is never really a great omen. But hearing from Robert has me on edge, especially after he saw me tonight. Robert rarely called me when we were dating.

"Robert's thinking about getting married to Katrina. He wanted to talk to you about if you thought he should. He says he trusts your opinion."

I set the coffee cup down with a bang. "I don't think I really feel like coffee after all."

"You had quite an impact on Robert, Lilly. It's a bit flattering, don't you think? That he cares about your opinion?"

As I'm heading behind the screen, I look at her. "He could have asked me what I thought of Katrina when I was dating him. It would have saved him the phone call now."

"It turns out *you* were the other woman while they were getting serious. He thought it was good not to put all his eggs in one basket so he wouldn't get hurt. You actually came *after* Katrina. He thought you should know that."

"He told you this?" I never heard Robert that chatty in the three months that we dated.

Kim nods. "He called to find out if you were still angry with him, and asked me to tell you that he was really sorry for not telling you earlier about Katrina. He just wasn't sure if he was ready to commit to her. So he was testing things with you. He never meant to hurt you, and he sounded totally aboveboard."

"Peachy. I'll give him my blessing if that's what he wants." Now I'll admit, I wasn't exactly heartbroken when Robert moved on, but this does feel like knife-twisting, does it not? It isn't like we broke up last year! And here I see him with Katrina, while I'm sitting with Michael Sloan/Moore, the tax man trying to convince me I have an eating disorder.

"He wants more than a blessing, actually."

Nate's at my side again, clutching my shoulders, but I yank away. "Stop that, Nate! Just out with it, Kim!"

"It's good news actually. Robert wants Katrina's gown custom-made and wants you to design it. He said she has big ankles, and you'd know how to cover them. I thought it'd be great because it would keep you designing, and he'd have to pay for the fabric and time. It would be your first paid gig."

I shake my head. "Okay, bear with me here, but what fiancée would want the 'other woman' ex-girlfriend designing her dress? Doesn't that sound the least bit odd to you? What if I have some psycho episode and tear the wedding dress at the last moment? Or put itching powder in the bodice?"

"He knows you wouldn't do that."

My mouth is agape. "Right now, I don't know if I would do that or not."

"It's probably best," Kim says with the voice of authority. "When women catch themselves a man, something snaps. They believe every other woman wants him, and they were the only one to reel him in. Katrina's probably at home feeling for you all alone, without the love of precious Robert." Kim brings her hands to her throat, speaking dramatically and then pretending to wipe a tear. "It was an unrequited love…because true love came along for Robert. And ultimately, true love cannot be denied. No matter who gets hurt in the process."

"Are you done?" I ask, as I make my way back to the counter and try to stuff the coffee grounds in the machine. "Spare me the Shakespearean tragedy routine. He dumped me. He didn't even tell me he dumped me—that's the worst of it. I went over there looking for sympathy, only to get more garbage dumped on me. I didn't even have a chance to grieve because there she was: my competition. He so deserves off-the-rack when he gets married, and I hope she wears neon ankle-wrapped stilettos to show everyone her fat ankles. I hope his perfectionist tendencies focus on an unraveling thread in the middle of the ceremony."

Nate is laughing. "You've got to be kidding us. Lilly, you guys went out to dinner maybe once a week. If that. Suddenly, he's your ex-boyfriend? I *so* do not get women. They call it commitment when it's over. Where's the reality here? The reality is that you could have cared less what he did, where he went. You're a hypocrite! I'm staying single for the rest of my life."

"I think you should do the gown," Kim perks up. "For one thing, it's money in the bank, and in case you haven't noticed, two unemployment checks are not going to pay our rent for long."

"Why don't *you* design it?" I say to Kim.

"You know my specialty is computer work. You design it on paper. I'll put it on the computer and print the pattern. Teamwork, just like you had with Katrina and Robert—tag-team dating." Kim starts to laugh again.

"Where are we going to do this design work, Kim? It's not like design software and pattern printers are available to us."

"So we'll do it the old-fashioned way. We'll make the pattern," Kim says. "Duh," she adds, rolling her eyes. "When Mammy made curtains into Scarlett's gown, do you think they had computer software?"

"I'll invest in the computer portion of the business," Nate says, out of the blue. Judging by the way he was staring at the television, I never knew he'd been listening.

"No." I shake my head. "Nate, we're going to do this on our own. You don't need to rescue us. As far as I'm concerned, my track record with men speaks for itself. This is going to be a women-only business. That will be my headline in *Vogue*."

"Maybe I don't see it as rescuing. Maybe I know a good

investment when I see it. This has nothing to do with testosterone, and besides, I can sue you for gender discrimination if you don't let me in. Where's my lawyer?"

The phone rings, and I stumble over the chair getting to the phone.

"Good thing she never modeled," Kim quips.

"Hello?"

"Lilly, it's Sara Lang."

My stomach is fluttering, like it's suddenly home to a thousand butterflies. "Sara—"

"Don't say anything, Lilly. I'm calling to tell you I've heard you want to go it on your own, and I've decided to invest in your company." I'd like to feel a warm fuzzy, but Sara makes her call sound like she's calling to diagnose me with something. My mouth falls open in disbelief.

Are you kidding me? Am I dreaming?

Now she's waiting for a response. After all, the queen has spoken. I snap my gaping mouth shut and sputter, "Sara, you won't be sorry. You—" But in my heart I'm thinking, *Why? Sara has never done a kind deed for anyone in her life; there's something more to this.* Sadly, I realize that I don't even care. It's the offer I've been waiting for, praying for even!

"Of course I won't be sorry," she says icily. "This is a loan, and you will pay it back regardless of your failure or success."

"I will. Completely. Don't see it as doing me a favor, Sara. Think of it as a wise investment." I ball my fists, thrust one into the air, and jump up and down silently. Kim and Nate are both watching me with their mouths open.

Sara brings the joy level down, as she does with such finesse. "I don't know how wise it will be, but trust me, I do see it as an investment. And you will pay back every cent within the year. I'm fronting you $20,000. That should be enough to get you started. You won't be able to afford trips to the finer mills in Europe, but I know you've always been very good at being economical. You'll find a way to get the better fabrics, and perhaps with your background, you might want to think of going more mainstream, rather than high-end. It's seemed to work for Mossimo, at wherever that is."

"Target. Mossimo's at Target. I'll definitely think about that." My finance education quickly calculates that two people living on $20K a year in San Francisco and trying to start a business with it is less than paltry, less than poverty even. I actually feel a bit poorer than I did five minutes ago.

Sara's still barking orders. "I'll have the paperwork written up and a check cut. There will be no mention of my name in this business publicly. Do you understand? This will come from my private finances, which are under my maiden name, so there will be no connection to Sara Lang Couture."

"I understand implicitly." She means, no connection to Jeff Lang, who she is only probably trying to stiff of alimony cash.

"If I were you, Lilly, I'd keep Kim on the payroll, but with no access to the business accounts. Her elevator doesn't always reach the top floor, if you know what I'm saying."

I look over at Kim, who has eyes as wide as the San Francisco Bay. "I understand, Sara." And I do. Kim doesn't have the self-control to stay away from the money, and though I hate that fact, it is a fact, and a smart business woman puts business before emotion. At least Sara does, and I'm following her lead here.

"I'll have a courier drop the papers off. Again, I do not want to see your face at Sara Lang Couture. Do you understand me? I am a silent partner."

"Yes, Sara. And thank you. You won't be disappointed."

"I'd better not be." *Click.*

"Ahhh!" I start to jump up and down. "We're in business! Sara's fronting us the money!"

"Don't forget me," Nate says. "I'm buying the computer equipment. Gender discrimination, remember?"

I laugh. "Fine, you can buy the computers, but they will be the first thing I pay off."

And just like that, my life does not look like complete rubbish. Although I have yet to tell my grandmother that my pipe dream is now a little more than a silver-lined fantasy floating in the San Francisco fog.

The phone rings again. "Hello," I chirp happily.

"Lilly, it's Morgan."

"Morgan, you're not going to believe this, but—"

"I can't talk long, Lilly. I called to tell you that I'm getting married soon. That was my fiancé you saw me with in the restaurant. Obviously, it's a long story, but I can't tell you just now. He'll be back in a minute, and I don't want him to know my reasons."

"That old man I just saw you with?" I rush a hand to my mouth when I realize what I've just said. "What are you talking about? Why wouldn't you let me talk to you? What's gotten—"

She cuts me off. "They'll be announcing it in the papers tomorrow, and I didn't want you and Poppy finding out from someone else. Pray for me, Lilly, and call Poppy and tell her."

"Morgan, what on earth?" Now I know she lives a completely different life than I do, even though we're in the same town. I know that her world revolves around acting glamorous at the right parties, but I also know that the real Morgan is nothing like that. The real Morgan is tenderhearted and easily bruised. And she would *only* get married for love. I believe that with my whole heart. So what's up here?

"Morgan, you've got to tell me the truth," I say worriedly. I'm a bit panic-stricken, and I can't imagine what would possess Morgan to marry a man twice her age without notice.

Think Dr. Emmett Brown from *Back to the Future* marrying a mentally, spiritually, and emotionally healthy Paris Hilton, and tell me that adds up. One doesn't need a background in finance to know this account doesn't balance.

"It's a long story, Lilly." Morgan sniffles. "I just need you praying, all right?"

"Morgan, you can't leave me dangling here." My throat catches, and I can barely talk. *Morgan is not getting married.* Not without a good, long talk and possibly cryogenics for the groom to allow her to catch up. "What if I just announced I was marrying Robert this weekend? You wouldn't be asking questions?"

"Just trust me," Morgan says, and I can hear her voice cracking. She can't lie to me. "Lilly, this is for the best." But I can hear her soft sobs, and my heart just grieves. My own tears are forthcoming.

"No, Morgan, you're not getting married. Were you supportive when I wanted to down a gallon of pickles? Were you supportive when I thought it was getting serious with Robert? I mean, if I remember correctly, you actually cheered when he broke up with me. Good friends don't stand by their friends' bad decisions."

"I want you to design the gown, all right?" Morgan asks, ignoring me. "I have to run. Put me on your design calendar, and I'll explain everything later. Love ya." *Click.*

The world has gone completely crazy. Is there something in the air? Why is everyone getting married? Is there some run on tax credits or something? Maybe I should have asked my date tonight. Or not. Definitely not!

chapter 10

Morgan, purveyor of all I wish I could be, is getting married. Somehow I thought that when such news reached me, I'd have to fight massive friend-envy for her choice of an incredibly gorgeous, wealthy, Christian, Orlando Bloom look-alike (the guy I couldn't marry due to his lush, full locks of hair, so fantasizing about him is good).

It's just wrong that I can't even be jealous, seeing as how her beau looks more like he should be set up with my Nana than any one of the Spa Girls. I tossed and turned and prayed all night, but I never found comfort or sleep. I never even thought about my business. Morgan...getting married...it consumed me.

This morning, Morgan's not answering her cell, nor Poppy's and my calls to the house. We even tried talking to her father, "San Francisco's Jeweler, Richard Malliard," as he calls himself. He never says, "Good to meet you. Richard Malliard." He says, "Pleasure," as he thrusts a moist hand at you and "San Francisco's Jeweler, Richard Malliard." But apparently Richard's conspicuously missing this morning, in addition to Morgan. The newspapers, contrary to Morgan's predictions, are eerily quiet of news on her impending marriage.

Regardless of the perilous possible weddings surrounding me, this new business venture has got to be good news to my Nana. I've felt the need to patch things up, and what better news than the announcement that I have obtained financial capital to act as fabric glue of the relational sort? At least, as I stand here outside her doorway, I'm hopeful it's good news to her. (Granted, I'm not sure she even saw the end of World War II as good news, but her granddaughter on the verge of success? Call me an optimist.)

I'm about to ring the doorbell when the door flails open. Max is standing there. He's taller than I remember him, at least six feet. I guess I've never stood right next to him before.

"Hey, Lilly." He says with a genuine smile. His deep brown eyes wrinkle at the edges, and his entire face shows his expression. It's very endearing. I can see how he's charmed my Nana completely. (No easy task, trust me.)

"Hi," I say, looking at the aluminum ladder in his hands. "What's that for?"

"Your grandmother had a light bulb out. She's a slave driver, that one."

Tell me about it.

Nana laughs cheerily behind him. "He's only trying to charm this old lady, Lilly. I'll bring you some cookies when they're done, Max."

I break out as much of a smile as I can manage. There's a bit of animosity in me toward Max. He watches television for a living and gets my Nana's full approval, while I finish two degrees at Stanford and work for San Francisco's leading designer, and I'm still seen as a failure. Definite inequity going on here. Logically, I know better than to try to please Nana for the rest of my life. I know this; I'm a smart girl. Yet something snaps in me every time she gives me a look—or even a sniff—of disapproval. I just want to make everything right.

"What are you doing home in the middle of the day?" Nana snaps at me.

"I came to tell you that I have officially started my own business. I have investors and two pending wedding gown orders." *And yay, color isn't a factor here!*

"Investors? You mean Morgan, I'm assuming," my grandmother chirps.

"No, actually, Morgan has nothing to do with the company. The investors are asking to remain anonymous though, so I can't tell you, as part of the contract. Only that I have the capital, and soon I'll have the equipment to get started."

Max nods his head. "Great news, Lilly. Isn't that great, Mildred?"

"Sure, it's great news for you. It means you'll have a tenant forever," Nana says. "Unless she can't make this rent either after this jump, and I'll be living in the Tenderloin district next thing you know." Nana then starts mumbling to herself. *Loud enough for all to hear, naturally.* "Always a dreamer…she's just like her father…can't be bogged down by reality."

I smile pathetically. It's not that she means anything by these words. It's the form of manipulation she uses to get me to do what she wants. Only this time, I'm not budging. I just read the book *Boundaries*, so bring it on!

"Mildred, your granddaughter is amazing," Max says with a twinkle in his eye. I watch him suspiciously, waiting for the other shoe to fall, but he continues. "Lilly found capital in less than a week, and she's a fighter, not to mention a great designer. You told me so yourself." Max gazes at me for a long time, then turns back to Nana. "What's wrong with this place, anyway? You have a great landlord. Think of all the supermodels who would die to live on the floor beneath mine, international hottie and television reviewer that I am." *Big smile from both of us here.*

"I'll tell you what's wrong with it—"

Max holds up a palm and smiles. "Never mind. I'm not up to it. I was up late watching bad television pilots last night. Complain to Lilly, and write it down. You'll need proof for any legal matters anyway. If you sue me, you'll want to have your ducks in a row. I know a good lawyer." Max laughs as he struggles to get the ladder out of her apartment.

It occurs to me that "Geek" was definitely too harsh an assessment. *I'm learning, Lord.*

"Nana, really, I'm a good designer, and my investors believe in me. That's proof that you should too. I even have two pending orders."

"No one has invested more in you than I have, Lilly. I just don't want you to end up like your father. You have a degree in finance."

So I'm reminded, daily. I mean, it sort of makes me happy I didn't major in gynecology. Can you imagine hearing, "Lilly, you have a degree in gynecology!" all day? "Nana, my father didn't even have a high school education. I have two degrees from Stanford. I will not starve; I promise. Besides, if things get really bad, I can move in with Max." I laugh, but Max turns around and winks at me. Now my body betrays me and suddenly feels as though I'm floating. *What the heck?*

"My door's always open," Max says.

"Aren't you tired of living with that strange girl?" Nana asks me. "You should have your own place by now. Shouldn't she, Max? And where do you think you're going?" Nana turns her wrath on Max. "I need my garbage disposal looked at."

I open my mouth to tell her I would have my own place if I wasn't paying two rents, but then I'm not up for the suggestion we room together. I love my grandmother, but being around her 24/7 is toxic on the system. Dr. Poppy said so. In fact, it's probably a lot worse than pickles and diet soda.

One might wonder why I put up with her, but she loves me like nobody else, which is why she nags me like nobody else. When my dad died and my mother abandoned me, there was one person who stood by me—Nana. When there's a gaping hole in your heart and someone stands in the gap to stop the pain, they earn the right to nag.

"Nana, we're doing all right, aren't we? Why do you think I'll be happy if I'm rich? Morgan's not any happier than I am, and she's always been rich." Even mentioning Morgan's name makes my throat constrict. *I'm worried sick!*

Nana takes a broom to the front porch, swiping at the floor like a machete through the sugar cane. "You're just too smart for this, Lilly. You're like a bull, plowing full force, but you've never looked where you're going."

Just like your father. Granted, Nana didn't say it, but she's thinking it all the same. Evidently, my father was not a brilliant man. Or even barely a man. He was only eighteen when he fathered me with a sixteen-year-old girl. Before I was even born, he'd been drag racing on the street, and he arrived first, although not at the finish line. Head-on into a tree. Nana never really got over the loss of her son, which is understandable, but I believe she thinks that if Johnny Jacobs had been educated, he'd be alive today.

The fact is, he and my mother would probably have been divorced, and who knows if he would have been able to settle on a job. My mother left me with Nana to raise me and went off to make her fortune. We never heard from her again. Somewhere about the age of fifteen, I stopped wanting to hear from her. I figured if she was so great, I'd read about her in *People.* Since I never did, I figured God left me with the right mother for me, my Nana.

Although Nana is a staunch believer in Jesus, she's never been one to allow Him to do the job without her help. But it's time we all moved on from my father's death and my over-education. The fact is, I never asked Nana to sell her home for my degrees.

I pull the broom from her grip and force her steely blue eyes to mine. "Nana, I'm a fashion designer. You have to deal with that. Maybe I'll never be Robert Cavalli—"

"Who?"

"He's a fashion designer. One who makes lots of money."

"And your dad was a race car driver." I see a tear glisten in the corner of her eye. Nearly thirty years later, and her pain is still an open wound.

I wanted to be everything Nana had hoped for. I wanted to make up for my father's failings, but how long do I have to pay the price? I did it through six years of college and two years of finance work, and I just feel like it's over for me. I can't deny my real self anymore. But then I look at her tears, and my resolve wilts like yesterday's lettuce.

"Nana," I say gently, "if my business doesn't take off in one year, I'll get a job with real benefits."

Her eyes narrow. "Six months."

Max comes back around with a wrench in his hand. "I've got an interview at the paper in an hour, but let me look at that garbage disposal." He smiles down at me, and I can see he knows exactly how to handle my grandmother. It charms me immensely, and we share a small moment. I smile softly at him, and his grin brightens the day. Max Schwartz, TV reporter at large, appears to harbor a secret so enticing, I find myself completely mystified for a moment. He is definitely sprinkling some salt and light. At least I think he is.

Nana leads him into the house, and I notice the over-whelming stench of artichokes. Going closer to the sink, I see a wretched display. Artichoke leaves in the garbage disposal. Now, my grandmother has been warning me about the ills of artichoke leaves (they're fibrous) in the garbage disposal since I was four!

I watch her, and she won't meet my gaze. "This just isn't a quality disposal, Max," my grandmother accuses. "It won't chew up simple vegetables."

Max smiles at her and goes to work. We're silent while he finishes, and as he walks out, I trail behind him leaving my grandmother to rake up the mess in the sink.

"Does she do this to you every day, Max?"

"She's fine, Lilly."

"No, she's not fine." Nana is lonely, and I was too caught up in myself to see it. "I abandoned her," I say to myself, but obviously, aloud.

"She cooks for me quite a bit, and she keeps the place up well. I figure God has His plan. I like having her here. I've got time, and you don't."

His words sting me like a needle to the thumb. *When did my grandmother ever not have time for me? When was she not there for me when I needed her?* Guilt bubbles within me like chocolate in my grandma's double-chip cookies.

"Lilly," Max takes his thumb and lifts my face to his, "this is your chance. You need to take it. Your grandmother is fine here, and she doesn't bother me. I'm a television writer and hopeless bachelor. What do I have but time? If it wasn't for your grandma, I'd have too many cats and eat at the corner diner every night."

I laugh. "No one dating a girl who looks like Valeria is a hopeless bachelor."

Max smiles.

"I didn't know you were a Christian. You are, aren't you?" I ask, completely stepping in it, because if he says no, it's not going to be pretty.

He nods. "Became a Christian through Jews for Jesus. But

I'm also a spinster, as my mother would say—bachelor when I'm feeling macho."

"How does my Nana get along with your mother?"

"My parents are in Florida, so I like having your Nana here. When she bakes cookies and nags, it's like having a bit of Mom here." He laughs. "Not that my mother ever baked cookies. But the nanny she hired did."

"Doesn't Valeria mind?" I ask, curious how his well-endowed girlfriend would feel about him calling himself a bachelor.

"Why would she? You know, every woman that meets Valeria is obsessed. She's just a friend, Lilly."

I shrug. "I just thought—"

"Do this for yourself right now. Go start your business. It might be the only chance you get." Truer words were probably never uttered, but that doesn't dissuade my guilt. Nana has trained me well.

Nana's phone rings, and we hear her answer it. "If you're selling something, I'm on social security and still have all my faculties, so I'm not giving it away."

Max laughs out loud. "You want to deprive me of moments like this?"

"Just a minute," Nana says into the phone. "Lilly, it's for you. That odd duck you hang out with."

"Poppy?" I say breathlessly into the phone.

"I think I'm offended. You consider me the odd duck?"

"No, I just know my grandmother well." I purse my lips at Nana, and she flicks her wrist and walks away. "Did you find Morgan?"

"I did, and you're not going to like it."

chapter 11

Morgan has been spotted at her health club in Union Square. It definitely crossed my mind that she might have been there, but I didn't know what could be done about it. Square One is not the YMCA. You can't just walk in wearing standard sweats and carrying your punch card. (I think proper attire is a Juicy Couture hoodie and coordinating pants—taut belly and implants required.) Morgan is naturally built like a Victoria's Secret model, so she's allowed in on a technicality.

Considering that Square One's monthly fee probably amounts to more than my rent, I was slightly intimidated about calling and looking for one of their clients. Even if she is my best friend. I knew the result I'd get. Measuring Sara Lang's clients, I've been witness to many Union Square hissy fits, and let's just say, as much as I'm worried about Morgan, I'm not anxious to go into their lair. Very wealthy people have this delusion that life is under their control. This *has* to be why a size six in couture would really fit the average size ten. If you pay enough money, the dress is whatever size you want it to be.

But I digress. Poppy Clayton is too ill-informed about the high-society social graces to be embarrassed. Ever. I don't say that as a bad thing. Poppy is so confident, she just doesn't care what people think of her. Therefore, she gets away with a lot. I would be the lead designer at Sara Lang if I had Poppy's force of nature. I know I'd have a more fibrous diet!

Poppy is now in my view. She's running down California Avenue, her face flushed and her locks bouncing. The first thing you notice about Poppy is her luxurious red hair. It's the color of a fall maple leaf changing to crisp rusty-red. The second thing you see is her clear, glacier-blue eyes. She can make it appear she's staring gamma rays right through you.

But soon after noticing God's fascinating color palette, your eyes drift to the definitely-not-God-given clothes. Poppy swims in wild, gauzy skirts that flutter in the wind and are adorned with enough pleats to bankrupt even the cheapest Indian fabric mill. Her ensemble is always topped with an oversized sweatshirt which never seems to match the plethora of colors in her skirt. She's a fashion nightmare, the eternal "Don't!" in *Glamour's* "Do's and Don'ts" section.

Poppy sprints down the hill in her tie-up suede moccasin boots, and I have to admit, I'm a little embarrassed we're going into Square One. Me, in my own jeans and Rebecca Beeson T-shirt (a partial trade for one of Sara's gowns) and Poppy looking like *Dr. Quinn, Medicine Woman*. We're a pair. If I were still working, I might have borrowed something more appropriate, but a ball gown at a gym wouldn't go over any better.

"Sorry," Poppy says breathlessly as she reaches me. "I had to park the car."

"Where on earth did you park?" I ask, knowing it takes more than the steep hills of San Francisco to take Poppy's breath.

"Other." Wheezing breath. "Side." Breath. "Grace Cathedral." Multiple gasping breaths.

"Poppy, that's blocks! Why didn't you call a cab or hitch a ride on a cable car?"

"No time. Morgan might have left. Do you know how long it took me to drive up here?" She opens the door to the club and allows me to walk in first. I look back and see her bent over, forearms on her knees, trying to catch her breath.

"Poppy!" I say through clenched teeth. "Come on."

She fans her face. "I'm here." She stands straight. "Let's go."

"Oh my goodness." I look up at the glass walls that part us commoners from the elitist health club members. The cavernous glass and slate room is like a modern art museum. I'd be embarrassed to sweat in here. I feel guilty enough for inhaling any of the rich people's oxygen.

There is the sound of flowing water rushing down a rock wall behind the man at the counter, and he greets us with disdain. "Ladies. We have no public restrooms."

Poppy reaches her hand out, palm up, and "scans" him. "Very bad energy flow. Do you have someone doing the Reiki on-site? You should really get that checked out."

I have to put my hand over my mouth to keep me from laughing out loud. Just when she manages to get people completely off-kilter with her alternative healing talk, she goes in for the proverbial kill, with Jesus being the source of all light and energy. But with those piercing blue eyes and intense speaking gift, she's led more than her share of people to the Lord.

Poppy hands insolent desk-boy a card. "I'm Morgan Malliard's personal chiropractor. She summoned me here. Terrible pain." Poppy looks down as though suffering. "Terrible pain," she repeats, and I'm half expecting a *Camille* deathbed scene before she straightens up.

He reads the card. "I'm so sorry. Dr. Clayton, Miss Malliard is in the whirlpool salt bath. Do you need directions?"

"Heat? She's in bubbling heat? Do you hear this, Lilly? When she needs ice! I'm glad we came right away." She yanks me to the glass door, and desk-boy presses the magic buzzer. We're over the moat.

"Where's the whirlpool?" I ask Poppy.

"How would I know? I've never been here. But I wasn't going to tell bad-energy-boy that." We endure the stares of all the members. We're missing the Juicy hoodies, and our taut bellies are well-covered, so it's obvious we don't belong here. Poppy actually looks like she's meant for the Haight-Ashbury reunion costume party.

"Excuse me," Poppy says to a man wearing a black Callaway golf suit.

He glances at his watch. "Yes," he says before emitting a deep sigh, as though this second is costing him a fortune.

"I'm Dr. Clayton, and I have a patient waiting in the women's whirlpool. Would you be so kind as to direct us?"

At this point, the Tiger Woods-wannabe notices Poppy's eyes and her striking looks, and his expression immediately changes. Maybe her clothes are the first thing people notice after all!

"Let me show you personally. It can be confusing." He leads us down a long hallway decorated with small glass tiles creating a colorful, metallic mosaic of the ocean. We pass a three-lane swimming pool, then the cardio room where people are watching stock market TV and CNN and working out on all sorts of contraptions. They could go outside, run up Powell Street, and get far more exercise for free. I bet Poppy's choice of parking place lowered her blood pressure more than the combined lot of machines in there. Outside, they'd even have natural hurdles, what with the multiple homeless camped along the sidewalk. Then again, running on Powell doesn't have built-in Internet—and their treadmills do.

Callaway stops in front of a frosted glass door. "I can't go in—it's the *women's* whirlpool—but I'd love to take you to lunch one day if you see your client again." He pulls a card from his golf warm-ups. *People sure are at-the-ready with the business cards these days. I definitely have to get some made!*

I push Poppy in the door before she answers. *One friend marrying a man old enough to be her father is quite enough.* "We do have to run," I say to him, snapping his card up. "But thank you for your help."

"Lilly, that was rude," Poppy says after I shut the door. "That was the first time I've been asked out in a year!"

"Listen, I'm not sitting in the hospital with the two of you while your husbands get their third face lifts. This has got to stop!"

"Lilly? Poppy?" Morgan emerges from the whirlpool in a Tommy Bahama suit, and some woman hands her a towel. "What are you doing here?"

"Someone hands you a towel?" I ask incredulously. Looking around at the waterfall wall and scent of lavender mixed with chlorine, I'm a bit shocked. And envious. I start to walk around the whirlpool. "Why on earth do we drive down to Spa Del Mar? You've had access to this and haven't shared the wealth? Morgan, Morgan, Morgan."

"Lilly, do you want to get back with the program here?" Poppy crosses her arms, trying to appear angry. "Morgan, Lilly needs to know why you're getting married to that man. Do you want to explain?"

"How did you two get in here?" Morgan asks.

Poppy is suddenly not with the program either. "I wish I'd brought my swimsuit. This conversation would be much better in the hot tub. It would help ease our stress points."

"Would you excuse us?" Morgan says to the towel lady.

I wonder how you get that job? She has beautiful skin, standing in this steamy room all day. The towel lady nods. She doesn't speak. Just like you'd see in that old Cleopatra movie, she exits like an Egyptian slave. I should definitely apply. I could *so* do that! I practice looking at the floor when Morgan speaks.

"So you've tracked me down," Morgan says.

"What kind of friend doesn't answer her cell phone when her friends are concerned?" Poppy asks. "If I believed in karma, you'd be in bad shape, Morgan. You're lucky I'm a Calvinist."

"Yeah!" I say, crossing my arms, not having the least idea what Poppy is talking about. "What kind of friend ignores her best friend in a restaurant?" I ask. "What if I had been trying to impress my date?"

"You had a date?" Poppy asks.

"Yeah, with Robert's brother," Morgan says.

"Wrong. It was a mercy date. And he had no mercy on me whatsoever, trust me. Now, Morgan?"

"I'm ignoring you both because I don't want to hear it." Morgan towel dries her hair. "I'm getting married, and you have no control over this situation. So get over yourselves! Lilly, this is perfect timing for your business. My dress will be in every paper in the city, and probably some national rags too."

"Who *does* like to be told when they're wrong?" Poppy says, sitting down on the teak bench. "You think you've got a corner on that market? Did Lilly like being told Robert was an idiot? Or that Steve Collins just wanted to sleep with her, but didn't want to pay for a date?"

"I thought this wasn't about me!" I croak.

"It's not!" Poppy and Morgan shout back in unison.

"Then could we leave my relationship humiliations out of this?"

Morgan steps back down into the whirlpool, throwing her towel at me. "See, this is exactly what I was afraid of. You've both made up your minds, and you don't even know the story behind my engagement. You just assume it's like Lilly and her cache of bad men."

"Ahem!" I say. "This isn't about me, Morgan. Just explain to us why you're marrying someone your father's age whom we've never even met or heard about. That's all we're asking. If I was to marry one of Nana's beaus, wouldn't you be a little suspicious?"

"I know the truth," Poppy says. "So don't try to get around it. Your father told me this man needs his green card. The question is, Morgan, when you could marry anyone, why help this man get his green card?"

Morgan gives us a look of resignation. "I'm marrying Marcus Agav. That's all you need to know." She slinks down for a moment under the water, and her hair splays on the surface. *Dang, what I'd give to have hair like that.*

"Who is this guy?" I ask when she emerges.

"He's a friend of the consulate general for Russia," Morgan says authoritatively. "I have a great love for all things Russian. You know that."

I look at Poppy and shrug. "Since when?"

"Morgan, we know there's something behind this match. This is not a love connection. You can trust us enough to tell us. We're your Spa Girls. We're in a spa. How much more appropriate do you think it's going to get?" Poppy asks.

Morgan pauses for a moment, like she's about to unleash, but snaps her mouth closed. "I can't tell you why. But it's something I have to do in order to continue to call myself a Christian. You'll like Marcus, girls. He's a fabulous man, and he treats me well. Love will come. Look at Ruth in the Bible. She fell in love with Boaz when given the chance. I just need a chance."

I cross my arms. Morgan appears the cynical ice queen, but she is extremely gentle-natured, and she needs a man who understands her. I've watched her dad parade countless wealthy men before her, and she's never been tempted. Her first love, a music pastor, was poetic and artistic. Perhaps a little too artistic. Andy left her for Nashville, hoping to make it big in the Christian music scene. He sent her his poems for a little while, before his complete and utter failure in the music industry halted his long-distance quest for her heart.

San Francisco's Jeweler has never understood Morgan's genteel nature; he's only pushed her to become the brand he created. With the right finishing schools, nannies, and the Stanford School of Business, Morgan's exterior is nothing like the artist within. I always wondered when she'd snap. Maybe this is it.

"I won't design this gown," I announce.

"And I won't come to the wedding," Poppy threatens.

Morgan's bright blue eyes fill with tears, but she won't look at us. "Please, girls. I'm fighting my dad on this tooth and nail. I can't fight you too. You have to be there for me, because that's what friends do. Even when it seems their friend has lost her mind." She grabs us both by the hands and looks at us both. We stand there with our hands dripping and clenched. "I haven't lost my mind, but I have to do this."

Poppy pushes back her red hair. "Morgan, what are you doing?"

I feel like I'm talking to a complete stranger, not my best friend since college, not the one who dissed a guy for me just to show her loyalty. *Where is that Morgan?* "What do you know about Russia?" I ask.

"I know all about the Fabergé eggs. My dad took me to see them once when they were on display in New Orleans."

We're both just staring at her.

"Well, Lilly, what did you know about Ireland? Did that stop you from chasing after that Steve Collins?" Morgan shouts—*completely not like her*. "I'll learn what I have to about Russia. Haven't I always?"

"We know you're capable; that's not the problem," Poppy says calmly. "Do you remember how you felt every time you got a poem from Andy?"

"I don't want to talk about Andy! Don't bring him up!"

"Does Marcus make you feel that way?" Poppy asks.

"They're apples and oranges. Marcus is a nice man. Really. That's all I can say. I'll never feel about another man like I did Andy. His poetry is etched in my mind forever, like Roxanne who longed for Cyrano." Morgan searches the ceiling, then her eyes pierce mine. "Not Christian, whom she *thought* she loved." Morgan shrugs. "I'm a realist though. If I've learned anything from my father, it's to be practical. Living around diamonds has taught me that all that glitters is not the real thing. There are definitely the four Cs of men. Right now, I have complete clarity about Marcus."

Morgan lets go of us, and I watch her sink back under the water. I've never seen Morgan yell before. The only time I ever saw her show deep emotion is when Andy dropped her via a letter. A twenty-seven-cents postage-due letter! I thought she'd cry until there was nothing left of her. One thing is certain; Morgan is drowning. What she forgets is that Poppy and I will inevitably head into the deep waters after her. Because *that's* what friends do.

chapter 12

We don't get any further information out of Morgan, who stays submerged until we leave after watching her for a few seconds. I figure her getting oxygen is more important in the long run than us knowing right this minute why she's getting married. Poppy shrugs, decides it's up to us, and we make a hasty retreat from the excessive health club.

Poppy heads for the Russian consulate, but sends me home to get to work. "You can't run a design business if you're not designing."

I start to argue, but if there's one thing I've learned over the years, it's that Poppy on the job is more than enough manpower for any given task. I've got a good dose of guilt happening for leaving her alone, but we'll regroup tonight and compare notes. Doesn't it sound so *Alias*?

I wait in line to take out a business license, and the magnitude of what I'm doing begins to take shape. I am going to have a business. *Based on my talent.* I've been hearing my whole life that I'm not good enough. Not in those exact words, but in little soundbytes that mean the same thing. Now, as I stand here with every other hopeful business-person, that voice starts to talk to me again.

You can't design.
It's an artistic business. You aren't artistic enough.
Stick with math. Math is an absolute.
A Stanford degree to play with a sewing machine?
You never were a good judge of your own abilities.

And then I hear the cackling, and I unwittingly grasp for my hair.

I struggle with my self-image while waiting in the snaking bureaucratic line and listening while all the immigrants starting their businesses speak in their native tongues to annoyed Americans behind the counter.

"They are the American spirit!" I want to yell. Look at them. They barely know how to say "yes" in English, and they're embarking on the adventure of a lifetime: to make it or break it in the American business world—in their new, capitalistic society. That's impressive. But of course, there aren't any brownie points for trying and failing, and I'm more than aware of this.

"You start business?" a man in front of me asks.

I nod. "Fashion design. I make dresses."

"Ah, very nice." He pats his chest. "Pho Noodle House in Tenderloin. You come; here's coupon."

"I love soup!" I take the coupon from his hand. "Thank you so much," I say, waving the paper. "I'll visit."

Another line opens, and he's off. I'm a little awestruck at how prepared he is. I mean, no business license yet, and he has coupons! He hands another coupon to the city clerk. *Lord, I hope I know what I'm doing.* The voices start back up again.

As the city clerk beckons me toward him, my stomach starts to rumble at the mere thought that *this is it.* Or maybe I'm just hungry. You know how they say skinny people forget to eat? And that it's a special kind of stupid? It's not stupid really. It's just that life gets in the way, and my stomach doesn't shout for attention until the dizziness starts. Perhaps if I had some-thing more than work in my life, food would be more impor-tant. As it is, which soup can I'm going to have a relationship with tonight is definitely not worth much brain activity.

"I'm starting a business," I tell the clerk, a slender, middle-aged woman without much regard for fashion.

"Honey, you're all starting businesses. Look around you at all the ahn-tree-pre-newers," she says sarcastically. "Forms?" She holds out her palm.

So it's not new to her. Must she stomp on my heart? I hand over my forms, which are apparently filled out wrong, and I almost go home at this point, but I wait through the line again and—*Ta da!*—I have a business license!

I grasp the paper from "Miss Happy." Here it is. I hold in my hand the last opportunity to make something of myself in design, and it's all on other people's dimes. I know this isn't exactly as fear-inspiring as, say, impending death by Amazonian snakes or anything, but I hear the *Indiana Jones* music anyway. *Gulp.* Lilly Jacobs Design is officially open for business.

Failure now means Starbucks would no longer be a luxury. Eating would be. Still, you can't wipe the grin off my face the whole way home on the bus—which, incidentally, I've learned is as good as bug spray in warding off unwanted seatmates. Smile, and people evidently think you're scary. But back to the job at hand: I think even more important than the busi-ness is the fact that I have taken a stand! I'm going to live my own life! I'm not looking backwards at what I maybe *should* be doing, but looking forward to what I think I'm called to do. Now, if I can just get Morgan to follow my lead, find the man of my dreams, and tame my hair, all will be good.

My answering machine is beeping as I unlock the latches and enter the loft. Kim is asleep under a mountain of tangled blankets. *At least, I think she's under there.*

I press the blinking machine. *Beep.* "Lilly? I trust you received my check today. Let me see your sketches before purchasing any fabric. I want approval of colors as I know it's not your strong suit."

Beep. "Lilly? There's a contest for up-and-coming designers in *Vogue* magazine. You'll need ten sketches with the designs finished for the show. The deadline to enter is next Friday. I trust you'll look into that today. I will sponsor you if a sponsor is needed."

Beep. "Lilly? How on earth do you expect to run a business if you're not there to answer your phone? First rule of business: be available. Get a cell phone. That's an order."

I roll my eyes. Like $20,000 for goods/services and two people's living expenses is going to purchase the luxury of a cell phone. I don't mean to be ungrateful, but I'm not exactly living at the Ritz just yet. In San Francisco, California, that's pocket change! Granted, pocket change I didn't have, but still. I pick up the check with my name on it, and all those zeroes. What an amazing feeling this is before the actual work starts!

"Lilly, turn that thing off!" Kim emerges from the mountain of blankets. "I thought I was having nightmares! Listening to Sara Lang invading my sleep is like hearing the Freddy music in those horror movies. That woman's like nails on a chalkboard, screeching at me all day when I don't even work for her! She's crazy, and you invited her into our world. This is *your* business. Don't you forget it!"

I pause at her advice. It's so much easier to let people tell me what to do, but Kim is right. If I'm going to take the dive, I have to jump in head first. "Didn't you hear the phone ring?" I ask, wondering why Kim didn't answer.

"I did. I wasn't answering it when I heard who it was. Unlike you, the sadistic one, I'm in no hurry to welcome that woman back into my life. We escaped, and you've put us right back into bondage. Lilly, you didn't even take the time to think about this. Where are you going to sell your designs? Who wants couture from some unknown? You need a business plan."

I yank her out of bed. "Come on, Kim. We're in business." I wave the license in front of her.

"*You're* in business, Lilly." Kim plops back on her mattress and covers herself in blankets.

"Come on. It's noon, Kim. We're wasting daylight."

"I agreed to go into business with *you*, not with Sara's money and not today. A normal person would at least allow one unemployment check to come. You didn't take it as a clue that we escaped evil, did you? Is it necessary this business start now? Today?" She's muffled under the blankets. "She's the devil, Lilly, and you've sold your soul."

I yank the blanket off her. "I've done no such thing. She's an investor. She doesn't have any say in the business."

"Approval of colors before you ordered? Get a cell phone? Right, she has no say. I've done nothing but heard her *say* all morning. What I haven't heard is your plans."

"Listen, we've got no other choice, Kim. Without Sara, our capital currently includes five cans of kidney beans and a twelve-pack of Diet Pepsi. I don't think we're in a position to be picky. We've got a week to make ten designs and one wedding gown for Morgan that will not be used." I roll my eyes. "Hopefully, we'll have one more for Robert's bride-to-be if they make it down the aisle. I'm having a hard time feeling the love there."

Kim jumps out of bed in yesterday's clothes. "Count me out of this business venture. I'm taking at least a week off. If you don't like it, find yourself a new employee." She runs into the bathroom and slams the door on me.

I get out my sketch pad, hoping Kim's over her tantrum before it's time to transfer them to the computer—when we get a computer. There's a pounding on the door. I open it to see Nate standing alongside a million Dell computer boxes. "I got them shipped overnight. Are you ready to set up? The design software is going to take a while longer to get here. Maybe tomorrow or the next day."

"Nate, what on earth did all that cost you?"

"It's really more packaging than product. Don't be too impressed. Tell me where to set up."

Like there's a lot of choice. "That would be on the one table we have in here. I'll clear Kim's dishes." I rush over to the table and pick up the empty Cup-o-Noodles and food-encrusted forks. Disgusting.

"Where's Kim?" Nate asks, a little more nonchalantly than usual.

"She's holed up in the bathroom now, hiding from me and anything resembling work."

"She had a hard day yesterday," Nate says, while pulling the boxes into our studio.

"Your point?" Considering I've recently been dumped, fired, and told by my grandmother I'm destined to be a hunchbacked spinster, I'm not inclined to muster much sympathy for Kim at the moment. Especially when I can only see her presence in terms of the mess made in the loft today. She obviously wasn't in bed the whole morning.

"Not everyone is driven like you," Nate says, as if *ambition* is a dirty word. I step back, wondering what's changed about him, why he's standing up for Kim and her attitude. Unemployment wouldn't be such a problem if we didn't live in the country's most expensive housing market.

"I'm driven? To what exactly? Are you saying I've given up my ethics to live this life of luxury? Pardon my sarcasm, but what do you think I'm selling my soul for, exactly?" I ask, scanning the room. "Morgan's gym has a hairdryer amounting to more than my current net worth. I went to Stanford, Nate. Shouldn't I have an ounce of ambition?"

"Yes, we know that, Lilly. You seem to be reminding us of that a lot. I went to MIT. Did you know that?"

I straighten at this. "Well, no, but you never mentioned it."

"Because no one really cares. Does it impress you?"

"Sure it does."

"I rest my case. Your education may mean something to your grandmother, but really it means nothing to us. This is San Francisco, and like Wall Street, people only care about results. Show us the results. Don't you watch *The Apprentice*?"

I shake my head. "I just want to shave off that comb-over, so I can't bear to watch."

"Just have some understanding for Kim. She's not like you."

"What does that mean exactly?"

"I'm just saying your dream is obviously different from hers. You can't force her to feel like you do. I'm putting my money up behind you because I know you will make it, Lilly. I believe in you, or I wouldn't have done this." He looks at all the boxes. "But Kim's different. You have to let this be her idea. She doesn't have anything to prove, and she needs to know she's valuable. She's in a hard place right now."

I drop the plate I'm scraping into the sink. "I'm not forcing her to do anything. I'm giving her a job. I'm playing her personal maid every day. How valuable does that make me exactly?"

"Kim feels judged."

"Well, call Dr. Phil. She's wasting her life, giving out our phone number to any number of leeches at the local bar, and when's the last time she did laundry? I'm not here to judge her, but I'm not her mother either."

"It's her life to waste, Lilly."

I'm aghast. Is he kidding? "Just the other day you were telling me to get her help. What happened to the tough love, Nate? Did you wimp out on me before we got started?"

"I talked to her, and she just seems like a lost puppy. Like she needs some time to find herself. She's not ready to start this business."

"News flash: neither am I. But I'm not ready to live on the street or with my Nana either. This is *it*. I design, or I find a clerk position doing accounts payable. With my résumé, those are my options. Yesterday, I would never have agreed to let Morgan wear one of my designs. Today? I want to design her monthly wardrobe because I've got nothing here. A wing and a prayer." I kiss his cheek. "And, thanks to you, a computer system."

Kim comes out of the bathroom, and I notice Nate stand up straight. "Kim, are you all right?" Whatever's going on between the two of them doesn't appear romantic, but what it is mystifies me.

"I'm hungry." Kim rubs her face like a toddler before bedtime.

"Let's go get something to eat." Nate grabs Kim by the hand. "I'll be back to set this up tomorrow when the software is here." Without giving me time to respond, they're out the door.

The roar of the freeway bothers me all the time, but especially when I'm alone in this damp loft. It makes me feel like everyone has a place to go, and I'm only left with their fumes. The constant noise reminds me I'm not living on the ocean, designing for Hollywood's elite, but that I will soon be eating on my only workspace, the one table we own, wondering if my life will ever get to the next level.

The phone rings, and I'll admit, I'm leery of answering it and hearing Sara's angry bark at the other end. Her husband may have left her, but there are a few of us without the option of eliminating her completely from our world.

"Hello. Lilly Jacobs Design. How may I help you?"

"Quite impressive," Poppy says into my ear. "I could totally feel your positive vibe. You are on fire with adrenaline. You are a couture designer! You rock! You—"

"Actually, I feel like dirt. Nate and Kim just escaped me like I was Sara herself."

"What are you doing right now?"

"Mulling over my food options: three-bean salad from a can or cream of mushroom soup," I open the fridge. "With water instead of milk," I say despondently.

"You can't eat that stuff. There's MSG, preservatives, hydrogenated oils, and heaven knows what else. Pick up the can. I want you to tell me how many things you can't pronounce."

I put the can down. "I give, Doctor. I'll fast and pray tonight. Is that better?"

"When's the last time you went to the grocery store?"

"I don't even remember. Sara had us working late recently to make the gowns for San Francisco Fashion Week. She ordered Chinese or pizza most nights."

"How you stay so skinny is really a mystery to all of us with normal bodies."

"Want to trade? While we're at it, can I have your hair too?"

"Listen, can you come out? I have a great idea. Can you meet me at Morgan's church? Tonight is the singles' group. Can you get there easily, or should I pick you up?"

"Sure, I can get there easily enough. You just have to bring me home when it's dark. I have to be home early. I have to do at least two sketches tonight." Just the thought of church makes me feel guilty. It's been almost three weeks since I've been to my own.

"Meet me at the church. Seven." Poppy clicks the phone.

Ah, the singles' group. Just what I need today: more rejection. This time, with a Christian flair.

chapter 13

One sketch. That's what I've done for the day besides getting my business license. I never realized how hard it would be, working for myself, to actually find the time to work. The sketch, however, is perfection. A gathered, pale pink silk chiffon, very dainty in design and with a tiny black ribbon gathering the three-inch strap of chiffon over the heart. Perfect contrast. It has a free-flowing skirt that evokes something Ginger Rogers might have worn in her day. It's elegant in a minimalist way—and, as far as coverage goes—a maximalist way. Personally, I find the female form extremely beautiful. I find showing too much of it extremely tacky. But that's me. Michael Kors…yes. Hooters…no.

I look at the sketch one last time before rushing off to meet Poppy and cash my first significant investment check. The phone rings, and before I can pick up, I hear Sara's voice on the answering machine: "I have two words for spring: sunflower-yellow corduroy."

"Or not," I say back to the machine. I don't even want to mention the fact that, really, this could be three words, depending on your use of punctuation. I figure corduroy is enough of a hit against her today. Sara may be a genius at color, but texture is my game, and corduroy will not happen on my watch. However, it sounds like an excellent reality show: *Crimes Against Fabric*.

I slam the door behind me and get ready for the bane of the Christian's existence: the church singles' group. The place where one goes to feel God's unconditional love in diluted, sparsely parceled-out fashion. At least that's been my perception. Sure, it's on the pessimistic side, but one doesn't get to be twenty-nine, standing next to two women who look like Poppy and Morgan, without realizing that my chances of being noticed while surrounded by friends like this would be about, oh, one in not-gonna-happen—*ever*.

Morgan's church is a beautiful cathedral on San Francisco's Nob Hill. The singles' group that meets there is not actually part of the church, but a bigger church down on the Peninsula. They use this building during the week when everyone is overworked and unable to get all the way down to the Peninsula.

The actual congregation has very little use for the singles' activities, but a bingo hall, yes. A place to hold the latest Junior League event, absolutely. Still, it's nice of them to lend the building to the younger single folks and allow the workaholics to keep up their pace, factoring Bible study into the week's work. As I approach the church, Poppy is waiting for me on the stone steps, glancing at her watch.

I rush up the stairs. "I'm here. The bus was late."

"It's all right; you're still early. Are you ready for this?" Poppy asks.

"To walk in next to you? I'm used to it actually. Men like redheads." *Men like women with actual figures too. Not that I don't own some really great bras.*

"You really need the emotional freedom technique. It's from acupuncture. Take the outside of your palms and repeat the negative things about yourself while you tap them together.

They're not true, and you have to make yourself believe it. You need to tap the meridian points while repeating the lies." Poppy starts to hammer away with her hands, thumping the outsides of my hands together, then the top of my head with her fingertips, and then my forehead. "Now repeat after me: all of my friends are more beautiful than me. I am thin and unattractive."

I still her hands. "You know, I'll do your voodoo when we're at the spa. Not in public. In public, I have to be seen as a designer next to a best friend who only wears gauze. Is that not enough torture for me?"

"We really need to pray you through your insecurities, Lilly. The emotional freedom technique—"

"I'm cool with that. It just looks like we're playing *See, See, Oh Playmate*. Can't it wait? We're here for Morgan, right? I'll still be skinny and unattractive with atrocious hair after the singles' meeting."

"I didn't say that. I said the opposite is true. See, you repeat the falsehood and then—"

"Never mind. Morgan?"

Poppy nods. "Let's go."

The singles' group meets in the back of the stone church, and the room is colder than a night on the Bay, even in the middle of summer. As we walk in, we all get the once-over from the sea of faces. Poppy's clothes are the first thing that's noticed, and probably the next is: is that skinny girl old enough to be here? Let's just say, if we weren't saved when we walked in here, our collective redemption value to this group would probably amount to less than an empty two-liter bottle. Our audience quickly loses interest and goes back to the rumbling.

"Bad energy," I say to Poppy before she can blurt it.

"It's probably rooted in deep-seated insecurity," she whispers behind a cupped hand before shouting, "Hi, we're friends of Morgan Malliard's." The entire room turns to face us.

We come in peace. Take us to your leader.

The room is silenced. A woman gets up, dressed to the nines in Chloe. A singles' group in couture. I need this like a hole in the head.

She stretches out an unbearably white arm and flicks her dark hair behind her back. "Welcome. I'm Caitlyn Kapsan." At first her voice is so breathy, I think she's teasing, and I wait for her to say, *Kidding, great to have you.* But no, just more breathy words: "Of Kapsan Properties."

"Dr. Poppy Clayton." Poppy sticks out her unmanicured hand.

"Lilly Jacobs." I thrust my hand toward her. "Lilly Jacobs Design."

"Do you know our friend Morgan, Caitlyn?" Poppy asks.

Caitlyn giggles a breathy laugh. I swear it sounds like a cat trying to get a hairball up. *Is that supposed to be attractive?* "Everyone knows Morgan. If they don't, they have to be living in some type of hole. Make yourself at home, girls. We'll be starting with Bible study soon." Her Chloe-clad self then turns and, nose in the air, walks briskly away.

"Ah, she exudes warmth, doesn't she?" I laugh. "I'm feeling so cozy, so absolutely enveloped in God's love. Gee, I hope there's an altar call tonight." We look at one another and laugh.

"It doesn't matter. We're here for answers, not spiritual sustenance. Thank the Lord. Someone here must know why Morgan is marrying that old man, or at least who he is."

But we both know that if *we* don't know, there probably isn't another soul on earth besides Morgan who can shed light on this. If being wealthy has taught Morgan anything, it's how to put up appearances and play her cards close.

"Someone here at least might know who he is. We're going

to have to piece things together—there's no getting around that." Poppy sits down and stretches her gauzy skirt around her. My eye catches on the Indian-gone-awry design, and I open my mouth to say something snotty when something stops me. Something pulls my gaze away, and I feel time stop.

There have been three moments in my life when I felt as though time stood still. One was when I saw my first copy of *Vogue* in a hair salon and realized that there were other emaciated girls like me. (Not that I was emaciated, exactly, but I did look a lot like a World Vision ad. Only the distended belly was missing.)

The second time was in college when I laid eyes on Steve Collins, a rugby player and Irish cad. He was heavenly to look upon, with blond curls and emerald eyes like the isle he came from. With his beautifully hooked Roman nose (hooked after being broken during rugby, of course) making him thoroughly masculine and yet completely approachable, Steve was the type of man whose looks should be immortalized in marble. Time quickly started again when he asked Poppy if I was the type that "put out," because he was considering dating me. *Ewww.*

This is the third time. Right here, today, in this stone church, time is standing still again. And the reason is behind the small podium. *Am I breathing?* He's got a full head of dark brown locks pushed haphazardly off his forehead, deep chocolate eyes that appear as if they hold a secret only for me, and a rugged jaw that's square but softened by a gentle smile. *Must remember to breathe*—but I feel this man's presence as if I'm entertaining angels unaware.

"Lilly? Are you okay?" Poppy asks.

I feel my head bob in answer. I don't find very many men attractive. I think there are many who are handsome, but feeling their presence? It's only happened to me once before—with

Steve Collins, a man who thought intimacy meant staying a full night. So…I can't say my feelings have been altogether proper…or that they've ever amounted to anything more than adding to my suffering. Still, this breathtaking moment is magical in its own way. Makes you buy into the thought of a soulmate.

Nana has always told me that it's dangerous to feel that way about a man. It's better to be in control and not care whether they stay or go. I try to remember that as I look at that full, wavy hair, a definite no-no. I just want to rake my fingers through it without bothering to introduce myself.

"Lilly?" Poppy says again.

"Shh." I feel my finger at my mouth, and then I see his eyes catch on mine. They hold there, and I slowly drop my finger into my lap.

"A warm welcome to our guests," he says, looking directly at me. I feel this girlish blush spread all over my face.

I lean over to Poppy. "Did he just speak in a British accent?"

"I am from England, yes," he says.

I look at Poppy in horror. Judging by her expression, I did indeed say that out loud.

"Kent," he says. "A little town near Canterbury. And will you share your names with us, ladies?"

He looks straight at me, and I fear my mouth is standing still with the moment. "P-P-Polly," I stammer.

"Lilly," Poppy says. "Her name is Lilly Jacobs. She's from San Francisco. I am Poppy Clayton, formerly of Santa Cruz and now, Cupertino. We are best friends with Morgan Malliard and hoped we might find her here tonight. To surprise her."

"Well, it's a pleasure to have you both here. Morgan hasn't been with us for some time, but you are always welcome. If we don't have any further announcements, I'll ask you to turn your Bibles to the Book of Romans."

I didn't bring a Bible, and suddenly I feel completely exposed sitting here with no Bible and an inability to speak. But I'm also lost in a dream world, so I'm not really caring either. Someone at the end of the row hands me a church Bible, and I murmur a thank you before rifling through the pages quickly to get to Romans.

When the sermon is over—and I did manage to focus on the fact that it was about living in God's will, even when life doesn't go your way. As if it ever goes mine!—Poppy stands up. "Valuable sermon, but I'm afraid in terms of Morgan, this night wasn't much help. Let's go mingle and see if we can find anything out."

I look at tonight's teacher, and my gaze captures his own. His eyes are so expressive, and I could swear they are saying, *Don't leave.*

Poppy grabs me by the arm. "What side of the room do you want to take?"

"The front," I say absently. My eyes never leave those chocolate brown eyes that seem to be conversing with my own. For the moment, I can't think of a better use of time. I straighten the pink cashmere hoodie I made from Sara Lang scraps. *Dang, I love design.*

"So I'll take the back?" Poppy asks.

"Yeah," I say, and I see a very slight smile lifting the corner of his mouth.

"Friends of Morgan's, then?" he says, reaching a hand out for my own. I grasp it, and he cups the other around mine. I clutch my hand against his, feeling the pulse pounding in my throat.

I nod. "Best friends since college." *I did it! I spoke intelligibly. It's a sign from above, I tell you!*

"Stanford then?"

"Yes. Excellent lesson, by the way. You're a gifted teacher."

"I grew up in the shadow of Canterbury. My grandmum would say I ought to be."

Can I bear your children?

"Are you the singles' pastor?" I finally ask.

He laughs. "No, I'm afraid the pastor's life isn't for me. I'm in pharmaceutical sales. Mostly over-the-counter products. We're just getting our American sales force in play."

Poppy is at my side just as he says this. "What kind of products?" Her eyes narrow, and I fear we're in for a natural medicine sermon. I cringe at the thought. I swear, I will shred that favorite gauze skirt of hers if she embarrasses me.

"Weren't you going to take the back of the room?" I whisper with lowered brows.

She ignores me. "What kind of products?" she asks again.

His face goes bright red. "We're just expanding our market from mostly UK generics to over-the-counter products here in America."

"What kind of over-the-counter products?"

Ugh, here it comes. The drugs as the devil speech.

"Pregnancy tests, mostly."

I'm gonna die. My Brit angel is now the color of the Netflix envelope: bright red.

"Poppy's a chiropractor," I blurt, hoping to shut her up on the evils of antibiotics and a good/bad yeast balance. "She believes in natural healing. But nothing unnatural about a pregnancy test, now is there, Poppy?" I ask through clenched teeth.

"I believe in natural healing too," my Brit angel says, "when natural healing is called for. But there are times when nothing can replace pharmaceuticals. Better life through chemistry and all that."

"The body is an amazing healing machine," Poppy says in distinct challenge.

"So are sales good here in America?" *Oh shoot me. Was that the stupidest question? Do I really want to know how the rest of my country is faring in offspring production when I can't get a date? And is it any wonder why? Ask his name, Lilly!*

"Quite good," he says. "I haven't properly introduced myself. I'm Stuart Surrey. I do hope you two will join us again."

At this point, Chloe-clad woman approaches us. "I see you've met my *boyfriend*, Stuart. Isn't he an incredible teacher?"

There are times when that word *boyfriend* is used as a weapon. This is definitely one of those times. And I feel my back curl like a cat's looking for a fight.

I look at Stuart as if he's betrayed me. "He's wonderful," I say, while keeping my eyes on his, but now my stomach is stirring.

"We really should get to the group in case there are questions, Stuart," Caitlyn says, clutching *my* short-lived angel's elbow. "It was a pleasure to meet you both. Do say hello to Morgan. It's been so long since she went off and took up with the Russian. We never see anything of her."

"You know her boyfriend then?" Poppy asks.

"He's a Russian diamond broker, right? We have so many internationals with us, and the diamond connection was obvious with Morgan's dad and all. I introduced them, I believe. They met and I guess it was an instant connection."

"He was coming to your singles' group? Isn't he sort of, um, you know, older?"

"Age is relative, darling," Caitlyn says. "A man is only as young as he feels."

Poppy looks at me with a sullen expression clearly visible in her eyes. "Thank you all for making us so welcome here tonight. Great sermon, Stuart. I do hope we'll get to hear you again one day."

"Please do come back," Stuart says, looking straight at me.

"We will." I grab for his hand one last time and feel his fingertips on my wrist.

Poppy grabs my hand and rushes me out the door. "I knew Morgan's father was behind this. That man would sell his soul to drape a diamond around someone's neck."

"Poppy, we don't know if this is arranged. She said she was fighting her dad. Maybe Morgan loves this man." But I know, even as I say it, that San Francisco's Jeweler probably has a great deal to do with this marriage. Morgan has never been able to break free of his clutches. If this marriage happens, she probably never will.

"Lilly, don't think I didn't see you and Mr. Surrey having your own private conversation, by the way. His girlfriend apparently noticed too."

I swallow the lump in my throat. "Stuart probably was feeling sorry for me, wondering when I might be entering puberty. It was nothing." But I feel thoroughly nauseated now. Maybe I have unrealistic expectations for what love is supposed to be like, but shouldn't it make you feel like that? Shouldn't it be wildly passionate, and shouldn't you be unable to talk properly when you meet him?

"Stuart was wondering how he might escape the clutches of that woman and get alone with you. Don't let my gauze fool you. I see more than you think I do. I'm just not fashion-oriented. There's nothing wrong with a skirt that lasts more than a decade," she says, sweeping her skirt around.

"There is something *so* wrong with a skirt over a decade old. Where do I begin? The only thing that's worse is that horrid tie-dyed one you wear. You look like you stepped straight out of Santa Cruz. How do you ever expect a man who isn't into medical cannabis to ever look your way?"

"I don't believe in medical marijuana," Poppy says. "They can get the medical benefits from pills and not sear their lungs."

"I know you don't, Poppy. My point is that you look like a burnout in those clothes."

"They're comfortable."

"They're like a flashing warning signal to normal men."

"You're one to talk, Lilly."

Poppy's words bring a smile to my face. "I've got to get home. I have ten designs due by next week, or I can kiss my investor goodbye."

"He's got bad energy and a girlfriend! Don't say I didn't warn you."

"How did I know you were going to say that?" I say, knowing full well that the church calls Poppy's gift *discernment*, and she most certainly has it. Sometimes though, I'm not in the mood, and I want to live in my fantasy world where a man with an English accent takes a distinct interest in *moi*. "Besides, it was probably Caitlyn interrupting his energy message."

Poppy drives me home and pulls up to the red curb. "Spa weekend. Don't forget the wedding drawings. Our only hope is getting Morgan out of San Francisco and away from her father. That man will have her believing her troubles can be solved with the right diamond pendant."

"We can't jump to conclusions." *But our best friend has gone completely silent. What's left to do?*

Poppy waves goodbye, and her gauzy skirt blows in the cool San Francisco summer night. She's a vision of Haight-Ashbury.

As concerned as I am for Morgan, I'm still floating from the brief moment with Stuart Surrey, British hottie and, *sigh*, someone else's boyfriend. I can't even blame my hair this time. It's as straight as a toothpick.

chapter 14

Poppy and I have wasted the entire evening, and really, we're no better off than we were this morning. As private detectives, we're pathetic. Charlie's Angels' jobs are, for the moment, safe. But the question is, is Morgan safe?

I always knew she'd be the first of us to get married. I never doubted it. I mean, do the math. She *has* dates. Poppy and I don't. Just by sheer probability, she's ahead of us. But somehow, I pictured her married to a suave capitalist her father knew, not an elderly foreigner, most likely in need of a green card.

As I enter my apartment hall, I'll admit, my mind is not completely thinking of Morgan and her secrets. My mind is on Stuart Surrey, and I feel a smile stretch across my face. I close my eyes and I picture those deep brown eyes and their ravenous intensity. Of course, I know he belongs to another. Technically. But somehow Caitlyn doesn't exude warmth, and *she* called *him* her boyfriend. It wasn't the other way around. I can't help but think he's with the wrong woman, and I must rescue him. However, I'm sure many a mortal sin started with that thought, and I try to repent to Jesus without allowing my mind to wander back to those dark eyes. *But those eyes.* It was as though they were only for me.

The light bulb in my apartment hallway is out, giving the

building an even more eerie feel. It's not enough we have to live in Bernal Heights, but we do it without windows and now in the dark of night. It feels like a truly creepy horror film, and like the dumb heroine of the film, I'm walking straight into it. Just waiting for the knife to plunge from a psychopath—who will be heralded as a misunderstood child when the court case comes to fruition—into my heart. High-profile attorney Mark Gerragos will be there to attack my character and use my grandmother to say I never made anything of myself.

"Lilly?"

I scream.

"Hey, it's just me, Nate."

"Nate, what are you doing creeping around here on my floor?" I try to catch my breath.

"I was trying to get the light bulb changed before you or Kim got home. I didn't want the two of you coming home into the dark. I came down to get my espresso machine, because I was craving a good cup, and you're holding it hostage."

"This building has no maintenance. It's really disgusting," I say, rather than the obvious, *You scared the life out of me!*

"Where ya been?" Nate asks, scraping the ladder down the hallway like Freddy Krueger's nails on the chalkboard.

"Morgan's church. She wasn't there, but it was interesting just the same. I have a question for you."

"Shoot."

Bad choice of words here in the dark.

"If a guy has a girlfriend, is he completely off-limits? And how do you know he's her boyfriend just because she called him that?"

"Was he there when she called him her boyfriend?"

I cross my arms. "Yes."

"You have your answer then. He's her boyfriend. Otherwise he would have taken you aside and corrected the error."

Like I'm giving up this easily. "Okay, another question. Is it acceptable to see where things go? If maybe they break up?"

"If maybe they break up?"

"Just never mind!"

"I'm just saying."

"Maybe I didn't want to hear the truth. Maybe I wanted you to lie to me and tell me that true love rules over all. Did you ever think of that, Nate?" *Did it ever occur to you I'd ask a Christian guy if I wanted the truth?* "Maybe I needed for romance to reign for one moment in time? I'm so sick of everyone making reality plain enough for me. Don't you all think I live in reality as it is? Dating men who hate women and look like Michael Moore? What more reality is it you think I need?"

Nate is quiet for a minute. "I don't think you need any more reality. I'm in the same boat, right?"

"At least we have each other to be pathetic with. What happened to your newfound George Clooney scenario?"

"I asked a girl out today."

"You did?"

"But she said no. She said her parents were in town."

"Maybe they are."

"Maybe they aren't. Anyway, it doesn't matter. I did it; that's all that matters. Getting over that first hurdle, that's the big problem. That's why I set you up with Michael Sloan. I was doing you a favor, preparing the way. I think I need to leave my apartment more. George Clooney doesn't stay holed up in his place."

"I'm proud of you, Nate."

He slides the ladder under the light fixture. "Will you hold this for me?"

"Yeah. One bulb. How does one expect a single bulb to light an entire hallway? I bet Morgan never has to deal with this."

"She just has to deal with that psycho father of hers. Every time I see her in the newspaper, there's her dad lurking somewhere behind. He's her Hitchcock. Everyone has their cross to bear, Lilly." He screws in the light bulb, and the hallway is once again dingily illuminated. "You should really get a heavy flashlight in case this happens again. It can also be a good weapon if you ever need it."

"You're not making me feel any better."

"I'm not trying to. You live in San Francisco."

"Where's Kim?"

"I don't know. She was acting strange when I called for my espresso pot. She said she needed a few minutes. I figured she was late for a date or something. By the time I got down here, she was gone."

"It's not like this couple is engaged or anything," I say, going back to the subject of Stuart Surrey.

"Still wrong. You're better than that."

"If you could have seen the way he looked at me, Nate," I sigh dreamily.

"Are you looking for the moral answer, the truth, or neither?"

If I were looking for the moral answer, I wouldn't be asking Nate.

"If I'd been born into a rich family like Morgan, I'd have a shot at men like Stuart Surrey with his British accent and wavy hair. Oh, Nate, you should have seen his hair!"

"Men of Morgan's society want a trophy wife. She's going to have to be careful she doesn't end up as one." Nate's all business with me. We used to sort of flirt, but ever since I looked straight into his eyes, he's avoided me like public transit.

Nate stacks the ladder up against the wall. "Can I get my espresso maker now?"

"Only if you make it down here so I can have one too," I

say, as I unlock the latch. "How come I can't ever have what I want, Nate? Why did God give me the ability to tell good clothes from bad clothes but not the money to buy them? How fair is that? He might as well have made me blind."

"Why did He allow Paul to go to jail? Or get shipwrecked? Or beaten?"

"You're *so* not helping." But I have to say, it always amazes me how much Nate knows about the Bible and yet denies it as the guidebook for his life.

"Hey, I went to Sunday school. There's a reason I don't go anymore."

I look up into Nate's hazel eyes, and my heart breaks. Have you ever known anyone who seemed so completely upstanding? So wonderfully polite, and there for you no matter what? And yet they repelled God like Off does mosquitos? That's my Nate.

"I'm certain I'm not just supposed to forget Stuart," I say, wondering if my mentioning another man has any effect on him whatsoever.

"Like you were certain you were getting the job at work? Or that Robert would stick around even though you didn't care one iota about him?"

"Why do I let you into my house?" I flick on the light. The house is a shambles. My stuff is thrown everywhere. The table is knocked over. "Kim? Kim?" I shout.

Nate pulls me back. "Wait here."

He goes into the room and looks around. I can hear him moving things around and swearing under his breath. When he comes back, his face is completely ashen. "She's gone." He holds up a note.

"Who's gone? Kim? I told you she probably had a date."

"Her stuff is gone, Lilly. Her closet is cleaned out."

Frantically, I run to the table. My heart pounds, and I can

actually feel it in my throat. "The check. Nate, help me find the check!" I tear through my purse to see if I took it with me.

"I don't think it's here." He hands me the note, which reads simply, "I'm sorry. I had to get out of here. I'll find a way to pay you back."

"She wouldn't have done this. She wouldn't have." But there's a note in my hand, indicating she did.

Nate looks away. "She borrowed money from me a while back. A couple thousand. I knew I might never see it again, but I wanted her to know I trusted her, and that I believed in her."

"Just today you told me that I needed to give her time, that she wasn't like me." *Which I guess is true, because I wouldn't steal $20,000.*

"And she's not, but I never thought—"

I slide down onto my futon, still unable to believe Kim could do this. "How am I going to explain this to Sara?"

"You're just going to have to call her and put a stop-payment on the check."

"But what if Kim just went to the bank for me? What if she's just doing me a favor, and I call the police?"

"She didn't clean out her closet to go to the bank, Lilly. What does this note mean if she went to the bank for you?"

I drop my face in my hands. "I can't believe I would be so stupid as to leave the check here. To not deposit it. I keep acting like everything bad happens to me, but sometimes I just don't think. Sara even warned me, and I was too proud to listen. No," I shake my head. "I still don't believe Kim would do this. There has to be an explanation."

Nate sits beside me and puts his arm around me. "I was taken in too."

"She just didn't do this, Nate. I can't believe she would do this to me."

"I think she probably did do this," Nate says, scanning the

loft. "At least she didn't take the computers," Nate says, a slight smile on his lips, and I pause to look at him.

"Leave it to you to look for the silver lining in every cloud." It's then that I notice Nate's hazel eyes haven't left my own. I feel myself being pulled toward him, and before I'm fully aware, my lips are on his. He kisses me, deeply and tenderly. And I must say I'm returning the gesture with entirely too much enthusiasm.

"Nate!" I pull away. But in my heart, I'm thinking, *George Clooney has nothing on you, babe!*

He moves toward the door quickly, as though he was someone else two seconds ago. "I'm sorry."

"About?"

"Listen, I got you something else today. It was supposed to be a surprise for the official launch of the business."

"What business?"

"Wait here." Nate leaves the apartment, and my heart is still pounding like the rumble of an approaching earthquake. He has a million things to offer a woman: he's sexy, he's generous to a fault, and he works all night on the phone with China but has most of his days available. He's like a walking Ken doll, and my heart is literally aflutter. *He's not a believer.* Yeah, I hear that voice, but I'm not exactly open to it at the moment. *I'm tired of being alone, God. Do You hear me?*

Nate comes back with another huge box, not yet acknowledging that he kissed me like the end of a Cary Grant movie. "Nate, what did you do?"

"It's a sewing machine," he says, setting the huge box on my now tilting table. "It transfers your drawings from the computer and helps you sew them faster."

I fall into his arms, and I feel his warmth surround me. We don't speak for a long time, and I'm afraid to look up. Afraid we'll fall into another kiss and be unable to stop this from exploding. Yet I don't pull away either. I just rest in his arms for a long time, the missing money being so far away it's like a disappearing space shuttle in the morning sky. Only a dot of despair remains.

"I'll help you set it up tomorrow." Nate pulls away.

I just look at him. My eyes say, *Are we going to talk about this?*

I can see by the stunned deer look that Nate isn't quite sure what's just happened either.

"Thank you for the sewing machine," I say like a complete idiot who's talking to her business professor. But how does one say, "Thank you for kissing me like Cary Grant in *Notorious*"? Nate knows what that kiss means to me. That I think it's the best screen kiss in history, one where you felt the film might melt on the projector. How do I say, "Thank you for helping me remember that I'm not completely repulsive to the male species"?

"Call Sara now." With that, Nate slams the door and I'm left alone. I look at the table tossed aside in this mess. I can't believe after two years of working with Kim, of cleaning up her dishes, she would do this. It seems utterly impossible.

Nate Goddard kissed me.

chapter 15

pick up the phone, then put it back down. I lost $20,000 in less than twenty-four hours. If this doesn't prove to my Nana that I am woefully bad with finance, I'm just not sure what will. Sadly, it also proves to Sara that her fears were correct. She even warned me about Kim. How could I be so stupid as to leave the check? It's like leaving a dimebag in front of an addict.

I look around my loft, at the tornado of fabrics thrown around, the table tipped. Kim had to have help in her crime. Even *she* couldn't make this big of a mess, and I'm just glad I really didn't have anything to take. Why would she even leave a mess? She knew where the check was. I can't for the life of me imagine why she left the computer. Maybe as a peace offering. I notice that Nate's espresso machine is gone. He never even said a thing about it. But it's gone, along with the contents of Kim's closet and my money.

I pick up the phone and dial Sara's number. I hear the line ring and Sara's clipped voice, "Hello."

"Hello!" she says more urgently.

"Sara?"

"Who is this?"

"It's Lilly, Sara. I have bad news."

"It had better not involve my money. Why are you calling so late? Lina is sleeping, and I don't appreciate you taking such liberties with my private line."

Oh Lord, where will I ever get this kind of money to pay her back?

"I'm afraid it does involve your money." My voice is shaking.

"It's not my money anymore. Read the fine print, Lilly. You owe me $20,000, plus interest at the end of the year. No matter what. Is that all?"

"I realize that. I will pay you, but I need for you to try and put a stop-payment on the check. I'm begging you."

"Lilly, where is the check?"

I hate with all that is in my being to say this. "I think Kim may have taken it, though I'm not certain about that and I don't want to falsely accuse her. I left it here in my loft, so—"

"I'll call my accountant, but I make no promises. Kim is probably in Mexico right now with what's left of your company. Didn't I warn you, Lilly?"

"You did," I say like a repentant child.

"Do you think I speak to hear myself babble? Did it ever occur to you that I've been running a successful business for years and that I might know more than you? Perhaps I've seen things in Kim."

"I'm sorry, Sara. You're right. You obviously know much more than me."

"Which is why I wanted you in finance."

I can't help it. I laugh here. "I lost $20,000 in a day. Why on earth would you want me in finance?"

"Because you're honest to a fault, and it's so hard to find an employee to trust with the books. I couldn't trust my own husband, so when I told you to watch out for Kim, didn't you think I might have been speaking from experience?"

"It never even crossed my mind. I've lived with her for two years. I thought we were business partners."

"See, honest to a fault. Innocents never recognize how harsh the world really is. I'm doing you a favor, Lilly. Take off those rose-colored glasses, or you'll end up the loser every time. Successful people see the world as it really is."

Another speech on reality.

I hope I never see the world through Sara's eyes, where no one can be trusted and the world is just out to get you. The fact is, yes, Kim stole from me, but at the same time, Nate brought me a brand-new sewing machine and a computer to create my designs. One can view the world through Sara's warped eyes, or one can see the silver lining. I choose silver.

"Please just try to get the check stopped," I implore. "If the money is gone, it's gone. I'll work around it," I say, like I have any idea just how that will happen.

"You do realize this isn't my problem," Sara says.

"I do." *But for one—okay, the second—time in your life, do something decent, will you?* "I made a mistake. People make mistakes." *Luckily, my God is more forgiving than you.*

"I don't make mistakes." *Click.* But I know Sara; she'll do what she can to stop that check. If there's one thing Sara is, it's in control. She will control where her money goes at any cost.

The money is gone, and I have no job. But I have everything in front of me to make a business. I just need to get fabric. Looking around the loft, there is fabric everywhere, and while the combination might make a stellar colorful skirt for Poppy, I'm thinking the couture crowd will probably pass.

The day's angst has worn me out, and I feel my eyelids getting heavy as I think about cleaning up this mess. I fall on my futon and fixate on the orange glow of the streetlight below. *Nate Goddard kissed me. I wonder what that was about?*

I wake up to the harsh sunlight beaming through my soaring windows, highlighting the shambles of what's left of my career. There's a knock at the door, and I look at my watch to see it's nine-thirty a.m. Nine-thirty!

I look through the peep hole to see a UPS man with clip-board in hand. I open the door. "Good morning."

"Morning to you, Miss. I have a package here for Lilly Jacobs."

"That's me."

"Sign here."

I do, and he hands me an enormous package from San Francisco's Jeweler. I rip open the package, and inside there are yards of cream shantung silk. I pull it out, admiring its perfect form and luxurious feel. Underneath it is more crepe paper and another box. I hang the fabric up in my closet and look at the box. It's a brand-new Italian ionic hairdryer like the one at her gym. There's a note pinned to the box:

> Lilly,
> I hope this hairdryer will make the upcoming winters more bearable for your gorgeous, thick hair, which you simply must stop straightening. The silk is for my wedding gown. I know you'll do something incredible, and my father will provide any seed pearls or crystals you might need. But something fairly simple, all right?
> With love,
> Morgan

She can't possibly believe I'm going to design her wedding dress without speaking to her first. I take out the gleaming silver hairdryer. *I choose silver*, I think to myself. I plug it in and feel the power, as even my thick mop blows easily under it. I put the hairdryer aside and start to clean up my loft.

As I finish, I'm just about to spray Lysol when I think of Morgan walking down the aisle with the subtle scent of

Mountain Breeze disinfectant in her shantung silk. The phone rings, and I answer it, praying it's Sara with word of my recovered check.

"Lilly, it's Nana."

I sigh. "Oh hi, Nana."

"Is that any way to talk to your grandmother?"

"I'm sorry. I just thought you might be someone else."

"Is that supposed to make me feel good?"

"It's a long story, Nana. What's up?"

"Max fell off a ladder this morning. He's got a broken leg, and I was wondering if you could help me get him home from the hospital."

"How'd you get there?"

"He drove with his broken leg. Of course, we didn't know it was broken yet, although thinking back, it was bent pretty funny. I'm sure *he* knew it was broken."

"Nana! Stop. What hospital are you at?"

"Mercy General."

"I'll be right there. Max has a car, right?"

"Of course, how do you think we got here?"

I hop into my jeans, modeled after Sevens, and oh so well-fitting. I actually appear to be shapely in them. Topping the jeans with a long-sleeve silk T-shirt I made from scraps, I am downright couture. Hospital attire never looked so good. Of course, I'm anxious about Max being on a ladder, as I have little doubt who had him up on the ladder. Can you say, *lawsuit*? The good news? I'm in the hole $20K, and I've got nothing else left to take.

As I walk out the door, Nate is outside about to knock.

My demeanor softens, and I feel a little giddy. "Hi, Nate," I say girlishly. "Did you have a good sleep?"

"A little. I was up with China most of the night, but I'll get a nap before I have to call London."

"I know how you feel. I talked to San Francisco last night, and I'm probably going to call Poppy in Cupertino today. It's just overwhelming sometimes. Dialing that 408 area code really gets the better of me."

"Listen, I just wanted to say no hard feelings about last night, huh?" He doesn't smile.

"Excuse me?"

"You know, we were just both wrapped up in the emotion of the night. I was upset about Kim leaving. I didn't want you to think we couldn't be friends after what happened. All right?"

"Right. Sure." I try to laugh, but it comes out more like a goose honk. Here I had this great kiss, this magical kiss that I actually dreamed about, and today I'm being told it meant nothing. It was nothing. I *so* don't get men. "George Clooney, here you come, right?"

"No, it's not like that. It's just that we're friends. I don't want to mess with that. I'd do anything for you, Lilly, but it's not like that."

I thought we already messed with things, but that's me. "Friends." I thrust my hand toward him. "I've got to catch the bus. Max and my Nana need a ride home."

"Do you want me to drive you?"

"No, actually you've done enough already." He looks at me sulkily here. "With the computer and the sewing machine. You've done quite enough."

"Right." He stands in the doorway.

"Excuse me," I try to walk around him, but we meet chest-to-chest as I do. He looks down at me, and I'd swear he was about to kiss me again, but I move around him. "I'll let you know if I hear from Sara about the check."

"That would be great."

"See ya later."

"Hey, Lilly, I Netflixed *A Fish Called Wanda*. I know it's one of your favorites."

"Thanks, but I've got to get some work done. Appreciate the offer though." I try to be as cool as possible, but naturally I don't feel it. I feel jilted, used, and like a complete moron.

After locking the door (all seven locks this time), I start to walk down the hallway. Looking back at Nate, I just want to burst into tears. *That's what a girl gets for giving away the milk,* I hear my Nana taunt.

But Nate had part of my heart all along, I guess. And I never knew it. Oh I know the arguments: he's not a Christian; he doesn't share my faith; we don't have a solid foundation. I know the facts, but tell them to my heart. Because after his kiss? I want nothing more than to forget who I am for Jesus, and be who I want to be for Nate Goddard. He waves me good-bye, and I can't help but think of the one Shakespearean line I remember. *Parting is such sweet sorrow.*

chapter 16

The bus to the hospital seems to consist of several homeless people and myself. Now you might ask, where is my Christian compassion? Shouldn't I be handing out sandwiches and used coats? But those questions are irrelevant, because of course, you cannot smell what I smell. And they do not allow Lysol on the bus. I've tried before. I don't imagine Calcutta smelled much better, but Mother Teresa was a better woman than I.

Once I'm on the BART train, the world looks—okay, smells—a little brighter, and I'm dropped off right in front of Mercy General. I tuck my sketch book under my arm and head to the emergency room.

I used the time on public transportation and actually did some drawings that I think might work for my collection. In the back of my mind, I'm thinking of Morgan's lithe figure and how it will look best in a wedding gown. She could wear any style she wished, but I want the gown to be perfect. More than that, I want the groom to be perfect, and that aspect definitely needs work.

I walk into the emergency room which is a zoo, like something out of the *Animal House* movie. I almost expect to hear, "Food fight!" There's so much activity. Kids are screaming, moms are spanking, wives and husbands are fighting, patients are yelling at nurses. It's like one of those disaster movies where they've just announced the world is being nuked in five minutes, and there are four spots left in the bunker.

I see my Nana sheepishly sitting in the corner with Max in a full cast up to his thigh.

"I could have driven," Max says when he sees me. "It's probably a lot less dangerous than sitting here like decoys. But of course, we had to wait for you once you'd started."

"You're welcome," I say. "How's your leg?"

"Broken in three places."

I cringe. "Don't tell me anymore. Here, let me help you up."

"I can get up." Max pushes himself up off the arms of the waiting room chair. He looks down at me, annoyed that he should be so babied. *Hey, you know, I didn't exactly sign up for this gig.*

"Where's Valeria?" I ask and see Nana shake her head.

Max just rolls his eyes. "Let's get to the car. I don't want to be on this leg too long."

We start to walk to his car, which I'm picturing as a Pinto or an Escort or something equally in poor taste, and he stops at a sterling silver Jaguar.

"This is your car?" *Dang, the TV critic business pays all right.*

"I didn't pick it out, if that's what you're thinking," Max groans as he tries to maneuver into the backseat.

"Nana can sit back there, Max. It's your car. Why wouldn't I think you picked it out? I picked out the bus and hold myself fully responsible for the choice."

"Valeria picked it out," Nana says as she tries to squeeze into what there is of a backseat. Italian cooking and riding in the back of a Jaguar are not a great mix. Eventually, Max gets tired of watching her maneuver and somehow gets himself and his cast back there.

"Don't mention that woman's name," Max says about Valeria, his eyebrows lowered menacingly.

I slide into the driver's seat. "You know, Max, the best of us get dumped. Welcome to the real world. She was too young for you anyway." *Some of us get dumped without actually realizing we had a relationship in the first place, and doesn't that feel good?*

"I didn't get dumped," he snaps. But inside, I'm thinking, *Yeah, she did dump him, and what do guys expect when they're twice someone's age, and they are only slightly better than a troll, and the woman is a swimsuit model? I mean, call me naïve here, but DUH!*

"How's unemployment, Lilly?" Nana asks.

"Liberating."

Here Max laughs, and my grandmother *harrumphs*.

I start up the car, and it just purrs like a kitten. Granted, a powerful, lion-like kitten, but still. I wonder if now is a good time to tell him I've never driven a car worth real money before. Seeing his scowl in the rearview mirror, I'm thinking probably not.

We're silent as we drive home. I assume Max doesn't want to talk about getting dumped, or whatever his macho name for it is, and I'm not keen on speaking of my unemployment or my loss of $20,000. So silence is definitely golden. As we drive up to his house in the Marina, it's obvious that Max has time to take care of the place. I don't know why it never dawned on me before, but this place has to be worth two million at least for its location. Its façade is much grander than those in the neighborhood, with ornate iron gates leading to the entrance and carefully-planted landscaping giving it a designer's touch. Even the paint job is elaborate, like the City's Victorian-era Painted Ladies.

He's got an incredible view of the Bay from his place,

although he usually has the plantation shutters closed for better television viewing. He's also got a totally redesigned kitchen with granite counters, but you never notice any of that because the TV is so disproportionate to the rest of the place. It definitely makes me wonder how everyone in this city seems to have money except me. He sits and watches TV and makes more than I do! Obviously a lot more! It's clear that my degree in finance translates into a complete loss when you look around at Bay Area success.

Nana speaks first as we reach the small driveway. "I'll be inside making some soup. You make sure Max gets settled, Lilly. I'll be up in a while."

Max and I scowl at one another. "Sure, Nana." Thankful the car is still in one unencumbered piece, I come around to the passenger side to get Max out, and rescue him from being wrenched in the backseat. Have you ever tried to get the first pickle out of a full jar? Um, yeah, it's like that.

Max takes my help this time, as the Jaguar is extremely low to the ground, and having a straight leg for the maneuver is more than he can handle. He puts his arms around my neck and I help him to his feet. He steadies himself on me, and I hand him the crutches.

"There. Could Valeria do that?"

"She's a black belt in karate."

"Would you give it up? She's a child," I say angrily. "You know what happens to those girls? They turn thirty, grow up, and think, *What am I doing with this old guy?* It happened to Rod Stewart; it can certainly happen to you."

"She wasn't my girlfriend."

"I never said she was." But usually, when a woman hangs out and watches TV and makes you dinner she's generally your girlfriend. Unless she happens to be my Nana.

"Valeria was sponsored by my father to come to America

and work in one of the hotels. My father was a Russian-Jew. He tries to do a lot for the old country."

Like get his son hot-looking women? "You don't need to say anything more," I say, silently praying he will. "Wait a minute. What do you mean your father's hotels?" *Emphasis on the plural.*

"She found out who I was and made her move for marriage. I didn't fall for it, but I ended up looking the fool just the same. Maybe she knew all along. I don't know. Your Nana figured it out."

"Who *are* you?" I ask, as he leans on me on the driveway. His eyes are so expressive. They seem to talk without even a hint of a smile on his face.

It's obvious he doesn't want to talk. "I'm a TV critic."

Somehow, I don't believe this is all he is for a second, but I figure I can ask Nana later what he means. His father owns hotels. *Big deal.* If he's an heir, is that a crime? I'd be shouting it from the rooftops and looking for my monthly handout!

Getting up the tiled stairs is a trick all its own, and more than once, I thought we might both tumble to the bottom.

Max gets to the door and opens it without unlocking it.

"You don't lock your door? In San Francisco?"

"I lock the gate."

"Let me help you get settled."

"You've done enough." He starts to close the door on me, but taking after my Nana, I push it open.

"Don't be so difficult. You've got no reason to hate all women because of Valeria. She has to grow up first before we can technically call her a woman anyway."

"I don't hate all women; don't be ridiculous. And she didn't dump me. I told you."

"You didn't tell me anything. Typical male."

"I just don't know what you women expect. You come on

to us guys, using your wiles, and then once we take the bait, you cut the line and run off to the next guy."

"I don't do that. None of my friends do that. *Girls* do that. You were dating a girl."

"Your Nana liked her for a while. And we weren't dating. I keep telling you."

"My Nana likes anyone with naked ambition, especially if they can turn it into cash."

"That's a harsh assessment of your own grandmother." Max lowers himself onto his leather sofa.

"It's said in love," I answer truthfully. "If I didn't love her, I wouldn't have tried finance in the first place. I wouldn't have a useless MBA from Stanford. I don't think being rich is in my blood because I just don't really care that much, you know?"

"All women say that."

"I'll give you that. I'd like to buy nicer fabric for my clothes, have a place that's lit by more than a single light bulb in the hallway. But I don't want to crunch numbers to get it. Does that make sense? I'm capable of making money, Max. I just want more than that."

"Yes, you're waiting for Mr. Right to make your dreams come true and bankroll your life."

I laugh out loud. "You cannot possibly believe I think *that* living in San Francisco. In case you haven't noticed, most of the men here aren't exactly looking for a *damsel* in distress."

"So, do you want to live like that forever? In some dumpy loft you can barely make rent on? You got out of Stanford. You have to have a touch of ambition."

"You don't think I'm ambitious?" I'm dumbfounded after Nate and Kim both accused me of being practically ruthless.

"I'm just saying I see your grandmother's point of view, but as one who turned down the family business, I understand more than you think."

"I wasted eight years, all counted, with school and working in the industry. What did you go to school for?" I ask, wondering how one prepares for a life of professional television-viewing.

"Journalism."

"Can I open these?" I ask, perched over the shutters.

"As long as you close them again," Max grunts.

"Did they give you any happy pills for pain?" I ask. "You need some."

I open the shutters, and a magical view of the San Francisco Bay, sapphire-blue from the afternoon sun, appears.

"Oh, Max," I say wistfully. "You have the most amazing view. I'd never get anything done if I lived here. How can you keep this window closed?"

"It's not shut all the time, Lilly. Just at night. I didn't get a chance to open it this morning."

"Does my Nana know your dad owns those hotels?"

"Yeah, why?"

"I'm just surprised she never tried to set me up with you. She must like you."

"Did you want to be set up?" he raises an eyebrow.

Hmmm. An interesting question. I think on it for a minute. "No, I'm just sort of curious why she gets herself a certified heir in her presence, and the thought doesn't occur to her. I'm not good enough for you apparently."

"I never said that."

"You don't even have much hair, Max! You'd be perfect. So I don't really get it. I'm definitely asking my Nana."

"You're telling me I'm bald? Am I supposed to say 'Thanks'?" he says questioningly.

"Well, I'd better get going." I close the shutters. "It's going to be something catching the bus at this hour. I hate Muni in the middle of the day."

Max sits up. "You are not taking the bus home."

"I'll be fine. I have a little Vicks for under my nose." I pull the jar out of my purse to show him.

"Take my car home. I can't drive it anyway." Max tosses me the keys.

"Max, you can't park a brand-new Jaguar in my neighborhood and expect it to be there in the morning." I'm laughing at the thought. "I'm used to using Muni. Are you going to be okay?" I sit next to him on the sofa and he suddenly plops his broken leg in my lap.

"It's fine. Doesn't hurt that much. They say I'll have to do some physical therapy. So it's good that I watch television for a living."

I look straight into his eyes. "I hope you weren't on that ladder for Nana."

Max looks away. "I wasn't."

"I'd better get going home," I say, waiting for him to remove his leg.

"Lilly, take the car. You're not getting on the bus when you came all the way over here!"

"If I take your car, you won't have one tomorrow morning when it's sitting on jacks without its wheels or stereo system. I've already lost $20,000 today."

"What?" Max laughs. "How'd you do that, if you don't mind my asking?"

"My roommate stole the check because I am, apparently, honest to a fault. Do you need anything before I go?" I pat his leg, trying to give him more of a hint.

"I'll give you the $20,000."

I just laugh.

"I'm serious."

"Where would a TV critic get that kind of money? I thought you weren't working for your dad."

"I'm not an idiot, though I know you prefer to think of me that way. I may not be exceptionally smart with women, but I have my strengths." It's here that I see he's completely serious.

"No, Max, I wouldn't want to put you out."

"I'm serious," Max says. "Lilly, I want to do this for you. I've been where you are. I want you to follow your passion in life. I love real estate, but I never had a passion for the hotel business. Too much pressure for occupancy. Did you know you need a 50 percent occupancy rate every night to make it? And that the restaurant in the lobby is just a loss leader?"

"Interesting," I say, patting his leg again. "I still can't take your money. I can't take your car. Is there anything else you want to give me? Because I might be open to the house with the view. You could still live downstairs." I wink at him, but he doesn't even crack a smile. Suddenly, I feel very guilty for taking Nate's gifts. Everyone obviously thinks I'm completely inane, or they wouldn't want to take care of me like this!

"I'm not asking you to *do* anything for it," Max says.

Well, that goes without saying. "Why does everyone want to give money to me? Am I that pathetic? I got myself into this mess. I don't want your money. I want to be a grown-up. It's time I started bailing myself out instead of people rescuing me. And why is it everyone in this town has money except for me?"

"Maybe you're supposed to take it. Did that ever occur to you? You know that old story about God sending the helicopter and the man drowning because he didn't get on it?" Max scoots over on the couch until he's sitting right next to me. His proximity is warming and completely frightening. *What is up?* Have I suddenly developed something? Does he want to kiss me and act like it never happened as well? All while giving me gifts to soothe his tortured soul? *I wonder if Vicks has an aphrodisiac effect.*

"Listen," I say, moving his leg gently and jumping up. "I've got to get back to the loft and set up my computer and sewing machine. I appreciate the offer, Max, but your looking after Nana is more than enough of a donation to my cause."

"You'd pay it back. You're good for the money. I can tell you if there's one thing about Mildred that never wavers, it's her unflinching honesty; and I see that trait in you."

"You're *not* saying I'm like my Nana?"

"More than you know."

"If you need anything, I'm writing down my number so you have it handy." I bend over a pad of paper near the phone and scratch my name with my charcoal pencil. "I'm getting a cell phone today, so I'll call you with the new number as soon as I get it. Please don't let Nana put you to work. Rest."

"Lilly, don't go just yet. I have to tell you something. Come sit down." He pats the space I just left.

Just the way his face is solemn makes me stop in my urge to get out the door. "You should know I won't take your money. We're a proud people, my Nana and me."

"It's not about the money." I sit beside him on the sofa, and I have to say, there's something very endearing about his tone. He covers my hand with his own. "We weren't at the hospital for my leg. I broke it two days ago. Your grandmother drove us to the hospital, and I swore she would never drive me anywhere again. That's why we called you. I should have figured something else out, but by then—I just wanted to get her home."

"What do you mean?"

"Your grandmother is not well. I'm not exactly sure what's wrong, but I drive her to the hospital every third day."

I feel breathless. Like someone has literally sucked the oxygen from the air. "Not my Nana. She's as tough as a horse." I hear myself laugh, but stop immediately when I see Max's face.

"She's not, Lilly."

"Why are you telling me this?" I stand up.

"Because I want you to know that your grandmother wants you settled. That's all she wants. Take my money. You'll pay it back. I know you will. I'm doing it for her. Does that help?"

"You're lying! You're a cruel man, Max Schwartz."

He keeps on talking, but I don't halt to hear another word. I run down to Nana's, anxious to see her back hunched over the stove, the smell of her chicken soup filling the apartment. There are tears blinding my eyes when I reach her stoop, but the warmth of the vision soothes me. She is there, bent over the pot.

"Nana?" I say, my eyes still filled with tears.

"Lilly, what's the matter?" She drops the ladle and runs to hug me. "Did something happen?" she says into my hair. My Nana comes across as one of the most coldhearted people you know. Until you really need her. Then, her true character comes out like the sun on a cloudy day.

I realize if Nana is sick, the last thing I can do is tell her that I know. If I tell her, she'll go out of her way to hide the truth. I swallow the lump in my throat. "Max is in so much pain, Nana."

"He is, but he'll be fine. He's young and in good shape. Sure, he might be off the dating market for a while." She taps her chin. "Although, with his money I imagine he'll have more than his share of nurses. You should go and sit with him."

This makes me laugh through my tears. "Will you ever give up?" I say, though I'm actually thankful she *does* think I'm good enough for her beloved Max.

"It's just as easy to fall in love with a rich man as it is a poor man."

"It really isn't, Nana."

"Will you stay for dinner?"

"I'd like that."

"Just us girls." She grabs my hand. "Let me just run this up to Max. It's been a long time since you've had time for this old girl."

"Too long."

I grab a handful of homemade cookies and get the familiar warning about ruining my appetite. Max can't be right. He's got to be delusional from pain meds. *Please Lord, don't let her be ill. As harsh as she can be, Nana means everything to me.*

never did ask Nana about what Max said. The truth is, I can't stand for it to be true, so it won't be. The life of an ostrich is sometimes quite rewarding. My mind hasn't let it go, though. I can't imagine that whatever challenge my Nana faces, she won't scare it off with just that look she gives me when she's disapproving.

If I learned anything today, it's that my pride needs to take a backseat to reality, or poverty, depending on your view. It's time for me to be an adult. Time to earn a living, and quit living for everything I *wish* for. If it is true about her health, Nana needs me to be an adult now, and the time for tired excuses has long-since expired. I lost $20,000? An excuse. A simple part of the challenge.

It's ten o'clock at night when I finally get home after a visit to the woefully overpriced fabric store, followed by mega-transfers on several buses. The loft is cold and empty when I unlatch the locks. Even though Kim and I were complete opposites, I have to admit I miss her presence. Oh, I could argue I miss the check more right now, but I do miss her entertainment value. What would she wear tonight? How does she manage to match so well when she can't tell blues from greens? Did Nate really want her like she claimed? The last question stops me as I put a tea bag in water, then into the microwave.

What did poor girls like me ever do before the microwave? I don't think I could have been poverty-stricken before the era of the futon and the microwave.

Because it's so late, I think twice about calling Sara and getting another earful about her precious (twenty-five-year-old "baby") sleeping daughter. But Sara never told me if the check was stopped, and call me an optimist, but I'm ever hopeful. *Remember, I choose silver.*

I dial her number. The phone rings, and for some reason it just seems excessively loud in my ears, like Sara's serenity is being destroyed by her hapless apprentice. Trump would never put up with this garbage.

"Sara Lang." I hear classical music in the background.

"Sara, I'm sorry to call so late. It's Lilly again. I was wondering if—"

"Did you get a cell phone today, Lilly?"

"No, actually I had—"

"I don't want to hear your excuses. Didn't I ask you to get a cell phone today?"

"Yes, but—"

"You have to learn to respect authority. If you can't smile at the investors and do as they say, you will never make it in this business. I'm trying to do you countless favors, and I feel like I'm banging my head against the wall. First, I lend you $20,000, which you manage to lose within the first day. Then, I try to call you all day and say that I've recovered the money, and can I reach you? No. What did I say about being available in this business?"

"The money's still there?" I sputter. I can't feel my fingers. I'm so thrilled, I want to dance and sing, but I hold steady, knowing more emotion is not what Sara needs at the moment.

"Kim tried to cash the check at one of those check cashing shops. She has your driver's license, in case you're not aware. It's a good thing you called and told me the check was missing. We're just lucky she waited as long as she did to try and cash it."

"Where was she?" Call me a sucker, but I'm worried about Kim. She has no money and I'm just worried about what she might do if she's already stolen $20,000. Truly, it's not like her.

"She was in Emeryville." *Just across the Bay.* "My accountant won't be in for another week, and I don't care to write that kind of check without his approval, especially with you bungling it so badly the first time. I'll have the money for you next Tuesday. In the meantime, I still expect ten designs in full for the design competition. I'll choose your best design for display at Fashion Week under mine."

"Sara, you would do that?"

"I'm feeling very jovial today. My ex-husband is filing for bankruptcy. I actually have you to thank for it, Lilly."

"Me?"

"You're the one who told me to make sure his name was off the corporation and settle with him before the divorce. That was a costly day, but it turns out not nearly as costly as it might have been. So I'm investing $40,000 in your company; I need the write-off, and I'm sure you can use the cash."

"Oh my goodness, Sara, I promise I won't let you down! And this time, I mean it." It's probably not a good thing to be rejoicing in Sara's revenge on her husband, but the man had to know better than to betray his wife since she was his paycheck. And all to date a woman younger than his daughter? Oh yeah, my sympathy is just *so* not with him.

I get off the phone and jump for joy. *I am in business—again—almost!* I run up the steps to Nate's loft. I can't wait to tell him. We can set up the computer, and I can get some fabric tomorrow. It's going to be fabulous. I bang on the door. "Nate, open up!"

He does, and sitting on the sofa is a beautiful girl with long, luxurious, and *straight* brunette hair. She has full Jennifer Lopez lips, among other attributes, and I feel my strength wilt and my shoulders fall. I can't feel my limbs.

"Hi," I manage. "I'm Nate's downstairs neighbor. I just came to tell him something about my business he invested in." As I peek my head in, I get the final blow. They're watching *A Fish Called Wanda*, paused on my favorite part, and she is sitting with Charley (draining-ear dog) on her lap. Doesn't she have a sense of smell? There's not even the lingering scent of Lysol. He has found the perfect woman.

"Excuse us, Christina." Nate steps out into the hallway. "The business?" he asks brightly, as if I shouldn't be the slightest bit concerned about the Miss Shampoo model in his loft.

I shrug, the wind thoroughly sucked from my sails. "Yeah, the business. Sara's lending me more money, and she recovered the check. Who is that?" I try to ask as casually as possible.

I want to tell him about my grandmother, but he's antsy, clearly worried he's upset the beautiful lady waiting inside for him. And I'm feeling a little ill myself. I'm not exactly sitting by the phone for him, but it was just yesterday he kissed me, was it not?

"Just a friend. That's amazing about the check, Lilly. I'm so glad for you." Said on same frequency as *I think of you as a friend, Lilly.* I can feel myself blinking away any emotion I might feel. But I want to scream at him, *How could you kiss me like that?*

"Well, have a good time." I back down the hallway and realize that what I really miss about Kim is not Kim at all, but Nate being there waiting for me. It takes everything I have not to whisper, "Let go of the doorknob and come with me, Nate."

But he's not my type, I remind myself. And clearly, I'm not his. This is just wrong.

"'Night, Lilly." Nate waves.

"'Night." My heart is pounding. She probably has hair extensions and caps on her teeth; when you get them off, she's like a "Swan" before the makeover. *Look at me, Nate. You know I'm all about reality, because no one would pretend this.*

"I'll call you tomorrow," Nate says as a token offering.

"I'll be out at the fabric store," I say with more sharpness than I'd planned.

"That's okay. Just let me know when you're going, so I can set up the computer. You don't need to be there."

I shake my head. "I can handle it. Dell color-codes it, and while color is not my expertise, I'm not completely oblivious. I can tell purple from green." I start down the stairs and punch the wall. *Jerk.*

Practice. Maybe that's what I was for Nate last night. A practice kiss, so he wouldn't screw up with Miss Shampoo! I stomp down to my loft and realize I don't want to go in there, but I hear my phone ringing. If it's Nate, I'm going to tell him where he can connect his computer!

"Hello?"

"Lilly, it's Morgan."

"Oh Morgan, I forgot to call you today." I have a brief blip of guilt, but it's soon buried under thoughts of Nana and Nate. "Thanks for the hair dryer. Your fabric for the gown is perfect."

"Thanks, that means a lot if you like it. We'll work on the design this weekend, okay?"

"You're coming to the spa?" I ask, surprised.

"I wouldn't miss it, but I have a change in venue."

"A happy one, I hope."

"We're not going to Spa Del Mar."

"Why not?" I ask, disturbed that my little world is being messed with. *Anything else?*

"I can't get away to drive that far from San Francisco. So I know of a really quaint little place in the Napa Valley. I thought we were due for an upgrade. We're nearly thirty. We can afford a better spa." She pauses for a minute. "Oh, I didn't mean—"

"Morgan, get over it. I'm quite used to the fact that I'm the only person without money in the San Francisco Bay area. Do you know how many people offered me $20,000 today? What is up with that? People just have $20,000 sitting around."

"It had nothing to do with money, Lilly. I meant I'm going to be married soon, and who knows how often we'll get these trips. It's time we upgraded."

My annoyance has quietly disappeared.

"Max says my Nana is not well, so I'm glad we won't be far."

"What's wrong with her?" Morgan asks.

"I didn't have the nerve to ask her. I'm not actually sure what's true, but if I asked her, you know she wouldn't tell me if she thought it would worry me. I know it has to be something fairly significant, or she would have used it to guilt me into a real job. Remember when she did that gout thing? *Oh Lilly, I have the gout. I sure hope you'll have a job before it takes me over.* I thought gout was worse than cancer until I went to work and Googled it!"

"You have to ask her what's wrong."

"And *you* have to tell your father you're worthy of more than being a diamond mannequin, but we both have boundary issues, Morgan. That's why we meet at the spa, so we can whine and commiserate on what wimps we are."

"*Touché.* You're planning to do gowns for you and Poppy, right?"

"I get to dress Poppy? Oh man, bring it on! I'm going to tell her I need a gauze skirt for sizing and then shred it for my own personal pleasure." I'm picturing the before and after of Nicole Kidman, from frizzy-haired anorexic to glamour queen.

"By the way, I heard you made quite an impression on Stuart Surrey at my church, and I won't even comment on why you and Poppy were both there. I'm sure you were minding your own business."

For the moment, thoughts of Nate with Miss Hair Extensions are left behind. "Who told you that? Did Stuart mention me?" Little giddy here. The man remembered me!

"I have my sources. You always were a sucker for those sorts. I should have known. English men are so pasty, Lilly. Really. Your taste." She clucks.

I giggle at the thought. "Need I remind you that my crushes are not members of the AARP, nor do they qualify for the Denny's senior discount menu?"

"No, you're just into the snooty accent type."

"He didn't seem snooty."

"He's dating Caitlyn Kapsan. Did you meet her? I would assume you did because she doesn't much let him out of her fake-blue-eyed sight. She's tried to drag him into my father's store a million times, but he never takes the bait. I'm sure he couldn't afford it anyway. If she does manage to drag him anywhere, it will be to the mall jewelry store on credit, or on her own dime. Mark my words."

"Why's he dating her?" I ask dreamily, ignoring her assessment of his finances, remembering only his smoldering gaze and how little I thought of Nate at the time.

"Lilly, you have the weirdest taste in men. Really. Stuart Surrey has to be the most full-of-himself bloke I have ever met, and trust me, I've met egotists from all nations in my Dad's business. He's a total social climber, or he wouldn't have any interest in Caitlyn. But you'll do what you want, and I'll be here to pick up the pieces."

"Seriously, he was a good Bible teacher, and—"

"There are lots of Bible teachers who preach well but don't live it. Are you getting my message?"

"Loud and clear. Nate said he was off-limits because he has a girlfriend, anyway."

"Nate, your neighbor? I always liked him."

"Want me to set you up? He seems to have turned into George Clooney overnight. I think he has an opening at ten."

"Are we bitter, Lilly?"

"I don't want to talk about it. Listen, Morgan, I need to ask a favor. You know I wouldn't ask if I wasn't desperate, but I'm most definitely desperate."

"Go ahead."

"I need to borrow some money for fabric. It's just until the new check comes through and—"

"What new check?"

"Kim, my roommate, sort of ran off with my start-up money, but she didn't get away with it. It's going to be replaced soon. But right now, I've got time and ability and no fabric."

"I can't believe it. She lived with you for two years!"

"Yeah, but things were never the same once Jen moved out and left us to ourselves. We were like oil and water trying to blend. She was a slob, and she never did get my need for clean or understand the Lysol."

"That's because your Lysol fetish is weird. I'll send you the money tomorrow. And I'll call and put my credit card at the fabric outlet you like so well. That's where I bought my silk."

Could I feel more like dirt? "Thanks, Morgan." I start to tell her how I'll pay her back, but I imagine that's getting a bit old.

"Listen, the reason I called you is that the wedding is scheduled for a month from Saturday. It's top secret. My dad is letting everyone think it's a sale night for special customers.

When they come in, they'll be seated quickly and the wedding will start."

"Three gowns sewn in less than a month? I mean, it wouldn't be an issue if they weren't for us. I want it to be perfect, Morgan." At Sara Lang, it takes four hundred man hours to make a couture dress. There are generally three fittings and countless attention to detail. You could say the dress is more of a piece of architecture or fine art than clothing. I don't want anything less for Morgan, but clearly, I won't make her time frame.

"Three gowns, plus the flower girl's. That's why we're going away for the weekend, Lilly."

The weekend? "You know, we've been pussy-footing around this subject, Morgan, but I just have to say it, I'm concerned about this groom. This guy is too old for you, and it looks like you're out with your father. Quite frankly, it makes you look like you're not in your right mind—"

Click.

She hung up on me!

I get up and finger the expensive shantung silk in the closet. If Morgan doesn't believe I know her well enough to comment on her fiancé, she's about to find out the truth. Besides, she's wrong about Stuart. English guys are hot. No one looks at another woman that way when they're serious about someone else. Stuart just isn't that into her. Hey, just like all *my* boyfriends! Maybe Caitlyn and I should bond. I close my eyes and try to remember how I felt when Stuart looked at me as if I was the only woman in the room. It makes me forget that Nate is up in his apartment with another woman.

I know what I should be thinking. Nate's not a Christian. He's not an option. I know all this, but I still can't stop feeling maybe Nate was my last chance at a husband, and God has forgotten about me altogether.

called Nana first thing before I left, but she wasn't home and neither was Max. Those two seem to have their own underground society! And certainly more of a social life than me. I try to put out of my mind that they might be at the hospital.

I spent $7,000 this morning on more fabric. That's the excruciating news. The good news is I'm completely ready for Morgan's wedding and the *Vogue* contest. I'm making coordinating gowns for the wedding that will be complementary, but not match like a bad JCPenney catalog. It always bothers me when the bride picks gowns not thinking of her friend's figures, and while there's little to think about with Poppy's fabulous figure, mine takes a bit of creativity. Okay, and strategically placed padding.

And another thing: you know when you have a stick figure bridesmaid standing next to a plump gal, both in some clingy, body-hugging satin? It definitely takes your eyes off the bride because people can't help but think, *Oh, that girl just shouldn't be in that dress. What was she thinking?* Like it's the bridesmaid's fault she's been stuffed like an Italian sausage into a satin casing, or that the thin bridesmaid actually *chose* her low-cut, push-up bodice with nothing to push up! (My worst memory comes flooding back from a cousin's wedding.

When dancing with my aisle partner, the starchy, built-in bra indented. So as I pulled away for a picture, my concave shape appeared where actual breasts should be. So humiliating.) Not this time. Now I control the fashion universe, and when I sew in padding, baby, it stays where it's supposed to.

Poppy's gown will be a soothing (meaning not bright and/or tacky) emerald green shantung silk to play off her red hair and coordinate with Morgan's gown via the fabric. Mine will be a very subtle floral of green, coral, and ivory like Morgan's gown to tie the three gowns together. Now, all we need is the appropriate groom and we're all set.

I know some women wish for Prince Charming, but for me, that dream seems so far away. My dream is to design the princess's gown. Prince Charming probably doesn't pick up his underwear, anyway.

Speaking of Prince Charming—*not*. When I get home, I see that Nate has set up my computer, and my new sewing machine is right beside it. He's like the Christmas elves in that he's long gone, and the only evidence is his good deed and a fresh coating of Lysol. My sorry little table is tilting further to one side from the strain of the new equipment, and I realize that, along with a cell phone, I need a real work table today.

I set up my computer with cheap Internet access. *Ah, Lilly, welcome to the twenty-first century and this amazing new concept: e-mail.* I search and buy several small IKEA tables to push together and find the best cell phone deal for me. They actually have a Web site that does this for you. Technology is my friend.

This, however, is the problem with shopping online: there's always one more upgrade that seems so necessary and really not that much more at all. It seems so crucial while Web surfing. I mean, a picture phone would really help me when shopping in Bloomingdale's to remember what the competition was up to. But wait, then another alternative pops up: a

BlackBerry really would keep me organized and in contact with the Internet as well as by phone. Sara would love that! But the reality of debt looms, and I go for the cheapest option. No camera phone, no BlackBerry, just a step-up from the rotary dial in cell phone technology. I'll pick it up on Market Street tonight after six, all programmed and ready for prime time.

The phone rings, and I put on my best business voice: "Lilly Jacobs Design, Lilly speaking. How may I meet your apparel needs?" *Okay, the last part—a bit over the top. It definitely needs work.*

"Lilly?"

Hmm. A man's voice. With an English accent. Hold me back!

"Yes?" I say as casually as possible, while clenching my fists and jumping up and down, yet trying not to breathe too heavily from the exertion.

"This is Stuart Surrey. I met you at church service the other night."

"Right." *Right? Could I have a little personality here?* I remind myself I am not chattering like a monkey and therefore reducing my chances of making a complete idiot out of myself. *Lack of personality definitely a better option than too much.*

Stuart continues with that heavenly baritone accent. "A week from Friday, we'll be having a singles' night mixer at the big church down on the Peninsula. I wanted you to keep your calendar open."

Can my social calendar get any more open? Because if it had a bigger hole, I believe it would be a black hole, and suck me out for all eternity.

"Really? You want me to come?" Calm down. *He probably wants me to bring the rolls.*

"I hope you don't mind my calling, Lilly."

"Mind?"

"I'm bumbling here," Stuart says dreamily. "Will you come—with me?"

If I learned anything from Nate's kiss, it's to play my cards close. "Actually, I'd love to go to the mixer." *Will you be bringing the Chloe-clad girlfriend?* "But I'm afraid, Stuart, that I'm without a car presently." *Okay, without a car forever, unless I make this work!*

"I'd be most happy to pick you up. If you're not uncomfortable with that? I know you've only just met me."

I pause to just let that accent sink in. "Morgan knows you, and I'll be taking fingerprints at the door," I joke. Badly. "I think that would be nice, thank you." Morgan's warning rings in my head, for oh, about a second, and then the accent's power takes over. Take that, Nate!

"Would you be so kind as to e-mail me directions to your home?"

E-mail. I can *so* do e-mail now! *Sure, could you just say that again, so I can salivate a bit longer?*

"Certainly." *Certainly? I sound like the Three Stooges.* "What's your e-mail addy? And do you mind telling me how formally I should dress for the occasion? What do you think Caitlyn might wear?" *Oooh, that was certainly coy. And catty. Meow! Bad, bad Lilly.*

"Caitlyn won't be joining us. We've decided to take a break, and she's going to be working on a fund-raiser that night. She suggested I make other arrangements."

Now, I may be naïve about men, but women I know. And I know if Caitlyn suggested he make other arrangements, she most certainly was not suggesting female arrangements. If there's one thing Caitlyn, the ice queen, and I have in common, it's that we know better than to let gorgeous men out with other women unless we're done. And even then, we like them to wallow a bit, don't we?

"I'm terribly sorry about Caitlyn." And I even manage to sound so.

"In case you were wondering, Lilly, I took your name and phone number off the church registration card the other night. I hope you don't mind."

"I don't." *Would you like to know my blood type?*

"So I'll see you at church next week, and if not then, on Friday."

"Cool." *Cool? What am I, twelve?* "Looking forward to it." I try to salvage the moment by not acting like I just finished watching *Sabrina, the Teenage Witch.*

We hang up, and I decide that I'm actually fairly eloquent on the phone—well, perhaps not as my own administrative assistant, but for the rest of the conversation. I didn't say too much. I knew my name. Always a good thing. But of course, here's the situation in the dating world. At some point, you have to face the guy in person. Even in Internet dating, eventually the day of reckoning comes. *What is going to happen when I'm standing face-to-face with him, and I have to speak coherently? One word of that accent, and I'm sure I'll be toast.*

Someone knocks at the door, and I prepare to pretend with Nate. It will be like I never kissed him, per his request. *That's comfortable.* However, after Stuart's call, I'm a little more prepared for that. I mean, the fact is, I came home gushing after meeting Stuart. It was probably just Stuart's kiss that I accidentally gave Nate, so caught up in the moment was I.

I'll just thank him for setting up the computers, show him the fabric I bought. Go back to the way things were. Tell him British hottie called, and may Miss Shampoo Commercial make Nate Goddard very happy. *After she coughs up a hairball.*

I straighten my shoulders, and open the door to see my former roommate Kim. I feel my shoulders slink back down. She looks like heck. Her hair is plastered against the side of her head, her clothes are disheveled, and she is carrying a pillowcase full of heaven-knows-what. She's not wearing any make-up; her pock-marked skin is sallow with a distinct yellow hue in her eyes.

"Kim?" I say, a tad unsure what the proper greeting is for someone who stole $20,000 and half this month's rent when disappearing.

"Look, I know what I did sucked, but I need your help."

"You don't want to stay *here*?"

"I do. I need to, Lilly," she says through tears, and call me a sucker, but I can't hack her tears. If Kim yelled at me, I'd be good and strong, but her tears get to me because she is so not a crier.

First, though, I have a few questions: "Kim, would you want to fall asleep at night next to someone who stole everything you owned?"

"Please," she begs. "I've been out on the streets, and I'm tired and hungry. You were right about that guy. I'm sorry, but I was afraid what he might do. When he saw that check sitting there on the table—you know you just left it out—something snapped in him." Kim keeps looking over her shoulder, and I don't know if it's for my benefit or part of the sob story.

"You didn't bring him here?"

"No, I left him in Berkeley. He was a user, Lilly. He stole your check. I didn't do a lot to stop him, but I was in over my head."

"Allow me this. I was right?"

"You were right, okay? I just wanted to get him something so he wouldn't be so angry. I thought they'd give him some type of advance on the check, and I figured Sara would be covered. I knew they'd never cash the whole thing."

"You took my license. So clearly, you had a little thought process going there."

"That was his idea," Kim says, and I can tell this conversation is wearing on her. "I wouldn't have thought of your ID. You know that." Kim's forehead is brimming with sweat, and her coloring appears to be getting worse before my eyes.

"Why on earth would I trust you?" I allow my gaze to focus intently on her, trying to see if she's lying to me.

"I can't think of a single reason, but I just don't want to go back out there. Do you think Nate would take me in?" Kim starts to back away from the door.

"I have no idea, but Nate seems to be busy lately. What would I have done if you got that money? I couldn't pay the rent. I didn't have a job, and you know my name is on this lease. You knew that when you left me holding the bag. Did you think Sara would just forgive a $20,000 debt?"

"I told you I didn't think they'd cash the check. We've been friends a long time, Lilly. I made a bad error in judgment, okay? Two years and one really bad decision. That doesn't seem completely awful, does it?"

I sigh aloud. Mostly because I know I'm going to forgive her. I can't stand to see her like this.

"I didn't want to fail again, Lilly, and you weren't listening to me. Just like Sara. You were just going full-steam ahead, doing what you wanted to do. If I stayed, you would have just trampled me to get what you need so your grandmother would approve. I'm sorry your Nana doesn't support you, but it's not my problem."

I'm losing a little compassion as she speaks. "You're actually trying to blame this on me?"

"No, I'm not. Please, Lilly, let me in. You know I wouldn't come back here if I had anywhere else to go. I'm sorry."

I open the door a bit wider, knowing I'll probably regret the decision. "One night. And we're going shopping at six. You're coming with me, because I'm not leaving you here alone with my computer and sewing machine."

"I wouldn't steal those things from you. I only took the money because he needed a fix. If I wanted to steal those things, I would have taken them the first time."

"Somehow, that doesn't ease my troubled mind, you know?"

"Just tell me how to start making it up to you? I've got nowhere to go. You know this wasn't like me."

"First off, I want my ID back." I hold my palm out, and she reluctantly digs through her pocket and hands me my California driver's license. "Then I want you to go upstairs and leave something of importance with Nate. As collateral."

"Like what? Don't you think if I had anything, I wouldn't be here?"

"Your mother's locket." I glare at the one thing of value she holds dear. An ivory cameo that couldn't be more out of place on her tattooed self, but she wears it every moment on a black leather cord. I've never seen her take it off.

She shakes her head. "No, please, Lilly."

"Nate has a safe, Kim. You either put it there, or you're not staying. You can go camp out in the Theater District, like all the other homeless."

She sighs and turns around, pulling her hair off her neck. "No, I'll leave it. I need you to trust me again, but I'm sure you'll want my firstborn too."

"No, just a lock of his hair." I grimace at her, and go back to finishing my drawings, having the pressure of the perfect wedding gown hanging over my head. Without the four hundred man hours I need, it's going to have to be fairly simple.

Scratch that. I toss the sketch book aside. *What am I thinking to send Kim up alone?* Like she's going to hand over her most prized possession without me watching the transaction.

I run up the stairs and see Kim at Nate's doorstep. She's shuffling her feet while he yells at her. "Lilly trusted you, Kim.

You should have seen her face when she realized you were gone. She wouldn't believe it!"

"I didn't want to be in the design business anymore, Nate. You don't know what it's like being color-blind around a group who needs the perfect color. It's like realizing my handicap every moment of every day. This guy offered me a ticket out of California. At least, I thought he did."

"You are not going to try that with me. You had a choice. Lilly never left you without a choice. She thought you needed a job, and she made one for you. How do you repay her?"

"Look, I didn't come here to be judged."

"Why *did* you come here?" Nate snaps.

"Lilly says I need to leave some collateral with you." Kim reluctantly hands him the cameo. "This was my mother's."

"How do I know your mother isn't in Topeka with a pile of these? Or this isn't some eBay junk?"

Kim's voice cracks. "She's not in Topeka, okay? You just have to trust me, I suppose. Lilly does; she sent me up here by myself."

Um, oops.

Nate takes the cameo from her. "If you hurt Lilly again, I'll tell Sara Lang where you are, and trust me, she won't be nearly so kind as Lilly."

If *she* hurts Lilly again? *Hello! Did my knight in shining armor not just pierce my heart with his very own sword?*

"I'm trying to start fresh. I won't harm her again."

"She deserves better, but I'll shout the truth from the rooftops to Sara Lang if you hurt Lilly again."

"Deal." Kim thrusts her hand toward Nate, and they shake on it.

I silently creep down the back stairs wondering what to make of Nate Goddard. No, that's not what I'm thinking at all. What I'm thinking is how can I get him to kiss me again? And how can I make the Miss Shampoo Commercial ride out on the horse she suddenly came in on? And then, of course, I'm having guilt because I know better. *Yes, Lord, I know better. But I'm only human here.*

call Nana and she's not home, so I try Max's place. I need to give them my new cell phone number.

"Max Schwartz," he answers, far too professionally for a television writer.

"Max, it's Lilly. Is my Nana there? I wanted to give her my new cell number."

"No." He pauses. "But I'm here. I'll take your number," he purrs flirtatiously. *What did I eat this week?* Or maybe it's my sense of freedom and unemployment that's turning all these guys into flirts.

"Where is she?"

"Your Nana?"

"No, Valeria."

"That was just mean," he tells me, and he's right.

"I'm sorry. I'm specializing in mean this week, and I'm not proud of it."

"I've got a pen."

"For?"

"Your number."

He writes it down. "Mildred is outside gardening. You want me to call her?"

"You are trouble. Is she feeling okay?"

"She seems fine, Lilly. Whatever had her going back and forth to the hospital seems to be over."

I let out a gasp. "Oh thank you, Jesus," I whisper. "Just tell her to call me when she gets in, will you?"

"I will. Hey, Lil—" I hear Max start to say. But it's too late. I've already hung up on him. I reach for the phone a few times to call him back, but ultimately decide our conversation was done enough.

It's Friday afternoon and time for a whirlwind Spa Girls weekend. We don't usually do this—cluster our spa visits so close—but we don't usually have so much drama either. Hasty marriages, fashion design crises, and the sudden need for couture gowns. Oh, my!

As I stare across my loft, I'm looking at Kim knowing I don't have the guts to kick her out of the house. *I'm a wimp.* Nate is still not talking to me. Avoiding me like the plague might be a more appropriate term. Miss Shampoo Commercial hasn't been back, so I choose to think it was the lingering memory of my kiss that made him unable to follow through on his designs for those auburn waves of hair. I like the idea of him up there pining, wishing he had the strength to come down and kiss me again.

In a new development, Kim has decided to feel a little guilt and is working on computer patterns for me until she finds "a real job." I'm very proud of the gowns I've sketched. They're better than anything I did for Sara Lang, so I'm grateful to have the help. When I'll find the time to actually sew them is still a mystery.

Kim is bent over the computer watching *The View* and yelling in agreement at the TV as the women take some anti-male stance. "Kim? I don't want to ruin your lovefest with the gals here, but I've left all the designs and the fabrics numbered that go with each pattern."

She nods and doesn't tear her eyes from the TV. "Men are dogs."

"The patterns are hanging in the coat closet, so don't put anything in here. I don't want the fabrics touched. I just need you to put the designs on the computer," I say to Kim as I store the last of the fabric. "The drawings are on the sketch pad next to the computer. Don't cut any of the patterns. I know you mean well, but that fabric cost me a fortune, and I haven't paid for it yet. I'll have a sewing frenzy when I get back."

"It'll be fine, Lilly. Just go, will you? You can trust me."

Actually, I can't, can I? I think. Then I shrug. It's too late to fix it now, and I've got my driver's license well-hidden in my wallet and no more money for her to take. I pack my new sketch pad and Morgan's wedding fabric, plus the material I picked out for Poppy and myself. I'm hoping we'll have a bridesmaid gown at the end of this weekend and approval for the design and fabric of the wedding gown. If all goes well, I can cut fabric and pin while the girls get spa treatments.

"I'll be on the cell. The number is right here over the phone," I point. "Don't answer the phone. It's forwarded to my cell, and Sara can't know you have any part in this, or I'll never get the money. Just do me a favor and work on the computer, will you?"

"It's fine. Everything's fine. Just go, will you?"

I back out of the door with one outfit for the entire weekend, as my bag is packed full with Morgan's wedding fabrics. The last thing I need is my common stuff mingling with her material that's fit for a queen. So my stuff—the riffraff—is in a plastic bag squished in with Morgan's fabric.

"Need some help?" Nate's standing over me as I try to shut the door.

Well, look what the cat dragged in. "I've got it, thanks."

"Are you ever going to talk to me again?"

Oh, isn't that just like Nate to play innocent?

"I've been here," I shrug. "I'm paying you for this," I nod to the sewing machine. "The computers, too. I'll have your money next week. We'll talk then. It's my policy to not talk to investors until they're paid in full." *See, this is the great thing about your own business. You make the rules as they're convenient.* "See you, Kim!"

"Lilly, this is stupid."

Nate picks up the suitcase, an old hardshell Samsonite in avocado that once belonged to my Nana. He hefts the sewing machine too. I'm left with only my cashmere sweater tossed over my arm. The one I made from Sara Lang scraps. We hike down the stairs.

"You have to talk to me someday. I shouldn't have kissed you, all right? I'm sorry."

"It's me who shouldn't have kissed you. You caught me off guard," I say. "I was just too polite to turn you down. I think in actuality I was kissing Stuart Surrey, and you just happened to be in between us."

"You *are* too polite, or you wouldn't have Kim back in your place. I can't believe you. I know about doing the decent Christian thing, but don't you people have missions for that?"

"I'm wise as a serpent, gentle as a dove." *Stupid as a sheep.* "My choice. My problem." We reach the bottom of the stairs, and Morgan's waiting for me in her BMW. She opens the trunk without getting out of her car. I never look at Nate. "Thanks for the help. See you Monday."

"Ugh!" I shout once I'm in the car, looking back at Nate.

"That was nice of Nate to help you down," Morgan says, waving at him.

I grab her hand and force it down. "Stop that. He's a jerk, all right?"

"A girl could do worse than him," Morgan says.

"Not really, no, she couldn't," I say, as she just stares at me waiting for an explanation. "He kissed me the other night. No, he snogged me full on," I correct. "Actually, he kissed me, then the next night had a cozy date up to his loft. Then he said he hoped I understood we're just friends. Of course, this was after I saw him with the girl." Okay, maybe it wasn't after I saw him. I just can't remember. It *feels* like it was after Shampoo Girl.

"Oh," Morgan says. "Well, he's not a Christian." Morgan starts to give him a wave involving a single finger, when I shove her hand down again. "Speaking of jerks," she continues, "Stuart asked me to give this to you. He came into Daddy's store yesterday. Lilly, you need to run from this guy. I thought of not giving it to you. He sauntered into Daddy's store like you were the best of friends."

Morgan hands me a small, blue package. I unwrap a wad of tissue paper and find Stuart's business card and an English toffee with a note that reads, "Something sweet for someone sweet. Looking forward to getting to know you better."

"Morgan, look!" I show her the card, and she rolls her eyes.

"Gads, that's sickening. Please don't tell me you're remotely moved by this. He's smarmy, Lilly!" Morgan tosses the candy on the floor, and I retrieve it like a good hunting dog. "Stuart gives a bad name to English lit everywhere with that. The home of Dickens and Thomas Hardy, and he gives you that? I'm surprised he didn't start it 'Roses are red.'"

"What on earth do you have against Stuart?"

"Nothing. I just think you can do better, all right? And you're too old to use the word *snogged*. Can it, okay?"

"Morgan, I tell you when I looked at Stuart, something happened. You'll be embarrassed when you're the bridesmaid at my wedding to him, so don't say anything more. Your love for Marcus doesn't exactly make sense either."

"I'll leave it alone, but he just really seems like he wants to marry into money. Does he know you don't have any?"

"He knows I don't have a car and that I live in California. Does it get much more pathetic than that?"

"He probably thinks you have a chauffeur. We're picking up Poppy at the BART station."

I look down at my gold-foiled toffee and smile giddily. *Life is most definitely good.*

"Lilly?"

"Yeah, I heard you. Poppy…the BART station."

We drive for a short time, and a cell phone trills. "I think that's yours," Morgan says.

"Oh right, I've never heard it ring before." I pick up the phone, but realize I don't know how to answer it.

"Oh, Lilly, for crying out loud." Morgan grabs the phone and opens it. "Lilly Jacobs Design."

"Give it to me." I grab the phone.

"Lilly?" a deep masculine voice asks.

"It's me," I answer.

"Max here."

"Max? Is something wrong? Is it my Nana?" My heart begins to pound.

"No, I'd just like to invite you to dinner for rescuing me the other day. I'd ask you out, but you'd have to drive, and I thought it would be easier here. I'll have something brought in, something good."

I'll admit, I'm completely taken aback. It's the only explanation I can give for what I say next. "Why would you want to have *me* to dinner?"

Max is silent.

"Max?"

"I'm thinking about that question. Why *wouldn't* I want to have you for dinner, Lilly? Do you have an eating problem or something? I know Mildred says you don't eat, but I think you look pretty great, so you must eat something."

My first thought is Stuart Surrey and our impending relationship. "If Nana sees me, she may be planning our nuptials," I joke, but Max is eerily silent again. "Are you ready for that? Have you ever actually been to an Italian wedding?" He's still quiet. "The chicken dance? The accordion?" I say, hoping to scare him into thinking this is a stupid idea. Nana needs her apartment. I can't be seeing her landlord, however casual he thinks it is.

"So, Sunday night?" he finally says.

"I'm not going to be here this weekend. It's a Spa Girls weekend. We've had more than our share of crises this year. You understand. Sunday night is cutting it a little short."

"Right. So that's a *no*?" Max asks.

I look at Morgan, and suddenly I'm thinking, *if I tick him off is he going to kick Nana out the door?*

"Is that for a date?" Morgan whispers at me. I just shrug. *I'm not sure what exactly you'd call this.* "I'll have her home in time!" Morgan yells.

Max is laughing. I scowl at her. "What time should I be there?"

"I thought I'd send a car around for you."

A car around for me? What am I, the babysitter? "No, I can get there. Morgan will drop me off," I say, and stick my tongue out at her.

"Great. How's seven? Is that late enough for you to have a full weekend?" Max asks.

"It is. How's my Nana today?"

"She's doing well, Lilly. Hasn't been back to the doctor or asked for a ride. Not that I could take her anywhere, but I'd see if a cab came by. Whatever her crisis was, it appears to be over."

I breathe a sigh of relief. Thrilled I never had to have an

actual conversation with Nana about her health. She can be such a bear when things concern her private business. As if she ever lets me have any of my own personal, private business.

"Are you serious about this thing on Sunday? Why do I suddenly feel like there's some great mystery?" Maybe Nana is going to throw me a surprise party to celebrate leaving finance behind! She's been pretending to be under the weather, but really, she's cooking an Italian feast for the week. Everyone will be there, and I'll feel like a dolt that I thought I had a date. "I'll see you Sunday, Max."

"Who was that?" Morgan asks. "I know it wasn't Stuart because I didn't hear the full-of-himself accent. My," she says in a pretentious fake English accent, "Lillian darling, if you would but give me the pleasure of your company, I do ever so need someone to hold my mirror for me."

"It's with Max, my Nana's landlord. Sunday night." I don't say anything else. I don't want to let on that I know about the party.

"That should be fun. Especially if your Nana likes him. He must have some charm!"

"Max Schwartz watches TV for a living." I suppress a giggle.

Morgan's smile dissipates. "Max Schwartz? *Max Schwartz* is your grandmother's landlord?"

"Yeah. He broke his leg this week climbing on a ladder." I roll my eyes. "When men are interested in me, I tell ya, it's like, roll out the geek-o-meter—"

"Get the newspaper in the backseat," Morgan says.

"I can't read in the car; it makes me sick."

"Get the newspaper." I lean over the lush, leather bucket seat and grab the paper. "Turn to the society page," Morgan orders me.

I hold my palms up. "Like I have any idea where the society page is. If Sara Lang is in there, she cuts it out."

"The Datebook section. Back page."

I find the correct page, and I'm stunned when I see a photo of Max Schwartz smiling in a business suit on the back. *Dang, he's sort of hot in a suit.* "What the heck?"

I read the caption: "Millionaire hotel heir falls, breaks leg." The smaller article goes on: "Max Schwartz, heir to the Union Square Sisters chain of hotels, broke his leg in three places when he fell through an air duct in the ceiling in the world-famous Starlight Hotel. He is recovering at home. Schwartz has a weekly television column in our sister paper, *The Peninsula Times.*"

"He watches TV for a living. He never said anything about being an heir. His father has a few hotels, but he's not involved in the family business," I explain while Morgan just smiles and placates me.

"Lilly, as a diamond business heiress, I can officially say that I don't wear a diamond brooch that reads 'Heiress' across the front. Max had a falling-out with his parents about not taking on the family business. I wonder what he was doing at the hotel."

Looking at him in the paper, standing there in his suit with his coiffed goatee, I am completely riled. "He's a total liar! If I want a liar, I can go upstairs and maul Nate." *Again.* I roll my eyes and finger the gold-foiled toffee. I read Stuart's card again and smile. *A gentleman. Precisely what I need.*

"You're being ridiculous. He's saying thank you for driving him from the hospital, not, 'Will you marry me?'"

I hold up the toffee. "It's time I got dumped by a better breed of man. If I'm going to get dumped again, I want it to matter. I want to be told with a sexy British accent that I'm only worthy of friendship. At least Stuart will make it *sound* good. Besides, I've got work to do. I'm tired of people with money. Maybe I need to move to a middle state."

"You are so weird. They don't buy much couture in Wyoming."

"In Jackson Hole they do. I could do cowboy couture."

We drive the rest of the way to the BART station in silence, and there's Poppy waving on the platform. She's wearing her neon-colored, tie-dye skirt. "She's wearing that ghastly thing on purpose. She knows I hate it!" I say to Morgan.

"It's comfortable for her."

"You are *not* defending that skirt."

"Johnny Cochran couldn't have defended that skirt."

Poppy dumps her bag, an awful tapestry thing, in the trunk and comes around. "Hey, girls, are we ready? Did you bring the designs, Lilly? I can't wait to see what I'm wearing."

"I brought the designs, all the fabric, everything. I thought I'd perfect the designs and take measurements while you each get treatments."

"Lilly, I signed you up for a massage and a papaya facial," Morgan says, tossing her hair back. "It's a Spa Girls weekend. You're not working all weekend."

I shake my head. "I won't have time, Morgan. I really have to get to these gowns if we're going to make your deadline. I usually spend more than a month on a specialty gown like your wedding dress, and you're talking three in less time than that." Then I look at her. "You're not pregnant, are you?"

"Of course I'm not!"

"That's what everyone's going to think with you getting married so quickly: shotgun wedding."

"She's right, Morgan," Poppy says.

"Nine months later, they'll know I wasn't then."

Ack. Foiled again. Nothing is getting through to her this time.

I lean back in the leather seat and close my eyes. *Something has got to happen to stop this wedding.*

chapter 20

There are women who have a hold over men, a magical essence that calls out to them like a swirling smoke signal over their heads. I am not one of those women. I am the kind of girl that men tell they just want to be friends. The "in-between" girl until they meet the one they want to marry.

First, it happened with Robert.

Then it happened, albeit briefly, with Nate. (I'm expecting his wedding announcement momentarily.)

But it will not happen with Stuart Surrey.

I was born to be the wife of a Brit—with my Italian heritage? Colin Firth's wife is Italian. You see, it's fate. Stuart and I will have to discuss adoption, as his full head of gorgeous locks will definitely be a problem I would not saddle our kids with. But maybe Poppy's right. Maybe he has a bald mother, or some recessive gene, and our kids will turn out fine. We'll just have to see. The point is, I will not be friends with him. I will tell Stuart point-blank: "If you're looking for a friend, go find a pub. I am a woman to be taken seriously." I am through being the "home for strays" everyone turns to when they're forlorn and have nowhere to go—like Kim…or even Max, fresh on the rebound from Valeria, despite what he says. I am not Mother Teresa. I am a serious fashion designer, and if you can't put up, then shut up—or something like that. Anyway, I'm done playing everyone's mother.

"We're here, Lilly." Morgan stops the car in a circular drive-way surrounded by vineyards and a golf course. *It's heavenly.*

I blink several times while I take it all in. It's magnificent! The drive leads to a gigantic building with stately rock and a bevy of dormers. Bellmen dressed in wine-colored uniforms with gold buttons circle our car like a NASCAR pit crew. One of them opens my door and reaches in to help me out. *Wow! This kinda rocks.* I feel myself smiling widely, thinking that there is no way Morgan can truly appreciate what this means to me. I may not have any strong desire to be rich, but being spoiled like this every once in a while? It's not such a bad thing.

One of the bellmen reaches into the trunk to retrieve all our bags, and I have to say, Poppy's tapestry number has nothing on my vintage, hard-shell Samsonite. Actually, *vintage* is too good a word. *Goodwill reject* is more appropriate. I slide over in front of the suitcase and play a sort of dance with the bellmen trying to keep it from him.

"I've got it, thank you. Very important stuff in here." I pat the hard surface. Then I lean over and whisper to the bellman, cupping my hand, "You never want to put valuable things in a valuable case. It gives you away immediately."

The bellman just nods, as though I'm speaking a foreign language. "It's not a problem, really, ma'am."

Ma'am? How old does he think I am? Granted, I'm going to be thirty soon, but that's hardly an excuse to break out the *ma'am*, now is it? I slide over closer to the suitcase until I'm standing right in front of it, but Superboy tries to grab for it. I lunge for the case, but as I do I kick it over, and I watch as it tumbles in seemingly slow motion into a step-down fountain.

"Noooo!" I hear myself wail, but it's too late. My clothes, and, much more importantly, Morgan's wedding fabric are now bubbling from the bottom of the fountain. I stand over the Samsonite corpse trying to catch my breath. I already owe Morgan $7,000. What did *that* fabric cost?

A group of bellmen scurry over, and out of the corner of my eye, I see Morgan's mouth drop open. I just allow my eyes to close. I'm devastated. My future was in that suitcase, and my stupid vanity just cost me a small fortune!

Morgan's clicking heels approach, and she looks at me as though trying to discern if I did it on purpose. It's no secret how I feel about her marrying AARP's spokesman. But one look in my eyes, and she knows. She places her arm around me. "It's all right, Lilly. We'll get new fabric."

We both just start to bawl and hug each other. The bellmen are mystified that anything in that worn-out suitcase could be worth this kind of blather. But looking at its dripping remnants as they pull it from the fountain, I think it pretty much sums up my life.

Poppy comes up behind us and stares at the suitcase. "Well, you won't be working this weekend after all, I guess. Good thing we've got the papaya mask scheduled, don't you think?"

We all three look at one another and just start to laugh. "It's not funny," I say through my laughter and tears.

Morgan shrugs. "It's sort of funny."

"It's not a good sign, energy-wise," Poppy says, shaking her head. "Maybe God is trying to tell you something, Morgan. At the very least, you shouldn't be rushing this."

"Come on, let's get our rooms." Morgan leads us into the travertine entry, and the great rock wall provides the focal point behind the massive granite countertop.

"Welcome to Laurwood, Miss Malliard. It's an honor to

have you with us." Then the uniformed girl lowers her tone. "I've heard on the radio there was an incident in the parkway. If you'll be so kind as to write your roommate's size down, we'll have a personal shopper attend to her needs right away. Will she be needing a new suitcase as well?"

"You're a four?" Morgan twists around and asks.

"Two," I say sheepishly. "You have to have hips to be a four."

"She's a two. She'll need something for bed, and then just a couple of casual sweatsuits for the rest of the weekend." Morgan looks me over and faces the clerk again. "She's a winter. Don't worry about the suitcase. I think we can replace that on our own."

The clerk writes everything down, and I feel like a child having someone go shopping for me. Me, a fashion designer, with no clothes and no income. Just when I think I've hit bottom, the floor gives way and I sink to new depths.

"Oh, I nearly forgot!" Morgan announces, and it seems like the entire foyer turns to gaze at us, like Alan Greenspan himself is talking. "She'll need something for a date on Sunday night. Not too sexy, but sexy enough. Maybe something in black."

"Morgan!" I protest.

She leans in closer to the clerk. "It's with Max Schwartz, the hotel chain heir."

The clerk gives me the once-over, probably wondering what Max Schwartz could possibly see in me. I'm sure if she knew the dinner was to give my Nana peace so she'd leave Max alone and be convinced that there's hope for me to avoid spinsterhood—or that Max is just the ploy for my surprise "I'm happy for you, Lilly" party—the clerk wouldn't be nearly so impressed. I know I'm not.

"Let's go." I yank on Morgan's arm, she gets the key, and we hike up to our cabin. The grounds are perfection. Green vegetation hangs sloppily over the pathway leading up to the Winecar Cabin.

"This is nice, Morgan. You outdid yourself," Poppy says.

"It's great, isn't it? The owner lives in Nob Hill. He comes in to buy gifts for his wife once in a while. My dad gives them to him just above wholesale, and we stay here for nearly nothing. We have to pay for meals and our treatments. The lodging is on the house, so I try not to take advantage and use it too often."

Poppy and I both nod, not wanting to mention how completely out of our element we are. Once the path ends, I see the Winecar Cabin is no more a cabin than my loft is luxurious San Francisco living!

The cabin is at the top of the trees and has a huge balcony. "Open the door!" I say excitedly.

The room is luxurious with a fluffy, white *duvet* on the magnificent bed and hardwood floors covered by a natural-weave rug. There's white wainscoting around the perimeter of the living room and windows everywhere overlooking the luscious gardens. It feels like we're actually living in the tree. I run into the bathroom and see a modernized, claw-foot tub with old-fashioned-looking Victorian plumbing. "Absolute perfection," I say.

"It is lovely, isn't it?" Morgan asks. "Mrs. Kapsan has a lot of style, and I think it shows."

"Mrs. Kapsan?" I question, swallowing hard at the familiar name.

"That's right. You met their daughter Caitlyn. She's the one dating Stuart, Lilly," Morgan says, implying *money-grubbing creep* when she says his name.

Things just went from momentarily glorious to down the drain again, and all in the midst of such fine, luxury appointments. So wrong.

We all come out of the bathroom after sniffing the soaps and shower gels and see the message light is blinking. I plop down on the huge king-sized bed at the back of the room and rest my head on my hands. "The message light is on. I tell you," I say, putting the back of my hand on my forehead, "my fans give me no rest." Knowing full well that this call is no more for me than it is Johnny Depp calling.

I reach into the bedside table and grab a Bible. I open it to Acts and just start reading. It soothes my soul to think of the power of God, and it reminds me that though I tend to live day-to-day, He has a plan for me.

Morgan walks over, ever-so-elegantly, and calls down for messages with the touch of a button. "It's probably your clothes, Lilly. Maybe there's a problem. Who knows where they'll find size two in this one-horse town." She laughs her light, tinkling laugh.

Her words serve to remind me that I've not only ruined her wedding fabric but also my only paying design work. My heart falls as the reality of what I've done sinks in. Morgan would never say so, but this has to be hard on her. I know she searched long and hard for that fabric, and it's not easily replaceable. At least not in this country. It will dry out, but it will never be the same.

A finance job is sounding more and more reasonable. *Regardless of what happens*, I vow, *I'm going to design Morgan the most beautiful, lusted-after gown San Francisco has ever seen. Scratch that. That Paris has ever seen!*

Morgan listens to the message, and her smile dissipates. I watch her eyelids flutter, then close slowly, and Poppy looks at me worriedly. Morgan lowers herself to the floor, leaning against the bed.

"Morgan?" Poppy says. But Morgan just waves at us to be quiet.

We wait for what seems an eternity, and Morgan finally drops the phone onto the floor with a clunk and lowers her face into her hands. Soft, muffled sobs emanate from behind the French-manicured fingers.

"Morgan? What is it?"

She lets out a deep breath and finally meets our agonized expressions. Then she straightens, and the businesslike Morgan, reserved for her father's charity events, returns. "There's no wedding," she says, matter-of-factly. "You were right, Poppy. The suitcase was an omen."

Morgan can't keep up the appearance, though, and crumbles into more tears, burying her face into her hands again.

"I don't believe in omens, really. That was a bad choice of words," Poppy says. "What do you *mean*—there's no wedding? Did your dad get to the groom? Because if he did—"

"No, nothing like that." Morgan sniffles. Her face is moist and pink, with mascara outlining her eyes like a raccoon.

I've never seen Morgan's makeup in disarray. It's unsettling. Now I'm thinking I wish I'd been more supportive of her. She actually looks truly crushed. I thought she didn't know what she was doing, but now, seeing her pain, I feel like a complete heel who didn't listen when her best friend needed her.

Lord, forgive me for not supporting her, for judging her instead.

"I will make you the most beautiful gown, Morgan. There will be a wedding," I say, determined. "Whatever it is, we can fix it."

She shakes her head, and smiles sadly. "Bless you, Lilly, but there really is no wedding. Marcus passed away this morning."

Both Poppy and I gasp. Right. *We can't fix that.* I'm embarrassed. *He was old, but he wasn't that old.* I'd only been joking.

Morgan grabs our hands. "Marcus had a bad liver, girls. He was awaiting a transplant. That's why he was here. I thought with a quick wedding, we'd beat the deadline."

"I'm sorry." I hug her, and she just clutches Poppy and me for a good, long time.

"He was a great man. I'm just sorry you didn't get to meet him. He wasn't feeling well that night at the restaurant, Lilly, or I would have introduced you. I didn't think he was up to it, and he would have pretended and made it worse."

"I don't understand," Poppy says.

Morgan smiles. "Marcus thought he'd have a better chance on the transplant list if he was married to an American citizen. There's always an uproar when foreigners get transplants, but we thought...anyway...I wanted to help him. We owed him, and he deserved it."

"You were going to marry him to get him a liver?" Poppy asks incredulously.

"I thought you only had one liver."

"Not *my* liver!" Morgan says, as though I'm stupid. "I was going to marry him because it would have given him peace to be on the donor list." Morgan looks at me. "The list where the donor has to be *dead* to donate, Lilly. A partial liver wouldn't have sufficed in his case. Marcus saved my dad from rotting in a Russian prison—or worse. If anyone deserved to have the favor returned, it was Marcus."

"Back up," I say. My head is now thoroughly swimming. I always knew that Morgan had a big heart. I didn't know she was completely sacrificial.

Morgan's jaw tightens. "My dad went to Russia, even though all his colleagues advised against it, and he bought some black market diamonds—diamonds that come from mines that are illegal because there are no safety checks in place. They basically come illegally from a war zone, and often people die to get them to market."

"Did your dad know they were illegal?"

"No, but had he done his homework he would have

known. He was only ignorant because he chose to be."

"Did Marcus sell the diamonds to your dad?" I ask, knowing that Marcus was also in the business, according to the church group.

"Heavens, no. Marcus was a godly man. He found out that my dad had been suckered by some bad men in Russia, and he broke up the ring with the help of police and got my father released from prison."

"Your dad was in prison?" Poppy gasps.

Morgan nods. "My dad was too proud to ever thank Marcus, to ever admit he deserved to be in that prison. But I know who saved my father from himself. It was Marcus Agav." Morgan looks down again and cries some more. "The very least I could have done for him is save his life. I really am sorry we didn't make it."

"I know you are, sweetie." I put my arm around Morgan.

"Marcus wouldn't let me announce the wedding in the end. I think he knew he was getting worse."

There's a knock at the door, and I jump up while Poppy continues to comfort Morgan. There's a valet holding Morgan's shantung silk, drenched and dripping. "Take it away," I say quietly as I exit the cabin, shutting the door behind me. "Throw it away. Everything in that suitcase. Throw it out. We don't want to see it again."

"Right away," the young man says and scampers away leaving a trail of water behind him.

"Oh, Morgan, I'm so very sorry," I murmur as I watch the man disappear down the path. *I'm the bad omen, Lord. Help me.*

chapter 21

Morgan spends the entire afternoon crying, weeping that she should have done more for Marcus or married him sooner. I listen for as long as I can, and while I'm truly sorry for Marcus, I'm glad that Morgan will now have the opportunity to someday know true love in marriage. At least I hope she will. She has such a gentle heart, and I pray that the Lord will bring her someone to thoroughly adore her quiet spirit. Another artist—although this one might be employed. Not like Andy, who was more heart than ambition.

Outside, the sky darkens and dumps an uncharacteristic September downpour. The treehouse rooms feel more like a damp cave than an elegant Winecar Cabin, and I feel smothered by the anguish within these walls.

"I'm going for a walk," I say suddenly. "Before the sun goes down." The girls just nod, and Morgan gives a little hiccup.

"We'll watch *Benny and Joon* when you get back." Poppy takes a VHS tape out of her bag. "Or *Don Juan DeMarco*?"

Morgan starts to laugh and sniffle. "You didn't bring those movies, did you? Haven't we matured at all?"

"No, not really, and they will cheer you up, Morgan. Besides, Lilly loves them, and we'll make popcorn and make her forget there's no Lysol to inhale. Don't you love Johnny Depp, Lilly?"

"Isn't that blasphemy to watch our cult favorites in this place?" I ask, looking around me at the elegant surroundings and burning mint candles. "We should be watching a Shakespearian play or something."

"Perhaps, but when have *you* ever been one to mind the rules? People who mind the rules major in finance, and then get themselves a good job in finance. They don't leave a perfectly good career to be a fashion designer." Poppy smiles, and Morgan giggles through her tears.

"*Touché*," I say. Poppy left the life of medical school to be a chiropractor, so she knows all about not taking the beaten path. She and I are birds-of-a-feather in snubbing logical choices for a lesser-paying life of adventure. "I'll be back. I just need a bit of fresh air." I close the door behind me and look up to the gray sky, feeling the droplets pour down my face. It's not cold, and the wet weather feels more refreshing than bothersome. I *deserve* the rain.

I start down the paved path, not bothering with an umbrella, just allowing the rain to beat down on me. Water. *Living water.* As I feel the drops pelting me, this verse comes to me: *You will be like a well-watered garden, like a spring whose waters never fail. Oh Lord, where are You now?* I feel my feet beneath me start to run down the path, and I hold my arms out to embrace the rain. I'm glad to leave the cabin behind, and I don't imagine I'll covet an elegant spa experience again anytime soon. While I know it's important to share in Morgan's pain, I just needed a break from that cabin filled with grief. I needed to remind myself that all is not lost, and that God still provides the rainbow of promise somewhere in this storm.

I reach the hotel lobby and walk into the foyer, leaving a

little trail of puddles behind me. I'm breathing hard from running and dripping on the travertine floor, but there's someone behind me with a mop. I don't care at the moment what type of mess I make. I'm on a mission.

I reach the granite countertop and put my elbows out to rest on it. The woman behind the counter is pleasant, but she does take a towel to wipe the mess around me. "May I help you, miss?"

"I need my silk back. I told the valet to throw it away, but I actually need that fabric." I'm holding back tears now, and my voice is trembling slightly. I know the fabric won't bring Marcus back, but I want to do something for Morgan. Anything to make her feel better. I think back to all the times she's been there for me, as recently as picking me up the day I was fired, and I'm tired of always being such a leech in her life, on everyone's life. When, if ever, will being my friend not cost people? When will I earn my keep?

"Let me call the valet for you. Right away." She turns away and whispers into the phone, probably telling him to rush right down, that there is a complete vagabond-looking, half-crazed guest scaring the other paying customers. The clerk turns back towards me. "Jim will be here shortly. He seems to know just what you mean."

Stellar. After waiting mere seconds, the valet appears, his expression squirming. "I threw the fabric away, Miss Jacobs. Like you asked me to."

"I know. If it's not too much trouble, I need it back."

He shakes his head. "It's in the dumpster. I didn't think you wanted to see it again. I was only doing what I was told. I should have held onto it, but I didn't want to upset Miss Malliard. She seemed upset when I was by the room."

He is clearly getting nervous. "Right. No worries. No worries. Maybe I don't need it after all. Thanks for your help."

But as I exit, I see a woman cleaning out the ashtrays, and I ask her to point me in the right direction of the dumpster. She looks at me oddly, and I repeat it in Spanish. She points behind the drive.

"*Gracias,*" I say. "*Muchas gracias.*"

I run down to the dumpsters. There are three of them, and they all smell ripe. *Ugh.* I cover my face. *Where's my Lysol when I need it most?* I knew I shouldn't have listened to Morgan. I should have followed my excellent olfactory instincts and brought it along! She swore I wouldn't need it here. I pull myself up onto the first gray steel box and look down into the bin. There's absolutely no sign of the suitcase. Or the fabric. I hold my nose and jump onto the next dumpster. Again, no sign of life.

On the third dumpster, my heart starts to pound. The suitcase is not visible. I'm going to have to climb in, and I just try to visualize which one they may have used last. "One. Two. Three!" I shout, before bounding feet-first into the pile of old food and heaven-knows-what else. I gag and plug my nose tightly, fighting the rising nausea. It takes me a while to get my bearings, as the smell just makes me dizzy with disgust. Once I find my footing, I start the search, stopping every so often to allow a wave of queasiness to pass.

Climbing through the muck, keeping nostrils pressed firmly shut, I can't believe the suitcase wouldn't be more obvious. I pick up old rolls and torn towels, but the worst of it is the dead fruit and the rank champagne from all those spa lunches. It just smells like something flies live for, but luckily the rain has scared them away. It's just me climbing through the bin. *Ugh, and maybe a few hidden rats!* The soggy garbage envelops my jeans as I sink in a little further, and I feel the smell start to seep through to my skin. *Please God, please let it be here.*

At that very moment, I spy a corner of the fabric. I reach for it and pull, hard. Up comes the entire afternoon's garbage, but it doesn't matter. It doesn't matter, because the fabric is here! I can wash it. I can make pillows. I can do anything I can to earn money to get Morgan's investment back to her. I've got to do something.

I pull, and I yank until I have the fabrics—all three of them—in my grasp. I'm so giddy with excitement, I barely notice the smell now or the fact that my Nana's Samsonite that saw me through college is long gone. I toss out the fabrics and climb to the top of the dumpster. When I get to the top, I see there are golfers returning from the links. But it's too late; they've seen me. I cringe and start to lower myself back down, but I hear my name.

"Lilly!" I hear again.

I jump onto the ground next to the fabric and try to hold my head high. *Who on earth would know me here?*

My face goes white, as I see Stuart Surrey and his "former" girlfriend, Caitlyn Kapsan, both in full golf attire, staring at me as though...well, as though I've just emerged from the hotel dumpster covered in yesterday's fruit plate.

"Stuart," I say while dusting myself off. *Heavens, there's a banana peel stuck to my knee.* I scrape it off and toss it back into the bin. "What are you two doing out in the rain?" *Don't you melt in water, Caitlyn?*

"We got caught on the fifteenth hole when this surprise shower came," Caitlyn says. "Men, they'll golf through any-thing. I had to convince Stuart that we could finish tomorrow."

"Yes, well, are you all right?" Stuart asks, scrutinizing my appearance.

"I'm fine." I look at the fabric at my feet. "It's a long story."

"Quite right." Stuart gazes at me. I'm sure he's thinking, *I have a date with this woman? What was I thinking to lower myself* to this human trash? Actually, I think I can safely assume the date is canceled by the repulsion I see now in his eyes. "Caitlyn, shall we?" Stuart puts his hand on her back and they sashay away from me, under the umbrella he holds over them. Stuart takes one look back and shakes his head.

I want to believe it's an accident that he's here. Yes, it's a hotel her father owns, but I'm certain they have different rooms. Right? I want to believe he finds it somewhat charming that he just discovered me in a dumpster, but something tells me *that* is the stuff of fairy tales.

Time stopped when I met him. At church! What's he doing at a hotel? With a woman he told me he was "taking a break from"? All these questions circulate in my mind, when the valet comes running toward me. "I would have had it retrieved, miss."

It appears that my stint in the dumpster has not gone unnoticed. Morgan will never be allowed back here with me. *Why didn't we just drive to Spa Del Mar?* No, I have to pick the moment when everyone decides to congregate at the trash bins.

I look absently toward the distance. "Don't worry about it, Jim. But if you could have the material dry-cleaned by tomorrow," I say, handing him the mass of filthy fabric, "I would most appreciate it."

He takes the soiled material and starts to jog up the path. *I have the worst luck known to man. Correction: I have the worst luck when it comes to men.* There is no way I'm going to make it as a fashion designer. Designers are elegant, upstanding citizens who people want to emulate. I am a dumpster diver with bad hair and an inability to keep a date.

part II: wavy

ust when you think it couldn't get any worse...my hair has started to curl! Maybe it's just the rain, but I'm back in our cabin now looking in the mirror and I see it, the first signs of a curl sprouting from my part. I knew I didn't sit under the solution long enough. I tried to tell my hairdresser, but she swore no one's hair could fight the technology of modern science. Ha! She'd never met my hair. I'll bet you my hair has the half-life of industrial plastic! Biotech could sell my DNA with the tagline: *Cannot be damaged by weather, hormones, or even battery acid!* I'm every bald man's dream.

"What are you doing?" Poppy comes up behind me. "Oh, Lilly, what's that smell?" she asks as she gets closer.

"My hair's curling. Already! What a waste of money. I could barely make last month's rent to pay for this."

"It's not curling," she says matter-of-factly as she steps back. "I think you just have—" she pauses for minute, "—food in it?"

"Where's Morgan?" I ask, avoiding her questioning glance.

"She went for your papaya facial. We didn't know where you went." Poppy shrugs. "Besides, she needs the break. I think she's cried every last tear. Her father should be shot for putting her in this situation. I think we would have liked Marcus, Lilly. It's so sad. Morgan says there won't be a funeral service. He didn't want one, and besides Morgan's father—Jewelry Jerk—you and I are the only ones who knew there was a wedding planned."

"Poppy?" I say, shocked to hear from her gentle mouth the insult to Morgan's father. But we've all thought it. He never did one thing for Morgan that didn't take himself into account first.

"I'm serious." Poppy swings her skirt around in anger. "Marcus should have left him to rot in that Russian prison. And what's he ever done for Morgan but *use* her?"

Poppy is like the rest of us when one of her own has been hurt. She's all about peace and harmony until someone messes with someone she loves. Then her claws come out; and Lord have mercy upon the person who riles her out of her dove-like pacifism.

"He's been the only parent she's had. That's what he's done," I answer in his defense, even if I don't necessarily feel it. "He's treated her like a princess and never allowed another woman to come between them. San Francisco's Jeweler has his bright spots, and one of them is that he knows Morgan's the very best part of him."

"You're right. But let me bask in the thought of hurting him for a moment. I've spent all afternoon listening to his daughter cry on my shoulder, you know? Speaking of which, where have you been?" Poppy walks closer to me.

"I needed to do something."

Poppy clutches her nose. "Oh, Lilly, where *have* you been? And where is your Lysol when you need it?"

"Do me a favor." I turn around and face her, wishing Morgan the realist was here instead of Zen-mind-in-the-movement Poppy.

Poppy lifts an eyebrow. "It doesn't involve getting closer to you, does it?"

"Call the front desk for me, and ask for Caitlyn Kapsan's room."

"Caitlyn? That girl in the white suit at Morgan's church?"

"She's here at her daddy's hotel." I turn away from her prying eyes. "With Stuart, I think."

"I told you he had bad energy. I'm not calling. Save yourself some trouble and dump him before you date him, okay?" Poppy plops in a chair and crosses her toned arms. "Isn't it bad enough we have Morgan in utter turmoil this weekend? Do you think we want to pick you up off the floor too? He's a dirtbag, Lilly. I'll give you good-looking with a sexy accent, but a dirtbag, nonetheless. Have you ever heard Morgan say as many not-nice things about a guy?"

I whirl around. "Just call. I'd do it for you. I just want to know if they're together. I want to put this to bed, pardon the pun, forever."

Poppy stands up. With a hand on her hip, she acts remarkably like Nana. "What do I say when she answers?"

"Wrong number," I say. "Just like we did in college."

"Should I ask if her refrigerator is running while I'm at it?"

"Caller ID makes those days a distant memory," I say wistfully. "Ah, the good ol' days. Poor kids today." I can see Poppy's resolve weakening. "Please, Poppy. Do this for me. If you're right, you're right. Wouldn't that make you feel good?"

Poppy sits down on the bed, and I watch with relief as she punches zero. "Caitlyn Kapsan's room, please." Then she covers the receiver. "They're ringing through." Poppy starts to hum. "Oh hi, yes, Caitlyn?"

What's she doing?

"This is Dr. Poppy Clayton. I met you at church in the city. With my friend, Lilly. Right, Morgan's friends."

Stop. Stop her now. I run to the phone, but she eludes me with an old wrestling move.

"Yes," Poppy continues. "We're here at the hotel with Morgan." She giggles falsely. "I know. Incredible, isn't it? We girls thought you might like to have dinner with us. Lilly men-tioned that she saw you here on the grounds…I know …sure." Poppy covers the receiver again. "She's checking with Stuart."

I am going to hurt Poppy. But inside, my heart breaks just a bit, because Stuart *is* in Caitlyn's room and what Morgan said about him is, in all probability, true. My stomach hurts. *I do have terrible taste in men.* How does one ever trust her instincts when she obviously has such faulty ones? Except when it comes to detecting foul odors. Why can't I sniff out bad men? Dash them with a good dose of Bad-Boy Lysol? Even if I could, how do I erase the fact that he makes me feel like a princess?

"That will be wonderful. We'll see you at eight o'clock then. I'll call and let them know we'll be together. Fabulous, see you then." Poppy clicks the phone down.

"What are you doing?"

"Listen, if Stuart's thinking he can have his cake and eat it too, I'm about to show him that you are not a dessert pastry. You are the main entrée, a serious contender for his heart. And if he's intent on following this through, he's going to treat you with dignity. Or answer to me in the process."

I definitely feel sick. And it's more than just dumpster du jour.

Morgan walks in, her face clean and scrubbed red. "Hi, girls!" she says lightly.

"Hi, Morgan," Poppy says guiltily, sliding the phone into its cradle. "How was your facial? Are you feeling better?"

"I'm good. Better. What's going on?" Morgan asks, immediately sensing the tension in the room.

"Poppy is a traitor, that's what's going on. Why don't you ask her what she's just done?"

"Lilly, what did *you* do?" Morgan crinkles her nose. "You smell awful!"

My cell phone trills, and I reach for it. "Lilly Jacobs Design."

"Lilly? It's Nana. I need you to come home, dear. As soon as you can. I've had a phone call." Her voice is trembling.

"What is it, Nana?" She is not the type to be rattled by anything.

"Someone called." She pauses.

"Yes, I know, you just said that—"

"It's your mother, Lilly. Your birthmother," she corrects herself. "She's here."

I feel as if I've been sucker-punched. *Like I need this right now?* "I'll be right home, Nana." I look at Morgan and Poppy. "I've got to go to Nana."

"I'll pack my bags," Morgan says, sensing the gravity.

"No, no, you girls stay. Morgan, you need to grieve properly. Poppy, you've got to be with her. And you have a date to keep with Stuart and Caitlyn. *Sorry, I couldn't resist.* I'll find a way home. If there's one thing I've learned in my years of taking public transportation, it's that where there's a will, there's a way."

"I'll run you a bath first," Poppy says. "If your clothes aren't here yet, you can take something of mine." She heads into the bathroom, and I hear the faucet knobs turning.

I gaze after her, imagining the gauze skirts; and let's just say, my desperation is not quite that deep yet. I look at Morgan, my eyes pleading. "Yes, I have something you can wear, Lilly. Don't worry. Is Nana okay?"

"Yes," I reply, my mind racing. "It's just that she received some…news. It appears my mother, or rather the woman who gave birth to me, is in town."

Poppy hurries out of the bathroom, and she and Morgan both gasp.

"No way! What does she want?" Poppy asks.

"I have no idea, but I've been waiting for this day all my life, so I have to find out."

"Well, I'll say one thing for us. When our lives get screwed up, at least we do it together." Morgan smiles at me.

"Speak for yourselves." Poppy grins, and we all grab hands. Poppy leads us in a prayer, and I try to still my mind, which has taken off in a thousand different directions. I have a mother. Will she like me? Where has she been? Suddenly, none of the work deadlines or Sara's directives matter. I'm about to find out who I am.

Poppy finishes, and I turn and head for the bathroom, shut the door, and step into the steaming bath against the backdrop of the rain coming down outside. It's heavenly as I lower myself into the tub. The heat sears my skin, and I watch the steam rise off the water surrounding me. *My mother. I have a mother*, I think again as I smell the lavender-honey bath soap. I've always known I had a mother, but I stopped thinking about her so long ago. Now all those old questions are back. What does she look like? Do I look like her? Is she gentle? Is she interested in fashion? Does she have an eye for color? Is she healthy? Why didn't she want me all these years? What kind of car does she drive?

I soak for a few minutes, but I need to get going. I leave my hair wet and slip into a Juicy Couture sweatsuit that Morgan had brought and slipped into the bathroom. It feels like pure luxury, but I don't have time to focus on good gym wear. *I've got to get home.*

I come out of the bathroom devoid of garbage and actually refreshed to see Morgan tearing up again. "I'll be back," I announce as casually as I can.

"Go, Lilly. You've waited a lifetime for this day. We'll be fine," Morgan assures me.

I brush out my hair and look at Morgan who's still a bit ashen. "Are you sure you're going to be okay?"

"I'm fine. I knew this might happen someday."

I look into her gorgeous eyes, and I can't say I'm too disappointed she's not getting married, but I wish the man hadn't died to free her from the commitment.

I take my hugs all around and dash to the lobby to find transportation home. The clerk behind the counter is obviously upset at my appearance. I am Garbage Girl and certainly not the image they're looking for here in the wine country. Of course, my hair, starting to wave already, is straggled around my face, and it's so thick that it won't be dry before I reach home.

"Going somewhere?" Stuart appears behind me, and I feel my lungs fill up with air at the sight of him. If he truly is the creep Morgan makes him out to be, I see none of it.

"Home," I say in a rasp, trying to find my voice. "I was just getting a taxi," I say, not adding, *which I can't afford, but credit cards were invented for emergencies, am I right?* Of course, mine were also invented with this horrible thing called a low credit limit too. But how much could it cost to get home? It's only an hour or so. "Can you call me a taxi?" I say to the desk clerk.

"I'll take you home," Stuart says, his deep voice dripping with that heavenly English accent. "I've been called away for an urgent business meeting." Stuart tosses his bag, complete with zippered tennis racket compartment, over his shoulder. My stomach betrays me, doing that butterfly thing again at the sight of him.

If I have such incredibly bad taste in men, why can't I truly see it at all? See, he seems nice. He is offering me a ride. White knight rescues the princess and all that. Right?

"So what do you say, Miss Lilly? May I offer you a ride?"

"You're going home? I thought you were having dinner

with us." I thrust a hand to my hip. *He was going to stand me up!*

Stuart brings his hand to my chin. "Does dinner with the woman you're trying to leave behind along with the woman your heart cries out for sound cozy to you?"

I'm embarrassed to say that this cheesy line completely works on me, and I'm putty in his hands. *He is just so incredibly gorgeous!* And he says it with that English accent. *Did you hear that? His heart cries out for mine!* I think back to Nate's kiss. Excuse me—Stuart's kiss that I accidentally wasted on Nate Goddard—and I just don't know which way is up any longer.

"No, I suppose it wouldn't have been cozy," I whisper back, sort of breathy like Caitlyn. Maybe that's why she talks that way—it's Stuart!

"Where are your bags?" Stuart asks.

"Long story. I'm ready." I look into his chocolate brown eyes, and I see nothing that Morgan warned me about. Not one thing. If Stuart Surrey is bad to the core, I only see a plump, delicious red apple hanging in front of me, ripe for the taking. No core in sight.

"Does your having no luggage have something to do with your being in the garbage bin?" Stuart asks.

"Let's leave that alone, shall we?" The last thing I need is to relive my worst no-Lysol nightmare. Even the thought makes me crave a good spray of Green Apple Breeze!

Stuart leads me to his car, and I notice when we get outside he does look back over his shoulder. Sort of like Lot's wife. I cringe, as I feel incredibly like the "other woman." Morgan's voice is suddenly ringing in my ear. *You're not the best judge of men, Lilly.* Clearly. I wonder if my mother had that problem too. *Yikes! I'm meeting my mother.* The reality of that has yet to sink in because right now, I'm trying desperately to see what Morgan means about Stuart.

I'm having second thoughts. Being alone with Stuart is not

the best idea because, although I see nothing that Morgan is warning me about, I do trust her judgment and know she's really on my side. I just believe with my whole heart that Stuart wants to leave Caitlyn in the past, and she won't let him go. He's just trying to let her down gently, surely. *And playing a round of golf while staying comfortably ensconced in her daddy's hotel is letting her down how?* I try to ignore the niggling voice in my head.

"Are you sure you're ready to leave the hotel, Stuart? If not, I can catch a—"

"I'm ready, Lilly. I told you, I have a meeting." He looks down on me, my skepticism apparently obvious. "Caitlyn and I are taking a break. Really." He gives me a sideways smile.

"Why?" I allow my eyes to narrow threateningly at him.

He simply laughs. "Pardon me?" Stuart helps me into his BMW and leans over the open door.

"Why are you taking a break? How are you taking a break? Are you breaking up with her? Are you afraid to commit? Or are you worried there might be someone better out there?"

Stuart slams the door, comes around to the driver's seat, and slams his door behind him. "My, aren't you straightforward?"

Really now, what do I have to lose? Except my heart and my good reputation.

"Stuart, you asked me out. I see you at a hotel with another woman, playing golf. Then you're in her room. You owe me nothing, so I don't know why you'd bother with the façade. I appreciate the compliment you've just given me, but my life is complicated, and so is yours. I've enjoyed our little flirtation—"

"Wait a minute." Stuart slams on the brakes at the stop sign at the hotel's exit. "I think perhaps I've made myself unclear."

"Granted, you can't really dump someone that you don't

actually have a relationship with," I ramble. Then I remember Robert. "Well, technically, I guess you can, but I'm not dumping you. I'm just saying you're good-looking, you're charming, and you have a rich, beautiful girlfriend. I think you should stick with that. A bird in the hand, and all that—" I gaze out the window at the lovely vineyard on the rolling hills, proud of myself for my very mature stance.

Majestic oaks dot the canvas, and I wonder how on earth I get myself into these things. Although Morgan got herself into an engagement, Poppy got herself in a bad-fashion ditch, so maybe it's the three of us together. *What does a Christian call bad karma?*

"Lilly, I think perhaps you've misunderstood. I was looking for a friendship, not a romantic entanglement."

I'm gonna die.

"Well, with you, I mean," Stuart continues. He drives out onto the main Napa road with a thrust of German engineering. "Maybe I do want something better for myself, but I just felt like I knew you, like I could confide in you."

"About?" My heart is aflutter. I have the distinct feeling this is not something I want to hear.

"You really are unlike anyone I've met before."

And haven't I just made for a very long, uncomfortable ride home?

"So," I clap my hands together. "Then what shall we talk about? Are you a Forty-Niner fan?"

"Not really, no. Rugby, actually."

I'm now having a visualization of Colin Farrell in mud-drenched shorts. So wrong.

"Rugby. I don't know anything about rugby, other than it's violent."

"It is," Stuart agrees.

"So, how did you meet Caitlyn?"

"I met her at church. Lilly, I really feel I should explain something."

"Must you?" I mumble. "What did you like about Caitlyn when you met her?" Bringing up the old girlfriend definitely serves my purpose. It reminds me that Stuart is a bit of a louse and helps me avoid whatever dire news he seems anxious to share with me.

"Her confidence. Do you want to know what I liked about you when I met you?"

"No," I answer severely. "Not really."

"I'm not the player you think I am. I've been seeing a woman that I think highly of, but I don't think it has the potential for much more than that. Do you understand what I mean?"

I laugh. "Men who don't see potential? They move on quickly."

"That's what I'm trying to do. That's why Caitlyn and I were here today. I had no idea you'd be here with Morgan."

"I was up last night working. I'm a little tired," I say, changing the subject. "I think I'll just take a little nap." And I lean my head back against the BMW's lush leather seat. My eyes are fluttering, as I'm far too nervous to sleep, but I can't bear to hear what Stuart wants to tell me. Not today. Not right now.

chapter 23

"Where are you headed?" Stuart asks.

I open my eyes and see we're on the Golden Gate Bridge under a crisp blue sky with the bright red bridge thrust into the scattered clouds. The ocean to my right, the San Francisco Bay to my left, the world's most beautiful city before me, and the heavenly cliffs of Marin County behind me. I breathe in deeply. *I'm home.*

"Where to?" he asks again.

"I'm going to my grandmother's. She lives in the Marina."

Stuart turns toward me. "Your grandmother lives in the Marina? Impressive."

"She rents a room there." I have to admit, I never once thought about Max Schwartz, television critic, owning a home in the Marina. It's one of the most posh areas in San Francisco, and *why* did it not occur to me that a newspaper salary and that home didn't go together? Sometimes I think I'm the most selectively nonobservant person alive. I can notice the tiniest stitching detail on a Coach handbag but miss an entire mansion—pardon me, *estate*—that Max shares with my grandmother. My fears are confirmed. *I am an imbecile.* What is Max going to think when I drive up with a man in a BMW? When he knows I've been in the wine country for a respite.

That's all I need—him telling my Nana I've been on some sort of sordid getaway with a man in a great big foreign sedan.

I give Stuart directions from the bridge to my grandmother's place. I'm completely paralyzed at the thought of meeting my mother. *Will she like me? Will she think I'm loose for coming back with a man to meet her?*

"Will your grandmother drive you home?" Stuart asks. "Do you want me to come back for you?" Just by the way he offers, I can tell it isn't really an offer. It's his way of saying, "I'm a gentleman, and that's what gentlemen do; but please find your own way and spare me any more of this chauffeur business."

"No!" I swallow over the lump in my throat. "I don't know how long I'll be here. Thanks for the offer though." *As false as it was.*

"Call me on my cell if you need a ride, all right?" Stuart slides me another business card, and half of me wonders if pharmaceuticals are all this man is selling. He's as smooth as a freshly Zambonied patch of ice.

"Thanks." We pull up in front of my grandmother's place, and Max is outside the house, trimming a small hedge while he balances on his good leg. "I really appreciate the ride, Stuart." I try to race out of the car, and Stuart grabs my arm.

"I'll prove it to you. What I said is true. I am moving on."

"Thanks again!" I wave at him and slam the door. "Max!"

"Lilly," he says, without emotion.

"Well, that was quite a trip. A whirlwind tour and all that!"

"Who was that?" Max nods toward the taillights of the BMW.

"Morgan's friend, Stuart Surrey. He was at the hotel with—with his friend, and he offered me a ride home when Nana called."

"I would have sent a car for you," Max says, his eyes meeting mine. "You didn't need to resort to *him*."

"He was there at the hotel. With his girlfriend," I finally admit.

"I heard about Mildred's visitor. Don't worry about Sunday night. We can call things off. We'll just reschedule when the timing is better."

I feel real disappointment here. Nothing will ever happen with Max, but at least something was happening with me. A few days ago, I had three men I thought were possibilities. Now, I have none, and while I probably should be focusing on putting food on my table…heck, *having* a table…it's still a tad deflating.

There's something about the way Max looks at me, like he understands what I'm about to face. I don't for a moment get him, or his unlikely concern for my grandmother, so sure, I question his motives. But right now, I have no one else.

I grab his hand and look him straight in the eye. "I'm scared to go in there." I nod toward my grandmother's apartment. "What's she like?"

Max shrugs. "She's…she's sort of…hard-looking."

"Hard-looking?" I ask.

"Like she's lived a hard life. She looks older than she must be if she had you so young."

Max's words don't soothe me. I'm trembling now, and the idea of going into that lion's den is the last thing on my agenda. "Take me home, Max. Please? I should be back there with Morgan. I never should have left."

"I can't drive, Lilly." Max looks down at his broken leg apologetically. "Come on." He puts down his pruning scissors behind the gate. "We'll go in together. I have a very commanding presence," he winks. "It's the journalist in me. Scares people." He laughs.

I take his hand, and I feel everything within me shaking. I can't catch my breath, and I cling to his hand tightly. *Put one foot in front of the other*, I tell myself. Max walks with one crutch and leads me into the doorway where Nana is hunched over the sink, scrubbing the finish off it, no doubt.

"Nana?"

"Lillian," Nana exhales. "You're here."

"Where is she?"

"She's in the bathroom freshening up. She'll be out soon."

I look to Max, and I know my face is panic-stricken. *This is my mother.* The woman who gave birth to me, then left me with someone she barely knew. "What do I tell her I do for a living?"

"You're a designer, Lilly," Max reminds me.

"Not an employed one." I try to laugh, but it only comes out a muffled sob. Max wraps his arm around me, and brings my hand to his lips. He brushes my hand with the softest kiss, and for a moment I completely forget where I am. *Lord in heaven, I just want out of here.*

"You're the best designer I know," Max says.

Again, I try to laugh through my tears. "And you know how many designers?"

"You'd be surprised who I've met in my father's hotel. Maybe you're better than Donna Karan. Did you ever think of that?"

When I look up at Max, there's something in his eyes that makes me all of a sudden want to kiss him. There are moments in life when God puts just the right people in place. This is one of those times. I pull my gaze away. I know it's just the emotion of the moment and needing to be wanted. Isn't it? I mean, an hour ago I was lusting over an Englishman with a girlfriend, who seemed more than anxious to ditch me in some special way. Clearly, I'm having major issues and mass confusion. This is not the time to be thinking about romance, a subject which I fail at regardless of my timing.

The bathroom door slowly opens, and I swallow hard,

trying to calm my beating heart. I fear she's going to know how nervous I am, just by hearing my throbbing pulse. She walks toward me, and I clutch Max's hand until I see his fingers go white. I force myself to let go and allow my eyes to swallow the vision: she's nothing like I imagined all these years.

"You're blond" is the first thing out of my mouth. She has lovely, long blond hair and deep hazel eyes. There's not a sign of frizz or the need for John Frieda anywhere on her person. And her skin…it's not olive like mine. It's ruddy with a pink tinge; and she has full, round cheeks. She's not a small woman, and I'm beginning to wonder if I might have been switched at birth. Because she also actually has a bust. *All right, Lord, what happened?*

"I used to be blond," she says. "Now I pay dearly for the privilege."

We both laugh nervously. I see that she does look like life has taken her down a rough path. Lines are etched strongly in her cheeks and around her mouth, and I smell the cigarette smoke on her and maybe just a touch of pine-smelling gin. *Where's my Lysol?*

"Do you live in San Francisco?" I ask her, thinking about how many times I've searched the crowd, wondering if she might be out there somewhere. Wondering if I'd see my own eyes staring back at me one day in the city. I never would have looked for a blond, though. Or a woman with a bust. I clearly got robbed.

"No, I live in Missouri."

I laugh, thinking about my lack of geographic knowledge, and my friends saying I should know where Missouri is on the map. *I guess they were right.*

"What do you do there in Missouri?"

"I have a family. Two boys and a girl."

I gasp. These words hit me hard—really hard. I never

once thought about another family, but of course she has another family. My mind races to process this. "I have brothers? And a sister?"

"They don't know about you yet. Here are some photos I brought for you. Alisa is sixteen. Jeremy is fourteen, and Joshua is thirteen." She hands me the pictures, and three towheaded blond teenagers stare back at me. "I didn't want to tell them in case you didn't want anything to do with me. But my husband knows. I came with his blessing. I've kept you a secret all these years. But as you got older, I wondered if you might seek me out. I decided to be proactive."

Nana is busying herself in the kitchen. I have no idea what she thinks of this meeting. This is the woman who slept with her eighteen-year-old son. Right before he died. The woman who abandoned her granddaughter one Sunday afternoon without warning and left me for her to raise. She left to get some diapers and never returned. Nana slams a cookie sheet on the countertop. *All right. I guess I have some idea what she thinks.*

"I'm going back to my hotel." She grabs my hand and shakes it like we're at a business meeting. "It's been a long day, as you can imagine. My name is Tammy. Well, I guess you know that. But Jamison is my last name, and this is where you can reach me if you want further contact." She hands me a wrinkled sheet of hotel stationery with her information scrawled across it. "I wanted to meet you for so long, but especially before your thirtieth birthday. Neither one of us is getting any younger, you know." She tries to grin, but it looks more like a grimace. I just stare at her.

"No," I whisper. "We're not."

"I want to give you time to digest all of this. You're a mighty beautiful girl. Your grandmother tells me you're a fabulous designer, and that you have a master's degree from

Stanford. I couldn't be more proud of you, Lillian." She runs her hand along my cheek and quickly heads for the door as if I'm following her with a meat cleaver.

I want to say something, but my mouth doesn't work. I watch her leave. I turn and snuggle into Max's chest, desperately needing to be hugged. She didn't hug me. My mother didn't even hug me. I feel Max's mouth beside my ear, and his breath is warm against my hair. "You *are* a beautiful girl," he whispers.

"Ever the drama queen, that Tammy," Nana says, and I quickly pull away from Max.

"What did you say?" I asked in a daze, trying to focus on my Nana.

"It's all about her. She's got a daughter with a master's from Stanford and her own design business, and what does she do? Calls you home from the spa, stays five minutes, and makes it all about her: Her family. Her husband. I don't know what I expected from a woman who would abandon her own child."

My jaw muscles tighten. "But I have siblings, Nana. That's exciting."

Nana smiles a little then and nods her head, "So you do, Lilly. Maybe you'll get to meet them someday." She goes back to cleaning, and I know she's hurt. My grandmother has always been harsh with me, but harsher still on anyone who would dare hurt me. She wanted the best from me, and I think she's missing the actual warmth gene, but as for consistency? There's no one like my Nana. She'd come back from the grave to help me if she could.

"Do they actually have planes that go to the middle states?" I wink at her, and she really smiles then. It's a small gesture, just between us, that says: *Everything is okay, Nana. You are my one and only mother. And you are still my daughter—fashion dreams and all.*

"Now, I've got bingo tonight." Nana breaks up the sentimental moment and begins bustling around. "You okay? Madeline is picking me up in a few minutes, and there's leftover pasta in here," she bangs the fridge, "if you and Max are hungry. You do know how to use a microwave?"

"I'm fine, Nana." And surprisingly, I am. I have a birthmother. But if the truth is told, I'm more interested at this moment in what's going on with this quiet TV reporter in front of me. If only because his warm whisper was just what I needed a few seconds ago, and I'm wondering exactly how he knew that.

But back to my birthmother: she has a family. Wow! I sort of imagined her living on the street somewhere, crushed by the terrible mistake she'd made so many years ago, you know? Someone sort of drinking out of a paper bag and all. Well, I guess we know where the drama queen comes from. Emotionally, she seemed pretty detached, which I guess makes sense. She doesn't know me from Adam, but it still rubs me raw. I guess I hoped for something a little more maternal. Like that there would be this deep emotional bond that couldn't be broken by time or distance. *But yeah, didn't really feel it.* You know, maybe she actually felt bad for abandoning me as a baby. Is that too much to ask? I start to feel anger begin to build, before I remember—like the Bible says—that I can capture every thought. I struggle but stamp it down.

I bite my lip and look into Max's eyes. He smiles. Not with his lips, but with his eyes. Suddenly, without any warning whatsoever, the fascination with Stuart Surrey completely evaporates from my mind, taking the momentary fixation on Nate Goddard with it. My attention is fully focused on Max. He was the one who was here for me. Just like Nana.

See, my Nana and I have never had a man around, and we did okay. But that didn't stop me from wanting one of my own. I have the sappy dream of the white picket fence and Mr. Right bringing flowers home as he hops over the little fence, and I yell, "Honey, watch the pansies!" But inside, I'm laughing at his curious ways and the flowers in his hands, while the children gather at my feet to welcome their dad home. It's a bad 1950s sitcom. I know that, but it doesn't stop the dream.

There's this weird thing that happens when your mother doesn't care enough to raise you, a sort of deep-rooted insecurity that no one will ever care enough to stick around. There's this fear that you're not good enough to keep, not special enough for anyone to want you that way. But the yearning for it never goes away.

"Lilly, did you hear me?" Nana asks.

"Yes," I say, still looking at Max. "Leftover pasta in the fridge. Are you hungry, Max?" I raise an eyebrow.

"Ravenous," he says with a sideways grin. "Why don't we take it upstairs, so we can see the city lights while we eat?"

"It's not dark out," I remind him.

"It will be," he whispers.

Nana plops the cold bowl of pasta in my hands, which pulls me out of my thoughts. "Ah! That's cold!"

"I taught her to cook, Max. Don't let her play dumb with you. Lilly, make him a vegetable and some French bread to go with that. There's starter for the dough on the counter."

"French bread takes for—" I clutch the bowl of pasta tightly. "How about if I take your Jaguar to get some bread at the store?" *Because I could really get used to driving a little horsepower without the need for disinfectant spray.*

"I'm in no hurry. Homemade bread sounds divine, and I'll wait. Where do I have to go?" He looks down at his leg. There's a horn blaring now for Nana.

"Bake the man some bread," she barks. "It's good practice

for you. Someday a man's going to want you to cook for him, and Max is good practice. He likes everything." She grabs her coat and her purse, and she slams the door behind her.

"Yeah, someday a man's going to want you to cook for him," Max grins.

I slap his arm. "I'll have you know, I have—"

"I know, you have a degree in finance. From *Stanford*, no less! But I'll be more impressed if you can bake bread like your grandmother." Max winks. "And do the laundry without turning my shorts pink."

"Chauvinist!" I roll my eyes. I'm really not in the mood to cook anyone's dinner. I want to go home and wallow in the fact that *my mother*, the woman I've dreamt of every day of my life, just breezed in and out of my life again. Leaving me standing here alone and feeling disoriented. Well, alone except for Max, who interrupts my thoughts again.

"Are you all right?" He meets my eyes once more.

"I am, I think. But that was sort of weird, wasn't it? That she had me come all that way home for a five-minute introduction to her family? I've imagined this day my whole life, and that so wasn't it. I thought I'd find the reason for my hair, hear why she *had* to leave me. I wanted to hear about my dad from her point of view."

"She was in here for some time with your Nana. Maybe she'd reached her limit. Or maybe just seeing how gorgeous and accomplished her daughter was, she felt inadequate."

I can't help but laugh. "That must have been it."

"I don't imagine being here with Mildred was easy on her."

"Good point. Still, I would think I'd actually want to know what my daughter loved, what her dreams are, what kind of dresses she designed."

"You will know all those things, because you will raise your daughter. Am I right?"

I nod. "Well, if I ever procreate at all. The world can probably do without another generation of my hair."

Max pulls at the tips of my bangs. "I love your hair. It's whimsical and fun, just like you. So, are you making me bread?" Max is looking straight into my eyes again, and I'll admit his gaze unnerves me. I'm a bundle of nerves after this day: death, a dumpster, a mother who doesn't live in a dumpster, siblings, and a man who likes my hair. I mean, it would be a lot for an average year in my life.

I notice, not for the first time, that Max has very little hair. If he lost the glasses and got a cowboy hat, he'd look strikingly like Tim McGraw with a lighter goatee. He'd be handsome if I were into the slight, intellectual type who wastes his talent on television reviews. But I'm not; and I can't trust my emotions anyway. Not today. Less than an hour ago, I thought I was falling for a man who only wanted to be my friend— and you know, getting dumped didn't sound any better with an English accent. *Tim McGraw is awfully good-looking. He makes me almost want to like country music.*

"But I don't like country music!" I exclaim, out loud, and with entirely too much force.

"Okay." Max shrugs. "And this matters to me, because—? I'm not planning to serenade you with Johnny Cash."

"I'll make you dinner." I point at his chest. "But there's nothing going on here, all right?"

"Did I say there was?" Max raises his eyebrows at me.

"Come on, all that talk about the city lights? I remember the submarine race offers when I was in school. I may be naïve, but I'm not completely dense."

"The last time you were at my house, you really berated me for keeping all the curtains shut. I've heard you complain that you have no windows, so I just thought I'd share mine. That's all."

"And you're in no hurry for dinner?" I say breathily, like he had. "What was that about?"

"I'm not in any hurry." Max grabs his crutch and hobbles toward the door, looking back at me. "Why are you so suspicious of everything, Lilly? What do you think I would have to gain by hurting you?" He shakes his head. "You should know I'd never do anything to harm your Nana's granddaughter." He steps out the door and attempts to slam it behind him, except that his crutch gets caught. He pulls the crutch out and slams it again. Hard.

The way he looked at me, so hurt. Wounded, almost. *Forgive me, Lord. Why do I have to be man poison?* I put the spaghetti back in the refrigerator and remind myself that I have designing to do! Let Valeria come cook for him. I've wasted this entire day, missed the proverbial boat—not to mention my facial and massage—at the spa, reconnected with a mother who treated me like the bag boy at Safeway, gotten two dates completely canceled, and left my friends like toppled bowling pins in my angry wake. I'm definitely better with fabric.

But as I look into the fridge and see the dough starter, I'm reminded that I have no way home, and Max *should* eat. I can catch a cab anytime.

I reach for the dough, plop it on the bowl, gather what's left of my self-respect, and open the door. Max is leaning against the wall. He smiles at me. "Are you ready to cook now?"

"I'm taking this home. I was waiting for my cab." *Total lie.* I hope God has better things to do at the moment than listen, but I know He's up there just shaking His head at me—again.

"You called a cab in that minute and a half?"

"I didn't say I called one. I said I was waiting for one."

"Well," Max stares down the completely empty street, "I sure hope one just happens by for you." He laughs.

"You think this is really funny, don't you?"

"I don't see what you have against making dinner for a fine Christian boy like me. One: I would appreciate dinner." He holds up a finger. "I would like your company." Two fingers. "I would provide you with a gorgeous view of the Golden Gate Bridge." Three fingers. "All for a little warmed-up spaghetti and a fresh loaf of French bread. You're a business woman, Lilly, and it's a good deal. A solid investment." He smiles, and his eyes just twinkle.

It is a good deal because I really don't want to be alone, and I don't want to face Kim or Nate either. "I'll come up and make your dinner, since you can't get around very well, but then I'm going home. I should have never left my loft this weekend. I have work to do, dresses to make, a business to run." But in my mind, I'm thinking, *Will I ever see my mother again? Morgan's lost her fiancé, and I'm not there to help her. What kind of friend am I? And why am I worried about making dinner for my Nana's landlord?* And underneath it all, the running mantra: *I have bad hair that sealed my fate long ago in a galaxy far, far away.*

"I appreciate that. You are a busy woman." Max motions with his hand. "After you." As I start up the stairs, he starts to whistle. "Ah, yes, the view is just fabulous from here."

I whirl around and glare down at him. "What did you just say?"

His entire face fills with a slightly wicked grin. "The view from my place," he says, all innocence. "It's just incredible. Wait until you see it."

"That better be what you meant."

We climb the stairs, with Max actually doing pretty well for a leg that's straight as a board. When we reach the top, I help him up the last step. "You made it."

"We made it." He stops in front of me. He towers over me.

I always thought of Max as smaller in stature, but as he stands right here with me, I see that he's not at all. I just thought he was because he seemed insignificant to my life, kind of like a hovering gnat. In reality, he's probably nearly six feet, and he does look like Tim McGraw. This is not good. He moistens his lips.

"I need to get this spaghetti going," I say nervously. I open up his door, and his place is like I've never seen it before. Yes, there's a huge television screen, but the wall of windows, the expensive furniture, the house in the Marina. *Selectively unobservant—that's me!* "What is it you really do for money, Max? Do you sell drugs?"

He laughs. "No, that would be your friend, Stuart."

I whirl around. "How did you know Stuart was in pharmaceuticals? You know Stuart?"

"I go to church with him. And Caitlyn Kapsan. Haughty bunch, Lilly. You can do better."

I feel my breath leave my body like a rogue wave rushing back out to sea. "Just never mind. You're changing the subject. I asked you what you do for a living."

"I write a newspaper column about what's on TV. Maybe you've seen it?"

"You don't own a house in the Marina with a journalist's salary. And you offered to give me the money for my business. What do you do, Max? Tell me, or I'm not making dinner." Granted, I know his parents own a hotel chain, but I want to hear it from his mouth. I want him to admit he's been lying about living on his TV reporter salary and not taking anything from his wealthy parents.

"I'm an heir, Lilly. Like Prince Charles without the ears. Sound romantic?"

I shrug. "You could have said like Prince William. It has more *oomph*."

"I'll remember that the next time I'm confessing my sin of being wealthy."

I slam the bowl down on the table. "It's just that you lied by omission, Max. You made Nana and me believe you were this pathetic loser who does nothing but watch TV. You even got my Nana to help you watch TV so you could write a better column."

"I never lied. I *am* a pathetic loser who does nothing but watch TV—oh, and occasionally climb into and fall out of air vents in my father's hotel. Having money makes me no less pathetic, if that's what you're thinking."

"It makes you more pathetic." *What am I saying?*

"Because I didn't earn it? Well, you've got me there, pal. Thanks for the reminder."

"No, you can't help how you're born. I know that more than anyone. The pathetic part is that you push away who you are."

"Sort of like you straightening that hair?"

"How do you know I straighten my hair?"

"Your Nana has pictures of you since you were a baby—I know your secret. What is it you have against men with money, Lilly? Are you afraid your degree in finance will go to waste if you find a rich man?"

"I don't like money. I don't like what it does to people," I say, thinking in particular about Morgan's father and Caitlyn Kapsan.

"What's it done to me, Lilly?" He pulls open his shutters to reveal the Golden Gate Bridge over a crystal blue bay. "Got me a great view, right?"

"It has made you a liar. You pretended you had no idea who that was who dropped me off tonight, and you knew all along it was Caitlyn's boyfriend. You told me some long-winded story about that drop-dead gorgeous Valeria, when she was really your girlfriend who dumped you. You lied."

"I didn't lie. Okay, it was a sin of omission, if you will. But she wasn't my girlfriend. She was a woman after me for my money. You were right, okay? I should have known a twenty-year-old wasn't interested in my mind or my heart, but I chose ignorance, okay? Feel better now?"

"Well, most men would have taken the bait, so why wouldn't you? I can forgive you for that. You're living here alone, having dinner with my Nana, of all people."

"Lilly, *really*, what do you have against rich people?"

I think about this for a long time before I answer. It seems my life has always been missing what mattered at the time: jeans when they were in style and I had miniskirts; Jennifer Aniston hair when I looked like Bon Jovi; and Stanford money when I was in school on a government grant.

"Money ruins people. It takes away the essence of who they are, and covers it with a fancy house or a gown." *What am I saying?* "Wait, I don't believe that, Max. I don't know what to believe." I don't even really know what I think. I just want to be away from my feelings. I just want to work on clothes and not have to deal with any of this. I want my mother to go away, I want my Nana to care what I want, and I want Max Schwartz to come clean and tell me who he really is inside. But as I gaze into his eyes, I wonder if that's really what I want. Max is a straight shooter, and I'm just not sure I'm ready for his version of truth.

"So, if I take a vow of poverty, would you be interested?"

I can't tell if he's serious or just baiting me. "I'm not interested, period. Men confuse me. I'm married to my work, and I don't have time for relationships." As I say the words, I feel the tears starting to sting. Max walks towards me, and I don't trust myself. "No!" I hold up my palm. "I don't want your pity. Sit down and watch some TV. I'm cooking, and then I'm leaving."

He starts forward again.

"I mean it, Max. Sit down."

So I open his fridge, where he has organic produce for a salad. I take out the ingredients, and as I chop the onion with a vengeance, I cry until the first lights come on across the Bay. Blessed are those who mourn, for they shall be comforted. *Where is my comfort, Lord?* Blessed are the poor in spirit, for theirs is the kingdom of heaven. *Okay, God, can we get the heaven part started? Because this part sucks like a Hoover.*

'd like to say the rest of the evening was completely void of
romantic emotions and that I wasn't the slightest bit tempted
by Max's charm. But that would be lying. While he did stir
something in my heart, I prefer to think it was just indigestion
from Nana's sauce. Max was there for me tonight, and that
means a lot, but that's probably it. I am the world's worst judge
of men, and the only good that will come of finally learning
this life lesson is if I stay single for all of eternity. Like Saint
Paul. *Only I don't want to go through that shipwreck, stoning,
unidentified thorn-in-the-flesh business if it's okay with You, God.*

Leaving my love life in the dumpster where it belongs,
there's the financial woes of late to think about instead. I realize that I owe everyone and their brother money, and I have a
business that amounts to little more than—speaking of
dumpsters—formerly drenched, now-hopefully-dry-cleaned,
canceled-wedding fabric, along with the other fabric purchased
on Morgan's credit card. So when I enter my loft's dark hallway, after forcing Max to let me take a cab (he insisted on
paying, and I didn't fight him; he got a good dinner), my
exhausted mind is back on the work that awaits me.

When I get to the door, it's slightly ajar. None of the seven
locks is latched. *Danger, Will Robinson. Danger!* the voice in my

head cries. Still, I ignore it and push the door open, only to see a huge flatscreen television playing Spiderman and Nate munching on popcorn, while Kim sews at the table behind him.

"What are you *doing*?" I shriek, looking at my beloved fabric in Kim's hands. "I asked you not to touch anything!" I feel a sense of hysteria rising, and it is definitely not because of Nana's sauce.

"I wanted to save you some time. You've been so busy, and I thought I owed you. Nate got this TV for next to nothing from China. He says we can have it!"

"We cannot have it. Nate, we aren't Goodwill." *Take your guilt offering, and shove it!*

"Speak for yourself," Kim says. "I'm *so* Goodwill. No wait, I'm his cheaper cousin, the Dollar Tree."

I rush to the table to look at the stitching, and my mouth drops in awe. "This is good, Kim."

"I have more incentive to do a good job for you than I had with Sara. You let me live here, and I still have nowhere else to go, Lilly."

"What are you doing home?" Nate asks.

"I got called away from the spa."

"Did you get the wedding gown drawn for Morgan?" Kim asks.

"There's no wedding. Morgan's fiancé died."

"Dang, I know you said he was old, but dang!"

"He wasn't that old. He had a bad liver."

"Ah, that's awful, man. Well, at least you can use her fabric. Maybe Robert will want it for his bride."

"Kim, do you mind? I'm not making a gown for Robert's fiancée. She already got my man."

"Oh, here we go," Nate pipes up, without taking his eyes off *Spiderman*. "The *woe is me* story of Robert. Remember in science how there are protons, electrons, and neutrons. Robert was a neutron, completely void of any charge."

Kim starts to crack up. I mean, she's giggling giddily at this geek humor. What is going on? And then I see the closet, with dresses, *yes, plural, dresses,* hanging in it. I rush to the doorway. "What is this?"

"A few of the gowns you designed. I did all the patterns this morning, and I had some people from Sara Lang come help sew this afternoon. Everyone wants you to make it, Lilly." She says this like she's shocked. I grab the gowns and study them carefully. They look just like I imagined. Maybe better! I can't believe it.

Kim goes on. "I only took a short break when Nate and I went to get everyone coffee. Otherwise, I've been here all day. We had a great time. People brought their machines, Nate brought in the television and Chinese takeout. It was fun, actually. I forgot how much I really do like to work with clothes. Nate put the designs on the computer and printed out the patterns. He made sure I had the right fabric, and that the thread matched. We were a great pair, weren't we?"

"You bet," Nate says with a wink.

I pick up one of the dresses in the closet. "Kim, the stitching is perfection."

"These are your best designs, Lilly." She picks up the pad. "I think we should put them for sale on eBay, as a couture shop. We can put in the listings that we both worked for Sara Lang for years and that your expertise in gowns is renowned. We can say these gowns would be $5,000 in Saks. Plus, I thought you might go around to some of Sara's boutiques and see if they'd carry them."

"Kim," I say breathlessly. I mean, I'm just stunned. Just when you think your life is completely falling apart and there isn't a speck of blue in the cloudy sky, someone surprises you like this. "I could kiss you!" Normally, it takes at least a week for a gown, so I know they're not exactly couture or Sara Lang quality, but they're good. They're really good. Good enough for a show, or even a shop on Geary.

"Nate worked up a business plan for you today, and he just spent the day brainstorming while I sewed. He says we can have Sara completely out of the business in four months, according to his projections."

I look through the papers, and I'm completely stunned silent.

"Lilly, you're an excellent designer. We just have to find a place to sell these things," Nate says. Truthfully, I don't know what to think. Once, I played this game called *Fact or Crap?* This is like that, and I can't tell which one this is.

"You mean you're going to help?" I ask Kim. Wasn't she just yelling at me to leave her alone? I know all of this is probably only a guilt offering on Kim's part, but I'm in no position to look a gift horse in the mouth, now am I? Besides, it's really good to see her energy going into something positive, rather than deciding on where her next tattoo should be.

"Everything's a perfect size eight. We can take things in or out depending on the customer, or better yet, custom-make copies and sizes to order." Kim pushes her hair back, revealing the small ladybug tattoo on her forehead next to the hairline. "Nate, I'm going to go up to your place for a minute and get Charley. I'm done for the day, and the poor dog needs some company. I finished his new bed today too." She holds up the doggie bed I'd started.

"Yeah, yeah, you go," Nate says.

Suddenly, I feel as if they're trying to leave me alone with Nate, and I'm not exactly comfortable with the notion. I've never been kissed like that. Not once in my poor twenty-nine—okay, almost thirty—years of existence, and I don't want to know why he was with another woman less than a day later. I don't want to know why he'd give Kim a $3,000 television set. Regardless of what it costs in China. Ignorance is really bliss here.

Kim leaves and shuts the door. Nate stands up and stares at me, rubbing his hands together nervously.

"Is there something wrong?"

He scratches the side of his neck. "Sit down, Lilly. There's something I need to tell you."

I don't like the sound of this. I am suddenly inexorably weary from riding the day's emotional rollercoaster (not to mention the physical effort exerted climbing in and out of dumpsters); I don't think I can face any more. "No, no more today. I've heard more than you can possibly imagine today. Please, no more." My whole brain just shuts down at the thought of more bad news.

Nate just nods. "Fair enough. We'll talk about it another day," he says anxiously.

I look into his eyes, and I wonder what he's thinking. Does he think I'm in love with him? Because my kiss *had* to make him believe that. Well, it at least had to make him think I was desperate. It had been so long since anyone kissed me, and I guess there was pent-up emotion. Plus, I did have Stuart's gorgeous baritone accent in the back of my mind. Didn't I?

I mean, the fact is, I barely see straight men in the realm of my existence. What I am used to are clean-cut, well-dressed, good-looking men with exceptional manners who have absolutely no interest in women. *Sigh! Of course* my feelers are off when it comes to heterosexuals. Gay men do tend to have more charm, with the exception of Shane Wesley. Okay, I can face up to it. I was a little overzealous with my Nate kiss. What of it? I am a straight, Christian woman, living in San Francisco, working in the fashion industry. Does that not tell you I'm a little desperate?

"If this is about us, I know that the kiss was a fluke, Nate. Okay? Enough said?"

Nate nods. "Good. Enough said." We both look at the expansive television screen where Kirsten Dunst has just removed a hanging Spiderman mask and is kissing Tobey Maguire hard under a rain-drenched night.

This is uncomfortable.

"I'm going to take a shower," I announce, hoping Nate will get the hint and make himself scarce.

"Yeah. I'll let Kim know when she comes in." He flicks off the television. "I might just check on her and Charley."

"That would be good." *Don't let the door hit you on the way out.*

I run into the bathroom and slam the door, banging my head against the back of it. *That was so humiliating.* "Okay, you know, Lord, I'm good with the fact that I am not a prom queen. I'm okay with the fact that I never even got asked to the prom. I'm even okay with the fact that I'm still dateless after being asked out twice this week. But must You bring me face-to-face with each of my latest mistakes continuously?" *Maybe that's the point. Maybe I need to learn from these mistakes before I can move on and not have to face them again.* I slide down the door to the bathroom floor and find a lone can of Lysol disinfectant. I spray at will, and soon the manufactured scent of apples washes over me and my new Juicy sweatsuit. Life is good when it's freshly disinfected.

chapter 25

Men come in threes. Like bad luck. God never sends a man with a big red arrow pointing down on him, as if to say, "This is him. He's the one." No, instead, you get mass confusion, where it's raining men in buckets, or total silence, where the dating scene is as dry as a creek bed in the Mojave. Those are the choices. Feast or famine.

Which I could completely handle if I was having a feast, but all I have is three men who have filled me with deep and utter confusion. This only adds another pitiful dimension to the girl with bad hair and an unprofitable business. On the one hand, there's Stuart, who drives me crazy with his accent and the way he looks at me. Although he asked me out, he really just wants a friend. *Can't he just go to the pound, like Nate did?*

On the other hand, there's Nate, whom I never would have looked at twice until he kissed me like Bond. James Bond. The result of which is that he now cannot stand to be alone in my presence for longer than ten minutes.

And on the third hand (yes, the *third* hand; see the problem?), there's Max. This ridiculous hotel heir, TV reporter who lives in the Marina on his parents' money, watches television like it's a sport, and flirts like the high school jock who never grew up. And, I have to admit, was there for me when I needed someone—and who looks like a balding Tim McGraw. So I have to ask: which is worse—feast or famine? Or more appropriately feast that still feels like a famine?

It's Saturday morning, and I'm feeling like I wish I was in Napa with the Spa Girls, but I am so grateful that I have gowns for an actual collection that I could jump up and down. I call Morgan on her cell, anxious to tell her about my mother, and how anticlimactic it really was. *I waited my whole life for that?*

"Hey, Lilly, it's Poppy. Morgan went for a run."

"Of course she did. Why didn't you go with her?"

"I'm having a sloth day. I already watched *Pirates of the Caribbean*."

"That's my girl!"

"Well, what was she like?"

"Blond, buxom, and bored."

"With life, or what?"

"With me, I think. She didn't give me more than a passing glance. There was no 'I carried you in my womb for nine months' emotion or anything."

"Were you expecting that?"

"I was a little hopeful, I guess. I thought maybe I'd endured all those years of ridicule because…ah, I don't know. I thought I'd find some answers, but I'm just as ignorant today as I was yesterday. Oh wait, that's not true. Now I have a definite beef with God about my hair."

Poppy laughs, and I have so much more I want to tell her. I want to ask her about Stuart and Nate and even Max. But there isn't time. There's an anxious Sara Lang at the start of my week, and I don't want to keep her waiting.

"They called from downstairs. Your fabric is cleaned. It actually looks pretty good. We're bringing it home. Oh, and

Morgan is over most of her crying jags. Just a few sniffles once in a while."

"Great news on both fronts. I know just what I'm going to do with that fabric now. See ya soon." We hang up, and I look at my fabulously clean apartment, and all the beautiful creations surrounding it. This is how I imagined my future. Only, now it's here!

I start fingering the gowns that Kim and crew made from my designs, and I have to say, I didn't know she had it in her to do such careful work. The stitching is impeccable, and it truly looks like a labor of love. It makes me feel like I'm actually in business.

"Do you like them? Are they as good as you imagined?" Kim comes out from behind her screen.

"They're perfect, Kim. I don't know what to say."

"I know you told me not to touch anything, but I knew there was no way you could have done these gowns by yourself, and Sara would have had your head. I knew we could do it, and I wanted you to come home to something tangible. You've been so worried about money, and I was afraid you might go back into the money business. I couldn't bear it."

I look her in the eye. Somehow I have a hard time with the concept that Kim is suddenly so worried about my going back into finance. It was a guilt offering, and I know this, but I'm cool with the charade. It makes us both happy.

I hold up a pale green chiffon gown, with a small cashmere half-sweater to match. "I imagined it looking just like this, but there's something so strange about holding something you created. Not for Sara Lang, but for a customer I don't even know yet. She could be out there ready to buy, needing the perfect gown for the Oscars or the Grammies, and I have it right here." I look around my loft. "Right here, in this scummy apartment."

Kim throws back her head and examines it too. "I cleaned it, at least."

"I noticed that. Any reason for it?"

"Well," Kim looks down at her feet, "there is, actually."

I can tell what's coming by the way she won't look me in the eye. "You're moving out."

"Lilly, listen. I know when Jen left, you and I never quite hit our stride here in the loft, but I totally think we make great business partners. It's just that you live like a nun, Lilly. I can't handle your judgment, and the way you roll your eyes when I happen to get drunk—"

"I was never judgmental. When I was in those shady bars, and scared to death, I wasn't judging, I was fearing for my life actually. Would you rather I hadn't picked you up? That I let you drink to your heart's content or get killed while driving under the influence?"

"Yes, you should have. Because I'm a grown-up. I don't drive drunk, and I don't bring guys home here. Even if I did, you're not my mother, Lilly. You're my roommate, and just because you choose to live a chaste existence doesn't mean the rest of us have to."

Her words sting me. Maybe I do act like her mother. I never meant to be judgmental, but *hello?* Was she not planning to go to Angel Island with a guy she didn't even know? Okay, that's just stupid, and while I'm not one to buy into Darwin's theories, "survival of the fittest" seems to fit here.

"I *used* to be your roommate, right?" I correct her. Then she drops the bombshell.

"I thought if you moved in with your Nana, you'd have more money and more time to get the business off the ground. Look at these preliminaries Nate has done for you." She pushes the paperwork in my face, trying to make me believe that moving in with Nana is the answer to my woes.

"You can have this business profitable in six months. You won't be able to pay back Morgan yet, but Sara will be free and clear. You can just give her back what's left of the check. Nate's done all the spreadsheets. You just follow these."

Oh, so simple. Except that it would ruin what's left of my life! "I am not moving in with my Nana!" I laugh. "When are you leaving? I'll find a new roommate." *There has to be someone out there who likes the scent of Lysol as much as I do.*

"You do what you want, but I am moving. Nate and I—"

"Wait a minute." I drop the paperwork. "What did you just say?"

"I'm moving into Nate's place. He's going to cover me on rent until I get back on my feet, and I think with the business, that won't be long." She pauses here. "If you still want me, naturally."

I can't think of a thing to say. I just stand here staring at her. Awestruck. I reach for the door, exit, and slam it behind me. I stomp up the stairs to Nate's loft, ready to strangle him the moment I get my hands on him. I pound on the door.

Nate opens the door. "Kim told you."

"How could you? If you want to be someone's knight in shining armor—" I stop short of what I want to say. *Why couldn't you be mine?*

"It's not what you're thinking. I'm happy to have her company. She's happy for the safety factor, not to mention the security factor. We said we wanted to get her help, right? I think I can do that for her, and she'll have a job with you, right?"

I get a whiff of Charley's ears. "Nate, can't you do something about that? Do you think I want Kim working with my material when she smells like your sewer-rotten dog?"

The dog whines, and Nate grabs his ears. "Do you mind, Miss PETA? This isn't about you, Lilly. It's about Kim and me."

"No, it's not about Kim at all. It's about you, Nate Goddard."

"If this is about us…"

"Don't flatter yourself. This has nothing to do with that. This has to do with Kim. Less than a week ago, she ran off with my money and a guy she met in a bar. She needs help, Nate, not another shack-up partner."

"I'm not a pastor. Kim and me, we have an understanding when we're lonely."

His words hit me like a sledgehammer. I never thought they would be more than roommates until he said that. The week's load comes tumbling down on me in full force, and I sway, bracing myself against the door. I haven't got a friend on earth. That's what it feels like, and I know what I have to do. I have to try to get some sleep, then get back to the spa. Morgan and Poppy are like Jesus in that they'll never forsake me. At least not for $20,000 or a flatscreen television.

chapter 26

never got back to the spa yesterday. I spent the day whimpering and sewing, trying to keep my tears from staining the fabrics. I slept long and hard after that. I needed time to digest the news. I knew nothing would come of Nate and me. I knew what my Bible had to say about such a relationship, but I never thought it would end here. I never thought I'd be tied to him financially. And I never thought I'd have to watch my former roommate and now employee have some kind of relationship with him that kicks me in the gut every time I witness it.

Sunday morning shines brightly, and I have a long prayer time, since I am forgoing church to return to my Spa Girls. I apologize for ever allowing my feelings to get the best of me. *I knew better.* It's all I can think, and I imagine God gets tired of hearing my mantra before my quiet time is over. I rush to pack a new bag for the spa when the phone rings. I pause, thinking it could be my mother and I might have to cancel my day's plans, but I pick up anyway. "Lilly Jacobs Design."

"Lilly, it's Sara Lang."

I'll never learn.

"Sara." *My boss. Maneater. Daughter's boyfriend stealer and all-around negative energy impulse.* "I was going to call you about all you asked me to do for the new business. I've done a business plan, and I just can't work the *Vogue* contest into my schedule." I'm doing my best Erica Kane impression. (Who says soap operas aren't good education?) "I need to get a collection built as soon as possible, and I just thought that was a more efficient use of my time than the contest."

"Lilly, I don't have time for this."

Welcome to the club. The Vogue *contest is a risk, and time I just don't have.*

Thoughts of my Nana's investment in my education come rushing to the forefront. *There are some deals that just cost too much.* "I'm completely overwhelmed, Sara," I say, my chin tilted up in the air for added confidence. "You should really just have your accountant hold your funding." Nate did one thing for me. His projections and estimates of what I *have* to sell were brilliant, making my creations a matter of simple math. Sure, I could have done it had I sat down and not panicked, but I was so not in that place.

"Quit your crazy talk. It's Fashion Week coming up," Sara says, clearly not hearing anything I'm saying.

"I know. I have the gown I promised you, Sara. I'm just saying I don't need your capital." *And that would mean I don't have to take your garbage.*

"I'm not calling about the gown. The gown was doing *you* a favor. Now I'm asking for one of my own."

Sara Lang asking me for a favor? Is the earth's crust feeling chilly to you? I have to admit, I have the distinct notion to let her beg a little. Is that so bad?

"Lilly, did you hear me?" she says impatiently.

"I heard you, Sara," I say, with a hint of a smile. *Let me revel in this, Lord.*

"Well, I expect an answer when I speak to you."

That's it! "Sara, I don't work for you. I have my own

employees. I have business equipment. I have capital." I start to hang up the phone when her tone changes.

"Wait, Lilly! Look, I'm just a bit stressed, and I need some assistance with the Fashion Week show. I know I fired you, but I was also willing to lend you the money for your business, right?"

At what cost? "Right," I agree reluctantly.

"Look, the jeans we designed are a bust. You were right. *Women's Wear Daily* is skewering me, and if I show only those jeans next week at the fashion show, I'm done for. I'll be the laughingstock of society. I only have two gowns in the whole show." She takes in a sharp breath. "I'm begging you, Lilly. I know you've been working, and I need gowns. And a finale that will drop them to the floor. Please. I'll do anything. Your name can be on everything. Lilly Jacobs for Sara Lang. And that capital funding? Consider it your bonus, your commission. Not a loan. I've got people working here around the clock, but it's not going to be enough. I need *you*."

Now, I'm not inclined to do Sara any favors. Heaven knows I put up with her insults and attacks on a daily basis for three years. I've sat in the front row of fashion shows where she let models go out dressed only in a skirt and boots for attention, and I've endured the ridicule of her clients in the Union Square store. It's not that I haven't truly tasted humiliation with this woman. But at the same time, this feels so good. She's my ticket out of this dump, and I am smart enough to know it. Getting a spot in Fashion Week any other way would be impossible for a nobody like me.

"How many gowns do you need? I'll do what I have to."

She lets out an audible sigh. She has to be desperate, because normally you never see any reaction from her. "I need at least six, preferably with a show-stopper at the end." She's all business, now that I'm agreeable. Her confidence wavers suddenly. "Can you do it? They don't have to be perfectly stitched. You can take care of that if they sell."

I look in the closet and count four dresses made by the little fashion elves—Kim and Sara Lang Couture's disgruntled employees. "I can do it. What do you think about the show-stopper being a wedding gown?"

"I'm not known for my wedding gowns, Lilly."

"Or your jeans," I counter.

"Fine," she says sharply. "Make me a wedding gown. Perhaps that will help us with the next generation—they don't support the arts as heartily as their parents."

"I need size eight models. Except for the finale. I'll take care of the bride."

"No, no. I'm not trusting just anyone to my show-stopper."

As if Morgan Malliard is just anyone. "It will stop the show. Trust me."

I think about Morgan and her lithe figure, the stir we'll cause about her possible wedding due to the gown, and who the groom *could* be. Most importantly, Morgan will get to wear her fabric (okay, and probably some of San Francisco Jeweler's finest ice; but that will only highlight the gown), and she will glow. She'll get to walk down the "aisle" knowing she would have gone through with a wedding to help her father and a Russian she barely knew.

"I'll take care of it," I reiterate.

"It's not easy for me to trust you," Sara reminds me.

It wouldn't be easy for her to trust Mister Rogers, but that's her problem, isn't it?

"But you *can* trust me, Sara." I hang up the phone, anxious to get started.

"You're talking to Sara?" Kim comes in and slams the door behind her.

"Exactly when is having my own place going to come to

fruition? Because I'm assuming that means that someone else doesn't just walk in the door."

Kim laughs. "You'd think that, wouldn't you?"

"How's life upstairs? With a view?"

"It will be fine. We're getting used to each other. You know, men don't actually clean their showers." She makes a face.

"Neither do you."

"Yeah, but you did. That's my point. I think he expects me to do it."

"For free rent with a view of the San Francisco Bay? You're lucky if that's all he expects you to do." I say it jokingly, but my heart aches. Nate can be very charming. And it's not like Kim completely values herself at this point in her life. I look at her questioningly, wondering about all the unspoken conversations that went on around me.

"Yes, Mom." Kim rolls her eyes.

"Sara just called. I guess you heard." I change the subject.

"You didn't tell her I was here, did you?" Kim panics.

"You *weren't* here."

"I mean that you know where I am."

"Sara needs six dresses from us, plus I'm going to make Morgan's gown for the finale for fashion week. She's allowing me to use my name: Lilly Jacobs for Sara Lang!"

"She must really be desperate."

"She is. So can you and the elves make at least two more gowns? While I work on the wedding gown?"

"Has Morgan agreed to this?"

What kind of question is that? She's my best friend—like she has options here. Besides, she's heard me whine for the last three years. Morgan will do it just to shut me up! "Will you make the two dresses, Kim?"

"With the designs left?"

"Yes, only nix the sash on the yellow one. I've been looking at it again, and I think it's too much." *Wait, Kim doesn't know red from yellow.* "It's the one with the covered buttons down the back."

"Will do."

"I'm off to the spa. I need to convince Morgan about the fashion show."

"How are you getting there?"

"Right. First I need to convince Nate to lend me his car." I slam the door on my "office/loft" and run upstairs to Nate's apartment. I can smell the dog from the hallway. I try to wipe all traces of distaste off my face, wishing I'd brought some Lysol, just for the hallway. But he'd know, and I'm not exactly on his favorite list at the moment.

He swings open the door. "Let me guess. PETA wants me to pose naked in their next calendar."

"I'm sorry, all right? I'm worried about Kim, and that's fair. It's not like you're a beacon of morality to me at the moment."

"I kissed you, Lilly. I didn't take you to bed and not call the next morning, all right? And I put together a stealth business plan for you, in fact. Isn't that enough of a penance?"

"Fair enough. If I can borrow your car."

"When will you bring it back?"

"Tonight. I'm just going to Napa. I'll be back before you wake up. Weren't you up all night with China?" I ask, hopefully.

"No, actually, I never slept better in my life."

"Please, Nate."

He pulls his keys off a hook. *Yes!* "No later than seven."

"I'll be back, I promise."

"And fill it up!" he shouts after me, as I'm running down the stairs.

I love driving in San Francisco. Some people get nervous at the constant tension, the weaving in and out of traffic, the honking, but I live for the adrenaline. You will never be "let in" in San Francisco. The point becomes to "get over at any cost." And with my mood this morning, I'm more than willing to play chicken with a few cabs and BMWs. *Bring it on! I'm on a mission!*

In odd contrast to my driving mood, I listen to praise music and Third Day and let it blare, thumping my palms on the steering wheel while lane-changing to the beat. Before long, I'm nearing the Bay Bridge, heading for the pristine Napa Valley and my friends. I can't wait to tell them about the fashion show. I can't wait to pitch my idea to Morgan. I've never bothered her before to wear anything because I didn't want to be anything like her dad. But today, with this fashion show, I believe she has the distinct opportunity to be her own woman. To separate from the man, if not from all that glitters.

It's at this small moment in time that I hear the enormous squeal and a crunch, while my neck snaps backward, then forward. Even after the car is stopped, it seems I continue to hear the noise from the impact and feel the car moving without my help, jamming into a place as I try to brake and steer to no avail. The scraping, whining squeal and my first glimpse in the rearview mirror at the metal that has made contact with Nate's Saab. It's some American make, from another era when big cars ruled the landscape. We're near the Fourth Street exit of 101, the last exit before the Bay Bridge, and traffic is honking, with a few shouts of "Get off the road!" among other expletives.

I know I'm not hurt. Not physically, anyway. But when I see the size of this great American gunboat, I know Nate's car cannot be in good shape. I step out of the car, since traffic has slowed to a crawl, and meet the face of the man who hit me.

He stares at me, then takes off running.

This is not good.

So here I am, stranded on Highway 101, with Nate's car

scraped and leaking yellow fluid. I endure the wrath of Sunday morning traffic. (Apparently no one is on their way to church, judging by the language.)

After what seems like an eternity, a CHP comes up beside me, turning his flashing lights on and taking up yet another lane which is oh, so very popular with the lanes trying to get to the bridge.

"Are you all right, miss?"

"I'm fine," I say, though I hear my voice shaking. I'm not as fine as I would be if I was still on my way to the beautifully serene wine country, that's for certain.

"License and registration." He holds his palm out.

"That's it? That's all the sympathy I get? This idiot hit me, and ran off, and I'm stuck out here all by myself."

"License and registration, miss." Behind him, I see the huge tow truck that's come to clear both cars away.

"This isn't my car!"

"Ma'am, you'll have your opportunity to give your side of the story, but I need to see your paperwork. We've got to get this cleaned up. It's Sunday morning!" he says, his voice rising, and I feel completely guilty. I'm hearing my Nana shout that if I'd been in church where I belonged, none of this would have happened.

I rifle through my new Marc Jacobs handbag and pull out my driver's license. Getting the registration, I just cringe. *Nate is going to kill me!* The only thing he loves more than this classic Saab is Charley. And now, both of them are leaking.

chapter 27

After giving my statement on what CHP kindly deemed "the accident," the officer gives me a ride to the cable car, and I grab a ride down to Fisherman's Wharf, then walk to the Marina. I find it funny that it's called a hit-and-run, because at the moment, while I definitely got hit, the places I can run seem pretty limited. I have to call Nate, there's no getting around that, but I'm not exactly wanting to see him face-to-face yet. I dial his cell, and he's not answering. For this, I'm grateful. I call Morgan and Poppy, but they must be enjoying an elegant Sunday brunch because they don't answer either. This leaves Nana's place as the only refuge I can think of, even if I do have to face her worried frown.

I reach the top of her hill, and my legs are shot from walking—even the slight hills in the Marina. Clearly, sitting at the computer and the sewing machine has done nothing for my physical prowess. But if I had to take an anatomy test right now, I'd be set, because I can feel every muscle in my body. So much so, I remember their names. And I thought I'd never use that information. I owe my anatomy teacher an apology.

I knock on Nana's door. Nothing. *What is with my Nana? Where does she go? Church should be over by now. Why can't I have her life?*

I hear a car pull up behind me and whirl around to see Max getting out of a Mercedes convertible, a fake blonde behind the wheel. Well, the woman is real, just the blonde part is fake.

"Thanks again, Jenna!" He waves at her, and she peers over her sunglasses to check out whether or not I'm any competition. Apparently, I'm not. She speeds off. "Lilly, what are you doing here?"

"My Nana lives here." I don't know if it's fatigue, the fear of telling Nate, or feeling so utterly alone, but I have to fight back tears when I look at Max.

"Her church was putting on a family potluck today. I don't think she'll be back for hours."

I sigh, and slide against the door until I reach the ground. "I'll wait." I put my palm over my eye, as it's throbbing.

"Come upstairs. I'll make you something to eat. Are you all right?"

"My head hurts."

Max bends over at the waist and gently lifts my bangs off my forehead. "You have a red mark here." He brushes his thumb over my eyebrow.

"Ouch!" I yelp as he touches it.

"Come on up. We'll put some ice on it. What have you been up to this weekend? Did you get caught in a mosh pit again?"

"I got in a little car accident when I was driving to Napa."

"You don't have a car."

"Exactly. Aren't you glad I didn't take yours? Because now, Nate doesn't have a car either. At least not one in working condition."

Max reaches down, leaning with one arm on his crutch, and pulls me up. He follows me up the stairs, and we reach his landing. I just look into his dark espresso eyes, and I forget all about my head. It's the only excuse I have for what comes out next. "Are you busy this Saturday?"

"It depends," he says. "Are we talking busy, as in *I don't have a television show to watch*, or busy as in *I can TiVo it, because this is an offer I can't refuse?*"

"Definitely the latter," I say.

He unlocks the front door and hobbles up the two steps into his living room where he opens the shutters and lets the sparkling blue bay and skating sailboats invade our view with the morning sun. "Do you want something to eat?"

"Just that ice would be good."

Max opens a Sub-Zero refrigerator, and pulls out a package of frozen peas. "Here, this works great. Let me grab one, and we can nurse our wounds together," he jokes.

I put the bag over my eye. "I didn't think I got hurt."

"I thought the same thing when I broke my leg and tried to stand on it." He continues to brush the hair off my forehead. "So, what's the offer I can't refuse?"

"It's almost Fashion Week."

"I know, believe it or not."

"Don't tell me, Valeria's modeling?"

"No, the hotel is booked solid with New York media. San Francisco fashion is finally on the map, apparently."

"Max, I need some buzz."

"What?"

"I need the media to take notice of me, because this is my last shot at fashion. If I can't make it next week, I'm going back to a desk job. I've lived the dream long enough. If it doesn't happen now, it's not going to, and my Nana deserves to know I'm well taken care of. If seeing the woman who abandoned me taught me anything, it's that Nana allowed me to have a childhood. It's time to have an adulthood."

"Meaning?"

"I want you to come to the fashion show with me." I nibble on my lower lip. "I want you to be my date." *I could die.* This is exactly like the time I talked to Steve Collins in college and asked him to a football game, only to have him tell me American football was hardly worth his time. *And neither was I.*

"Well, well." He falls on the sofa and crosses his hands behind his head. "Yeah, they all come around sooner or later."

I force myself to refrain from rolling my eyes. "You can even break up with me in some dramatic way after the event. It'll help your playboy status with the Valerias of the City.

"As if I need help."

I can feel the sting of tears again. "Please don't make fun of me, Max. I saw your picture in the society page in the Datebook section of the paper. I know you're some hotshot around town because your family owns the hotels. Anything I can do to create conversation, even if it's about me being with the City's playboy, I could use."

"My pastor wouldn't exactly appreciate the *playboy* description. Neither would my mother, frankly. Besides, what have I ever done to you to deserve that title?"

My voice is timid here. I had the feeling he'd like the title. "I just thought because of Valeria…and that girl that dropped you off just now—"

"So let's see, because I had a woman make me dinner, and a friend from church drop me off, that makes me a player? If you want to know the truth, Lilly, your Nana had more to do with Valeria being here all the time. She invited her over to cook, because she was so certain I needed a wife to keep me company. I don't think it mattered to her that the girl's IQ and her bra size were about equal, in actuality."

This just makes me laugh. I try to stop, but I'm giggling like a schoolgirl, and every time I try to stop, it gets worse.

"So you see, I'm not really the player you think. I have an

ex-girlfriend or two, sure. Would you really trust me if I didn't at this age?"

Not answering that question. "Morgan Malliard is going to be my finale, and I want you to be my date, Max." I press the peas tighter against my head. "No, wait, you don't even have to really be my date. I want you to pretend to be my date. We'll have our picture taken. We'll smile for the camera, and then, you're on your way. One of your hot, little chauffeurs can come rescue you from the after-party." I shift the icy peas on my forehead. "Maybe Tara Reid is available," I mumble.

"Boy, since you're asking me for a favor, I hoped to find you a little more humble." He laughs. "Let me give you a hint: when you want a favor, usually it's a good idea to warm up the room a bit first. You know, feel the love."

I get down on my knees, drop the peas, and clasp my hands together. "I'm begging, all right? How's this for humble?"

"Lillian, what are you doing on Max's good rug?" I whisk myself off the floor and face my Nana in the doorway.

"Nana, I thought you weren't due home for a while."

"I'm home early. Everyone made mashed potatoes. How can you have a potluck with four types of mashed potatoes and no meat?" She catches a glimpse of my head. "What did you do?"

"I got in a little accident."

Nana comes toward me and puts her icy hand on my forehead. "Well, you don't have a fever. That's good."

"Speaking of which, what have you been doing at the hospital, Nana?" *When the going gets tough, the tough always shift the focus back.*

She purses her lips at Max, as though he's betrayed her confidence. "Getting a flu shot. They were out of them the first time. I had to go back a couple times until they had stock." She points her finger at Max. "Must you tell everyone my business?"

Max shrugs. "I'm just sitting here, waiting for golf to start. In case you haven't noticed, Jacobs women, this is my place!" He clicks on the set.

"We'll go downstairs. Max, I brought you some leftover spinach casserole. I put it in the fridge."

As we start to exit, I feel myself getting anxious to the point of near-panic. I wait for my Nana to start on the first step, and then I turn back into Max's house. "Please, Max. Will you do it?"

He beckons me with a finger. "Come here, first."

I get close enough to him where I can smell his woodsy, expensive cologne. It's light enough to incite my senses, but not overwhelming enough to make him smell like an overeager teenager. Oh yeah, Max is easy on the nose. No Lysol necessary.

I gaze at him, face to face, and I watch the corner of his lip curve into a smile. "I wouldn't miss it, Lilly," he growls. Growls!

I pick up a pillow and throw it at him. "You made me suffer for nothing!" I start toward the door.

"Hey, wait a minute. What day?"

"This Saturday night, at your father's hotel."

"Which one?"

I just look at him. "You know, you could figure that out. Is that your way of letting me know he owns more than one?" I shake my head. "Call your concierge," I joke.

"I'm just asking. Should I get a limo for this gig?"

A little giddy rise of the pulse. "A limo, really? Definitely. Can Nana ride with us too?"

"What's a date without an obvious chaperone, Lilly? You'd think we were living in the Victorian era, for goodness' sakes."

"Thank you!" I bend over to kiss him on the cheek, but he turns his face and kisses me full on the lips.

"You're welcome."

I can't help smiling down on him, and capturing the glimmer in his eye. *I don't know what to think of you Max Schwartz, but I'm most definitely intrigued. Plus, you smell fabulous!* I skip down the steps to my Nana's place, and she's already cooking. I think that woman would explode if there wasn't something in the oven. I get four steps into the living room when I realize I have to tell Nate about his car. *And* I realize that my cell phone must still be in it. After I called them all while the cop was writing up the accident, I must have put the phone down when I reached in to get my purse.

"I have to use the phone, Nana."

"Is it long distance?" Okay, what is up with older people and long distance? I know they lived through the Depression and all that, but *hello*? Long distance is not going to drain your social security check these days.

"No, it's local."

She hands me her telephone with the extra-large numbers, and I dial Nate's number. He answers on the first ring. *Ack!* "Nate Goddard."

"Nate—"

"Lilly, are you all right? Kim and I have been worried sick. You aren't answering your cell phone, and we heard about the accident."

"I must have left my phone in your car. How did you know about the accident?"

"They called from the police station to tell me my car had been involved in a hit-and-run on 101."

"Nate, I am so sorry. It wasn't my fault, I swear! I didn't know what to do, so I went to my Nana's."

"It's cool, Lilly. The car was on its last legs, and I was going to sell it soon. You probably got me more than trade-in."

"You're not mad?"

"Well, I'm not thrilled, but we were so worried about you this morning, the car paled in comparison. Don't do that again, all right? When you're in an accident, call!"

I rub the frozen peas deeper into my skin. "I did; you didn't answer...I'm going to pay to rent you a car until the insurance kicks in, all right?"

"No offense, but you know, I think I'll just take care of it myself. Bad luck seems to be your sidekick."

"Not anymore, Nate!"

We exchange pleasantries. Well, as pleasant as you can be to someone who once kissed you ruthlessly, then had your roommate move in with him. And I did just destroy his car. Nana plops a chicken salad sandwich in front of me, and I say good-bye and hang up.

"Eat," she says.

I'm starving, and my first bite is sheer heaven. "Nana, this is so good."

"Extra pickles, just the way you like it."

"I *have* to get to Napa this afternoon." The thought occurs to me to ask Max for his Jaguar when common sense over-rules. I pick up the phone and dial Morgan's cell again. I look at my reflection in my Nana's toaster and see the red raspberry mark left by Nate's steering wheel.

Morgan doesn't answer, and I hang up, strategizing my next move. I've got a fashion show, a date, and a limo. Now all I need is a bride and her dress.

fter three bus transfers, I arrive home to see Nate's scraped car parked on the side of our street. I now see that the car that hit me was blue, because Nate's silver Saab has a blue stripe. The reality that I caused the damage just makes me feel sick. It's such a physical manifestation of the havoc I seem to wreak lately.

At the moment, I owe my working life to Nate for the computers, the sewing machine, and my first payment that will come in the form of his own insurance settlement. He'll probably be on one of those Geico commercials touting how he had to trade for better rates when his friend ruined his car. Maybe I can get them to put the gecko in one of my gowns when it airs.

Certainly, I don't owe Nate anything for stealing my roommate, or for stealing that kiss. (Well, okay, so it wasn't exactly stolen. Can't a girl preserve her dignity here?) But as long as we avoid these subjects, we're good. He'll probably have more of an appreciation than I did for the barely-there fashion shows one gets from Kim before she parades out for a bar-hopping trip. You know, Nate is a decent guy, and if he thinks the "taming of the shrew" is imminent, he doesn't know Kim at all. I just have to let the chips fall where they may. Let the Superman complex die on its own. As Kim has told me countless times, she's a big girl. I'll work on her from my knees from now on. She doesn't have to know. For that matter, a few prayers for Nate wouldn't hurt either.

Speaking of Nate, he steps out of the building onto the sidewalk and sees me checking out the car. "It wasn't that bad," he yells over the traffic up above on 101. "I thought it would be worse." He nods, taking in the sight of his car, now sort of lurching to one side. "It's leaking anti-freeze, and it's not as much of a chick magnet as it was this morning, but—"

"Wait a minute," I correct him. "The Slob was never a chick magnet."

"You don't speak for all women. In fact, the *Saab* says, 'Casual, yet stylish and sophisticated.'"

"Or not."

"Kim loves the car. She loves my dog. She even uses Q-tips to clean out Charley's ear."

They say that smell is the strongest memory indicator, and they must have something because now I think I'm going to hurl. I put a palm up. "Please, don't go there with me."

"It's cute. She puts Charley on her lap and takes a Q-tip and—"

"Stop! I'm begging you. I'm having visions of the dog's gooey ears. Please, have mercy!"

Nate is laughing. "I'm just messing with you. I figured it was the least you deserved for crashing my car. I was tempted to let Charley into your loft this afternoon, just as a little healthy aromatherapy, but I worried you'd ruin my investment gowns by spraying Lysol everywhere."

"Technically, you know, the accident wasn't even my fault."

"And technically, now I don't have a good-looking chick mobile."

"Technically, you never did."

"Technically then, the accident *was* your fault because you were driving my car instead of hoofing it on Muni."

"Muni doesn't go to the wine country."

Nate points at me. "Neither one of you goes to Napa!"

I grimace at him and pound my hand on the hood. "Aren't they going to fix it?"

"I'm taking the insurance money, probably. I'll get an estimate tomorrow, but even though it *is* fixable, I doubt it will be worth it. I was hoping they'd declare it totaled so I could use it as a down on a new one."

"The money? You already have more money than Moses. Go buy yourself a new car if you want one."

"He who dies with the most money wins. Haven't you ever heard that?"

"Except what happens when you die? It ain't going with you. Great theology you got going there, Nate. You sure you don't want to come hear about Living Water with me? Jesus? True victory?"

"You can't even pay your rent, Lilly. You don't have the answers I'm looking for." An ambulance drives up the street with its siren blaring, and we're both quiet until the wail dissipates.

"I never claimed to have the answers, just eternal life." But yeah, could that sound any more hollow at the moment?

"One time around is good enough for me, okay? In case you haven't noticed, this place ain't all that great to begin with." He reaches into his pocket. "Here's your cell phone."

"You really know how to make a girl feel like a loser, you know?" I can feel the tears coming on, but I'm so not giving in to them! "I'm sorry I crashed your car. I'm sorry I got fired. I'm sorry you feel the need to rescue me, and then hold it over my head like a noose!"

"Lilly, I don't know what you want from me. You're a great

designer. If I didn't believe in you, I wouldn't have put my money where my mouth is. I wouldn't have lent you my car this morning, and I wouldn't have worked things out with Kim so you'd have employees working like honeybees in a hive. I care about you, but we are fundamentally different."

"For example?" I ask.

"I think sex outside marriage is a good thing. I relish it, in fact. I don't believe in self-denial to the point of feeling any pain." He glares down at me, waiting for some reaction, I suppose. "You never know when your day is up, and living like that—with some pleasure—doesn't seem like a bad idea."

"I respect your honesty," I say calmly.

I question everything at the moment. I feel like no one will ever want me. No one will ever cherish me. I can see why Kim goes for the moment. For one night, to be in someone's arms and feel as if I'm his whole world? I covet that with my whole being, and maybe a lifetime is too much to ask. I wonder if I'll get over feeling like I'm always in someone's way. I'm always the one people have to stop and deal with for a second when they are really on their way to do something else. I am never anyone's final destination. I feel like nothing more than the human version of a Greyhound bus stop.

"But you don't respect me," Nate says.

"I don't know what I think about you. Does that make you feel better? I don't have all the answers, and I never did. But I do think you are a decent man, Nate Goddard. You've always taken care of Kim and me. Come to our rescue with money and cappuccinos when the going got really tough. I think you're a hero in your own way."

"But you don't respect either Kim or me for our decision to live together. That makes you judgmental."

"Or prophetic. I guess we'll see." *Like I haven't learned something living with the girl for two years.*

"I live for the right-here, right-now," he says, while doing some macho jig. Nate won't let the subject drop. He seems determined to bait me into a debate.

"I don't really care how you live. If you want to have Miss Shampoo Commercial up—heck, a *different* Miss Shampoo Commercial up every night, you do so. Just stay away from Kim, all right? That's all I'm asking." I kick the car's tire. "I know you'll get ticked at me for saying it, but you're a nice guy, Nate. Regardless of your actions lately. What's your perfect ending with Kim? Two kids, a dog, and a picket fence in the suburbs?"

He ignores my question. "Do you promise me this isn't about *us*?"

I make an *X* over my heart. "Cross my heart, hope to die. I promise."

"You *really* don't think Kim wants me? Or are you just jealous of our arrangement?"

First off, they don't have anything. I can't imagine why Nate *wants* Kim. I know that sounds harsh, but he's like Opie to her goth revival. It makes no sense. I think back to the myriad of times Kim rolled her eyes at Nate, how her annoyance at his mere presence made her leave the loft. She wants someone—I believe that wholeheartedly—and Nate is simply convenient.

"I don't think so. If I'm wrong, she'll tell you, and you'll know it. You can dance on my tabletop, and tell me I was wrong."

"Fine."

I gaze over the wreckage of the Saab in front of us. "You're right. It doesn't look all that bad, but I'm still sorry I ruined your car."

Nate comes alongside me and puts his arm around me and I shudder at his touch. I don't know who he is anymore, but I do have an overwhelming urge to slap him silly. "I'm not. It sort of looks cool now. Like you might want to stay away from me on the road. I bet it helps with city lane changes."

My cell phone trills, and I see Morgan's cell number in the lit-up box. "Hey, Morgan, how's the spa?"

"It's me, Poppy. What did you do?" she accuses.

"What do you mean?" I look at Nate and swallow hard.

"Stuart Surrey came back here this morning to the spa. He gave Morgan a bouquet of orchids and then stuck his tongue down her throat! He then said *you* told him the feeling was mutual!"

"What? What are you talking about?"

"Stuart Surrey, your creepy Englishman?"

"Yeah." Not in agreement about the creepy part, but apparently it's not up for discussion.

"He came here for Morgan, thrust some flowers in her face, started macking on her, and she slapped him—"

"She slapped him? Wait! He did *what*?!"

"Stuart said *you* told him Morgan had feelings for him."

"I never said any such thing! Morgan can't stand him!" I turn away from Nate, lest he see I've managed to screw something else up this weekend. "How is Morgan feeling?"

"She was better until Slimy showed up. What did you tell him, Lilly?"

I can hear Morgan in the background. And she doesn't sound happier than when I left her sobbing and bereft. *Oh my gosh, what did I do?* "Poppy, let me talk to Morgan."

"It's Lilly," I hear Poppy say to Morgan. "Do you want to talk to her?"

"Lilly?" Morgan squeals. "They took a picture of us...kissing," she cries. "Oh, I am completely grossed out! Him and his huge, pink tongue. What on earth could you see in that jerk?"

I lean against the wall of my building, not comprehending any of this. "Who took a picture of you?"

"Some photographer. I'm sure it was probably set up by Stuart himself, the slimewad. We'll be in tomorrow's paper, with me linked to that letch. Hopefully, no one will find out about that fabric purchase, or they'll be planning our wedding. What did you say when you drove home with him?"

"Well, I didn't say, 'Please come maul my best friend,' if that's what you're thinking." I start to check my mind. *What could I have said?* How could Stuart possibly get the idea that Morgan wanted him? I'm hearing Stuart's gorgeous accent, the line I fell for hook, line, and sinker…When he whispered to me, he said he didn't want to stay for dinner at the hotel, and he brushed his hand on my chin.

"What did he say, Lilly? Think!"

"He said dinner with the woman you're trying to leave, and the woman your heart cries out for didn't sound cozy," I repeat verbatim. *Hey, when a guy gives me poetry, I remember it.* Then, I feel the breath rush from me as I listen to the words again. "Oh my goodness. He wasn't talking about *me*." I say this more for myself than Morgan. "When he called for the potluck. When he didn't want to go to the dinner at the hotel. None of that was about *me*, was it? It was about getting close to you. That's why he wanted to be my friend."

I try to let this all sink in, try to make myself understand that just because I wanted this so badly, I wasn't reading Stuart correctly. I run through the specifics in my mind: the toffee, the phone call, the drive home…it was all a way to get closer to Morgan. Rejection does *not* sound better with an English accent. Trust me on that one.

Nate comes beside me and takes my hand, and I crush his in my own. Even though I want to slap him, too, and the rest of mankind at the moment.

"Morgan, I thought...I'm so sorry."

"I told you he was a creep, Lilly. What possible reason do I have to lie to you? I hate what your mother did, because you don't trust anyone because of it! It's just not right! We stand by you, no matter what, and yet every time you're given the choice to trust us or yourself, you go with you! Even though you've been wrong about men *every single time!*"

I swallow hard. The last thing I need is a now-weeping Morgan yelling at me. I'm happy she's aware enough to yell, but disturbed at how right she is. "What can I say? When I saw him preaching that sermon, and heard his English accent... and worst of all, when he stared right at me into my eyes. I felt it, Morgan! I felt it in my entire being. It was like he woke me up from this dead state I've been in, and he made me feel wanted." Suddenly, it makes me question everything in my life. "Am I really a bad designer, and no one tells me? Do you guys whisper behind my back that I'm a design nightmare?"

"Your fashion instinct is impeccable. Your finance abilities, incredible. But your man-scouting skills are very, very rough. I think you've inhaled too much Lysol, and it has affected your how-to-find-a-mate brain cells."

We both start to giggle. Somehow this makes me feel better.

Well, I guess now is certainly *not* the time to ask Morgan if she'll dress up in a wedding gown for me and parade across a stage in front of San Francisco's elite.

chapter 29

My loft is a whirlwind of activity when I step into what appears to be a downtown sweatshop. *Thanks, God, for each and every one of them. When You say You'll provide for all of our needs, You always have an interesting way of doing it—usually just in time too. Guess that's to keep me leaning on You.* Hannah and Cheryl, my former workmates from Sara Lang, are bent over machines, working on two gowns for the collection. Kim is managing things by blaring Green Day on a borrowed stereo system, which I can only assume is Nate's, and watching one of her plastic surgery shows, muted. One has to give Kim credit; she's got delegating down. *As if I should talk.*

As the surgeon on full-spectrum, plasma-screen HDTV slices into a patient in vibrant and graphic color, I see Kim smile. She apparently takes some sick pleasure in watching the suffering of vain women. Years at Sara Lang Couture will do that to a person.

"If it isn't Dale Earnhart Jr.," Kim says when she notices me.

"Cute, Kim."

Hannah stops sewing. "You buying us dinner, Lilly?"

"It's the least I can do. Thanks so much for coming, you guys." I pick up the gowns, and I have to admire them. One is a canary-yellow crushed silk with a scooped neckline. And, okay, I'm hoping to get Morgan's dad to lend me canary diamonds for the model. It gets his diamonds exposure, while setting off my gowns. A win-win for everyone, right?

The other is a romantic, pale tangerine gown with long, wispy sleeves. Its lines are so airy it will practically float with the model. I can't wait to see it in action! Still yet to be made: a creamy-yellow mid-calf that fits snugly until a spray of tulle brings the skirt out at the knee; and finally, a crimson, spaghetti-strapped crepe wonder. I'll be hand-embroidering the tangerine gown, but first and foremost is the wedding gown and its wearer. I have a week to make my best gown ever, and less than that to get Morgan to agree to wear it. And it wouldn't hurt if her father would provide a big honkin' diamond for her left hand.

"You know, I think Nate is an alien robot in disguise." Kim looks away from the television.

"Do you?" Note, I don't ask why. I'm hoping this will end the conversation.

"The guy does not possess a temper. He's like the calm before the storm, but without the storm."

"Profound."

"You don't think he's one of those psychos who is just going to lose it one day, do you? The kind where his neighbors come on camera and say, 'He was the nicest guy, would do anything for ya'?"

"Shouldn't you have thought about that before you agreed to sleep in the same house? When you moved your stuff in, did you see his mother's skeleton in the closet?"

"Very funny."

"Do you think these gowns are going to be okay, Kim? We really rushed them, and I wonder how creative I've been lately."

"These gowns are beautiful, Lilly. The colors are right. I love how they're spring colors for the fall. Everyone will be designing black for the season, and Sara will once again be the saving grace for those who want to stand out."

"These feel like my very first gowns...the first that will bear my name." I get giddy just thinking of it: Lilly Jacobs for Sara Lang. *It's really my dream coming true!*

"Have you told Sara I'm coming yet?"

Shoot. I hadn't thought of that. "I'm working it out."

"Just so we're straight, you're not working it out where Sara has me hustled away in a police car, right?"

"I'll fix it. Okay?"

Then my home phone rings. "Sara—I mean, Lilly Jacobs Design."

"Hi, it's Sandy." Sandy is my hairdresser, and with my hair that's no small relationship. She knows my cowlicks. She knows my texture. She is my Tom Ford. She takes the impossible and makes it workable. There is no making light of a good stylist.

"Hey, Sandy!"

"Lilly, did you happen to notice anything different about your straightening?"

Okay, now that she mentions it, it got a little curly in the rain...

"Why?" I ask, feeling the terror.

"Well, we got a bad batch of crème. The manufacturer recalled a lot number, and I noticed it's the one we used on you. But it can't be that bad. It didn't burn your scalp or anything. We can always redo, right? Apparently, the neutralizer was missing an ingredient. It didn't set properly."

Time, I think while forcing down the panic. *I do not have time to sit for five hours in a salon.* "Actually, how long do you think it will keep? Until this weekend?"

"Well, I used the CHI iron on it, so I'd say at least until you wash it a couple times. Maybe two weeks?"

Mentally, I start counting. I've washed it well past my limit already. All those stupid spa trips! I had to get the essential oils off. The countdown starts. I could keep it in a hairnet and probably only shampoo it once before the big night, but then I think that no one wants to be dressed by a designer who neglects bathing. Personal hygiene is sort of important to the couture set. *This is not going to work.* "Sandy, when can you get me in? I've got to have my hair straightened by this Friday!"

I hear her flipping through pages. "Hmmm. I'm pretty booked up with Fashion Week coming up. The best I can do is a week from Tuesday. I can work you around other people, but it will probably take longer. Like maybe seven hours?"

My mind goes to the wedding gown. It's going to take me days to sew, and I haven't even designed it yet. I force the words out of my mouth. "It's going to have to wait, Sandy."

"I'll send your money back until you reschedule. I'm really sorry about this, Lilly. I know what straightening means to you. Your hair just doesn't take product like someone else's."

Ah, the old hair-like-steel excuse. I love that one. But it will take me the full week to get the wedding gown done. I can't possibly spare five hours in a salon chair, even if it is free! I start to pace the loft. I know it doesn't sound like a big deal. It's only hair, but my hair is huge. I can use the CHI straightener and gallons of hair serum for the night. Oh sure, I'll look a little greasy, but as long as I don't drip on the clothes, it will be fine. I'm worried for nothing.

It's curly hair or your career, Lilly! A hat! I'll design a hat. "Sandy, you still there?"

"Yeah."

"I can't make it in before my big show with Sara. You'll save me a spot the following week?"

"Sure! I'll put you in for your normal Thursday morning appointment, all right?"

"Sure," I say absently and hang up the phone. "Bad hair ruined my life! It's a never-ending life sentence." I crash on the futon next to Kim. "I got some bad stuff," I say, tugging at my hair.

She starts to giggle. "Usually, when people say that, Lilly, it's a translation for—'I've overdosed on an illegal drug. Take me to the hospital.'"

I let my head fall in my hands. "You don't understand, Kim. I know everyone thinks it's my *hair*, big deal. It's not like I have three hands or something, but when you don't have a mother or a father, and your grandmother dresses you straight out of the Depression era, and your hair is so big no one wants to sit behind you or pick you for their team in P.E., it does something to you. It really does."

Realistically, I know I should be over this. I know that my God is bigger than my hair, but when my hair is curly, I remember the taunts like they were an hour ago, and for a while, I live there again, unable to crawl out. I remember everyone laughing at me, and my little stick legs and my Nana's answer: "You just tell them, Lilly, sticks and stones will break your bones, but names will never hurt you."

But they *do* hurt. And they do make you believe it. There's always the girl with the fashionable mother who took the time to clip her hair and make sure her tights matched, and that she had tights verses ankle socks. If Paula Hastings, fashionista of the fourth grade, had socks, they were the kind with little frills around them. They didn't come from the boys' section because they were cheaper.

I stand up from the sofa and realize this is getting me nowhere. I have the wedding gown of the year to design. It's time Vera Wang had some competition. "It's time I grew up!" I announce.

"Yes, it is…I guess." Kim looks at me questioningly.

"I'm going to wash my hair!"

"Okay? And this concerns me, why?"

"No really. I mean, shampoo, rinse, repeat. The full treatment. I'm going all the way!"

"You go, girlfriend!" Hannah shouts.

"Order dinner. I'll pick it up when I get out."

Nate walks into the room without knocking. "What's going on?"

"Lilly's taking a shower!" Kim says.

"That's big news."

"Shut up, all of you." I grab the fancy hairdryer Morgan bought me, and I put the diffuser on with a hefty click. "Shields up!" I grab the new product the hairdresser gave me. "Phasers set to stun." And finally, I shove the hairdryer at my hip. "I'm going in!"

I head into the bathroom, with my mind as full as my hair soon will be. How will I get Morgan to agree to wearing a wedding gown within the next day or so? I'm just praying that the photo of her and Stuart does not appear in the paper. Then, I've got to work out the whole forgiveness factor—what with Kim stealing $20,000 from Sara and all. Sara Lang probably hasn't forgiven her first-grade teacher for some minor infraction like not letting her sharpen her pencil right away, so this should be fun.

When I think about the most important aspect of the week though, designing a memorable gown, that doesn't inspire fear. That, I look forward to. Thinking about a gown for Morgan has been foremost on my mind for a week. I know just how I want the fabric to lay, just how I want the bodice to hug her tiny waist, and just how I want the sleeves to reach her tiny, elegant hands.

I turn on the shower, but my phone rings again, so I turn it back off and go to the table to answer it. "Lilly Jacobs Design."

"Yes, this is the Seven Seas Hotel on Van Ness." (Translated: red light district of San Francisco.)

"Yes?" I say, knowing they must have the wrong number.

"We had a Tammy Jamison staying here, and she left this number on her registration card as her local number. It appears that her credit card has been turned down. Originally it was preapproved, but when she left, the credit card had been revoked."

"I can't help you," I say, slamming the phone down. It rings again, and my stomach churns. "You've got the wrong number. This is Lilly Jacobs Design!" I shout, and hang up again.

This is who my mother is? The realization that her issues have nothing to do with me suddenly comes raining down on me. I am not her. I am not abandoned. I am Lilly Jacobs, Stanford graduate, fashion designer, and card-carrying Spa Girl! Loved by friends—quirky as they may be—and her Nana, grouchy as she can be. *I will repay you for the years the locusts have eaten.* I hear that scripture in my mind as if for the first time. I never missed a thing without *that* mother.

The phone trills again. "If you call here again, I'm calling the police!"

"Lilly? It's Max. Am I safe, or is the San Quentin warden coming for me?"

I breathe out deeply. "Max, hi. I have big hair. I'm going to have big hair next Saturday."

"I have a broken leg. I'm going to have a broken leg on Saturday. Anything else you want to lament?"

"My mother is a freak of nature from the non-maternal side of hell."

"My mother is convinced that I need a nice Jewish girl to settle down with—and soon—or I will turn into a pumpkin."

"I'm Italian. Christian. With big hair. Obviously, I can't help you."

"Close enough for government work."

"I suppose you didn't call to hear me whine?"

"No, but I like to hear you whine, Lilly. You do it with such flair."

"You think?"

"Listen, I'm going to be late for the fashion show. Is it all right if I arrive a few minutes after the fact?"

I'll admit, his question leaves me with a sting of rejection, even though I'm sure he has a logical and real excuse. I'm just not in the mood. "Sure. You arrive whenever. My Nana can ride with Nate."

"Nate?"

"My upstairs neighbor. He paid for my sewing machine and the computers. I'll see you if you get there, okay?"

I start to hang up the phone, when Max shouts, "Wait!"

"What?"

"I have something to do beforehand. I'll be there. I promise. There won't be a single after-party where I'm not there for pictures, all right? The *Chronicle* can announce our engagement the next day if it makes you happy."

I giggle and feel better, pretty much. "We don't have to take it that far. Thanks for calling, Max."

"Lilly?"

"Yeah?"

"Quit worrying. I'll have the limo pick up your grandmother and I'll meet you there."

"Thanks. Bye." I hang up, disappointed but not surprised. It's time for that shower. I'm going to wash away the remnants of civilization and revert to the cavewoman look—and then, I'm going to design a hat, followed by a wedding gown fit for a princess.

chapter 30

S tepping out of the shower, I feel relief. I am finally going to see my hair in all its glory. I am going to embrace the real me. It's the first step toward real and significant change! I slop smoothing crème on my hair and anti-frizz serum, and then I pick up the titanium hairdryer. "This is the first day of the new Lilly Jacobs!"

Bending over, I dry the back and roots, and just let the hot air cleanse me from all my negative emotions. (I feel like Poppy!) Bad hair did not ruin my life. Bad hair was only a figment of my imagination, made up to ease the pain of a mother who didn't love me, a Nana who didn't understand fashion, and a series of milquetoast boyfriends who didn't marry me. "I am Lilly Jacobs, woman of the twenty-first century!" I say out loud, and I flip my hair up and gaze into the mirror. "Oh my gosh! I am hideous! I am Simba grown up with a mane that would rival the largest African lion."

"Lilly," Kim pounds on the door. "Are you ever coming out? Hannah needs to go!"

When I emerge from the bathroom, I slink out of the doorway, waiting for the first glimpse at my true hairstyle. I think you'd call it "cotton ball with an attitude." No one looks up from any sewing machine. "Here I am," I finally say.

A quick glance, and then everyone's back to work.

"This is my real hair."

"Cool," Hannah says.

"What do you want, a standing ovation?" Kim asks.

Forget it. You can't get blood out of a turnip. I settle down on my futon with my sketch pad, and I start to dream about the perfect gown for Morgan's lithe figure. She's like Cate Blanchett, wispy yet muscular, and dresses were made for her little body. I don't have time for a lot of detail on the gown, so the shape will be everything. The shape and the placing of the darts so it hugs her perfectly. Kim and the girls are gossiping, and I close my eyes and realize nothing is coming. Nada. Zilch. Zippo.

I realize I need quiet. I can't be creative with the sewing machines buzzing, the stereo blasting, and more women being cut open on the big screen. There's something unnerving about the beauty of a wedding gown against the background of sliced human flesh. Call me crazy, but it's not working for me. I can't use Nate's place because the smell will get to me. I can't be creative smelling that dog.

I decide to do something that is completely not in my character. I am going to the spa. Okay, it's not completely out of character, but by myself? Just me? That's out of character. Not on Morgan's dime, but on my own (borrowed) dime. Granted, I guess it's sort of on Morgan's dime, since I am currently borrowing from her, and my various and assorted credit cards, but this time I am paying it back, and she will be thrilled when she sees the outcome. The wedding dress that will make her long for a groom she's in love with, not one she's saving from an impending death.

I throw a pair of yoga pants and a T-shirt in a bag. "I'm leaving. I need to work."

"Whatever," Kim says.

"See ya," the other two girls chime.

After a short taxi drive, I arrive at a local hotel. It has a spa that has always been like Calgon—it takes me away when I really need it. I have an overnight bag and my sketch pad. And most importantly, an old ski hat I wore in college.

The spa is not fancy by spa standards. It has linoleum floors in a world of travertine, and gaudy chrome fixtures in today's brushed steel environment. I get to the front desk, and Lars recognizes me immediately. "Lilly! It's been ages since we've seen you." He lowers his tone. "I imagine this means Sara Lang is not nice lately, no? She is such a bad, bad woman!"

"No, she's fine. I'm just very overwhelmed, and I need to come up with the gown of my life in the next three days."

"I have a room for you!"

Generally, the hotel is considered more of a day spa. But there are a few rooms, and Lars doesn't advertise them. I have actually cleaned the rooms before, as a way to earn my keep, and it has ingratiated me to him forever. He has always asked me about the scents of new products, and appreciates my "expertise" there as well.

"It's only for a night, Lars. And no spa treatments this time. I just need the quiet."

"Fair enough. I will make sure your room is sprayed, and the tabletop waterfall is running. Just give me a minute. I know you're my smelling girl!" he says, touching the tip of my nose. "What is the hat about? Not stylish, no? It's summer."

"Long story."

I get to my room and look around. *This is my secret.* My hiding place, where no one can find me, and my creativity can soar to new heights. When I'm here, I am not a failure. I am in the presence of God with my praise music playing, and the good scents flowing. I haven't made much time for God lately, but luckily I am not forgotten. Though I probably deserve to be.

Quietude is the way I can really hear. It's the way that design comes to me, and then flows through my fingers. After making myself a cup of chamomile, I light a candle and cuddle up in the French armchair by the window. Clicking Play on the CD, I allow the sounds of nature to fill the room… and I am in the zone.

Although the room smells divine, I have brought my own sensory therapy from the Origins store. It's really expensive, but the citrus infusion of their "Sleep Perchance to Dream" is just what I need as a muse. I spray it heartily in the room and feel the scent rain down on me. Morgan always puts a sprayer in my goody bag and says she gets it free, but I know she goes and buys it. One day, very soon, I hope, I'm going to show her that believing in me was worth all her investment.

I start drawing frantically, and within minutes, the form of Morgan's perfect gown emerges. It isn't shantung silk at all! It's a mixture of silk and satin, and strapless, no less! I wouldn't have imagined! It flows perfectly, and there's no veil. A veil will only get in the way. I'm so anxious, I reach for my cell phone.

"Morgan, you there?"

"Yeah, Lilly, have you set me up with anyone new today?"

"Can you guys come home? Not home-home but to my little hotel? Do you remember the one where I used to escape Nana?"

"That one on Sutter?"

"Yes!"

"We're on our way home now. What's up?"

"Just stop by, okay? I have to go out and get fabric. But I'll be back. When will you be here?"

"Six?"

"Shoot! I forgot to get dinner for the girls," I remember. "Okay, I'll be back. Just get over here."

I call and make arrangements to have Chinese food taken up to the loft. I will hate to see my Visa bill next month, but no good business ever happened without expending significant venture capital, did it?

The fabric outlets are closed today. *I'm going to have to pay retail.* But I can't afford to wait overnight. I need it now because once Morgan gets in the doorway, she's mine. I'll have her draped and pinned before she even has time to say no. In fact, the answer won't even occur to her.

It's then that the guilt comes like the seventh wave. *What am I thinking?* Morgan can't possibly get in a wedding dress this week. I suddenly remember all the tears, and the loss of the man she was going to marry. Then there's Stuart mauling her for a photo opportunity. Getting Morgan into a wedding dress is not going to be easy, and worse yet, it's not going to be easy on my conscience. I've lost it. Today, I *became* Sara Lang, San Francisco's Jeweler, and my Nana all rolled into one scrawny, frizzy-haired package.

chapter

31

No!" Poppy shouts. "There is no way I'm getting in a wedding dress! It's bad luck for the groom to see you before the wedding."

"What wedding?" I ask.

"Precisely! Do you want to relegate me to a life of no prospective grooms because I dressed up in a gown that I have no business in?" Poppy crosses her arm, and Morgan looks away.

"Sara is usually ready for her shows weeks in advance. I don't have the finale dress or a model, and I've got five days. I don't have time to beg. Please, Poppy."

"I'll help you get the diamonds from my dad," Morgan offers, and then for the first time today, she really looks at me. "What happened to your hair?"

I reach for my hat. "I thought you said I had great hair!"

"Yeah, well, I guess it's been a while since I've really seen it. I don't remember it being quite so...so..."

"Puffy," Poppy finishes for her. "You probably need more Omega-3s in your diet, Lilly. That would help the texture." She reaches out for my hair, and I push her hand away.

"Stop! When I told you I had bad hair, where was the support when I wanted pickles and some commiseration?

'Felicity made a mint on that hair,' I believe was what you said, Morgan."

"We thought you were exaggerating," Poppy says with a shrug.

Which apparently means I wasn't exaggerating. This is not good.

"What did you do to it?" Morgan asks, as if I tried to get it looking like this.

"I just blow-dried it with the dryer you gave me."

"Did you point the dryer down the whole time?"

"Well, no, I was in a hurry—"

"Lilly, no wonder you're frizzy. That hairdryer is not a toy. It's serious business. Go wash your hair again. You need to let it air-dry and then dry it a little after the serum has worked in. You know all this. You can't rush hair; it's like fine wine."

"My hair is definitely more like sour grapes. Anyway, I don't have time to worry about it, and if I go in there and wash my hair, you might leave, and you can't leave. Poppy has to be in a wedding gown Saturday night. A wedding gown that I can't make until I measure her in thirty-four places."

"Lilly, why can't you get a real model?"

I don't want to admit that I thought I was getting Morgan. I promised Sara Lang, in fact, because it just shows the kind of friend I am. I've done a lot of stupid things in my time, don't get me wrong. But I am not putting myself above Morgan. I've watched her dad do that to her for an age.

"Please, Poppy. I'll never ask you for anything again."

Morgan looks at me and lets out a ragged sigh. "Poppy, remember that Stuart Surrey rammed his tongue in my mouth because of her."

"I really thought he wanted his tongue in *my* mouth," I say sheepishly.

Poppy holds up her hands. "You're giving me bad energy here. Stuart Surrey needs to keep his tongue in his own mouth. Do you know the amount of bacteria he has in there? A human's mouth is worse than a dog's." She looks at our disgusted faces. "Really."

"I'm gonna throw up!" Morgan rushes to the bathroom.

"Thanks a lot, Poppy!"

"There are thirty-seven unique types of healthy bacteria in the human mouth to aid in digestion and kill disease-causing bacteria. But when you mix that with—"

"Stop!" I rush to the bathroom door and pound on it. "Let me in. I need Listerine, and now!" Morgan lets me in, and we both rinse with the Listerine provided by the hotel.

We come out minty-fresh.

"All right, Poppy. We have put up with this long enough. You don't get dates because you freak people out with your talk of energy and bacteria and yeast," Morgan tells her. *You go, girl.* "Let's just eliminate those words from your casual conversation, okay? You keep the alternative stuff at work, and we're all good."

"What are you mad at me for? Lilly's the reason Stuart had his tongue in your mouth."

"Which I didn't realize was quite so disgusting until you enlightened me."

"Poppy, stand still. I'm measuring." I take out my tape and go after her.

She runs behind the chair. "I'm not doing it. Gauze is back in, with Birkenstocks," Poppy says. "I saw it in a magazine, so I really don't need any fashion help at the moment, and I'm definitely not in need of a couture wedding gown."

This causes both Morgan and me to forget our current battle, and we both stare at Poppy. "It has to go *out* of style to come back in, and since you never did dismiss the style, its coming back in is irrelevant," I say.

"Why me, Lilly, really? I'm no model."

"I designed the dress for Morgan," I finally admit. "I can rework it if I have all the measurements, but I can't afford to pay a model to be here today, and I need them now."

"The gown's for me?" Morgan asks.

"I didn't think, Morgan. I'm sorry. I had a vision and I didn't think it through. I just saw you in that gown and the town of San Francisco in awe. I saw you walking down the runway and—"

"On one condition," Morgan says, and I start shaking my head.

"No, no. I'm not putting you in a wedding gown this week."

"When I'm introduced at the end, you say that I was engaged to Marcus Agav, that my fiancé was killed by liver disease, and you make a plea for people to fill out their donor cards on their driver's licenses."

It's here that I'm struck by how truly unselfish Morgan is. She has lived her entire life for other people, and granted, she lives well, but I wonder what she wants for herself. "Why would you do that?"

"Because I would have been walking down the aisle soon, Lilly, and that commitment meant something to me. It still does. Besides, I sort of like the idea of ending Stuart Surrey's quest once and for all. He knows that there's bigger fish in the sea than Caitlyn Kapsan. He started coming to our church specifically to bag himself a rich wife. He's no more a Christian than—well, just never mind. Will you make the announcement, or are we turning Poppy into a runway model?"

Poppy is currently sniffing the ylang-ylang oil, and curling her fingers to her nose like she's an ylang-ylang connoisseur.

"Morgan?" I say fearfully, and we both look at Poppy.

"Will you make the announcement?"

"No one knows about your engagement. Why tell everyone now that it's over? Isn't it better as water under the bridge?"

She comes around the chair and sits down. "I've been letting men take over my life by saying nothing for years. It's finally my turn. I want my father to think I'm just getting up there to be a fashion puppet, but then he will know that I know exactly what he did in Russia. I want him to know he forced me into that engagement in a way, and even though Marcus was a fine man, my father's mistakes have haunted me long enough. I want my father to know I am not depending on him anymore."

"This will also fire up the press to find out exactly who Marcus was. Do you want that now that he's gone?" Poppy asks.

"I'm not ashamed of my engagement. Please, Lilly, let me do this."

"Forget it." I drop the tape measure. "I'm not doing it."

"You're the one who's always telling me that my father takes advantage. Here's your chance to do something about it. Help me fight for my freedom, or I'll be wearing diamonds and walking around society parties for the rest of my life."

"This will make you the subject of gossip for weeks! I'm not doing it. You can't trade in your father for a whole different kind of annoyance."

Morgan bends over and picks up the tape measure, thrusting it at me. "Measure!"

"Fine!" I smirk at her and grab the tape measure. "But I don't know what good you think this is going to do," I mumble some more under my breath.

"Would you quit mumbling? I'm ready to shove a pickle in your mouth."

I look up at her. "Do you have any pickles?" I ask wistfully.

"Measure!"

"You know, the chances of this coming off successfully are nil anyway," I say out loud.

"No," Poppy says. "You are not going to get anywhere talking like that. This is your chance. You've worked for years to get here. This is your show. If you fail, at least fail on the runway—at Fashion Week. Get there and fail, all right? Take the risk at least." She starts spraying my sensory therapy scent, and I'll admit, I feel better by the end of it.

Deep breath in. Deep breath out. Life just looks better when it smells good.

My cell phone rings. "Shoot, I meant to turn that off."

"You better answer it, in case," Poppy says. "You are starting a business."

"Lilly Jacobs Design."

"Lilly, it's Sara. Listen, I think I may have been a little too fearful of the jeans. I've decided to showcase the denim after all and leave the gowns in my background. Shane has assured me that that particular journalist has been way off before."

"No, Sara!" *Shane! Bane of my existence.* "Sara, I've got *the* gown that will put you on the map again. It makes Vera Wang and Monique Lhuillier *passé*. Are you willing to let your legacy go so quickly?"

"I've thought about this—"

"Morgan Malliard is wearing the gown, Sara." I try to sound incredibly strong, and not like my whole life is riding on this Saturday night. But it's everything to me. With at least six gowns, plus a wedding creation, and no Fashion Week show? When I pay the girls for their time, and for the fabric I purchased, I'm in debt to the tune of nearly $10,000.

Sara is speaking to someone else, when I hear what I've said register to her. "Morgan? She's agreed to the show? She's never done a show before."

Poppy grabs my cell phone and wrestles it out of my hands. "Sara Lang? This is Poppy Clayton, Morgan's publicist and agent. She's cleared many things from her calendar to wear Lilly's gown on Saturday. If Lilly's gown isn't available, she'll have to take the Paper, Denim & Cloth show."

My mouth is agape. How on earth does Poppy know about Paper, Denim & Cloth? A competing San Francisco designer, and forerunner in the denim business. I am definitely impressed. What else does she have up her sweat-shirted sleeves?

"No offense, Ms. Lang, but I haven't…" Poppy takes her time, making the circumstances sound grave indeed. "Well, I haven't heard…great things about the denim in your collection. I'm very concerned. I couldn't possibly have Morgan wear them in public without some generally positive reviews. As you may know, she and Lilly Jacobs are friends, or I wouldn't let her do this show at all. We're here negotiating the terms of the fashion evening right now, and—" Poppy pauses. "Sure. Sure. I think that can be arranged. Let me discuss it with my client, and I'll call you back directly."

Poppy snaps shut the phone and smiles.

"You are holding out on me," I point at Poppy. "How did you know about the Paper, Denim & Cloth?"

She just smiles. "Believe it or not, there was an article in my *Organic Weekly*."

"You are amazing."

"Sara Lang had a lot of fear-energy." Poppy says. "I just had to massage it a little, and she was ours. Still think my energy talk is whacked?"

"Yes, I do. You sound distinctly like Yoda. But the Force is with you, and I love you, Poppy Clayton!"

"Of course you do. I feel ya, girl."

"To the Spa Girls!" Morgan says while opening a mineral water Lars put on the desk.

"To the Spa Girls!" Poppy and I echo in unison.

chapter 32

My adrenaline is bubbling over. I generally love the rush before a fashion show, but this time the reviews are mine. If the press doesn't like a gown, they will say something like, "Lilly Jacobs for Sara Lang, complete and utter failure!" Then, not only am I unemployed, but I'm $10,000 in the hole—and back to Nana and finance. So the adrenaline currently feels more like hyped-up angst.

I'm just pacing back and forth, listening to the rumbling crowd as they enter and find their seats. I have poked and prodded and pinned the models until not so much as a wrinkle is apparent on their tiny, shapely frames.

One good thing about this week. I literally worked my fingers to the bone, well the second layer of skin anyway. I've been stabbed by needles so often that my finger looks indented like the thimble that I should have worn. Models are wiggly creatures. Regardless, I worked so hard on the gowns that I simply didn't have time to obsess about my hair. I made a headband out of the leftover tangerine fabric, and it's tossed up on my crown like fresh fruit salad. I'm a modern-day Carmen Miranda (Nana's favorite besides Van Johnson and William Holden)!

Sara has seen the gowns and fitted the models with me.

She was pleased with my color choices, and for once, I feel like I finally did something right. I can tell she's pleased because I didn't hear how idiotic I am even once in the last three days. But of course, if the reviews come back negative, she'll have plenty to say, and it won't be good.

The Schwartz family hotel has been transformed. Most of the shows were at the Palace of Fine Arts, but Sara rented out the hotel so the media and society attendees wouldn't have to cross town for the after-party. More attendees equals more purchases equals more attention. The hotel walls have been draped with rich, colorful fabric to match the gowns, and the ballroom has been sprayed with a fresh citrus scent (my idea—as if I really needed to say so). There's a collage of expensive perfumes vying for attention, however, and I feel my lovely orange mist is all for naught. Old money and old cologne seem synonymous. *There is a shelf life on perfume, people!*

Sara managed to hire the models and take care of the musical score for the show, and she had her normal crew build the runway extra long so that photographers have time to snap pictures. Sara says one of the mistakes some designers make is rushing the walk. She says that although the music is fast, models should think of the elephant walk when they parade. Of course, the models are too young to know what she means, so one of the handlers usually translates: "Slow," he says, like a breeder speaking to puppies.

I found a use for Morgan's wedding fabric. I used it on the runway, and it's impeccable down there, providing just the right elegant contrast for the brightly hued dresses.

Morgan is backstage holding my hand. We're both so nervous we can't speak to one another. We just stare at each other knowingly. She'll break free from her dad tonight. I'll either break free of debt and my fears of unworthiness, or crash over the ledge. It depends on my success rate. If Morgan's appearance is any indicator, I am home-free. I took thirty-four measurements for Morgan's figure and fitted the clothing darts precisely where the dress would mold to her. I like to think my finance degree comes in handy here. Because the measurements are so precise—the understanding of math can create a perfect body illusion. Not that Morgan's body is far away from perfect anyway.

The other gowns are important too; don't get me wrong. They are an entire year's worth of work at Sara Lang, not to mention the last deadly week in my own personal sweat-shop/loft, but only Morgan's gown and the last six matter at the moment. They are officially in the program as *Lilly Jacobs for Sara Lang Couture*. They are the beginning of my own walk down the runway. Will I accept a hearty bouquet of roses? Or will there be tomatoes and rotten fruit thrown my way? *Okay, Lord, don't desert me now!*

I peek outside the curtain. My Nana is in the front row, with an empty seat next to her where Max should be. Nate is behind her, talking to a blond and tipping his head back in laughter. *Oh, brother.*

"Is the room packed?" Kim comes up behind me, and I whip the curtains shut. Morgan steps back.

"What? Yeah, yeah. The place is packed." I grab her hands before she peeks out the curtain. The last thing I need is for her to get nervous. "This is it, Kim. We've worked hard for this moment."

"You never did tell me how you got Sara to agree to drop any charges against me."

"I had my friend Poppy call her. She's got some special power over the woman, and Sara is completely under her control. I don't get it, but I don't ask questions either."

Sara's ex-husband is sashaying about the back room,

hoping to catch a glimpse of a model sans clothing, but Sara is actually pretty good about keeping the models well covered. I think she was married to the man long enough. He still owns part of Sara's business, but what she does with me is hers alone. Hence, the reason she's been so helpful.

We hold the show's start until the socialites in the front row arrive. They are generally late to make a grand entrance, and the problem is, every one of them wants to be later than the last. So it's very rare that a show starts on time, because the wealthier your audience, the bigger the press coverage.

Morgan is shaking her hands nervously, and I gasp again at the sight of her. "Morgan, you were born to be a bride."

"I know. It totally makes me want to get married—to the right guy. You outdid yourself, Lilly. You have a gift for understanding the shape of women. I never want to take this off."

"It's knowing the client. I've decided that I'm going to do custom-fit to the body, if this flies tonight. It's all the measurements, and knowing where to put the darts in the fabric so it lays right. I didn't do that with the rest of the models, and I see the difference. Maybe the audience won't see the technicalities. But they'll know when you walk out there that something is special."

I take Morgan's appearance in, and she is truly a vision. The gown is strapless with a small appliqué of beading and pearls on the bodice. Everything is in satin, with the exception of a ruched silk cummerbund at her natural waistline. The skirt is a narrow A-line with a small flare of fabric at the floor.

"Are you ready for this?" I ask her, knowing that both our futures are on the line here.

"I am. Anxious, actually. Are you ready?" she asks, and I nod. "This is what I want you to say." Morgan hands me a sheet of paper. "My father's in the back against the wall, and he's brought quite a few of his security guards for the diamonds."

"I know. They frisked everyone entering tonight. The press will certainly know the jewels are real."

"My father will be sure and let them know exactly where they came from, trust me on that."

"Sara!" I say, seeing my former boss walking in a daze. "Did you need something?"

"Your agent is amazing, Miss Malliard," Sara says to Morgan. "She brought her chiropractor table, and just put my spine in such peace. I have never felt so calm before a show. Can't you just feel the *energy* out there in the audience? Wait until they see you, Miss Malliard." Then Sara looks at me and slips her glasses off. "Lilly, don't you have something to do? We're about to start."

The televisions are on backstage in case we get any pre-show press, and I look at one of the monitors, and see Max Schwartz on the screen being interviewed in a tuxedo. I approach the set and turn up the monitor.

"This award means a lot to you, doesn't it Mr. Schwartz?" the announcer asks him.

"Yes, it does. It's always nice to be recognized for your work, but it's more important that the work continues." He smiles. "If you'll excuse me, I'm late for another engagement."

"There he is," the announcer continues, clearly flustered by Max's sudden exit. "The recipient of this year's Citizen Award for charitable giving. He raised hundreds of thousands for San Francisco's homeless this year, and that won't be soon forgotten. Back to you in the studio, Katie."

Morgan comes up behind me. "That's why he's late?"

I shrug, open-mouthed. "I guess so. *Hundreds of thousands of dollars.* Did you hear that?"

"No wonder he can put up with your Nana. He probably has really expensive ear buds custom-fitted in there or something."

Sara claps three times harshly. "Let's go, Lilly. Now!"

The lights dim lower in the ballroom, and the lights lining the stage brighten, while the music gets louder. My stomach is surging. "This is it."

"It's going to be great, Lilly," Morgan says.

First, I have to wait through the myriad of denim in Sara and Shane Wesley's collection. Even with the pounding music, the reception is eerily quiet. I can see Sara pacing the stage, yelling at the models to stand up straight. Sara is exceptionally cheap, and she's usually a model or two short for a show, so they are already not thrilled with the collection in the first place. Being seen in stilettos, black denim, and skeleton T-shirts is doing nothing for their mood. No one ever went on to übermodel status in skull-wear for anorexics.

I've found something worse than the silence. It's the negative mumbling roar that happens when an audience clearly doesn't like what they see. My heart begins to pound. The mood is not great out there, and I'm praying I won't be the beneficiary of a grumpy crowd. Worse yet, an absent crowd. I clutch Morgan's hand, and the music changes to the soft, flowing, dreamy *Rhapsody* by Rachmaninoff.

The first model steps forward in my canary yellow scooped-neck silk with a matching canary diamond tennis bracelet and huge canary pendant around her neck. Even though she must be all of seventeen, the brunette model appears sophisticated and assured.

"Remember, take it slow," I say to her. "Float with the music."

She pushes through the curtain confidently, and I feel her every step. The walk seems to last forever, and I look at my Nana's expression. She actually has her hand over her mouth. Is she astonished? Disgusted? What?

I see Nate, and he lets out a loud whistle, using his finger in his mouth. As the model makes her trek back up the runway, the crowd erupts in applause. The second model is in front of me, wearing the dress my tangerine headband matches. I tug at the waistline and straighten all the gathers as she steps onto the runway. Time is standing still. And this time, I mean it. Not like when I thought it stood still with Stuart Surrey, but truly, not moving forward and suspended in midair. With each model taking her place on the runway, my heart is in my throat, and I'm parched beyond measure. Every step is like a dagger held precariously at my jugular, as though I'm waiting for the model to fall, or the skirt to rip from the bodice. Impending doom is my M.O.

Finally, Morgan takes her place at the head of the runway, and the finale comes. We grab each other's hands, and what passes between us in the silence is a knowing comprehension and a quick, "Thank you, Lord." *This is our moment.* And like everything else important in our lives since college, we're doing it together. Poppy is giving massages with her table in one of the back rooms, but she comes out at the moment Morgan steps to the curtain. Poppy points to the ceiling to let us know she's prayed. And we give one last telling look to each other.

The curtain opens, and Morgan just stands there until the audible gasps die down. Slowly, she glides down the runway like the most seasoned of models, carrying herself with impeccable grace, the simple diamond earrings and enormous cushion diamond engagement ring sparkling under the stage lights. The room is silent, every eye glued to her form as if they are seeing an angel. Then, without warning, Morgan pauses in the middle of the runway. The music suddenly stops.

"Sara," I whisper. "What's up? Turn the music back on!"

It's then that I see Stuart Surrey at the end of the runway. He must have read the press release and known she was here.

He's gazing longingly into Morgan's eyes but she's not even looking at him. She's staring at…"Oh my goodness!" I exclaim, clutching my chest.

"What is it?" Poppy asks, coming behind me.

"L-l-look," I stammer. And I point. Andy Mattingly, the poem-writing, *American Idol* reject of Morgan's romantic past is standing at the end of the runway. The stage lights are highlighting *him* as though he's surrounded by some aura. His gaze is fixed firmly on the woman he loved, and her eyes haven't left him since she first noticed his presence.

"Go, Morgan!" I whisper, urging her down the runway. "Finish the walk! Finish the walk!"

The photographers are snapping at will, thinking it's Stuart Surrey who has her rapt attention, a trance that has suddenly made her forget to put one foot in front of the other. Stuart stands up proudly when Morgan starts to walk…and then…run!

"I can't believe she can run in those shoes," Poppy says.

At the end of the runway, Morgan leaps off the edge, and the security guards surround her. Stuart struggles valiantly to save her. I'm just really glad I glued the gown on so nothing else is struggling to get free. Morgan wiggles and maneuvers until she's free from the wrong man, and she rushes into Andy's arms. She closes her eyes, and even from here, I can see the tears streaming down her face. Andy tilts her chin upward, and the two of them fall into a heated kiss that is straight out of a sizzling afternoon soap opera.

"That is hot!" I hear Poppy say. "I'm feeling *that* energy."

"I think the whole room is feeling *that* energy."

Cameras are clicking madly, and I have to give her credit. Morgan just did more for my fashion career by her own weakness for mediocre musicians than a thousand Stanford degrees could have ever done.

Her father is going ballistic, yelling and trying to get across the room. Of course, the security guards think it's about the jewelry, but Poppy and I smile at one another, knowing it's the poverty of the man with his lips locked firmly on the lips of the San Francisco Jeweler's daughter that is the problem.

"Should we make Morgan's announcement?" Poppy asks.

"I think she just made her own."

I look at my Nana and her mouth is agape. She's just shaking her head at the whole scenario, which makes me giggle out loud. Poppy gives me a hug, and we start jumping around together. "We did it!"

Andy whisks Morgan up into his arms, while she simultaneously rips off the diamonds and hands them back to the security guards—who obviously have no clue who she is. Andy and Morgan are smiling at one another as though they've just pulled off the biggest crime spree in centuries. They rush out the door away from her father and toward— their future? My gown is with them, but I imagine that's good for *my* future.

"I told you that dress had power."

"You did. Maybe you should have worn it, huh, Poppy?"

As the young couple leaves our view, I see Max coming in, straightening his tuxedo collar. He acts as though nothing is amiss with a woman rushing off a Fashion Week runway and out the doors in a wedding gown with an unidentified man, and walks towards my Nana. Then he sees me on stage, and the utter chaos in the ballroom.

He keeps his gaze fastened on me and hops up on a step and then the stage, his broken leg straight in front of him. He winces a bit with the movement, but once he's on the stage, he comes toward me with those incredible brown eyes, not caring if everyone in the place is watching him. I start to giggle and wonder what on earth he's up to. I look down at Stuart Surrey, who is doing battle with Morgan's father, and there's nothing. Not a single feeling left in my bones—not even in my stomach—for that man. But there are definitely feelings developing for a slightly older television reporter with a goatee and receding hairline.

"Miss Jacobs?" A hand is thrust toward me. "Helen Wong, *Women's Wear Daily*. Where do you get your inspiration for your gowns?"

I look at her for a brief second and without another thought, I say *exactly* where my inspiration comes from. "God. My friends. The spa—usually in that order."

She nods. "And the colors? They're so unique."

"Bright is good energy," I say, smiling at Poppy. "Will you excuse me, please?"

I finish the walk towards Max, and we stop mere inches from one another. "Max Schwartz, *who* are you?"

He takes my hand, pulling it to his lips, and he brushes me with one of his gentle kisses. "I'm sorry I'm late." He takes both of his hands and slides my headband off. "I have a broken leg. You have curly hair. No fair, cheating."

I shake out my hair and let it explode to its natural girth. "It's a *lot* of curly hair, and it's *not* temporary," I say, looking at his cast.

He takes my face in his hands. "Lilly Jacobs, sometimes I wonder if you pay any attention at all to life around you. I have wanted you from the moment I laid eyes on you. Why do you think your Nana got such great rent in the Marina?"

I shrug. "I thought maybe you had an old lady fetish. Or maybe you were gay and didn't want to be tempted by some young guy, and then—"

Max puts a finger to my lips and starts cracking up with laughter. "Never mind, okay? I just have an 'old lady fetish,' as you so aptly put it, for one particular old lady, because she has a hot granddaughter. I'm a very patient man, Lilly Jacobs, but I think I've been patient enough."

I laugh and look down. Then he lifts my chin back up toward his. Max kisses me firmly on the lips, and I'll admit, if I had an objection I have no idea what it was.

I turn to see Sara loving the limelight of the fashion journalists, and I look at my Nana and see a mother. *Nana knew exactly what she was doing inviting Valeria to Max's place.* Nana's smiling like a Cheshire cat! I look at Max, whose dark, expressive eyes make me feel like I'm the queen of the castle. Then, I think about Poppy and Morgan. In all of these people who love me unconditionally, I see a mirror of who I *really* am—who God created me to be. Bad hair and all. To sum up Psalm 139, I am all that and a bag of chips!

Two Months Later:

I did make *Women's Wear Daily*, and I did make a business out of the scraps Sara Lang left me. Money will continue to be an issue until I can get my gowns made a little more quickly, but bad hair has not completely ruined my life, after all. I know that now. In fact, life is good. Max Schwartz assured me he isn't living an heir's life, and that's good with me. (But you'd never know it by the diamond brooch of his grandmother's that he recently gave me.)

For the first time, I'm in love with a man who has seen my hair in full bloom and isn't scared of it! And we're taking it slowly. I hang out at his place in the evenings, enjoying the view and his company, while he takes notes on television shows. I sketch and think about how I'm going to meet my fabric costs that month. Every now and again, I'll look over at him and wonder, *How did I get here? Me. Lilly Jacobs—actual designer and girlfriend.* What could be better than this? Oh wait, I can't go there. I may be all that…but I'm realistic too!

Nana seems to think I'm settled and has suddenly found a life of her own with a man she met—at bingo, no less. As for Morgan and Poppy—the best friends a girl could ever have— I'll let them tell their stories at the next Spa Girls weekend. This time, with pickles.

Look for the continuing
adventures of the Spa Girls in

spa girls
COLLECTION

a girl's best friend

Book 2 of the
Spa Girls Collection

from award-winning author

kristin billerbeck

Coming Soon from Integrity Publishers.

INTEGRITY®
PUBLISHERS

www.integritypublishers.com